PRASE FOR *SOMETHIN*

"A sparkling debut about frienc
and heartache of queer teenhoc
a witty, fresh new voice in YA."
Lex Croucher, author of *Gwen and Art are Not in Love*

"Full of passion and drama, with moments to make you
laugh, gasp and even punch the air with satisfaction!
It's a story about the power of friendship and the
importance of standing up for each other, making mistakes
and doing your best, and learning that we are always
stronger together. It's a message we all need right now."
Sarah Hagger-Holt, author of *The Fights That Make Us*

"This hilarious comedy will make anyone who is queer and
neurodiverse feel seen, uplifted and treasured."
Lauren James, author of *The Quiet at the End of the World*

"A study in the strength, determination, and love that
young people can bring to the world, *Something to be
Proud of* is both powerful and hilarious at once."
Anika Hussain, author of *This is How You Fall in Love*

"Inspiring, uplifting, and completely fabulous!"
Sinéad O'Hart, author of *The Time Tider*

"A funny, inspiring story about the importance of
friendship and fighting for a more inclusive world"
Sophie Cameron, author of *Away with Words*

To all the loves of my life – I'm so glad we're here together.
And to everyone who threw those first bricks, and anyone
still kicking up a rumpus today.

LITTLE TIGER
An imprint of Little Tiger Press Limited
1 Coda Studios, 189 Munster Road, London SW6 6AW

Imported into the EEA by Penguin Random House Ireland,
Morrison Chambers, 32 Nassau Street, Dublin D02 YH68

www.littletiger.co.uk

A paperback original
First published in Great Britain 2024

Text copyright © Anna Quirke, 2024
Illustrations copyright © Lucía Gómez Alcaide, 2024

ISBN: 978-1-78895-690-1

The rights of Anna Quirke and Lucía Gómez Alcaide to be identified as the
author and illustrator of this work have been asserted by them in accordance
with the Copyright, Designs and Patents Act, 1988.

The Forest Stewardship Council® (FSC®) is a global, not-for-profit organization
dedicated to the promotion of responsible forest management worldwide. FSC
defines standards based on agreed principles for responsible forest stewardship
that are supported by environmental, social, and economic stakeholders.
To learn more, visit www.fsc.org

10 9 8 7 6 5 4 3 2 1

SOMETHING to be PROUD of

ANNA ZOE QUIRKE

LITTLE TIGER

LONDON

CHAPTER ONE

I have long been aware that I inhabit a world that was built neither by nor for people like me. What I was not aware of, however, was that sometimes highly necessary wake-up calls come in the form of drag queens in lilac wigs brandishing silk handkerchiefs at you.

I'm not doing too fantastically. I'm at a pride festival in the city (the very last one of the summer, but the first and only one I managed to convince my friends to attend with me). Ten minutes ago, a marching band began bellowing its obnoxiously loud 'music' without any warning (rude), while pop songs still played over the speakers so loudly that I felt them vibrating through my veins. Add on the small matter of approximately three thousand people all talking and laughing and shouting within a one-mile radius and, to put it succinctly, my autistic ass couldn't handle it. I forgot how to talk, my brain doing the equivalent of a keyboard smash at even the vaguest threat of a coherent thought, and my supposed 'friends' Jen and Hannah left me alone in this random coffee shop, wearing my noise-cancelling headphones that, let me tell you, are not living up to their name.

This is where Auntie Septic finds me, offers me a literal silk handkerchief embroidered with *AS* to dry my glittery tears (and regular, non-glittery snot) and says, "Honey, if friends are people who leave you alone at a time like this, then I'm going to need Beyoncé to stop texting me because I want *none of that*, thank you."

And, not for the first time – albeit definitely the first time the thought's invoked by someone wearing a wig large enough and doused in enough hairspray to fit the actual *cast* of *Hairspray* inside it – I realise I need to shake things up.

"Are you going to be OK, sweetcheeks?" Auntie Septic says, blinking at me through vivid pink false lashes.

I nod, still not quite able to form words, and offer up a watery smile.

"That's the spirit." She pats me on the head. "I'll maybe see you out there, but if I don't, then good luck, and never forget to be fabulous, be gay and do crime."

I manage a laugh for the first time all day, and she blows me a final kiss before strutting back out of the café to rejoin the hordes of people outside.

I pull out my phone and examine myself in the black screen. Stray curls of the thick mess I call my hair are stuck to my clammy face, with patchwork pink blotches scattered across my skin for good measure. Hot, I know.

I pipe some white noise into my headphones to stop my head pounding while I text my dad to come and get me. I'd wanted to come to my first pride event so badly I thought I could handle the crowds, but obviously I can't. Not like this, not on my own. I draw my Bi Pride flag tightly round my shoulders and wait for my disgruntled father to text me and tell me that he's going to miss some kind of sporting endeavour on TV but he's on his way. Hopefully, the crowds will have dispersed by then and my sensory overload will have dissipated enough for me to move from this chair.

As if mocking me, a loud roar comes from outside, some performance evidently having started, and a shiver twitches its way through my torso. I don't think I'm going to forget the sheer, all-encompassing panic that I experienced out there in a hurry.

Or the feeling of my bones contracting inside me, shrivelling against the noise and smell and the act of being jostled and shunted from side to side by a crowd that seemingly had the sole goal of crushing me.

Or, for that matter, how a thundering boom cracked in the electric air, interrupting the sonorous honking of the marching band and the thumping of the speakers, and a confetti cannon erupted over the crowd sending scratchy shards of glitter shuddering down my back.

And I definitely won't forget how, when I grabbed Hannah and Jen's arms to get their attention, it wasn't only them that followed behind me through the crowd, but also their groaned words and loud complaints about missing the parade.

Watching a parade versus stopping their friend from exploding, actually physically exploding. Apparently, it wasn't the easy choice I thought it would be. But then I don't think like everyone else; that much is clear.

"I knew you wouldn't cope."

Dad's driving me home, windscreen wipers sweeping hypnotically across the glass. I feel a pang of guilty pleasure at the fact that Jen and Hannah will currently be getting soaked, their laboriously applied make-up running down their faces... All right, fine, so maybe I don't feel *that* guilty.

Dad flicks the windscreen wipers up another notch; they start flashing back and forth in a dizzying blur. "I'm missing the test match right now."

He should really be thanking me. I find cricket the dullest of the sports (which is saying something, given that golf exists).

"Sorry," I say, "but I didn't anticipate my friends

being assholes and abandoning me mid-meltdown."

He frowns. "Language."

"Sorry. *Twats.*"

"IMOGEN." He stretches his neck from side to side; I flinch as I hear the bones click. "You shouldn't have gone."

"Great," I say, staring out at all the red brake lights piercing the dismal grey of the dual carriageway. "That's super helpful, thanks, Dad."

His eyes flick upwards. "I'm just saying, if you knew your limits, then this would never have happened. It's not your friends' fault you had a meltdown."

"It's not mine either," I say, festering in mounting irritation. "And why shouldn't I be able to go to Pride and have a great time?" My voice grows in both volume and pitch. "It's not like I'm the only neurodivergent queer person who exists."

He sighs again. "You know, at some point, you're just going to have to accept that you're not going to be able to do some things like normal people."

"NEUROTYPICAL, not 'normal'." I fold my arms tightly across my chest. "And no, I won't *just accept that*. Nothing would ever change if people never got angry about things. But whatever, let's just sit in awkward silence for the rest of the way home, shall we?"

His face flickers in annoyance once more, but he stays quiet until we pull into the driveway.

"You're welcome, by the way," he says, turning

the engine off. "For me picking you up."

"Thanks," I say, my voice sounding as flat as I feel.

I head into the house, barricade myself in my room with a chair, put on some sweet, sweet tunes, change into comfier clothes and grab my blanket. What a perfect end to the summer holidays. I don't like transitions as a rule, they tend to make my back sweaty, but I'm kind of glad school starts again next week.

I throw myself down on to my bed. I'm so sick and tired of not being able to enjoy things just because they're only designed to be enjoyed by one specific kind of person. I reach for my phone to change the music to something angstier but my hand falters, hovering in mid-air as I get a thought.

The very first Pride was a riot. People got mad at the ways they were being treated and then they did something about it. They threw those first bricks and demanded to be seen as who they are, no more, certainly no less. Maybe it's time for me to start harnessing my rage in a more productive way too...

Ignoring my mum's calls to come down for tea, I eat some flapjacks from my secret snack drawer while I draw up plans in my 'gay agenda' notebook: first thing Monday morning I'm going straight to the headteacher's office to make a proposal.

★

I march to school twenty minutes early, burst into Ms Greenacre's office without knocking and announce my idea before she's even had the chance to tell me to take my denim jacket off and replace it with my school blazer (like she has done every other single day of my high-school career).

"I would like to start an activist society in school," I say.

Ms Greenacre takes a full ten seconds to compose herself. She was our head of year before she finally got her mitts on the headteacher position at the end of last term. She was probably hoping that being head would mean she'd have to see less of me, but unfortunately for her I have zero understanding of or respect for authoritarian hierarchies.

"Right," she says at last, straightening the lapels of her tweed jacket and carefully considering each word. "I'm not saying no, Imogen, but I'll need an idea of what kind of activism this group would be engaging in first. We can't have you throwing eggs at the police or vandalising property as acts of protest if you're going to be representing the school."

She has her *I'm trying hard to placate you, but I really don't understand you as a person* face on, but I'm not backing down.

"You shouldn't have given me the egg idea. Thanks, Ms Greenacre."

She inhales slowly through her nose.

"But," I bluster on before I hurt my cause any

further for the sake of poorly timed jokes, "I'm fully prepared to put it in writing that no one will engage in violent activities while they're in the group, if that would help? It would only apply while they were in our sessions, though," I add. "I'll take no responsibility if somebody decides to shank someone off school premises; that's their business."

"That would be a start," Ms Greenacre says, thankfully ignoring that last part. "How many members do you have so far?"

"Erm…" I haven't exactly spoken to anyone else yet. I only started plotting a few days ago. "It's just me as of right now, but I'm hopeful that plenty of people will want to join."

"Well," she says with an annoyingly knowing expression, "I'm sure you're aware that all school societies need a minimum of five members in addition to a faculty supporter, so why don't we put a pin in this conversation until it's more immediately relevant?" She closes the notebook in front of her and smiles falsely up at me.

"All right." I attempt to smile back with gritted teeth. "But if I get those five members and a teacher on board, it can go ahead?"

"Sure," she says, already typing something on her computer. "Put your blazer on and have a good first day back, Miss Quinn."

"I will."

Oh, I most certainly will (the second part, at least).

She made a fatal mistake in underestimating me. I'm far too competitive to not do everything I can to wipe that smirk right off her face.

I walk out of Ms Greenacre's office into the corridor, where students are starting to gather round their lockers. I spot Hannah's blond ponytail and Jen's brunette one swishing from side to side behind their fake-smile-clad faces in front of me and try to change direction, but ... ugh. Too late. They beckon me over.

"Hey, girl!" Jen says. "We missed you this weekend!"

I see we're brushing right past the fact that they abandoned me and couldn't even be bothered to message and see how I was. They had plenty of time to post innumerable photos on Instagram with matching *Love is Love* captions, however.

"Isn't this exciting?" Hannah says, sticking her new timetable up on the back of her locker door. "We're in Year Twelve now. It's wild – we're like fully adults at this point."

"Oh, yeah. I can hardly contain my excitement – I may just burst. And then go open a pension account."

"Right!"

Jesus Christ. And they say it's autistic people who don't understand sarcasm.

Jen rolls her eyes at me. "Imogen was just joking, Han."

"Oh, I knew that," Hannah says breezily. "I know what she's like. Little Immy, our favourite 'stand-up comedian'." She puts that last part in air quotes. "So cute!" she says, flicking me on the arm.

Gross. I don't want to be cute. I want to be terrifying. Less baby panda, more ticked-off grizzly bear.

"Our favourite *autistic* 'stand-up comedian'." Jen puts a hand on my arm, and I resist the urge to a) slap it away and b) slap her. "Because sure, those two things go hand in hand."

She murmurs that last part under her breath and my stomach twists into a knot of rage. I know exactly what she's implying: *You're autistic, so you can't be funny.* Or: *You're autistic: you can't possibly understand nuance and humour at a basic level, never mind at the level you need to make a career out of it.* And probably: *We were embarrassed by you and your freaky brain this weekend. So now, instead of actually telling you that, we're just going to be even more passive-aggressive towards you than usual. Capisce?*

Well, riddle me this, Jennifer – if I don't understand nuance, then how do I know that you're being an ableist twat right now?

"On that note, I'm going to head off," I say as I spin on my heel.

"Where are you going?" Hannah calls after me.

"*Away*," I toss back over my shoulder.

Maybe Auntie Septic was right – maybe having

14

no friends would be better than having terrible ones who abandon me when I need them and never seem to understand why the things they say upset me. But it's a scary thought. We've been friends since primary school – sure, maybe just because it was a small school with limited options – and the idea that, if I didn't have them, there would be no one to meet in the mornings or talk to at break doesn't exactly make me want to do a happy dance. Although I suppose that would mean that more of my attention could go to the activist group. I just need to find some people who aren't dickheads to join it first.

I'm heading down the corridor away from Hannah and Jen, flicking my fingers in and out of fists to try to make myself feel less antsy, when I see him straight ahead of me. Oliver Armstrong.

I tend to fixate on small details, so there are some facts that I know about Oliver Armstrong already. His dad is White British and his mum is Japanese – if I remember correctly from a horrible ice-breaker activity in a class aeons ago. He has a dimple, just the one, etched into his right cheek, a sweep of black hair with hints of warmer browns sneaking through in the light, and his smile is the kind that's equal parts teasing and affectionate. Although, curiously, today there seems to be something slightly forced about it, something strained about the way he's holding himself. And finally, as always, he's accompanied by a group – one star in a glittering constellation of friends.

I'm definitely not part of a constellation. I'm more of a meteor, something with too much momentum, something so threatening that you instantly feel you should move away from it. (RIP dinosaurs.)

Oliver would be an excellent founding member of the activist group. In addition to his constellation of friends who may want to join too, he's also the openly gay captain of the football team – a brave feat in this school (unfortunately). Maybe he'll want to join a society that's fighting for a better world for everyone.

I march up to him and tap him on the arm.

He swivels round from chatting to his group.

"Oliver Armstrong?"

"Um … yes?"

CHAPTER TWO

OLLIE

I always forget that my parents are people with entire lives just like mine, but then I see my mum crying like her heart is splintering inside her (because it is) and I remember.

"No one's to blame – people get divorced all the time – it's just how things turn out sometimes," my dad is saying, and his complete lack of any discernible emotion disturbs me just as much as Mum's tears.

My little sister Maya is crying too. She's only six and she's kind of like a dog – if other people are sad then she is too, even if she doesn't know exactly what she's sad about.

"Everything's going to be all right," Dad says and I laugh in his face. Mum's sobbing in the corner, unable to even speak, and he has the audacity to say that everything's going to be all right?

"Oliver?" Dad says, the creases in his forehead

framed by his angular receding hairline. "What is so funny?"

"Nothing," I say flatly. "Absolutely nothing is funny."

"Good. Now, your mum and I are going to work together to make sure you kids are always our priority, OK?"

That would make a nice change, for him, at least. I don't think I manage to conceal my derisive look because Dad sighs again. I'm just glad he's displaying an emotion, even if it is irritation.

"We've made plans, of course," he continues. "I'm going to be the one to move out. You guys are going to live here with your mum for now and come stay with me over weekends or holidays – whatever you'd like."

I look him dead in the eyes. "What I would like is to not be having this conversation."

A muscle jumps in his cheek. "If you have anything you'd like to get off your chest—"

"I'd just like to circle back to why exactly this is happening," I say, leaning my weight on the arm of the sofa. "Why are you getting divorced, and why are you telling us you're getting divorced in the worst way imaginable?"

"Listen," he says, eyes hardening, "I'm trying my best here. I'm sorry if that's not good enough."

Mum is still just sitting there, crying like it's the only thing she can remember how to do, and the longer I sit here and watch, the angrier I get with her too. Why isn't she saying anything? She's usually the one handing out reassurances and explanations while my dad sits back, stewing in his borderline impressive levels of apathy. I feel like I've somehow fallen down a rabbit hole without realising it.

"And like I said," Dad carries on, "sometimes things just don't work out, and that's OK."

That's OK? I'd love him to show me what exact part of this is *OK*.

Mum wipes her face with her cardigan sleeve, avoiding looking at me or Maya. There's a whole person's worth of space between her and Dad on the sofa and I wonder how I had no idea what they were going to say when they pulled us into the lounge today. I knew they'd been tenser than usual recently, but I figured it was just normal married-couple stuff, not – not *this*.

"So you're not happy being married to Mum?" I ask, unable to keep the aggression out of my voice.

"It's not about being happy; it's about things not working out and that being—"

"Dad, I swear to God, if you say 'that's OK' one more time, I'm going to jump out of the fucking window." (We're on the ground floor but the sentiment still holds.)

He tosses one hand up into the air. "I don't know what you want me to say!"

My jaw stiffens. "I don't want you to say anything.

In fact, if you could not say anything ever again, then that would be great." I stand up, done with him, with all *this*. "Maya? Do you want to come play upstairs? I'll braid Princess Moondust's hair again for you if you like."

Maya stops chewing the end of her plait and nods, scrambling up from her seat.

"I didn't know we were finished," Dad says, voice chasing us out of the room.

"Well, now you do," I say, closing the door firmly behind me to block out the sound of Mum crying and Dad's exasperated muttering.

"Ollie?" Maya says, her brown eyes gazing up at mine as we walk upstairs. "Is Mum OK?"

I attempt a reassuring expression. "I'm sure she will be. She's just upset right now."

"Can we make her a card with my glitter pens?" she asks, and if this wasn't such a shitty, *shitty* day, I'd have to laugh.

"She's not poorly, Maya – she's just sad."

"But I want to cheer her up," she says, wiping a snail trail of snot on to her dress.

Even though I know there's about to be glitter absolutely everywhere and I have no idea what we're going to write on the front of the stupid thing, I say yes.

We spend the rest of the afternoon in Maya's room making Mum a card that says *We hope you feel less sad soon* on the front in sticky glitter ink – a much better suggestion than anything I came up with. *Sorry you're getting divorced after eighteen years of marriage, that must suck, but also could you maybe stop crying because I need you to be OK so that I can work out how I'm feeling right now instead of sitting here and getting glue stuck to my hands* was a bit lengthy and kind of a downer.

I keep my door open just a crack that night in case I hear anyone crying, but the only sound is Dad padding across the landing to sleep in the spare room.

★

"Ollie."

"Ugh."

"OLLIEEE!"

"UGHHH."

It's morning. Again. This shit is relentless. You endure one crappy day and then *BAM*, here's another one, enjoy.

And not only is today a bad day because it will be the first twenty-four hours in which I'll have to exist knowing that my parents don't love each other or our family enough to keep it together any more, it's also the first day back at school.

People are going to want to know what I did during the two months between the end of our exams and the start of sixth form. And, even though we went water-skiing on holiday and I managed to stay upright the entire time, ate a pretzel the size of my face *and* made out with a guy who was on 'vacation' from Canada, despite my great flirting tactic being asking him whether he'd ever ridden a *moose* before, all I'm going to be able to think about is the fact that my parents are getting divorced and won't tell me why. No skiing, no pretzels, no kissing the Canadian guy in the changing rooms.

"OLLIE!" Maya calls from the landing again. "I can't find my school socks."

I roll over to face the door. "Ask Mum where they are."

"I don't know where she is. Ollie, *pleeeeease*."

I guess I'm getting up now.

We eventually find a new pack of socks in a carrier bag in the bottom of her wardrobe, and I return to my room to get dressed before heading downstairs. Maya follows me and runs over to the breakfast bar where Mum's sitting slumped over a still-full mug of tea. When I touch it, it's stone cold.

"Mum!" Maya prods her.

"Oh." She jumps, flicking her dark hair out of her eyes. "Hey, honey. Did you get dressed all by yourself?"

"I did most of it, but Ollie helped," she says, grinning as she tugs on the butterfly bobbles at the ends of her plaits.

"Oh," Mum says again, looking at me properly for the first time in twenty-four hours. "Thanks, Ol, I must have zoned out."

"Are you going to be all right, Mum?" I say, taking in the dark crescents beneath her eyes. "Are you ready for work?"

"Maya's lunch is in the fridge, yes."

"OK…" That's not even nearly what I asked. "I'll walk Maya to school. You just … keep sitting there, I guess."

I know I shouldn't be annoyed with her but I am. It might be her marriage that's ended but it's *our* family that's collapsing all around me. I still need her to be our mum.

★

I drop Maya off and walk through town towards school, greeting my friends at the gate.

"Oi, oi, Armstrong's here, lads!" Charlie calls out to the group. He likes to act like he's the ringleader of us all but really he's just the loudest and most irritating.

I force a smile and follow them into school to our lockers, listening to everyone chat about what they did over summer.

"Where's Hudders?" Charlie says. "Amelia's fit and all but what happened to bros before—"

Oh, good, someone's tapping my arm and interrupting *that* horrible sentiment.

"Oliver Armstrong?"

"Um…" I say, turning around to face Imogen Quinn, a short and very fierce-looking girl in our year who I've spoken to precisely zero times before today. "Yes?"

"OK, good, just checking."

I stare down at her. She's small in stature, but everything else about this girl is larger than the space allows – you can't help but get the sense that if you even just pinched her then chaos would come tumbling out, everything previously alphabetised surging into the air and scattering into anagrams. Her arms are folded across her chest so I can see all the patches she's sewn on to the arms of the denim jacket that she always wears instead of a school blazer. One appears to be a box of noodles with the words *send noods*.

"My name is Imogen Quinn," she says, "and I would like you to join my group."

There's a ripple of laughter behind me. I focus on retrieving my books from my rucksack and placing them into my locker. "What group?"

"The Ardenpool Academy Activist Society."

"I didn't know we had an activist society here."

"Well, we don't – currently," she says. "I'm hoping you and I will be the founding members."

"What?" It's too early in the morning for this. "Why me?"

She picks at a loose thread on her sleeve. "Because Ms Greenacre's being all *bureaucratic* and won't let me form the group unless I get five members and faculty support. Now, Mr Holland is a babe and will one hundred per cent be our faculty advisor, but I still need four students to join and I've heard tell that I'm not particularly approachable."

At least she's self-aware. I've noticed her around school before, parting crowds in the corridor with her chin tilted slightly towards the ceiling like she's saying to the universe, 'You want to try me, mate?'

"I need the support of someone popular to win more people over. People *like* you – they look up to you. And not just literally, even though you are super tall in comparison to my more hobbit-like proportions. You're still looking confused," she says. "You are Oliver Armstrong, right?"

"YES."

"OK… Can you maybe stop doing that whole vacant-stare thing, then? I'm happy to answer any questions you may have. I know it's a sudden proposition, so take some time to mull it over."

Jesus Christ. "I don't need to mull it over. I—"

"Take some time."

"Look, Imogen," I start, more than a little exasperated now, "I just don't think I want to join."

"All right…" She considers me through narrowed eyes. "That doesn't sound like an outright no. You don't even know the kind of things we'll be doing in the group."

"Fine, what will *you* be doing?" I ask, emphasising the 'you'.

"Lots of things, hopefully. My dad works for the

local council so I'm aware of a lot of areas that need improving for marginalised people in our district. Not that he elects to talk to me about these things himself. I mostly just read the news and then pester him with questions about it all until he tells me to go away. I'm not exactly his favourite child," she explains. "And there's only two of us, so it's not like there's stiff competition."

That's a whole mood given my dad is also a grade-A dickhead. But I'm not joining her group just because we both have shit dads. I try to fob her off again. "Look—"

"I also want us to organise a pride festival for next summer," she plunges on. "A fully accessible, inclusive pride festival for our town. We've never had a pride event in Ardenpool before, and I don't know of any pride festival *anywhere* that's accessible for all different kinds of LGBTQ+ people. I thought the group could go to protests and make changes in school and stuff, and then also do fundraising events to put on this festival."

I would love to see the look on my dad's face if he saw me marching past our house in a pride parade. That would almost make it worth joining a club with this unruly, obstinate girl. Almost.

"OK, I'm going to leave the idea with you and check back in tomorrow," she says. "Just think about it."

"Fine," I say, glad that she's finally leaving, even

if she's not taken the hint.

"Oi, Hudders!" Charlie calls out from behind me as Imogen swivels round and walks away in one direction and Josh Hudson-Scott approaches from the other with his girlfriend, Amelia. "Listen to this. You know that really intense girl in form four?"

Josh claps me on the shoulder in greeting before he replies, "Imogen something, right?"

"That's the one. She's starting some activist club and she wants our Ollie here to join."

Josh laughs awkwardly. "Good luck with that, dude. I wouldn't want to get on the wrong side of her."

Amelia removes her hand from Josh's and fiddles with the heart-shaped necklace she always wears. "Did you say an activist society? Imogen's starting one? That could be interesting."

"Babe," Josh says, somehow managing to both roll his eyes and look at her with so much affection that it makes my stomach ache, "you've got all your head-girl stuff going on now, and you're already captain of like a billion different clubs. You're going to be busy enough as it is."

"I know I'm busy," she says, the slightest hint of irritation in her voice. "I'm just saying it could be a good thing to be involved with. When's the first meeting, Ollie?"

"Whoa." I put my hands up. "I never said I was joining. Besides, she said she needs five members minimum, and we'd only make three." Like hell am

I doing this; I've got quite enough to think about at the minute, thanks.

"Well, Josh would join too, of course, so that would make four. And I'm sure some of my friends will want to join."

"Sounds like you don't need me, then," I say, trying not to annoy Amelia and risk her wrath (and then also the wrath of Josh for daring to upset her) while still making it clear that this isn't something I want to do.

"Yeah, we're going to be busy with football practice as well," Josh adds.

"I'm sure we could work around that," Amelia says quickly, clearly thinking hard. "And this group could be a really useful vehicle for enacting important change."

"Now, you can't argue with that, Armstrong," Charlie says, grinning broadly. Prick.

"I'm going to talk to Imogen," Amelia says firmly. "This could be really great."

Josh shrugs at me as if to say, *What can I do?* Everyone in school knows that Josh would probably kill a man if he thought it'd make Amelia happy. Normally, the hopeless romantic, cries-at-the-ending-of-*La-La-Land* guy within me finds them endearing, but recent events seem to have put a halt to that. I can't help but remember how my parents were high-school sweethearts just like them, and – great. Suddenly I have the urge to go and find a broom cupboard to throw up in.

The bell rings its abrupt, trill tune and I start making my way over to the sports hall with Josh for our first PE class. He chats away about everything he and Amelia did over the holidays while I surreptitiously blink away the sting of tears.

CHAPTER THREE

IMOGEN

"Imogen!"

Someone's calling me. I whip round, accidentally bashing a Year Eight kid with my overstuffed backpack as I do so.

"Oops, apologies." I crane my neck to see through the crowd, spotting Amelia Valadez striding towards me down the corridor. Her long, loosely curled hair, warmly glossy like a perfectly ripened October chestnut, bounces gently as she walks. Her movements are purposeful and neat, but I also can't shake the sense that she has practised exactly how she puts one foot in front of the other and the exact proportion of her face that her smile should assume.

What in tarnation does *she* want from me? She's been the school's 'It' girl since the second she walked through the doors in Year Seven, president of every club and society, and she's been dating

Josh Hudson-Scott since before his voice cracked and he learnt how to operate a deodorant can. And I— Well, I'm planning to start hanging out with Mr Holland in the Drama classroom during breaks while I debate whether or not I should formally dump my only two 'friends'.

"Imogen, hi!" Amelia says as she joins me in the stairwell. "I was hoping we could have a quick chat."

It better had be quick. She's so put together it's irritating – no one person should be allowed to be this perfect.

"I heard that you're starting an activist group, and I would like to join," she says matter-of-factly, causing me to blink at her in shock.

"*You* want to join?"

"Yes," she says. "The world can always do with more people standing up for things they believe in. I'm aware that we need five members – I've already messaged my friend Maryam and she's on board. Plus, I'm sure I can persuade Josh. Then we'll only need one more person. I'll spread the word around, but I reckon we could also get Oliver to join in the meantime if we both work on him."

Huh. She really is serious about this.

"I don't know," I say slowly. My brain is in overdrive trying to work out which would be worse – having to spend extended periods of time with Little Miss Perfect or having to find new people to join on my own. When I realise that the second option involves having to actually talk to my peers myself, and that having the head girl on my side may piss off Ms Greenacre even more, I make my decision.

I sigh. "Sure."

"Oh, great!" she says, clapping her hands together. "I'll go tell Maryam the good news, tell Josh the … news, and try to get him to have a word with Oliver."

"I'll work on Oliver too," I say while I attempt to ignore the slight flicker of the fluorescent light over our heads.

"Even better. And, as far as faculty advisers go, I can talk to—"

"I've got that sorted, actually," I interrupt, aware that it sounds rude as I say it, but Amelia looks unfazed.

"Of course. Well, we'd better get to class, or I'll have to write myself up for loitering in the hallways." She laughs. I'm too busy concentrating on not concentrating on the light to remember to even fake laugh. "Bye!"

And then she's off, regulation-height heeled shoes clacking on the linoleum floor.

Well. This'll be interesting.

★

The second my double Biology class finishes for break, I forge my way out of the lab and descend the stairs to the Drama classroom two at a time.

I burst through the double doors, accidentally slamming them back hard against the wall.

"MR HOLLAND?"

"Imogen! Glad to see your habit of making dramatic entrances hasn't altered over the summer holidays," Mr Holland says, using the sleeve of his knitted cardigan to wipe the whiteboard, even though the eraser is right there.

"Well, you know me. I like routine," I reply, moving into the room and pushing the eraser towards him.

"Ah, thank you." He pokes his circular glasses back up to the bridge of his nose. "To what do I owe the pleasure of your company – I don't have a Year Twelve class until last period, do I? And where are Misses Tate and Grimaldi?"

"Don't know, don't care," I say, causing him to raise a curious eyebrow that I choose to ignore. The uncertainty around what I should do about Hannah and Jen is making me feel antsier than *A Bug's Life*, but I have more pressing issues right now. "And I need to discuss something with you."

"Sounds serious."

"Yes and no," I say. "The idea itself isn't particularly serious but the side effects include getting back at Ms Greenacre, something I take very seriously indeed."

He lets out a spluttering laugh. "I can't possibly comment on your feud with Janine, but let's just say I'm interested. Proceed."

"I went to Pride in the city last weekend," I start.

"Did you?" he says eagerly. "It's a shame our paths didn't cross – Jacob and I were there all day. Did you watch the parade?"

"Nope, which is exactly my point. The whole thing was so inaccessible it was ridiculous – it was so overwhelming sensory-wise: it was all way too loud, too bright and too busy. I only lasted forty minutes. *So*," I say, placing my hands together in the classic evil-genius pose, "my plan is to put a proposal to the council to have our own *inclusive* pride festival right here in Ardenpool. And to help me do that I want to start an activist group at school. But, as Ms Greenacre so kindly pointed out, I need five members – something I'm working on – and a faculty advisor."

"Ah, I see," he says. This wasn't just an *I've missed my favourite teacher over the holidays so I should go to his classroom to see him* kind of thing. You're exploiting me for your own interests."

"I prefer to think of it as being for the benefit of the world *as well* as my own interests," I say, deciding not to tell him that I've already been thinking about how I could do stand-up at the pride event. "But yes."

"Hmm," he says, sinking into the chair behind his desk to stroke an imaginary beard. "And will the group have a snack budget?"

I roll my eyes. "I will buy you biscuits if that's a deciding factor."

"OK." He grins. "I'm in. Party Rings aside – and they'd better be Party Rings, *ooh*, or Jaffa Cakes – in all seriousness, it sounds like a great idea, Imogen."

"Jaffa Cakes aren't biscuits – they're cakes."

Mr Holland sinks his head into his hands. "We're not having this debate again, Imogen – I can't do it."

"Just because you know I'm right. But fine." I *am* right.

"Who else is joining?" he asks, in a blatant attempt to change the subject.

I allow it for once and count the people off on my fingers. "So far it's me, Amelia Valadez, Josh Hudson-Scott, Amelia's friend Maryam Kabir and maybe Oliver Armstrong."

"Wow, you got the head girl. Impressive."

"Uh-huh," I say with a tense smile.

"Well, I'll definitely be your advisor now. I'm excited to see two such –" he clears his throat – "*determined* people interact with each other."

I give him a withering stare. "I don't love how much the word *determined* in that sentence sounded like code for *stubborn, intense and a pain in the ass*."

He leans back in his chair, crossing his legs and grinning. "Any resemblance to anything derogatory was purely coincidental."

"Sure."

★

We spend the rest of break arguing about which biscuits are superior and making plans for the group; if I can convince Oliver to be our fifth member, we'll have our first meeting next Monday lunchtime.

And, speaking of Oliver, I'm on my way to Sociology when I spy a head of dark hair bobbing above the treeline of the crowd in front of me. I decide to seize the opportunity.

"Oliver!" I tug on his trailing backpack handle.

He jumps. "What the— Oh. It's you."

"Yep, me again, sorry. I just wanted to make sure that we're on the same page – I still need you to be the final member," I say, watching as his already sharp jawline hardens even more.

His nostrils flare as he runs a hand through his hair. "If I say yes, will you leave me alone?"

"Absolutely," I lie, trying to conceal my giddiness.

"FINE!" he says emphatically. "And make sure you spread the word around that I'm doing it. Josh was bugging me all through PE about not upsetting Amelia, and Amelia herself was guilt-tripping me during break and I think also hinting that she wasn't above blackmail?"

Annoyingly, I catch myself admiring Amelia's relentlessness.

"I'm just a placeholder, though. I'm not actually joining. You have to find another member before your first session," Oliver finishes, eyebrows in a harsh downwards arrow.

I do an excited little shoulder dance, despite his stormy face. "Of course, that seems perfectly reasonable. I'll go tell Ms Greenacre the good news now."

"*Fantastic*," he says, before storming off like he wants to put as much distance between us as quickly as he possibly can. Bless you, Oliver Armstrong. I promise I'll let you leave as soon as you can. Probably.

I mosey my way down the technically forbidden senior leadership corridor and poke my head round the door. "Ms Greenacre?"

Her face falls so far I'm surprised it doesn't drop off into the tea she's clutching. "Imogen. Back so soon?"

I smile innocently. "Well, I know how invested you are in my idea, so I thought I'd come and tell you straight away that I have five members and Mr Holland's going to oversee everything, so I think you'll find that we're *immediately relevant* now. Isn't that great? Anyway, I've got Sociology in a sec – better dash, bye!"

"Wait— Imogen!" I hear her call after me. I ignore her and carry on walking, grinning so manically that a couple of people do a double take as they walk past me. Everything's coming together.

★

Back at home, I'm still feeling jazzed as I bounce into the kitchen where my mum is making what appears to be a quinoa salad. Yuck.

"Hi, honey, how was school?" she calls over from the stove. "Are you hungry? I can make more quinoa?"

"School was OK," I say. "And you can make more if you like, but I'm definitely not going to eat it."

She takes a breath and plasters on a smile. "A simple 'no, thanks' would have sufficed."

"Oh. No, thanks then. I'm going upstairs."

I think I was a bit of a shock to my parents. They had my brother, Ben, and everything was fine. He got his A Levels in Law, Maths and Physics and went off to university in St Andrews to study to become a lawyer and play for the rugby team – he generally does exactly what he's supposed to. And then they had me. A chaotic, leftist, autistic bisexual who wants to be a stand-up comedian.

I honestly don't know how my parents' genes managed to manifest in me what with my dad being a grouchy, tie-wearing council worker, and my mum a stereotypical middle-class 'hippie' who claims to be all about doing yoga and being 'centred', but, in actuality, is frequently guilty of cultural appropriation and shopping at Waitrose.

I throw my backpack in the general direction of my bed, sit down at my desk and open my laptop. Time to do some research into how exactly one goes about organising a pride festival.

I pore over the council website and take notes from their event-planning pages, downloading all their guides and leaflets, getting slightly overwhelmed by how unnecessarily complicated everything seems to be.

I eventually find a link to a page where you can download forms to apply for grants to put on community events, and bookmark it for later. First, I need to come up with my pitch for the festival.

After a while, I zone out, staring at my laptop screen but not really seeing it, instead letting my head fill with daydreams of a space where everyone is included, where everything is planned and figured out, where loud noises and bright lights are still allowed, but so are calmer spaces. A space where everyone, queer, trans, disabled, neurodivergent, or otherwise, can come together to celebrate all aspects of their identities at once. Something I don't think I've ever really been able to do.

Yep, that's the dream. Now I just need to make sure it doesn't *stay* a dream.

CHAPTER FOUR

"I'm home," I call into the house, listening for any signs of movement. I don't hear any, so I decide to head upstairs. I want to plan a solo photography outing for this weekend to keep building my unofficial portfolio (with the added benefit of avoiding my family) and complain to Josh about how we've been conned into temporarily joining this stubborn-ass girl's group. I walk past the living-room door towards the stairs and then stop in my tracks, doubling back.

"Mum?"

She's curled up in a ball on the sofa, the woollen blanket over her rising and falling slowly and rhythmically. Her green tea leaves are out on the kitchen work surface, yunomi chawan next to them, but there's no sign that she progressed any further than this in the drink-creation process. I feel crushed that she clearly wanted her go-to comfort drink but this is all she could manage: an empty cup and some scattered leaves on the countertop.

I look over again at her, unconscious on the sofa, and sigh as I go to make the tea.

When the water is heated (but not too hot) and the leaves have steeped, I take the tea through into the lounge. "Mum?" I say, a little louder than the first time. "Mum – c'mon, wake up."

She stirs a little, letting out a slow sigh like a punctured tyre deflating. "Ollie?"

"Yeah. How long have you been asleep?" I hold out the tea to her.

She rubs her eyes, sitting up and looking around like she's trying to figure out where she is, then taking the tea off me with what might (almost) constitute a smile. "Oh, not long, I don't think. How was..." Her eyes go glassy, her voice trailing off.

"School?" I supply. I think that's the word she's looking for.

"School, yes. How was school?"

"School was fine. Have you eaten anything today?"

"Not yet, but there's still time. Where's Maya?"

How the hell would I know? "No idea," I say. "I haven't seen her since I dropped her off this morning."

She starts to rubs her forehead absent-mindedly. "What time is it?"

"Nearly four."

"Maya's school finishes at quarter past three."

"Yes, it does," I say, waiting impatiently for her brain to engage again. "Is she at a club tonight?"

"No, I don't think so."

Why am I the only person in this conversation that's connecting the dots?

"Right," I say slowly, really spelling it out for her, "so if she's not at a club, and she's not here, then she's still at school, waiting for someone to pick her up."

She stares into space.

"MUM. You're forty minutes late picking Maya up." My raised voice seems to knock her out of her trance and causes a steady stream of tears to begin falling down her face.

"I'm a terrible mother," she whispers, drawing the blanket up to her chin with clenched fists.

"You're not a terrible mother," I say, although, granted, today isn't exactly a great example of her parenting skills. "I'm going to run and get Maya, OK? You stay there."

I sprint across town, still in my blazer, my metal water bottle clunking with each bound as my backpack bumps up and down on my shoulders. I reach the school, sweaty and irritated, and apologise to the very disgruntled receptionist who says she's been calling Mum all afternoon. (Fifty minutes late to pick up your kid from school isn't great, I'll give you that, but it's hardly 'all afternoon'.)

"It won't happen again, I promise," I say tersely.

She huffs, her chair creaking as she finally gets up and lets me in to fetch Maya from the after-school club they parked her in when Mum didn't turn up.

I hurry through the hall to the classroom where she's waiting, gnawing at her thumb like she always does when she's anxious.

"MAYA."

She looks up and runs across the room, one of the straps of her shiny black shoes flapping around as she does. "Ollie!" She pelts into me at full speed.

"OOF," I groan.

"I thought Mum forgot me. I thought I was going to have to live at school forever," she says dramatically.

"No, don't be silly. Mum didn't forget you," I say, improvising wildly. "She just had something to do, and she didn't tell your teacher because she wanted it to be a surprise when I got here."

"OK," she says, accepting the lie immediately. Man, kids are gullible. "I didn't want to live here, but at least I wouldn't have any more homework. Or would *all* my work be homework if school was my home?"

I don't even know how to respond to that. "Jeez, you're asking the big questions here, missy," I say.

I take Maya's hand, slinging her book bag over my other shoulder. We traipse home while she babbles away about where exactly in the school she'd like to live if she had to. The hall wins initially because it's big – I think she's still annoyed that my bedroom at home is slightly bigger than hers – but then she decides on the kitchen because that's where they keep the yoghurt.

This is so not how I pictured the new school year starting.

★

I make myself and Maya some basic cheese-and-tomato pasta, put a bowl in front of Mum for her to ignore, and then plonk Maya in front of a film. I'm about to go upstairs to sort out my school things when Mum calls my name from the hall.

"I just wanted to thank you for looking after Maya the last couple of days," she says as I turn to face her.

"Oh." This is unexpectedly lucid. "That's OK."

"No, you shouldn't have had to. I know I'm not the only one who's upset by…" She looks distractedly around, swallowing hard. "By all this."

"No, you're not," I say, not quite managing to keep the harsh undertones out of my voice. "But it's all right. I didn't mind," I carry on, trying to sound more sympathetic. "Although it's probably best that you feed Maya from now on. I've pretty much exhausted my culinary capabilities over the last two days, and I wouldn't want her to get scurvy."

She smiles weakly. "Probably." She reaches out and puts a hand on my arm. "You're a good kid."

"Thanks."

Upstairs, the floorboards creak heavily. I jerk my

head up. "Oh, is Dad home?"

"Yes. He is." Mum looks down, focusing intently on fiddling with the ends of her sharply cut bob. She's been avoiding my gaze a lot recently, but something about this feels different. Pointed.

"What's he doing?"

"Nothing," she says, but she's still not looking at me. "Why don't you come back in and watch the movie with me and Maya?"

Her forced airy tone does little to convince me. I start walking upstairs, ignoring her call of, "*Ollie!*" behind me.

Upstairs, I stand in the doorway of my parents' room and watch my dad storm round the bed. It's strewn with what looks like every item of clothing he owns. His suitcase sits on the floor, already bulging.

"Oh!" Dad jumps as he spots me in the doorway. "Ollie, you scared me."

I ignore this. "What are you doing?"

He glances up briefly as he packs sunglasses into the pocket of a bag. "What do you mean?"

"I mean apart from acting annoyingly vague. You're packing," I state.

Silence.

"Are you going on a work trip?"

More silence, but this time I hear my answer in it.

"Oh." I guess this really *is* every item of clothing he owns. "You're *packing* packing. Like, to leave."

I stare right at him, imploring him to answer me, while the leaden feeling coursing through my veins further confirms the truth. When he remains silent, I try again. "Dad. Can you please audibly confirm or deny whether or not you're packing to leave the family for good?"

He has the gall to sigh at me. "Yes. I'm moving out. I'm going to do most of my packing on Saturday. I'm just getting a head start tonight. I spoke to your mother earlier and she said – among other things," he adds darkly, "that she'd take you and Maya out somewhere, so you didn't have to…" He stops.

"So we didn't have to watch you leave," I finish.

This isn't happening. It's too sudden, too ridiculous – it just *can't* be. I narrow my eyes at him. "Thanks for keeping me informed."

"Ollie—"

"No, don't *Ollie* me," I spit out. "I'm sixteen, I deserve to know about things that are going to impact my life like, oh, *I don't know*, my dad moving out and leaving our family."

I don't know if I've ever been angrier than I am in this moment. Everything's been slowly shifting under the surface for so long, and all I want now is an earthquake. It might be rough while it's happening, but at least I'll know that there's going to be an end point when I can stand on solid ground again.

I try to compress all the anger rising through me to get my next words out coherently. "Why are you leaving? I mean … why are you getting divorced? What happened?"

"It's complicated."

I fold my arms. "Try me."

He tosses a jumper down on a pile with more force than is necessary. "Ollie, this is between me and your mum. You don't need to get involved."

Wow. How comforting. "It's not just between you and Mum, though, is it?" I wish he'd look at me properly. "This affects me and Maya too. I have a right to know who I should be angry at and why."

"You shouldn't be angry at anyone."

"Right, so no one's done anything wrong at all?" I say, my hands shaking with anger, aware that my voice is too loud, clashing with the heavy, suspended waves of silence in the room. "This was a mutual decision and everyone's feeling great about it, that's what's going on? Because all the evidence is pointing towards this not being something *Mum's* feeling great about – she's hardly spoken for two days. You and Mum raised us to value shōjik – where's all that honesty now?"

Dad just stands at the wardrobe with his back to me, not saying anything. As per usual. Even when he does speak, he doesn't actually *say anything*.

"I'm not going to let this go," is my final addition to this very productive discussion. "I need to know what's happened."

I see his shoulders lift with tension just before

I slam the door shut behind me.

That went well.

This *has* to be his fault. But if it is then why isn't Mum saying anything either? I cross the hall to my bedroom, throw myself down on my bed and stare at the ceiling, my thoughts forming one giant ball of knotted strings, and the longer I lie there and try fruitlessly to untangle them, the more frustrated I get. I throw my pillow across the room where it smacks into my wardrobe and flops to the floor anticlimactically. UGH.

"C'mon, Maya – we're going to the beach."

It's Saturday morning and I'm trying to herd Maya out of the door so that we can leave before the van gets here to transport Dad's things to his new flat. So much for my avoiding-my-family photography outing.

"But – but why isn't Dad coming?"

"Because he's got things to do," I say firmly, stretching out my arms to try to herd her out of the lounge. "Come on."

She ducks under my arm and hurtles across the room to Dad, who's eating his porridge. "Dad, why aren't you coming with us to the seaside?"

Dad glares at me like this is all my fault. Dickhead. I just didn't manage to get her out of the house – he's the one breaking up a family.

"I'm busy, Maya. I'll take you to the beach another time, OK?" he says, patting her on the head, getting his watch caught in the French plait I've just finished doing for her and having to clumsily detach himself while Maya winces.

Once loose, she soon brightens up again, saying, "Mum said she'll let us get ice cream while we're out – we could bring you back some mint choc chip?" I think she's forgetting that she's the only one in the family that likes mint choc chip. The rest of us are in the (usually) rational group of people that think it tastes like frozen toothpaste.

"Another time, Maya. I won't be here when you get back."

"Why not?"

Mum makes a guttural, frustrated noise from behind me before pushing past and grabbing Maya's hand. "Come on, sweetie. It's time to go."

Maya lets herself be pulled towards the front door, but she looks back at Dad the whole time, her lip wobbling dangerously. Dad just sits there, slowly spooning porridge into his mouth like it's just a regular Saturday morning when no one's worlds are irreparably changing.

★

Maya sniffles in the back of the car the whole way to the beach, and when we arrive and I open her door, she climbs straight out past me and runs down the steps.

"Go after her, will you? I'll go get the ticket for the car," Mum says.

I nod coolly and jog down the stairs. The sand kicks up into every available nook and cranny of my shoes as I pace across the beach to Maya. I pull up next to her and see tears glistening on her bright pink cheeks. I wipe them off with my sleeve so that the wind doesn't make them sting. We stand facing the ocean in silence for a while, watching the waves crash and smooth out again like wrinkles in sandy bedding. It's beautiful – ordinarily, I'd whip my camera out to take some photos, but today isn't exactly a day I want to immortalise on film.

"Ollie," Maya says, and I'm so lost in my thoughts that it almost makes me jump.

"Yes?" I look down at her concerned, expectant face.

"What's – what's going on?"

I sigh. It should be a simple question. "I don't know, Maya. I really don't know."

She plonks herself down on the ground, her dungarees instantly coating themselves in sand. I sit down next to her, staring out at the horizon, imagining all the other people doing the same and wondering whether any of them are having a day as depressing as ours.

"But, Maya," I say, taking her tiny hand in mine, "you know everyone will always love you, right?

Some things might be changing, Mum and Dad might be splitting up, but you're still going to see them both all the time, and everyone still loves you just as much. Maybe even more."

She nods, staring at me solemnly.

"And I'm definitely not going anywhere, OK? You're still my favourite sister."

She lets out a giggle just like I knew she would. "I'm your only sister, silly." She shuffles closer to me and I put my arm round her.

I might be angry, really angry, but I don't want her to be. She's so small: she doesn't deserve to fill up with big, messy feelings like the ones I have. Not for as long as I can help it.

I hear footsteps approaching. Mum sits down behind us, wrapping us both in her arms. We stay like that for a while, none of us saying anything, just listening to the waves breaking and the seagulls cawing as they circle overhead.

I need to protect them both. I need to set an example, to be a good role model for Maya, to support Mum and make her proud of me. I won't let Dad ruin us; he can't damage the family beyond repair unless I let him, and like hell am I going to do that. Like *hell*.

CHAPTER FIVE

IMOGEN

Ding! My phone chirps at me from my desk across the room.

Ding!

"Oh my God, I get it," I grumble, extracting myself from my duvet where I've cocooned myself with my laptop to eat flapjack and watch a livestream of a drag show in New York.

"Huh," I say to the empty room when I pick up my phone. I have a message request from Oliver Armstrong. Intrigued, I click to open it, sitting back down on top of my unspooled duvet like a bird atop a nest.

> Hey, it's Oliver A from school
> I was just wondering if there's anything
> I can help you with for the group.

Curiouser and curiouser. Someone's changed

their tune. I accept his request and quickly type out a reply.

> hiii, that's very kind but just so you know you're relinquished from any obligations. Amelia convinced some other people she knows to join, so you're free to leave without either me or Amelia putting a curse on you and any of your potential future offspring.

I send the message and have just reached for my flapjack again when I hear another ping.

> As glad as I am to hear that my future children would remain uncursed if I did leave, I actually really want to be a part of this if that's chill with you?

Oh, it is very chill with me, Mr Oliver.

of course, I type, the more the merrier. And then, confused by this abrupt change of heart, what made you change your mind?

Oh, nothing really, he fires back. I just want to do some good in the world, set a good example for people, you know?

'What people?' I wonder, but I don't type it. After a brief pause, the three dots start jumping again.

So what's the plan? Do you have any ideas yet?

LOTS. I'm just not quite sure where to start.

Another message comes through a moment later.

Well, I really mean it when I say I'm here and willing to help with anything, planning, doing research, whatever

I still don't understand why he's so keen all of a sudden, but it would be kind of nice to have someone to bounce ideas off. I decide to just go for it.

if you want to come round to mine tomorrow, we could brainstorm and formulate a plan for our first meeting on Monday. that way we can assert our dominance over Amelia and Co. too.

The typing bubble disappears for a second.

Come round to your house?

yup, if you want to. I prefer to do things in person so that I can see people's faces and know what they're thinking.

There's another momentary pause as the typing bubble flickers on and off.

> OK, yeah, I guess I can come round.

Neat, an official planning session. I send Oliver my address and the plan is made for tomorrow evening. I look down at the remnants of soil scattered around my wooden floor from where I was repotting some of my plants earlier and grimace. I should probably tidy up the mess before my gentleman caller arrives.

★

At precisely five thirty the next day, the doorbell rings.

"I'LL GET IT!" I yell, sprinting down to the hall.

Dad calls out from the kitchen, "Imogen? Who's that?"

I stop, panting a little from absolutely pelting down the stairs. "A friend from school. He's helping me with a project."

"He?"

"Yes, *he*. Oliver."

Dad's eyebrow arches as he comes to loom in the kitchen doorway. "And what do you know about this *Oliver*?"

"You mean besides the fact that he runs a meth lab, kicks puppies for fun and is absolutely *riddled* with STIs? Nothing."

"IMOG—"

"Hey," I interject, "it could be worse. The meth

55

business is very lucrative, so you know I'll be well provided for, he only kicks the puppies that really deserve it, and STIs are extremely treatable these days – the real killer is the stigma surrounding them." I watch as the vein in Dad's forehead grows ever more prominent.

"Anyway," I continue slowly, "he's still waiting and it's a bit nippy outside, so can I go now? Oliver's just here to help me with a project, plus he's a homosexual so there's no chance of me having premarital sex today – with him, at least," I add, just for fun.

I don't wait for an answer because Dad's face is growing more and more akin to a ripe tomato and that's usually the signal that he's about to explode.

Giggles emanate from the living room where my mum and some of her yoga friends are having a 'namaste day', which as far as I can tell consists of them getting wasted on prosecco and doing zero yoga whatsoever. I scoot past the lounge and open the front door.

"Hey," Oliver says, hands shoved deep into the pockets of his corduroy jacket.

"Sorry that took so long. My dad was just enquiring as to who you are and what the nature of our relationship is. I told him that we're lovers and plan to elope quickly before this little one arrives," I say, stroking my stomach gently. "I hope that's cool. I thought it was best to be honest with him."

Oliver looks at me, trying to figure out whether I'm joking or not.

"Well," I say quickly, "come in."

He follows me into the hallway and gazes around awkwardly.

"My room's upstairs," I say, but as I put my foot on the first step I groan, remembering that I left my notebook in the lounge last night and now I have to face eight tipsy women in yoga pants.

I smack my palm to my forehead. "Oh, budgies, I forgot my book. Hang on."

"Imogen!" Mum says, looking very happily squiffy as I dive into the room. "Have you come to join us for a bit?"

"No, thanks. That doesn't sound like something I'd even slightly enjoy, but you guys have fun," I say, flipping over the cushions surrounding the yoga-pant-clad butts in search of my notebook.

"Who's your friend, Imogen?" Mum asks, deftly manoeuvring the conversation and surveying Oliver from behind her glasses. "He's very handsome, whoever he is."

I direct a smirk at the panicked-looking Oliver behind me in the doorway. "Gosh, yes, a real dreamboat. This is Oliver Armstrong; he's a member of the activist group I'm starting at school."

"Would you like to stay for dinner, Oliver? It's almost ready, we're just finishing up in here."

"Oh, erm…" Oliver looks uncomfortable and

I can't exactly blame him. I finally find my notebook and shrug.

"Sure," he says. "That's very generous, thank you."

"It's no problem, dear," Mum says, beaming, before speed-running her friends' (wobbly) exit from the house.

"You know, Immy," Mum says, pottering around in the kitchen, getting dinner ready while Oliver and I lay the table, "one of the girls was talking about something she read recently about people with autism."

"Once again, *autistic people*." She's not looking at me, but I fix her back with a glare anyway as she ladles steamed vegetables on to plates. "Not people *with* autism. My autism is a permanent part of me, not a disease. But do carry on," I say, readying myself for whatever bananas theory she's about to share.

"Well," she continues, "Sharon said that a gluten-free diet can be really beneficial for people with – for autistic people," she self-corrects, probably sensing my rage behind her.

"Did she really? And where exactly did she read that? From a very reputable source, I'm sure." This isn't my first rodeo with Mum and her friends' pseudoscientific bullshit.

"I think she said it was a supermarket magazine," Mum says carefully, finishing with the veg and turning round to face us.

I nod, in mock seriousness. "Ah, yes, because all great, lauded scientific studies are printed in *ASDA* magazine, right next to a recipe for chicken enchiladas. Ooh, wait, what are we having for tea?"

"Toad-in-the-hole."

"Ah." I twist my face into a grimace.

Mum blinks at me. "What?"

"Well, you see, I read that eating toads gives you eczema and I'm right out of E45 cream."

Ollie hastily stifles a laugh as my dad walks into the room, takes in my mother's vaguely baffled and exasperated expression, and glares at Oliver and me for our crimes.

After half an hour of alternating between my mother asking Oliver probing but friendly questions about his life, including what he wants to study at university (Photography) and what his star sign is (Taurus), my dad glaring at his male form, and me making quips about feeling itchy, we successfully extract ourselves from the situation.

"Sorry about all that," I say as I clomp up the stairs like a jovial rhino, Oliver following close behind. "My parents and I lack a basic understanding of each other and sometimes that depresses me so I make inappropriate jokes as – and I'm sure any therapist would agree – a very healthy coping mechanism."

I plop myself down cross-legged on my bedroom floor and gesture for him to do the same.

"You have a lot of plants," he observes, folding his lanky limbs underneath him.

"Ah, yes," I say. "All part of my dastardly plan to hoard oxygen."

Oliver rolls his eyes, but I don't *think* it's with malice, something that's confirmed when he says, "You know... You can be pretty funny sometimes. Even if I did hear you tell your dad I have an STI."

"Oh." I'm caught so off guard by that that I forget to be obnoxious and remind him that it was *multiple* STIs. "Thank you?" I recover slightly. "I mean, that's probably a good thing given that I want to go into stand-up."

"Really? That's cool."

"What about you? You mentioned photography downstairs," I say, realising it's probably the polite thing to do.

He nods. "Yeah, I did. I've always loved taking photos to preserve moments in time or to help people see themselves in ways they maybe haven't before. It sounds wanky, I know," he adds, cheeks reddening.

"A bit," I say. "But also kind of nice."

He smiles briefly in thanks, but then I watch him sink into himself a little, his gaze falling as he picks at the pompoms on the edge of my rug. "My dad really wants me to do something in sport, though. But then he's been a dick recently, so why would

I do anything he wants me to do?"

"HA, mood," I snort. "Hey, we should start that club too."

He looks up, confused. "What club?"

"The daddy-issues club. But we should probably use its full name and not abbreviate it when asking people to join. I have a feeling asking people if they would like to be a member of DIC might not go down too well."

Oliver laughs, I think surprising himself as well as me. "But at least I have a new pick-up line. 'Hey, would you like to be a member of THIS DIC.'"

We both chortle.

"The most exclusive membership deal," I say. "Gives you access to all areas."

"Never seen before benefits and perks! Get a free ballpoint pen when you join."

I sit up. "Ooh, I like pens – I want to join!"

Oliver looks at me, amused, as it dawns on me what I just said.

"Oh, wait. I forgot what we were doing. Yeah, no, I don't want to join, thank you. I'll buy my own pens. No double entendre intended."

We subside into silence as we survey each other. This is all very strange. If you'd told me a week ago that Oliver Armstrong, captain of the football team, would be sitting in my room as we cackled away together like old lady friends in a coffee shop, then I would have – very politely, of course – asked you if you were on the crack. Oliver still looks a tad wary about being here, but he still committed to the bit. Jen and Hannah never commit to the bit – they're more likely to exchange a knowing *she's off on one again* look and swiftly change the subject.

Oliver clears his throat. "So … what made you get into stand-up, then?"

"I just love the sound of my own voice," I joke, avoiding looking at him.

"Right," he says, but I can tell he's not convinced, and he sounds almost … disappointed?

My brain makes the decision before I'm aware it's done it that I should risk being honest with him. After all, he did the same with me about his photography and if he's a shit-bag about it then at least I've already been thoroughly desensitised to that by Hannah and Jen.

"And…" I pause to chew my nail. "Because I know what it's like to have people laugh, and for a second you think they're laughing with you, but really you didn't know what you'd said was funny at all until they started laughing. They thought I couldn't tell that they were laughing at me, they didn't think an *autistic person* had that kind of capability, but I always knew. If not when they started laughing, then definitely by the time they'd finished."

I swallow thickly, staring intently at the coffee stain on my rug. "So I decided to exploit people's laughter and control it for myself. I became the *funny* one, the *quirky* one, the *isn't she hilarious?* one. I figured that if my brain's unexpectedly hilarious anyway then I may as well cash in on that sweet, sweet hilarity and become a comedian. Plus, then I just fell in love with it. Performing's such a rush, I swear."

If I thought Oliver was surveying me earlier, then now he definitely is.

"That – that makes sense," he says. "I'm sorry that—"

"It's OK," I interrupt quickly. I'm not looking for pity. "It's totally fine." I cough. "Should we start working on our plans for the group?"

He looks at me for one more beat before replying. "Sure."

I open my notebook. "I've mentioned that I'd love for us to put on a pride event, right?"

"Uh-huh. I've never been to Pride – it'd be cool to go to my first one in our own town. I think it's a great idea."

"Good. I've been scouring the council website, and I've found a couple of grants that we might be eligible for, but the forms are super confusing. They wouldn't cover all the costs anyway, so we'll need to do some fundraising ourselves. A *lot*, really."

"What kind of things could we do?" he says, making notes of what I've said in a notebook with a fancy 'O' on the cover that he extracted from his bag. Adorable.

"I thought we could put it to the group and see what their ideas are – Amelia seems like the type of person who would get off on doing bake sales so that's a definite option."

Oliver laughs. "Harsh."

I raise an eyebrow.

"But also possibly accurate."

"Thank you."

"I could talk to Josh and try to come up with some kind of sports thing we could organise. Maybe we could have a football match or something to fundraise."

"Ooh, that's an option," I say. "And then we should also do some more immediate things that'll make a difference. Like attending protests and implementing changes at school and in the local community," I say.

"Sounds good," he replies. "I guess now we just see what everyone else's thoughts are tomorrow."

We continue talking about plans for a while longer, and then he heads home, leaving me with a whirring brain and notebook pages filled with mind-maps and lists.

CHAPTER SIX

IMOGEN

Our first meeting arrives on Monday morning and, when we're all gathered in Mr Holland's classroom, I get straight to explaining everything Oliver and I talked about.

We've ended up with an unexpectedly excellent turnout of seven people: me, Oliver, Amelia, Josh, Amelia's best friend Maryam, whose mint-green hijab matches the socks she's wearing over her tights, evidencing the kind of forethought that's very on brand for a friend of Amelia's, and two people Amelia knows from band practice.

There's Clem, a White, lanky, angular-looking person with bright auburn cropped hair, scattered freckles across their nose and cheeks, and a case containing either a long, thin musical instrument or a very straight, rigid snake. They've come with their partner Louisa, a Black girl who has dark, tight braids with a tinge of red to them, paired with a pink gingham headscarf and a multicoloured array of paint splodges on her arms and blazer sleeves, and who usually – as today – uses an electric wheelchair to get around school. As Louisa introduces herself, she mentions an environmental protest she's going to at the weekend and asks whether we'd like to join.

"It's to protest the council not following through on the clean-energy promises they made five years ago," she explains. "They made all these great plans and then didn't follow through on literally any of them, the dicks."

I laugh at that. I'm already enjoying the energy in the room. I don't mention that my dad is one of those 'dicks' as I (and the rest of the group) enthusiastically agree to join the protest.

I then move on to asking whether anyone has any suggestions for fundraising.

"What about having a bake sale?" Amelia says. "We could do one regularly even, maybe once a month? That's a sure-fire way to make a couple of hundred pounds: people love baked goods."

"Thank you, Amelia – what a wonderful suggestion," I say, and I have to turn a laugh into a cough as I spot Oliver's eyes starting to water.

She smiles serenely back at me, utterly oblivious.

"We could also think about creating a social-media presence," Maryam pipes up. "I'd be happy to help with that. It'd be useful for getting donations and marketing events, things like that."

I make a note on the pad in front of me. "I hadn't thought of that; that would be useful." I've seen Maryam's baking videos online – she makes ridiculously cool cakes that make me want to eat my phone and she's got, like, two hundred thousand followers or something similarly bananas. We can definitely use her expertise.

"I'll start setting something up tonight, and we can talk later about ideas for promoting the festival too," Maryam says, her eyes bright.

"Sounds great! Oliver, we could use your photography skills to record all the things we do too," I say. "You know … if you want," I add, but he's smiling.

"Definitely," he says. "I can do that."

"We don't have that long, really; there's only nine months to raise enough money to put on the pride festival, so we'll need to work hard," I say. "But I reckon we can do it."

Nods and general noises of assent ripple round the room.

"You said you wanted it to be an accessible pride thing, right?" Louisa says, voice cautiously measured. "What exactly do you mean by that?"

"Well," I say, "I mean that I want everyone to be able to attend, *including* disabled LGBTQ+ people. I want there to be BSL interpreters and audio descriptions, adequate seating available, quiet spaces, timetables and descriptions of everything so people know exactly what's going on and at what time, and some performances that are less demanding sensory-wise than most pride things." I finish my list off simply. "I want everyone to feel safe and included."

"Is it possible for *everyone* to be included?" Josh speaks up for the first time all meeting, brow furrowed. "That doesn't sound realistic."

I nod, trying not to bite back with something unproductive. "You're right – we probably will fuck up in some way and not do something that we could have. But wanting to fuck up the least amount possible still feels like a pretty good place to start from, don't you think?" I say airily and, to my surprise, he nods.

"Yeah. Yeah, it does."

"I think it sounds like a great idea," Louisa says firmly. "When Clem and I got together in Year Nine, we were really excited to go to our first Pride together, but it was a bit of a shitshow, really."

Clem grimaces. "*Cobbles*," they say. "The whole parade route was on very uneven *cobbles*."

"Which wasn't particularly conducive to not jolting out of wheelchairs," Louisa finishes. "We've not gone back since. So this whole thing is an *excellent* plan."

"Yeah, that doesn't sound like the ideal Pride experience," I say, making a note to think more about physical accessibility. "We'll make sure there are no cobbles on our parade route."

Louisa smiles. "Good. God, it's refreshing to think that we can come up with solutions for things like that. Most people, when you say something isn't accessible, just go, 'Oh, that sucks,' and leave it at that. Sometimes the inaction makes me feel like I'm being greedy for asking for the things that I need to literally exist. Very sorry for trying to survive out here. It was like that when I was trying to get my Ehlers Danlos diagnosis. Everywhere we went, it was like good bloody luck trying to get people to believe you're actually in pain when you're a young, Black disabled woman. The gaslighting was just..." She grimaces.

"Also," she continues, "the whole 'oh that sucks' spiel reduces me to this one thing – a thing that requires pitying. When actually I'm also really fucking smart, and I love art, fashion, driving my chair over the toes of homophobes – all the normal things."

A few people cackle at that. Clem swoops a kiss on to Louisa's cheek, a twinkle in their moss-green eyes that makes them look even more like a forest sprite than usual.

"I'm all of this *and* I'm disabled." Louisa grins. "That's the part that really blows people's minds. The idea that I don't view my very existence as a tragedy."

"Oh my GOD," I say. "Literally. It's like people

69

don't think being disabled in any way is compatible with anything positive. And that's exactly what I want to remedy. I want us to put on this pride event and tell the world that all queer people deserve to celebrate who they are, *all* of who they are. I can't think of a better form of protest than getting to shove all our joy and anger and whatever else we damn please in people's faces."

Louisa keeps grinning. "Hell, yeah."

"I'm in," Oliver says, and it's then I notice that his fancy notebook is out and he's been taking notes while we've been talking. We weren't even making plans for the festival – we were talking about our experiences. No one's ever really, properly listened to me talk about any of that before, never mind taken *notes*.

"Me too," Amelia says. "It all sounds wonderful."

Everyone else chimes in with their approval of our plans and I find that I can't stop smiling, even as Amelia launches into her plans for our first bake sale with more enthusiasm than is strictly necessary (even if the plans *do* involve cake).

"Well, that was a very productive first meeting!" Mr Holland says once she's done. "Shall we leave it there for today? Good luck with the protest at the weekend and see you same time next Monday. Oh, and make sure you message Amelia with what you're bringing to the bake sale next Tuesday!"

The sound of half a dozen chairs scraping against

the floor as people stand up makes me twitch and, after waving goodbye to Louisa and Clem, I head over to Oliver as he puts his notebook away and hefts his backpack over one shoulder.

"Hey, Ollie, do you want to meet up and make posters for the protest after school one day?"

Ollie. I replay in my head how it sounded to say that aloud. Familiar. Easy.

He blinks at me. "Erm … OK." He shakes his head at Josh who throws him an enquiring glance from where he's waiting by the door.

"Great first meeting, Imogen," Amelia calls over, arm linked through Josh's. "I think we've assembled a pretty fab team here."

She assembled it more like – without her, I would never have got five members, as I'm sure she's trying to imply. But she just stands there smiling at me, looking as sweet and innocent and infuriatingly pretty as she always does, like the evil mastermind she obviously must be.

"C'mon, hon. I need to eat my salad before English." She steers Josh out of the room.

"Friday night OK?" Ollie turns back to me. "It'll have to be at mine because I have to pick my sister up from school first."

"Sure, see you on Friday," I say, caught offguard a little by how easy that was. "I mean … I'll also see you now because you're right here. And also maybe before then because we go to school together, but you knew that already because here you are, at schoo—" I stop. "Friday's good," I finish quietly, wishing that I'd stopped at 'sure'.

Ollie nods and exits the room.

Mr Holland grins to himself as he collates his papers from the desk.

"Shut up." I glare at him on my way past.

He throws his hands up in surrender. "I said nothing!"

I step out into the corridor, feeling a whole bunch of different things, but the first emotion to punch through is annoyance when Jen and Hannah leap on me the second I'm out of the door.

"Imogen! There you are," Hannah says.

Jen reaches out to link arms with me. "Come on – walk to class with us. Or are you still in one of your moods with us?"

I look down at her hand on my arm and remember how different it was when Louisa and Clem touched each other in the meeting. They spoke a silent language, shifting for one another without even thinking. I remember what it felt like to hear people actually agree with me for once and not say I was being crazy or 'too much', both things that Jen and Hannah have always said, even after my diagnosis when I started trying to explain how my brain worked. And then I remember Ollie literally *taking notes* of what I said.

I know for sure now. I'm done with this.

I remove my arm from Jen's and stop walking. "If you don't mind, I'm going to go a different way. Actually, I'm going to go a different way even if you do mind."

They both turn back to face me, equal measures confused and irritated. "What do you want us to do, Immy?" Hannah says. "We've said we're sorry for whatever crime we've committed against you."

"I don't recall you ever saying you were sorry, actually, but that doesn't matter any more," I say cheerfully. "Thank you for your years of – well, friendship feels like a bit of a stretch, but I suppose it'll do – thank you for your years of *friendship*, but I'd like to terminate whatever unspoken contract we had to spend time in each other's company."

"What?" Jen says, twisting her hair around her finger, eyes narrowed. "You don't want to be friends? Would you care to tell us why, exactly?"

"One – nope! And two – I'm very glad you've asked. You don't understand me," I say, and it finally sounds as simple as it feels. "And I've given you ample opportunity to. I don't know whether I'll ever find anyone who understands me completely, but I've come to realise that maybe there are people out there who are at least willing to *try*. Now –" I nod once at each of them – "I'd better get off to class. I hope you both have lovely lives," I say, meaning it, so long as they live them a minimum of twenty metres away from me. "See ya."

I wheel round, not waiting for a reply, and walk through the crowds of students alone, a foreign kind of buoyancy rising through my body, a satisfied smile on my face.

CHAPTER SEVEN

OLLIE

"Will you play horses with me at home?" Maya skips the whole way back on Friday, swinging my hand wildly with each bound forward.

"I can't, Maya, sorry. My ... erm—" How do I adequately explain my relationship with Imogen? A person I was coerced into spending time with, who I then agreed to regularly meet with in order to help make the world a better place for people like the small, horse-obsessed one currently holding my hand, and am now spending time with voluntarily but not exactly enthusiastically?

I settle on 'friend' for brevity's sake. "My friend's coming round, and we have to do some work."

She looks disappointed for a moment, but then gets distracted picking a daisy from a crack in the pavement. What I wouldn't give to be so easily distracted by things at the minute.

Once I've set Maya up with her horses, and some

yoghurt for a snack, I go into the front room and scroll through my phone. After about a quarter of an hour, the doorbell rings.

"Hi," I say, opening the door.

"Hello," Imogen says, walking straight past me into the hall. There's a roll of something sticking out of her bag and her arms are full of … sticks? For some reason? "I decided to go home and get supplies – I brought card and sticks. The card was from home; the sticks I found in the garden. I thought we could Sellotape them together to make the signs."

"Great," I say. "Or, you know, we could use the planks my dad left in the shed?"

"Oh, that's much better. I'll take the sticks back home and give them to one of my crow friends," Imogen says, taking her shoes off and putting them in a gap on the shelf (along with the sticks) without being asked. "Are you sure your dad won't mind us stealing his wood, though?"

I clench my jaw. "Nope. Given that he doesn't live here any more and took all the things he wanted, I'm assuming he doesn't need or want it." *And he clearly doesn't want a few other things as well*, I add bitterly in my head.

"Oh." Imogen goes quiet for maybe the first time ever – or at least the first time I've ever been witness to. "Well, I made that awkward, didn't I?"

I exhale through my nose. "It's all good."

She peers at the family portraits dotted around the walls as we go up the stairs, the same portraits that I have to repress the urge to tear down every goddamn day now. I'm hoping Mum replaces them soon.

On the landing upstairs, I point to my door. "That's my room. I'll just be a sec."

I knock on Maya's door, Imogen still standing behind me.

"Hey, Maya?" I peer in. "Can I borrow your craft things, please?"

She says yes and I go to her dresser and remove a drawer that's full to bursting with glitter and felt-tip pens.

"Thanks," I say, trying to leave, but Imogen's just come in. Why.

"Whoa, you have a mighty cool room, kid," she says, looking up at all the fairy lights and the floaty fabric and stars that Mum stuck on the ceiling.

Maya looks up, beaming. "Thank you! I'm Maya. Who're you?"

"Imogen," she replies, sticking her hand out. "Nice to meet you."

Maya giggles and shakes her hand.

"C'mon," I say, not *un*amused by this interaction. "We have signs to make."

Imogen waves goodbye to Maya and I manage to usher her to my room. She sits down on my office chair and starts spinning it around. "Your sister's cool," she says.

"She's a good kid," I reply, but there's a sigh in my voice.

Imogen glances at me. "Why the sad-puppy expression?"

I hadn't realised I was wearing a 'sad-puppy expression'. "No reason."

She gives me a look that plainly says, *bullshit*.

"I guess," I say carefully, "we've just had a lot going on lately, and I hate that she's involved and upset by it all."

"What, you mean with your dad leaving?"

I guess I walked into that one with my outburst downstairs. "Yes," I say. "Exactly with that."

"That's not fun."

"Nope. Divorce is very not fun." I can't help myself. "Especially when there's no reason for it," I mutter.

Imogen chews her nail with a frown. "There must be a reason."

"Not that my parents are telling me."

"Oh, great." She rolls her eyes. "Because you're not involved whatsoever."

"Exactly! It's so frustrating, I feel like I deserve to know what's happening in my own family."

"You definitely do," she says encouragingly. "Not knowing things is the worst. I hate it. You really have no idea?"

"Nope," I say. "I mean, I feel like it's got something

to do with my dad because my mum's been a wreck. Whatever it is must have been a shock to her."

"That makes sense." She swings the chair from side to side like a hyperactive pendulum a couple more times. "You know, I bet we could figure it out if we wanted to."

"How?" I say, my forehead creasing. "My parents aren't saying anything. Believe me, I've tried to get them to talk."

"I'm not saying we ask your parents," she says. "I'm saying we could try to work it out ourselves. Maybe with some low-level espionage."

I look at her. She's joking. Isn't she?

She looks me in the eye, and I realise she's not.

"I … I'm not sure."

She goes to speak again, but I jump in to distract her – I know I was the one to bring it up, but I really don't want to talk about it any more. "C'mon," I say. "The protest's in the morning – we'd better get making these signs."

"That was quite the productive morning!" Amelia says brightly as we start packing up from the protest the following morning. We've spent three hours trying to convince people to sign our petition to present to the council, handing out leaflets for the environmentalist group that runs the protests, chanting and brandishing our signs. "We got plenty of people to sign our petition."

"Well, you did, at least," Josh says, trying and failing to roll up his poster to fit in his bag.

"Yeah, you were very persistent," Imogen says. "I wouldn't have been able to say no to you either."

"Thank you." Amelia smiles, deciding to take that as a compliment, even though I'm almost positive it wasn't meant to be one. "I could really use my powers of persistence for evil if I chose to."

"*If*," Imogen mutters.

Amelia takes Josh's poster off him and rolls it up neatly, her eyes mysteriously twinkling as she does so. "Come on," she says to him. "We've got a busy day ahead!"

I raise an inquisitive eyebrow at Josh.

"Art gallery," he says flatly. "And then the library."

A fun-filled day perfect for a guy that loves sports and has only ever read books when told to by school, and not always even then. I grimace at him sympathetically before they start walking towards the gallery across town.

Imogen skips up to me, looking more like a children's TV presenter than ever, her stripy turtleneck tucked into bright green trousers with a yellow anorak over the top and a section of her curly hair piled up on top of her head. I'm glad she seems more relaxed now. My mind flits back to a moment towards the end of the protest when I noticed that she was staring forward, her whole body seemingly frozen until she kind of shuddered, muttered – not necessarily to me, but in my general direction – that she'd 'just be a minute' and then disappeared. She *was* only a minute, but I do wonder what happened that meant she needed to leave like that.

"How are we doing over here?" she asks before leaning over and taking a slurp from the straw of my iced coffee without asking.

I pull away. "Erm, you're welcome?"

"Sorry, I'm remarkably parched after our busy morning."

"Parch yourself with your own parch-quencher, then."

"You sound ridiculous."

"You started it."

"Quite right, I did." She grins before seeing something that makes her eyes crinkle in the opposite direction. "Hey, is that your dad?"

I look across the square to spot what is indeed my dad, dressed in a starchy shirt and jeans, sunglasses on his head, despite the distinct lack of sun in our grey northern town, heading into the chocolate shop. "Huh. Yeah, it is." That's weird.

"I thought I recognised him from your photos. Is he also a chocolate fiend, then?"

I purse my lips. "Not really."

"Oh. That's odd. A masochist, then? Let's go over and see what he's getting."

"No," I say quickly. "I don't want him to see me,

then I'd have to talk to him. And I've been very successfully avoiding doing that since he moved out."

"OK…" Imogen says slyly. "But he's never met me, so I could still go."

I tear my gaze away from the shop window and glance at her. She's serious.

"No … that's not necessary." I stare back at the shop.

"You sure?"

I'm quiet for a beat too long.

"You're not sure?"

I don't say anything again.

"OK, I'm going," she says, jogging away from me, hair flinging itself in all directions. "Back in a sec!"

I stay loitering around the steps of the town square, trying to be inconspicuous. A minute later, my dad emerges from the shop with a carrier bag, Imogen following close behind him, licking a cone with two heaped scoops of chocolate ice cream.

I beckon frantically for her to come back over. My dad looks behind him and she immediately stops and changes direction, speed-walking back to me. Dad clearly decides he was imagining things and continues on his way, disappearing round the corner.

"He almost saw you," I say furiously to Imogen as she hops up on to the steps next to me.

"Yes, *almost*, and so? I'm just a dashing stranger to him."

I'm still annoyed at her antics – she could have

got caught. "Well, why did you get ice cream? It's September."

"Ice cream is for life, not just for summer, and how is it different from your iced coffee? I know you're gay and iced coffee is an essential beverage, but *it is September.*"

"Fine."

"Besides, I couldn't just walk in there and not buy anything. It's a chocolate shop: it would look weird if I went in and then went, *Oh, no, sorry, you don't have what I'm looking for.* They literally sell one thing."

"FINE."

"Do you want to know what he bought, then, or are we still being grumpy?" she says, licking the side of her dripping cone.

I fold my arms and stare her down, but she stares right back at me with comically wide eyes until I can't help but crack.

"That's better," she says with a grin.

I kick her (lightly) in the shin. "Shut up – just get on with it."

"Ouch, *violence.* But as you wish. He perused the gift selection for a while, then he purchased one of those heart-shaped gift boxes and got the man behind the till to put a big red bow on it."

"Heart-shaped," I echo. My mind begins to whir. "So it's definitely a gift for someone, then?"

"Or he's treating himself?" Imogen suggests.

"Maybe he's really into self-care."

"He doesn't even use moisturiser. Trust me, he's not into self-care," I say darkly.

"Is it one of your relatives' birthdays soon?"

"Nope. Dad's family all have their birthdays in spring and summer. And it would be weird if he was sending Mum's family anything now. Plus, most of them live in Japan."

Imogen starts chewing on her lip. "Then I don't have any more suggestions."

"I do."

She looks at me and sighs, almost managing to seem sympathetic. "Maybe it's not what you think."

"Or maybe it is."

"Or maybe it is," she repeats.

Heart-shaped.

I sink down on to the marble steps of the town hall, feeling the cool stone beneath me as I wrestle with my thoughts and try not to think about Occam's Razor – the theory that the simplest explanation is usually the correct one. But there's a big red flashing neon sign in my head that reads: *Your dad is dating someone. Someone who is not your mum.*

Imogen sits down next to me, watching everyone going about their day in the square. "You know, my offer still stands," she says carefully.

"What offer?"

"To play detective and help you get some answers. Even if they're not the answers you want."

I very much doubt that any answer would be an answer I want. But ... it would be good to know for definite. Then I can start being *really* angry with him and he won't be able to dismiss me. I'll know who exactly he's buying clichéd, pseudo-romantic gifts for.

"OK," I say quietly.

"OK?" Imogen says, drawing her head back like she can't believe what I just said. "Great! We can talk later and make a plan," she carries on. "I'm going to need to get a black notebook that I can flip open. And a tiny pencil. Why do detectives always use such tiny pencils?"

I shake my head. Tiny pencils aren't exactly my primary concern right now.

"Oh boy, I've been preparing for this moment my entire life," she says, frankly a little too gleefully given the circumstances.

What have I done? I think to myself, but as visions of my dad handing a huge heart-shaped box of chocolates to some mystery woman flood my head, I decide that I don't care. I need to know the truth and, given my parents' new tight-lipped philosophy, this seems like the only way to get it.

Game on, Dad, I think as the heart shape flashes in my head again like a light on a carnival ride. *Game fucking on.*

CHAPTER EIGHT

I'm storming through the hallway, trying to get to our session on time on Monday, when I spot Louisa and Clem huddled to the side of the corridor, locked in an intense discussion.

"No, you *shouldn't* have to, but it's not your fault that you do," Louisa's saying in a furtive tone. "It's fine, I promise."

Curiosity piqued, I head over. "Everything all right?"

They both turn to look at me. "Oh, Imogen! Hi," Louisa says. "Yes, we're just having our daily discussion about bathrooms."

"You have a daily discussion about bathrooms?" I frown. "You know there are lots of other more fun topics of conversation, right? Like, what you would do if you won the lottery, or what's the first thing you would do if you woke up in the body of a giraffe?"

"Probably hit my head on my bedroom ceiling,"

Clem offers sagely, before their expression returns to its perturbed setting.

"I *wish* we could talk more about giraffes," Louisa says. "Love those guys. But unfortunately this school is the worst and so we always end up right back here."

I tilt my head to the side, still confused. "Right back where?"

Louisa glances up at Clem. They shrug as if to say, *Go on*.

"Here," she says. "Staring at the toilets because Clem doesn't feel comfortable using either the boys' or girls' toilets. And even though I tell them it's fine for them to use the disabled one quickly if I stand outside and yell at them to hurry up and get out if anyone comes that needs it, they still resist it every day."

"I resist it," Clem says, twisting their hands together, "well, first, because I have anxiety and like to avoid conflict at all costs, but also because it's not fair. We've been dating for three years now, and I know how important access to disabled loos is. But…" They sigh a deep sigh and I watch their tall frame diminish in front of me. "But I'm just so tired of it. I'm tired of being misgendered by teachers and other students. We were told today to split into 'girls and boys' in Music and I just stood there and *panicked*, and I'm tired of either feeling dysphoric from using the girls' toilets or guilty for using the disabled ones when I don't need to."

"But you *do* need to use them," Louisa protests. "Your needs aren't any less important than mine: they're just different."

"Agreed," I say, having taken all of this in and found the resulting effect on my rage levels fairly similar to throwing vodka on to a fire. "I don't really experience dysphoria personally," I say, "but I also don't feel connected to gender as a concept – or any binary, really. The world feels much more fluid in my brain, that's why I use she/they pronouns." My eyes narrow as I get a thought. I face Clem. "What if we talk to the group about trying to get the school gender-neutral bathrooms?"

Clem laughs quietly and I follow their gaze past me to the office of a certain favourite teacher of mine. "Good luck getting that past Ms Greenacre," they say dryly.

Speaking of the literal devil, Ms Greenacre's voice comes from behind us and nearly scares me shitless. "Is there somewhere you could all be instead of loitering in the corridor, ladies?"

Clem's whole body tenses and I'm seized with the urge to run after Ms Greenacre, who keeps walking towards her office, oblivious as to how much we hate her, and give her a swift kick to the knees. Instead of doing that, however, I say firmly, "I think we're more than a match for Ms Greenacre. *Together*, at least."

"I think you're right." Louisa reaches to squeeze Clem's hand before releasing it and wheeling back as they open the door to the disabled loo. "Now go piss, babe. Then we'll go to group and talk about this some more."

Clem chews their bottom lip, still looking guilty, before nodding and disappearing inside.

★

I burst into the room so quickly that the door slams against the wall behind me and the others all look up from their seats. "Oops."

"Imogen?" Mr Holland crosses one leg over the other. "Do you have an announcement, or did you just feel like making a dramatic entrance? Wait, never mind. I already know the answer."

I shake my head at him. "Not today, sir – I do have an announcement." I gesture to Clem and Louisa who follow me into the room and position themselves at the table. "Clem has raised an important issue, and I think we've found our first act of change within the school. Ardenpool Academy –" I pause for dramatic effect slightly longer than is probably necessary – "needs gender-neutral bathrooms."

"Ooh," Amelia says, leaning forward on to the desk. "That's not a bad idea."

"No, it definitely isn't," Maryam says thoughtfully. "My stepsister's trans and she's had a lot of trouble from people in her school when she uses the girls' toilets. I know she'd feel more comfortable if there were gender-neutral ones she could use." She smiles across at Clem. They still look less convinced than I wish they did, the fingers on their free hand (the one Louisa's not squeezing) drumming rhythmically against the table. I hate that they've been made to feel like their existence is an inconvenience.

"We should take this to the school council," Amelia says, writing the words 'gender-neutral bathroom' in obnoxiously neat lettering on her notepad. "I'll raise it at our next meeting."

"Great," I say. "And if you get any pushback then just let us know and I'll make a PowerPoint to take to them to explain exactly why they're being bigoted and exclusionary."

"That hopefully won't be necessary." Mr Holland swoops in. "But I do think this is a great idea. Amelia, you take it to your school council meeting, and we'll go from there."

I smile over at Clem who looks cautious still but manages a smile back before I turn to address the whole group.

"I also think we need to start making plans for the festival," I say. "I've got some estimates for how much things will cost, and I think, as a *minimum*, we'll need to raise ten thousand pounds to cover it all. Hopefully, we can get council permission to do it in a public space if they offer us a grant. There's one, the Community Enrichment Events

Grant, that would be a huge help – I just need to figure out how to apply for it first – but there'll still be costs for performers, interpreters, sound equipment, programmes, and probably a million other things I've not thought of yet."

"We should come up with a fundraising schedule," Amelia jumps in eagerly. "And I'm happy to help with logistics. We can add budgeting and general planning to our session agendas, or you and I can meet to plan things outside of group to really get things going, Imogen."

We don't have a session agenda, and I'm sure as hell not meeting up with Amelia outside school so she can take over the entire project. This is a group thing, not an Amelia thing.

I force a smile at her. "Thanks. We can certainly discuss logistics in the group," I say vaguely.

"That sounds like a plan," Mr Holland says, glancing back and forth between Amelia and me. "Now, I've successfully cajoled my husband into making us his famous eclairs. Are the rest of you set for the bake sale tomorrow?"

Back at home, I chuck my things down in the hall, grab my blanket to wrap round my shoulders and head to the kitchen. I ice the cakes I made last night in a tired but determined frenzy with buttercream (the superior form of icing) and then drown said icing in sprinkles and edible glitter. They look 'rustic' as they'd say on *Bake Off*, but they taste good and that's what counts.

"IMOGEN!" a voice shouts, seconds before the front door slams, making the kitchen door tremor in its frame. I begin to go through a mental list of things I could have done to piss Dad off. I'm only up to eight by the time he yells again.

"IMOGEN!" Dad comes into the kitchen, an almost visible cloud of anger surrounding him. "What the hell is this?" He slaps a piece of paper down on the counter.

"Hmm." I rub my chin (and then rub it again with my other hand when I realise I've just smeared buttercream on it). "It looks like a petition to me."

He stares at me, mouth in a completely straight line. "You know damn well that it's a petition. It's a petition that found its way on to my desk this morning. And look at one of the very first names on it. What does it say?"

OK, he's in one of his *you've done something bad, kid, and I'm going to drag this out for as long as I possibly can to make sure that you know that* moods.

"It says 'Imogen Quinn'," I say.

"And why the hell does it say that? Were you protesting with the rest of the environmental lunatics at the weekend?"

A stab of anger pierces my chest. "First of all, there's no need for ableist language, and second, yes, I was. What about it?"

He puffs his pressed-shirt-clad chest up. "*What about it?* Yes, I wonder what could possibly have pissed me off about my own daughter being involved in a direct act of opposition to the council – otherwise known as my place of work."

"Well, if you'd just carried out the promises you made about clean energy *years ago* then we wouldn't have had to protest, would we?" I say. I'm pushing my luck, I know, but I've learnt over the years that nothing I can say will placate him so I may as well just say what I feel.

Dad looks positively apoplectic at this point. "Don't you DARE turn this back on me, madam. I can't have you pulling stunts like this. Do you know how it makes me look? I need my employees to respect me."

"Fear you, more like," I mutter.

Dad slams his hand down on the counter again and I flinch. "I forbid you to go to any more protests; it's not happening." His nostrils flare with his temper. "We never had any of this shit with your brother."

"Oh, yeah, *perfect Ben*. I'm sorry I'm such a disappointment to you," I say, voice laden with sarcasm in an attempt to cover the hurt that I wish I wasn't feeling.

"You should be."

His words resound into the room before slipping round the door of the section of my brain I prefer to keep locked up at all times. Very few people have the key to that door. My father is one of the few.

I stare straight into his eyes, swallowing hard to dispel the annoying lump at the back of my throat. "Let's just leave it there, shall we? I don't think either of us is going to say anything that the other one wants to hear. You think I'm a complete disappointment, and I'm neither capable of nor bothered about being the person you want me to be," I say. "Now, I'm tired, so I'm going upstairs. Don't bother calling me down for tea later – I won't be hungry."

I exit the room quickly so that he doesn't see that my eyes are beginning to fill with tears, leaving him looking stony, even more frown lines carved into his already densely creased face.

I wipe the tears away briskly as I hurry up to my room – he doesn't deserve to get to upset me. Only a few years ago, I would have started sobbing in front of him, but I refuse to do that any more. I realised that I was never going to be the kind of kid who would make him proud, and I was exhausted from trying and failing. If he's not going to like me, then I may as well be a version of myself that *I* like. I'm pretty fucking cool. I know that. I don't need anyone else to know it too.

The tears subside as I think of all this, and I unwrap a flapjack from my stash to eat in anger, trying to ignore the niggling thought at the back of my brain that's saying, *But wouldn't it be nice if other people liked you too?*

Still rage-biting off large chunks of flapjack, I grab my phone; I need something to distract me from my very-not-fun thoughts.

> hey, how are you doing? When are we commencing Operation Chocolate Box?

I stare at my wall, hugging my knees to my chest and lightly rocking from side to side until some of the overwhelming energy that's firing around my chest dissipates a little.

My phone pings with Ollie's response.

> I'm ready when you are.

> really??

> Really. I've realised it's best to give in to your schemes sooner rather than later, saves energy. Also my dad just casually invited me and Maya over to his new flat like he's our pal who wants to show off his new pad, so yes, let's expose the fucker

I smile. I won't lie: I'm kind of enjoying the evil-genius vibes.

> loving this energy, Armstrong. how about we meet at the weekend and start plotting?

Sure, d'you want to come here? Maya said she thought you were cool (high praise indeed) and asked whether I thought you'd play Just Dance with her next time you're round

um OF COURSE. we can all play

Erm I didn't agree to that, I will definitely NOT be involved.

we'll see

We will not.

It's adorable how he thinks he can win arguments against me. But I'm glad he's keen on the plan – hopefully this way he can get the closure he needs.

I spend the rest of the evening holed up in my room, wrapped in my blanket and watching endless *Schitt's Creek* episodes while I brainstorm more ideas for the pride festival. Heck knows what Dad'll do once he hears about that, but that's a problem for another day.

Mr Holland calls me over after Drama class the next morning, prising open a Tupperware box. "Here, what do you think of these?"

"Oh, fuck off," I say automatically, glowering

96

at the box of beautifully decorated eclairs. "They're amazing."

He laughs. "As you complimented my husband's baking, I'll overlook the fact that you just swore at a teacher. I'm sure he'll very much enjoy the fact that you were driven to such violent exclamations by his baking prowess."

"Good."

"So what did you make?"

"Cupcakes," I say briskly. "Come on – let's go set up."

"Show me them, then. I want to see," he presses, nudging me in the ribs.

"No… They're at the bottom of my bag. I can't get them out right now."

"Uh-huh," he says, looking sideways at me.

"There's no other reason, so you can quit looking at me like that," I say. "Although if you do happen to be called away on urgent teaching business in the next few minutes and miss the opportunity to see them then that wouldn't be too big of a shame."

We reach the entrance hall. Amelia and Maryam are there already, spreading out a gingham tablecloth over the tables we nabbed from the storeroom.

"Hi, girls!" Mr Holland says cheerily. "And what delectable bakes did you bring for our consumption today?"

Maryam lifts up a huge display container full of various baked goods and places it atop the table. "Here," she says. "Amelia and I baked these yesterday."

"Yes," Amelia says, a slightly strained smile on her face. "With varying levels of success. Maryam's are excellent, of course." Then she adds quickly, "Mine not so much."

I peer at the tray and see that there's a definite divide in the quality of decoration. Some of the cupcakes would look at home in any French patisserie and some of the others (presumably Amelia's) … would not.

"Well," I say, trying to be encouraging, "it's a toss-up between the garbage they sell in the cafeteria and what we've made, so we're going to win hands down. Their flapjacks are very dry."

Amelia smiles at me, more genuinely this time, but then as she looks down at Maryam organising the table and sees her handiwork again, I hear her sigh slightly. She really is a perfectionist.

I get out my own pathetic cakes, place them on the table and stand next to Amelia, biting my lip. Maybe I should have asked Mum for help; she's always overly nice to me after Dad and I have been fighting. Then they might not have looked quite so … like this.

I hear a quiet chuckle and Amelia and I both look up to see Mr Holland standing watching us. We glance sideways at each other, and I realise that we're both pulling the exact same expression. Huh.

"Oh, look who's here. Ollie and Josh," I say, in a transparent ploy to distract us all, spotting the two familiar heads coming our way.

"Hey," Ollie says, and Josh comes round to kiss Amelia on the cheek.

She kisses him back, but doesn't meet his eyes, instead focused on shuffling her cakes into neat rows.

I turn back towards Ollie. "So ... did you have a good lesson completing various sporting endeavours?"

"Yes, thank you. Our endeavours were very successful."

We finish setting up and start serving our excited classmates.

"People sure do love cake," I say and Ollie nods.

"Yep, it's pretty much a universal truth," he agrees, but I can tell he's distracted.

"Are you OK?" I ask. "Are you still feeling irked?"

He chuckles lightly as he takes some money off a tiny Year Seven kid (in exchange for one of Maryam's excellent cakes, not in a mugging incident) before breathing out. "I guess you could say that. I'm not looking forward to having to play happy families at the weekend."

"That's understandable, really. Dads can really be *shit* sometimes."

Ollie nods, matching my energy. "AGREED."

He fidgets, rearranging a plate of cookies. "You still down with coming round this weekend?

Maybe on Sunday – I might have more *intel* then, after seeing Dad's flat."

I grin. "Definitely. Make sure you're on the lookout for any clues, you know, pull some books out of his bookshelves and see if there are any secret rooms, or maybe some floorboards that look wonky like they might have been prised up and had body parts stored underneath them."

Ollie fixes me with a look. "I feel like I should emphasise that we don't suspect my dad of murder, just douchebag-ery."

"You can never be too careful," I say sagely, and as we make eye contact we both snort. It's going to be fun being a detective.

The bake sale ends before lunch does – they cleaned us right out and we raised about two hundred and fifty pounds. Not bad for a first try. I feel a smidge more confident that I haven't just roped six (mostly) willing bystanders into a fool's errand just because *I* have a dream. It's feeling more realistic, at least, but I still won't let up until it's *real*.

CHAPTER NINE

OLLIE

"It'll be fine!"

Mum's putting on a very brave face, smiling at me and Maya in turn as we get ready to go out to see Dad in his new flat for the first time. Her smile doesn't convince me in the slightest, however, and neither do her wide, unblinking eyes.

This is ridiculous. I don't understand how Dad expects us to go round and *ooh* and *ahh* at his crappy new digs. It's just all such *bullshit*.

"There you go," Mum says, tying Maya's shoes for her. "Ready!" she adds, in a cheery voice an octave higher than usual. "Have a good—" Her voice cuts off, either because she sees my stony expression or because she can't bring herself to finish the sentence. Either way, I'm glad. I'm pretty positive that I won't have a 'good time'.

I glance down at Maya and see her face, framed by her black hair in two tiny plaits, completely oblivious to the internal wars raging inside mine and Mum's heads, simply excited to go and see her dad. *Little idiot*, I think to myself, feeling both fiercely irritated by her and fiercely protective.

I take Maya's hand and kiss Mum on her cheek as we walk past. She looks surprised. I guess I've not exactly been the most affectionate son recently, but I know today can't be easy for her.

Maya chatters an endless stream of six-year-old nonsense as we walk across town and I say just enough to make her think I'm listening.

We reach one of the new blocks of flats down by the old mill and I double-check the address Dad sent me. Yep, we're here. Great.

I ring the buzzer and a fuzzy voice answers. "Hello?"

"It's us," I say, *your kids*, I add in my head. *Remember us? We're the ones still living at the house where you used to live, with our mother who you used to love.*

He buzzes us in, and we traipse up the stairs to find him standing in his open door, smiling as he waits to welcome us in.

"Dad!" Maya runs at his legs, and he pats her on the head.

I hang back and give him a cautious nod.

"Well … come on in, then!" he says.

We walk along a hallway with two closed doors and end up in his lounge/kitchen.

"So, this is it!" He gestures around the room proudly like it's a mansion with an inbuilt gym and swimming pool, and not a flat with three rooms, grubby magnolia walls, and a mismatched collection of shabby furniture sourced from friends' garages and IKEA.

"Nice," I say flatly, and his smile twitches. He proceeds to show us his bathroom and nods at the remaining closed door. "And that's my bedroom. Should we get something to drink?"

Hmm. Why can't we see in there?

Dad opens up his fridge once we're back in the kitchen. "Here, I bought you some squash," he announces proudly, brandishing a bottle of peach-and-barley cordial, i.e. the worst kind of squash and one Maya definitely won't like. He sees me staring and assumes I'm checking out his fridge for some reason. "It's big, isn't it? It's got lots of freezer space."

"Oh, yeah. Very roomy."

"And there's a balcony out there too It's got a view over the car park, but if you look closely you can see the mill in the distance."

Maya runs over to try to see the mill, even though we got a much better view of it on the walk over and have both been inside it on multiple tedious school trips. I stay silent.

He's trying so hard to impress us, it's like he's saying, 'Look, I know I left, but see how good my life is. I'm really living the dream over here; you can't resent that, can you?' Except joke's on him: I definitely can.

I stride over to Maya to stop her from leaning too far over the railing and plummeting to her death. The balcony's tiny, with just enough room for a tiny circular table and two uncomfortable-looking wrought-iron chairs. Something draws my eye, however. Atop the table is a small terracotta pot with a drooping marigold plant in it and an ashtray.

My dad hates smokers. His dad – my grandad – smoked like a trooper right up until he died of lung cancer. Dad always used to throw dirty glares at people smoking in public and would rant about how disgusting a habit it was behind closed doors. It was one of the only things I ever heard him talk about with any kind of fervour. Yet now we're faced with two options: he's either renounced his previously iron-clad standpoint on smoking and is doing it himself as yet another manifestation of his mid-life crisis, or he's renounced it because he's shagging a smoker. Neither option's exactly great.

Dad comes over and lifts up Maya, still smiling with well-rehearsed ease. I'm beginning to get a tension headache from clenching my jaw so tightly. I'm tired of being the only person in the room who finds this whole performance ridiculous.

"You a smoker now, then?"

Dad looks around, his now-blank gaze falling

on the glass ashtray on the table.

"Ah," he says. "No. It was here when I moved in."

"There's still a cigarette end in it," I point out.

"Yeah, gross, isn't it?" He laughs awkwardly, and then he puts Maya down, picks up the ashtray and empties it into the bin inside before putting it back. "That's better," he says firmly, like the fact that it's now empty means that I didn't see it in the first place.

We all go back inside and he pours us both some squash. I grab Maya's from him before he can give it to her, and dilute it a whole lot more. He doesn't live with her now – he doesn't have to try and prevent the whole house from getting covered in glitter while she's on a rampant sugar high.

She takes the glass, big and unfamiliar in her tiny hands, and immediately drops it, the liquid spilling out to form a growing wet stain.

Dad says nothing, but I can tell he's cursing in his head.

Maya's lip wobbles as Dad stays silent while he attempts to clean it up, so I poke her on the nose to make her smile like I used to do when she was a baby. She looks up and giggles, and just like that she's fine again. If wonder if I poked Dad on the nose whether he'd forget to be an asshole?

We don't stay much longer. Dad doesn't have any toys or games to entertain Maya and, after the spillage, his previously irritat*ing* smile becomes irritat*ed*. That's just like him – wanting us to be there and be happy, but checking out the second things aren't perfect.

Mum's waiting in the lounge doorway when we get back home. She hugs Maya as she tells her all about the stain on Dad's carpet that looked 'kinda like a unicorn'. As Maya prattles on, Mum looks over at me. I try to smile but don't quite manage it.

Her eyes soften. She pulls me into the hug, and I allow it for a second or two before removing myself and going upstairs, feeling her eyes follow me the whole way.

"That BASTARD."

Imogen and I are sitting in my room, her having far too much fun on my swivel chair again while I sit on my beanbag. She came over to plan festival stuff, but now I'm updating her on what happened yesterday.

"I mean of all the *lazy* mistakes an adulterer could make, leaving out something as obvious as that is just offensive. Make this harder for us, pal."

"I mean 'adulterer' is a strong word." I scratch at my arm. "We don't know that he was cheating on my mum with this smoker. Maybe they got together after they split up. Or maybe someone really did leave it there." *Wait, why am I defending him?*

Imogen looks at me with her bright green eyes

that say, *Come on, dude. I'm not buying that for a second.*

"Yeah, OK, fine," I say grudgingly.

"Besides, they're not even divorced yet, are they?"

I scoff. "God, no. Mum told me all the things that the solicitor said need to happen before it's final and it won't be for months yet."

"That bastard," she says again.

"And the worst thing is I can't even be fully angry to his face because he'd just deny it." I shake my head. "You should have seen him when I asked if he'd taken up smoking. He looked panicked for literally the briefest second and then he went straight to covering it up and pretending it was all in my head."

"Tha—"

"Yes, that bastard. I've got it."

She stops swinging the chair and grimaces. "Sorry. God, sorry, this already sucks. You don't need me telling you how much it sucks."

"It's OK. Anyway, I need you for part two," I say.

She wiggles her eyebrows in a ridiculous fashion. "Part two?"

"Yes. Get actual evidence of his *adultery* so that he can't argue back when I confront him."

"Oh my God, YES!" she screeches. "I'm so in, Armstrong. Let's have a full-on stakeout." She sees my *absolutely not* look. "OK, maybe not a stakeout. How about some light stalking?"

I snort. "That sounds better."

"All right – step one. You need to ring your dad and try to arrange a time for you and Maya to go over again one evening after school."

"What?" I splutter. "I've just endured one horrible afternoon and you already want to send me back. No, thank you."

"Don't have a cow; you don't actually have to go," she says. "You just have to *pretend* you want to go, make up some lie about Maya wanting to see him or something, ask what days he's free and, on the days that he isn't, we follow him after work and see where he goes."

Dear God. "An evil genius lives inside your tiny form. You know that, right?"

"I'm going to overlook the height comment and just thank you for appreciating my mad skills." She stops smiling and turns more serious. "You're going to be OK if we find out that what we suspect is true does turn out to be true, right? Because we don't have to do this if you don't want to."

My throat grows tight, but I nod to reassure her. "Yeah. Yeah, I'll be fine. I want to know for sure."

Maya drags us downstairs to play *Just Dance* with her as promised, and then we actually manage to do some planning for the festival. Imogen insists that we devise a fundraising schedule before Amelia can, so we come up with three concrete goals – we need to raise a third (so about three thousand pounds) of the budget by the end of November, two-thirds by February, and all of it, i.e. the full ten thousand, by the end of May, so that everything's ready to go for Pride Month in June. It's a lot of money to raise, and I don't know if we can manage it, but we can try. And the new fundraising page Maryam set up and showed us last session is bound to be a huge help. I know I was reluctant to join the group, but Imogen's passion has been kind of infectious and now I really want us to manage this.

After I'm all out of distractions, I call my dad at Imogen's insistence, making up some very unconvincing excuse about why I'm ringing, but somehow it works. He says he's busy at work next week because it's auditing season (we googled this to verify, and it seems like he's telling the truth), but that he's free the week after – our October half-term – besides Friday and Saturday. When I questioned why he couldn't do either of those days, he fumbled some excuse about seeing a friend.

I hang up and Imogen and I make plans to wait outside his work the Friday after next and see where he goes. Something inside me is impatient, eager for that Friday to come so that I can know the truth, but something else inside me screams, *Don't! Blurriness is better than hard edges.* But that's the thing: I don't know if it is.

I guess I'll find out in a couple of weeks.

★

Once we've finished with the group at lunchtime the next day, Josh and I head down to the sports hall where Mr Yarbury puts us through our paces doing sprints and then makes us run ten laps round the hall. Charlie speeds up and joins me and Josh in discussing strategies for our first match of the season next week.

"Are you talking about our game against West Overstone?" Charlie says. "My dad says he's coming to watch. His colleague's son is that Mitchell kid in the West-O team and Dad says he's a dick – he wants to watch us crush him."

"Ha," I say, wishing he'd shut up so I can focus on counting the laps.

He doesn't pick up on the annoyed side-glances I'm throwing him, however. "Are your parents coming to watch?" he asks.

"My mum probably will," I say. "Not my dad, though."

And that's when I realise that the only person I've told about my parents' divorce is Imogen. I've not exactly been chatty this term, but it's still weird that I haven't told anyone else.

I think about just coming right out with it and telling them both now. We've been friends since primary school after all, but I don't trust Charlie not to be an asshole and say something stupid.

Josh's parents have already been divorced for years so maybe he'd understand, but I don't want to make it into a whole thing. I try to think back to when I told Imogen and how it came out, but I honestly can't remember. She's kind of so ridiculous and unapologetically herself that it can't help but make you feel safer being the same.

"What are you smiling at?" Charlie prods mid-huff, dragging me out of my head.

"Huh?" I say. "Nothing. Come on, only four laps to go."

CHAPTER TEN

IMOGEN

It's the Friday of October half-term and, after finishing our busy week of Pride prep with an afternoon of scouting out potential parade routes for the festival, Ollie and I are now camped out in the window of a greasy spoon opposite the block of offices where Mr Armstrong works, waiting for him to emerge so we can see where the punk goes. We stare out of the window so intently that we fog up the glass and I have to wipe it with my coat sleeve.

"OOH," I say, suddenly remembering something. "Here, hold this." I thrust my backpack on to Ollie's lap so that I can root through it.

"Oof. Don't mind me."

"I never do." I find what I'm looking for. "AHA."

"Imogen..." Ollie leans forward in disbelief. "Is that – are they binoculars? We're stalking my dad, not a puffin."

"I know, I just thought I may as well bring them

along with all the rest of my gear."

"There's more?"

"Of course," I say, like it's the most obvious thing in the world that I have an entire backpack full of spy paraphernalia. "I went through quite the spy phase as a kid. If you ever need to covertly communicate, I can teach you Morse code. It's come in handy precisely never but, then again, I've never been on recon before so maybe it's about to become more imminently useful."

Ollie swirls the ice cubes in his coffee around before taking a sip. "Again, we're just stalking my dad. We're not going to end up tied to chairs in an abandoned warehouse, communicating through Morse code so that our assailants don't know we're going to escape by feeding them the wrong missile codes."

"You never know."

He takes another sip. "I think I do."

"Whatever." I narrow my eyes at him and start tapping on the table.

Ollie puts his mug down and fixes me with his disapproving stare. "What did you just call me in Morse code?"

"See, if you already knew Morse code, then I wouldn't have to tell you that I just called you a twat."

He rolls his eyes and pretends not to look amused.

It's weird: I know it's not been that long, but

I feel like hanging out with Ollie has already become part of my routine. Not just planning the festival but talking about anything and everything else, texting about our evil schemes, or bullying/admiring him for his clearly well-practised 'Shake It Off' performance on *Just Dance*, supposedly *Maya's* favourite game.

He makes me put away my binoculars, and we stare out into the courtyard opposite the café for another twenty minutes. Nothing happens besides an old couple letting themselves into their house (or committing a very smooth burglary), a blond woman with a well-groomed Scottie dog sitting down on one of the benches, and two men coming out of the offices and getting on bikes.

"Your dad needs to get a better work-life balance. He's late," I observe.

Ollie stays quiet.

I've just fogged up the glass with my breath again and suggested we play noughts and crosses when Ollie sits up straight. "It's him."

We sit and watch in a tense silence only fractured by the gurgling sounds of the coffee machine behind us. Mr Armstrong crosses the courtyard. The woman with the Scottie dog looks up from her phone and smiles.

I feel Ollie stiffen on the bench next to me as the dog bounces up and down at his dad's ankles in excitement while he embraces the woman. They pull apart from the hug and kiss for a very uncomfortable four seconds. The woman hands the dog's lead to Mr Armstrong so that she can light a cigarette, and then they walk away, their joined hands swinging.

I guess that's that, then.

I brave a look at Ollie. His face is pale and he's sitting so still that I worry he's forgotten to breathe.

"Ollie…?"

He finally takes a huge breath in, looking like he's inhaling pure rage, before he stands up so abruptly that it shakes the table. Some of his coffee splashes out and soils the stack of napkins.

I ignore the spillage. "Ollie? You OK?"

"I have to go talk to him."

That feels like a supremely terrible idea. "Ollie, no," I say. "You're too upset right now – it wouldn't be productive." I look up at him. "Sit down. Please?"

He gets even closer to the window, staring after his dad and the mystery woman with a dangerous glint in his eyes. I'm still worried that he's going to run out of the doors and challenge his dad to a duel, but then he falls back, slumping down on to the bench and staring at his lap.

"Ollie?" I say quietly. "What are you feeling?"

He makes no attempt to move for several seconds, and I don't think he's going to respond, but then he looks up, his face as blank as if he's a robot that hasn't yet been programmed with human emotions.

"What am I feeling?" he repeats. "I dunno,

what *am* I feeling?"

"It's OK you're upset," I say, putting a wary hand on his arm. "But this isn't a surprise, right? We knew that this was probably what was going to happen."

He blinks down at my hand; I remove it as quickly as if he was suddenly on fire. "No, it's not a surprise, Imogen. But it's one thing *hypothesising* that my dad cheated on my mum and broke her heart and destroyed my family forever. It's a whole other thing seeing the proof right in front of my fucking face."

My chest tightens. This is why I asked whether he could cope with finding out – was I an idiot to believe him when he said that he could?

"I'm sorry…" I say. "I know it must be hard—"

"Hard?" He lets out an emotionless laugh. "Yeah, hard. You should have let me go and deck him. And that – that *woman*."

"You're not punching anyone. I mean, you're definitely strong enough to take your dad, but you're better than that. You can't make bad things better by doing more bad things, that's not how it works."

"Oh, what would you know?" he bites at me. "You have no idea how I'm feeling right now."

"No, I don't," I say, frantically searching through my brain for something I can say to defuse the situation. "I'm sorry. I didn't think you'd react like this. I thought I was just helping you get your answer. I thought…" I scan his face but he's furiously avoiding looking at me. "I thought it would help for you to know one way or the other. You *said* it would help," I finish quietly.

He looks me in the eye at last, but I wish he hadn't. He looks so angry.

"Oh, sure, it's helped me a lot to know that my dad's a cheating, lying dickhead. Thank you so much for your *help*. This wasn't just a fun little puzzle for me, Imogen; it wasn't a *joke*," he says. "But whatever, you clearly don't understand."

"I'm sorry; I've said I'm sorry," I say. *Come on, brain, find something not idiotic to say.* "I knew that it mattered – matters to you. Let's go back to yours and try to forget about it."

"Forget about it?" he says in a dangerous tone of voice, and I immediately regret everything I've ever said. What was that I was just saying about not saying anything else idiotic? "I can't just *forget this*, Imogen; that's not how it works." His eyes go as cold as steel. "God, why can't you just be a normal human for once?"

Ouch.

I strain my eyes to keep them from flooding. "I…" I let my voice evaporate in the air. I don't want to make things any worse. "Maybe I should go and give you some space?" I offer.

"Yeah," he says flatly. "I think that would be a good idea."

I put my head down and pretend that I'm zipping up my backpack so that he doesn't see me wipe my eyes and know how hurt I really am. I walk out of the café and leave him sitting there.

I walk down the streets, squeezing my hands in and out of fists to try and quell the waves of anxious energy tumbling through my brain and body. I keep my head down to concentrate on where I'm putting my feet – I think tripping over in front of people would be enough to break me right now, and I'm already trying about as hard as I can to stop the tears coming.

When I was younger, I would cry all the time – usually at least once a day. I'd cry if anyone teased me for doing or saying something wrong or funny when I didn't mean it to be either of those things. I couldn't do what most people could and just brush it off with an 'oops' or a laugh. I was trying so hard to fit in and get everything right, and it was *exhausting*. I felt like I was constantly failing at something that I didn't have a clue how to be better at, no matter how hard I tried.

I feel like I've failed again today.

The sun has well and truly set now; the streetlights all come on as I walk down my cul-de-sac. The suddenness of it makes me jump.

I pull open the front door and drop my bag on the floor. I shed my coat, drop that on the floor too and hurry upstairs. Mum calls my name from the kitchen. I ignore her and go straight up to bed, hugging my knees to my chest and wrapping myself up in my duvet as tightly as I can.

How could I have been so stupid? *Obviously* Ollie was going to be upset. I shouldn't have pushed him, even if he *did say* he would be OK. I just don't understand why people say things they don't mean. Ollie's words – the *why can't you just be a normal human for once?* – echo in my head, repeating over and over like the world's worst broken record. He meant *that*, at least.

I could have handled finding that kind of thing out – the not knowing would have been far worse for me in a world where I already feel like I'm constantly fucking up from not knowing things. I didn't stop and really think about which would have been worse for Ollie – why didn't I do that?

What if I've messed everything up?

I thought – and a tear does fall this time, splashing hot and bitter on to the duvet – I thought that we were maybe becoming friends.

My mind plays me a lovely little montage of all the times Ollie and I have spent together over the past couple of months, ending with a static screen of his face from earlier, so angry, so *hurt*.

Maybe it was stupid to think that we were becoming close. Maybe people like me just aren't built to have friends.

"NO," I say out loud, taking even myself by

surprise. "No more self-pity, please," I say, quieter this time.

I refuse to go back to that kind of headspace; I won't do it. I worked my butt off to stop masking and pretending to be a person I wasn't – a person that I didn't even *like*.

And I do like who I am most of the time now. I'm far braver and bolder and unapologetic than I ever dreamt that I could be. And yes, I might have royally stuffed things up on this one occasion, but I still deserve to have friends just as much as anybody else, and to feel safe and supported and every other thing that most people take for granted.

I take all of my stubbornness and try to fuse it together, starting to feel like my fight-and-flight response has reached its crescendo.

I'll message Ollie later and apologise, see if he wants to talk. But for now I've got things to do. *Yes*, I think, less self-pitying, more planning, more doing.

I grab my notebook. First, I write a draft of a letter for Amelia to take to the next school council to chase up their progress on the gender-neutral bathrooms, before returning to my plans for the pride festival.

I flesh out some of the ideas I had about accessibility and add more ideas to the list, even researching some performers that I'd like to book for it once I've got the group's approval, focusing on queer and trans disabled and/or POC performers so that hopefully we can amplify their voices and talents, and then *everyone* in the audience feels seen. This is what I need to make sure happens – this is bigger than me.

I unwrap the duvet from around me so that I'm not just an Imogen head in a duvet molehill any more and sit at my desk. I try to move the chair and then almost fall off as I realise that it's not my desk chair but Ollie's that spins. My throat tightens but I shake my head from side to side as fast as I can to try to get rid of that thought. I'll text him later once he's had the chance to cool off and I feel less wounded at history repeating itself.

I spend the next two hours poring over the guide to applying for grants from the council that I found in September. Then, when I get frustrated filling out the form for the Community Enrichment Events Grant, I do something I really (really) don't want to. I swallow my pride, and video call Amelia.

She answers after two rings and is more than happy to spend the next hour powering through the form with me, drafting responses to particularly confusing questions and helping me write down calculations for all aspects of the festival budget, until we finally finish and send it off.

"We did it! How exciting." She beams at me from the screen and it's then that I notice Josh lounging on the bed in his room behind her while she sits on the floor in front of her laptop. Has he been there this whole time?

I force an answering smile, trying and failing to think about nothing but how great it will be if we get this grant from the council.

"We sure did. Thanks for helping out," I say reluctantly (but meaning it all the same).

"You're so welcome," she says brightly, and my brain comes up with a suggestion: *What if she's not an evil mastermind after all, and is in fact just ... a nice person?* What a highly disturbing thought.

Josh makes a grumbling noise in the background, probably to the tune of *I've been listening to you two talk about hiring stages and sound equipment for over an hour and I'd quite like my girlfriend back now*, so I let Amelia go. Frankly, though, I think in the ranking of things she loves, organisation takes the top spot above him, based on everything I know about her and the vague hint of disappointment I detect around her eyes when I press end call.

The room feels quiet without her voice ringing out in it, matching my incoherent rambles with her much more coherent ones, or reading out a piece of helpful info she found online, and I find myself wishing she was still there. Just so that I don't have to be left to my own thoughts (gross), obviously.

Now I am left to my thoughts in the silence of my room, I reflect on the day. At least it wasn't a *complete* disaster – I've started fixing one thing. Now I just need to figure out how to fix the other...

CHAPTER ELEVEN

OLLIE

> Hi Ollie. I'm really sorry about today, I'm sorry about what we saw and I'm sorry I wasn't more understanding. I hope you're doing OK (I'm v v sorry) x

I stare at the message that's just come through from Imogen. As I'm looking, another message pops up. It's a gif of David from *Schitt's Creek* wearing his top that says *I'm stupid*. It would normally make me laugh, but not today.

I read through the original message again – that's a lot of *sorry*s for two sentences.

I sigh, staring at the pale grey walls of my room from where I've been sitting for two hours, anchored to the floor as I go over and over the events of the day.

I feel awful for snapping at Imogen, for saying that I wished she could just be normal. I *like* that she's not like most people, I really do. But I saw her sitting there – this person who's so unwavering in who they are, who always says what they mean. And it scared me that who she is, is someone I will never get to be. Because there I was, here I *am*, still letting my dad upset me, still letting his emotions guide mine. That's not who I want to be. I want to be open and brave, like her. Colourful, like her.

I clench my jaw and kick out at the rug in front of me.

But I'm just so angry at my dad. Why hasn't he asked how I'm doing? Why hasn't he checked up on me? Does he not care that the angry red mess inside me keeps growing and growing until it's all I can see, all I can feel?

Why doesn't he care? Why has he *never* cared? Sure, he was an OK dad when I was growing up, but we never once talked about anything important. I told him and Mum I was gay when I was thirteen. Mum came over, hugged me so tightly that it hurt and told me that she loved me and was proud of me for telling them, and he just sat there and said, "Right. Well, if that's who you are, then that's who you are."

What the fuck does that even mean? Actually, no, 'I'd have preferred it if you were straight, but I guess I'm just going to have to deal with you being gay now' is what it means. He just sat there. Just like how he just sat there, emotionless, while the walls of the house collapsed around me, and my mum cried herself into oblivion.

I throw my phone across the room. It thumps face down on to the floor and I'm distracted for a second as I scramble across to see if the screen smashed.

Phew. It's fine. That wasn't the smartest idea I've ever had; I really should stop throwing things.

My phone's still open on Imogen's messages. Maybe I should reply. She treated this flippantly but my reaction was uncalled for. I was really mean. I think it's all still a bit too fresh to get into right this second, though.

"Ollie?" Mum appears in the doorway. "I heard a bang. Daijōbu?"

"I'm fine," I say. "I just dropped something, that's all."

"You sure?" she asks, still standing there.

"Yes," I say, in contrast to the tension in my voice.

She steps tentatively further into the bedroom. "Did you have a nice time with Imogen earlier?"

I laugh, a horrible hollow laugh that I wish I could take back before it's finished.

Mum's forehead creases into a concerned frown. "What is it?"

"You don't want to know."

"I do," she insists. "Whatever it is is clearly upsetting you and that means it's important, and if it's important to you then it's important to me too."

"It *is* important to you," I say flatly. "That's exactly why we shouldn't talk about it."

"Not talking never helped anything, kid. I know that's how your dad liked to 'deal with things' –" she puts that last part in air quotes – "but you know that's not me."

Now I'm torn.

"Come on, talk to me. Things always seem worse in your head than they do when you say them out loud. Just—"

"I KNOW DAD CHEATED ON YOU."

Fuck.

Mum's staring at me, eyes wide and mouth hanging slightly open.

FUCK.

"I'm sorry…" I'm such an idiot. "I didn't mean…"

She closes her mouth. "How did you…"

I stare down at my rug again. "Imogen and I saw him with this woman outside his work," I say quietly. I leave out the part about how we were there on purpose and how we'd been working on catching him out for weeks.

Mum drops down on to my bed and the sound of the springs in my mattress adjusting rings out into the otherwise silent room. (I think she's too shocked to coordinate standing and thinking at the same time.)

"Mum?" I venture tentatively. "I'm really sorry, I shouldn't have—"

"It's OK. I just… I didn't think you'd find out."

"I know you didn't," I say back, a little more

fiercely than I'd intended to.

Mum looks up from intently studying the palms of her hands.

"Gomen. I'm sorry," I say. "I know this isn't your fault. I just wish I'd known so that I could have, I dunno, supported you more. And got as angry with Dad as he deserved."

"You've supported me more than you should have had to, honey. And I didn't want you to be angry with your dad. That's why I tried to shield you from all of this – which I see now wasn't the right way to go about it and I'm sorry for that," she adds with an apologetic smile. "And why I went along with him when he asked me not to tell you why the divorce was happening. I wanted you to have a relationship with him. He's still your dad after all."

"He won't be after I murder him."

"That's not funny, Oliver."

I can't believe he was such an asshole. To not only cheat on her but then be like, 'Hey, don't tell the kids that I'm shagging someone else. Let them blame both of us for this. That seems fair, right?' I can't believe he would do this to us.

I glance at Mum, still sitting there looking like she's grieving and trying to keep it all together for me, and something deep in a cavern in my chest *aches*. I get up from the floor, sit down next to her on the bed and wrap my arms round her, as tightly as she did with me when I came out to her.

She needs me, just like I needed her then.

She stays sitting up, her back stiff for a few beats before she disintegrates. She leans her head against mine, and I feel her shoulders shaking with sobs. We stay there for a while, neither of us moving. She looks small – she's a few inches shorter than me anyway – but now it seems like she's been punctured, all the strength in her slipping silently out and making her deflate.

After a while, she lifts her head up to look at me. I wipe a tear off her cheek with my cardigan sleeve and she smiles a watery smile, wiping away a single half-dried tear from my own cheek that I wasn't aware was there.

"I'm so sorry, Mum."

She shakes her head. "You have nothing to apologise for. You've done nothing wrong."

"Neither have you," I say insistently, and she sighs.

"No. I don't suppose I have." She looks solemn, as though she's trying to convince herself that that's true. "I just never thought I'd be forty and divorced. Or divorced at all… I've … I've *failed*."

"Mum, no, stop that," I say fiercely. "You've not failed at anything. Dad's the one that caused this, not you. You loved him and he treated you like shit. You'd never do that, not to anyone. You're always kind; you're the best mum Maya and I could ask for. That sounds pretty damn successful to me."

She sniffs, raising her head to meet my fierce gaze with her own soft one. "Thank you, sweetie."

I know I should let the conversation end here, but there's something I need to ask her. I don't know whether I'll get an answer, but I have to try.

"Mum? Can I— Can I ask you a question? You don't have to talk about it if it's too hard but…" I bite the inside of my cheek and take in a breath. "Who is the woman? How did Dad meet her?"

Her chest hitches slightly but her face is serious and resolved as she replies. "Her name is Lisa. She works behind the bar at the racecourse. They met when your dad had his work Christmas party there."

That explains his sudden perverse interest in racing in the New Year. But wait…

My eyes bore into Mum's face. "So they've been seeing each other all year? All these months?"

She doesn't say anything, instead giving an almost imperceptible nod.

"GOD. That *bastard*," I spit, and then have to ignore a twisting in my gut as I think about Imogen.

Mum slaps my hand. "Oliver, *language*. I'm not saying you're wrong, but we don't need to use words like that." Her face softens as she looks at me, however. "We're going to be fine, you know," she says quietly, and I wonder who she's trying to convince the most – her or me. "One day this will all be fine."

I squeeze her towards me with the arm round her shoulder and reply (untruthfully), "If you say so."

She takes advantage of our closeness and reaches out to tuck a strand of hair behind my ear. "Come on then," she says. "Let's check on your sister and then you can help me finish making the gyoza for tea."

"Hai," I agree quietly.

★

Maya's still glued to a Barbie princess movie downstairs, her own Barbies in her lap.

"You all right, stinky?" I call out through the open doors between the kitchen and lounge as I sit down at the table.

She nods but doesn't remove her eyes from the screen. I don't blame her – the original Barbie movies are criminally underrated.

I sit and spoon the marinated minced-pork-and-vegetable mixture on to the gyoza skins and then pass them on to Mum to seal up in crimped crescent shapes.

The rain drizzles outside, droplets descending slowly down the windows, catching the light from the lamps in the lounge and shining in contrast to the shadowy darkness of the street outside. We eat the gyoza with white rice and steamed vegetables and then pile on to the sofa to watch *The Princess and the Pauper*. Maya falls asleep with her head on my legs, and when I glance at Mum I see her eyes are growing heavy too; it won't be long before she's asleep. I stay still and silent for the rest of the movie so as not to disturb them both while they're so peaceful.

I wish I felt more peaceful. I wish I believed Mum when she said that we're all going to be fine, but I just don't see how I will *ever* feel fine with this. I don't see these feelings ever growing smaller.

CHAPTER TWELVE

IMOGEN

People are loitering in the corridor before the bell rings. Everyone's catching up from the half-term break, their conversations bouncing around the walls. Ollie is standing at his locker, talking to Josh and Amelia. Amelia sees me looking and smiles like she's expecting me to go over there. I would, but...

Ollie didn't reply to my message. It's been three days now – it's not like he hasn't had the time. No, he's making a statement. He's letting me know that I messed up and he hasn't forgiven me yet.

The bell rings and I dawdle towards Biology, avoiding looking up at any of them as I go past, not wanting to see Ollie avoiding me too. I don't want to annoy him – if he's going to forgive me, then he's going to do it on his own terms; he's made that perfectly clear.

The following weeks pass quietly. I stay busy making more plans and going through the motions at school, and I carry on keeping my distance from Ollie. I don't talk to him or even look at him when he can see me. I even talk to Amelia and Josh more instead at the next protests and bake sales to avoid pressuring him in any way. It's a little lonely, and I think Amelia picks up on that because she messages me a few times with questions about the group that have super-obvious answers, and with much too frequent updates on our fundraising progress. (We've made a good chunk from all our bake sales, but not nearly as much as would be ideal at this stage – we really need to start booking things in.) It's slightly patronising but also nice of her, I suppose.

★

Somehow, it's the final Monday before the Christmas break, and thus also the final group meeting of the year. I'm there early – partly because I have lots to talk about, and partly because I have no one waiting for me in the halls to chat and procrastinate with. Mr Holland clearly notices I'm not on top form and offers to tell me a joke to cheer me up, but he stops talking when the others start coming into the room.

I put my head down and stare at the graffiti scrawled on the table. Apparently, someone called Chris is offering some kind of service in the boys' bathroom and for a very reasonable price too. How lovely.

I keep staring until Mr Holland nudges me. "I think everyone's here."

"Oh, right, good." I cough and shake my hair back, trying to appear in control. "Thank you all for coming and thank you for your participation this term – we've done some really great things. And, Louisa?" I turn to face her. "Do you want to tell the group what you messaged me about the other day?"

"Sure. Your support at the protests helped the environmental agency I've been working with to get the council to recommit to their clean-energy promises and come up with a timeline for those changes. So you've all helped enact real change!" She smiles round at us.

"And not only that," I add, "but all our bake sales and campaigning online – big props to Maryam especially there for her hard work—"

She looks bashfully pleased as I continue.

"—have helped us raise just over two thousand pounds. And Mr Holland says that the heads have been made aware of the need for gender-neutral bathrooms and are going to come up with a 'dynamic solution' in the New Year. God knows what that means, but hopefully it's progress."

Clem looks understandably wary of anything that involves the world 'dynamic', but gives me a nod, nevertheless. "Sounds good."

"But," I say, glancing down at my notes, my anxiety manifesting in my leg jiggling under the table and the slightly manic tone that creeps into my voice with my following words, "come the New Year, we definitely need to kick things up a notch. Amelia and I sent in a proposal for us to get a community grant that would be a huge help with the costs for the pride event, but there's no guarantee that we'll get it, and we're already behind on our first fundraising goal if we do have to raise all the money ourselves. Does anyone have any ideas for bigger events that we could do next term? Things that would make more money than bake sales?" I look expectantly around the room.

There's a pause and then Amelia raises her hand. "What about a talent show?"

"A talent show," I repeat, processing the suggestion.

"Yes," Amelia says. "We could get students to perform in it and then we could charge for tickets. Even if it was just five pounds, if we sold tickets for all three hundred seats in the auditorium, then that's already fifteen hundred pounds and we could give people the choice to pay more if they're able to as a donation."

Annoyingly, it's an excellent idea – I wish I'd come up with something similar myself. "That… That sounds like a great plan, thank you, Amelia."

She smiles a wide, glowing smile as everyone

else expresses their enthusiasm.

"I could play the flute?" Clem offers.

"And I could get the school orchestra to perform – I'm their violinist," Amelia says because of fucking course she plays the violin.

I'm busy suppressing an eye roll when someone else speaks up and makes me freeze.

"Imogen?" Ollie says quietly. "You should do stand-up."

I look over at him. "Oh!" I say, trying to play it cool, even though internally I'm freaking the fuck out. "Yeah ... yeah, I could."

He shrugs and goes back to staring at the wall opposite him.

I clear my throat. "When are we thinking for this talent show, then?"

"Ooh!" Amelia shifts to sit up straighter in her chair. "How about on Valentine's Day? We could make it a whole special themed fundraising day."

Hmm. On the one hand, I despise creepy little cherubs and teddy bears holding hearts. But, on the other hand, we probably *would* sell more tickets that way...

"Sure," I say begrudgingly. "I guess that makes sense from a marketing standpoint. And then we have a whole month to organise it and sell tickets after the holidays. But I draw the line at the performances being Valentine's Day themed. I refuse to listen to a Year Seven kid play 'Can't Help Falling in Love' on an out-of-tune ukulele."

Amelia lets out a laugh, and Louisa nods grimly. "Valid."

"Great!" Mr Holland says enthusiastically. "Let me present the idea to the heads and see what I can do."

The rest of our session is spent with everyone chatting and getting hyped about the talent show. I sit quietly, only speaking when I'm directly spoken to, half listening to them all, half thinking things over. This would be my first proper stand-up gig – I've written hundreds of routines over the years, but I've not delivered any of them in front of a big audience like this and there's a lot riding on the talent show as a whole – I should really get some practice in.

I get out my phone and google one of the pubs locally that I know does an open-mic comedy night. I scroll through their website and discover there's one coming up at the end of the week.

I take screenshots of the dates and times as the bell rings. Everyone gets up to leave for class. I say a few hurried goodbyes and head to Sociology where I ignore everything Miss White has to say and brainstorm ideas for my routine instead.

★

"Imogen, come here!" This is bizarre. My dad sounds almost … jubilant (?) as he calls out to me on Friday night. Something must be really wrong this time.

I sigh, stop doing my make-up for the open-mic night, only one eye glittery, and head downstairs.

"Immy, darling, look who's here!" Mum's beaming, gesturing across the kitchen table to— Ah. This explains it. My dad's favourite child is home.

"Oh. Hey, Ben," I say, making reluctant eye contact with my brother, who nods back just as reluctantly. I forgot he broke up for Christmas this week too.

"Sit down," my dad's voice booms. He's also beaming, like the cat that's got its favourite child back. "Ben was just about to tell us all about uni and his game against Edinburgh. Bet you scored the winning try, huh?" He claps Ben on the back.

Ben looks uncomfortable, ruffling his cropped curly hair and shifting in his seat. "Not exactly. I, erm, I was actually on the reserve bench for that."

My dad's brow furrows, creating a valley in the centre of his forehead. "Ah. Right. I'm sure you're busy with your studying too – you just need to manage your time a little better, then you'll ace your exams *and* be the star player, just like you did at A Level."

Ben slumps down even more in his seat. At this rate, he'll be on the floor before the night's up. Maybe university's turning out to be a trickier beast than he was expecting.

"Or not," I say helpfully. "Uni must be a whole different ball game – pardon the pun – right, Ben?"

"You could say that," he mutters.

"You shouldn't, though, Imogen." My dad's voice is a warning. "Ben's smart; he can do anything if he tries hard enough. Right, son?"

Ben's expression ripples with tension, his eyes flicking to mine like a hostage trying to communicate something. My brother and I have very little in common besides unruly hair, but we do both know what it's like to live under our parents' roof and expectations. And though, sure, I may resent him for being the favourite, for being everything my parents want him to be, I do also know that being 'everything' must carry pressure. A lot of it. I decide to change the subject to rescue him from this conversation.

"Well, I'd love to stay and chat," I say, "but I need to finish getting ready. I'm performing at a comedy open-mic tonight. You're all welcome to come and watch, of course," I add, purely for my own amusement.

"Oh! Well, we c—" My mother's eager tones are interrupted by my father's irritated ones prompting her face to become awash with frustration.

"We've got lots of catching-up to do with Ben," he says. "And besides we don't want to encourage this comedy thing. You're going to need to grow up one day, Imogen, and start thinking practically. The sooner the better."

"You are so right," I say, my tone airy and light.

"Hey, maybe if you put as much pressure on me as you put on Ben, that'd sort me right out. I'm sure I'd be happy, healthy and Oxford-bound that way."

"You're happy, aren't you, darling?" my mum asks, looking at Ben with desperate eyes.

"Of course," I say. "Look at him." I gesture to his hunched frame and withdrawn expression. "Happy as Larry, aren't you, Ben? Anyway, I'd best be off. Have a lovely catch-up. You'll have to regale me with stories later, Ben, sorry. I've got people to make laugh and parents to disappoint."

And with that I skip out of the kitchen, tossing a non-sarcastic apologetic glance to Ben on my way out, while – to my great surprise – I hear my mother begin to berate my father. "You could at least let me finish a sentence, Greg. And why couldn't we have…"

Her voice fades away as I exeunt back up to my room to finish my other eye before leaving the house, walking down the streets in the dark. I watch my breath billow out in front of me in the cold like I'm some kind of cool reverse dragon and try to get in the comedy zone.

The streets in the centre of town are lit overhead with strings of multicoloured Christmas lights and some slightly phallic-looking lights in the shape of candles with holly berries on either side. Clearly no one on the council decorating committee has a dirty enough mind.

I reach the pub where the open-mic night's

happening, *The Lock and Key*, and peer in through the window. It's a busy night, most of the tables are taken and there are no stools left at the bar. The small platform in the corner of the room is already surrounded by a swarm of people.

I take a deep breath, enjoying the cold now that I'm about to be thrust into the cloying clutch of several dozen people's body heat, and push open the door as a bell tinkles above me.

I approach the bartender who glowers at me like he's expecting me to ask for an alcoholic drink, but a) I don't think lowering my inhibitions even further than usual would be a smart idea and b) I'm well aware that, despite my being the ripe old age of sixteen, my height (or lack of it) will likely mean I'm going to get ID-ed well into my thirties. Instead, I order a cappuccino before hovering in one corner. Two old guys at a table in front of me make eye contact with each other and smirk. Twats.

A man with a moustache extracts himself from his group of friends and gets up on to the stage. "Hey, everyone," he half shouts, making the microphone redundant. "The open-mic night is about to start so if you haven't already then get your ass to the sign-up sheet on this wall here and put your name down."

Aha, that's where it is. I try not to spill my drink as I push through the crowd to the clipboard, where I scrawl my name beneath half a dozen others.

I ignore the feeling of people's eyes following me as I head back to my spot in the corner of the room and take a few big sips of my coffee.

The two men in front of me turn round and smirk odiously.

"You telling some jokes, then, love?" says the one wearing a large grey hoodie and sporting a scruffy beard. He takes a drink from his pint glass and wipes his mouth, largely missing the beer froth that's clinging to his already crumb-scattered beard.

"Yes," I reply stiffly. I think the coffee was a bad idea – the caffeine's making me even more jittery.

"You think you're funny, then, do you?" he says, shuffling his chair round to face me more directly.

"Pretty funny, yes."

"Go on, then." His friend leers. "Tell us a joke."

"I'd rather not."

"G'wan, you've said you're funny – prove it."

"I don't need to prove it to you," I say forcefully. "I already know I'm hilarious. I don't really give a fuck whether you think so too."

"Hey, hey!" The grey-hoodied one puts his hands up in mock surrender. "We just want to hear a joke; there's no need for a pretty young thing like you to use words like that."

Dear Lord. I pull a disgusted face and they both smirk at each other again. I think I might vomit. What a shame that they'd both be in the splash zone if I did.

Thankfully, the first person to perform starts talking and they swivel back round, leaving me to hate them in peace.

I try to listen to the man on the stage but all the other noises around me are also clamouring for top billing and I'm finding it hard to focus.

A few words manage to stray over to me, though. The man onstage finishes a line with 'and my wife has no idea', gaining a few throaty chuckles from the crowd. He carries on, making several more jokes about how stupid his wife is and how hilarious he thinks it is that he pretends he doesn't know how to do basic household tasks so that she'll get annoyed and take over from him and he can watch the rugby all afternoon.

"Love a bit of weaponised incompetence," I mutter to myself.

"What was that, darlin'?"

Oh, shit. The man onstage is staring right at me; a sea of bloated, red-faced heads twist around to face me, and I suddenly feel acutely aware of my body and the determination with which my heart is thudding in my chest. I take a sip of coffee and gather myself for a second before shaking my hair back and raising my gaze to meet his.

"I'm sorry?" I say, despite not being sorry at all.

"You muttered something. I wondered if you wanted to share with the group." The man smiles with far too many teeth. There's a ripple of amusement through the crowd infused with an undisguised desperation to see what happens next.

I take another sip. "If I'd wanted to share with the group, I'd have said it louder."

The man blinks several times before selecting his retort. "Wow, someone thinks she's clever."

There are a few more scattered laughs. I can practically hear the gross men I'm sitting near panting to see how this plays out. It's becoming very clear to me that this is not a place in which I want to spend my time. I stand up.

"Oh, you've finally realised you're lost, have you?" the man onstage says, his brow shiny. "If you ask behind the bar, I'm sure they'll give you directions to the nearest creche. Or have you realised you've got somewhere more important to be? The kitchen, maybe?"

"Ham and cheese on white, please, love," the bearded guy behind me practically *screeches*, and all the men in the audience lose their tiny minds at that shining example of wit, like baboons at the zoo. If they started flinging their shit around, I wouldn't be in the least bit surprised.

I weave my way through the crowd, mug in hand again, unfortunately having to dodge nearer the front to find a way out. I can feel my rage actually emanating from my body, so much so that the twat on stage notices.

"There's no need to get the hump, doll. I was just making a joke."

"Oh, really? Well, there's a first time for everything, I suppose," I say, putting a great deal of effort into sounding airy and not at all like I'm close to combusting in a fiery rage.

I get a few laughs from the audience at that and a few *waheyyyy*s.'

"Honestly, don't let me stop you," I continue. "Maybe if you get some practice in it'll become more apparent to your audience when you've actually started."

The head baboon onstage doesn't like that – he doesn't like it one bit. With a thunderous face, furious that the audience would turn on him even slightly, he spits out, "All right, who let the little bitch in?"

I'm now at the very front and there's a gloriously Imogen-sized gap between two chairs to my right. However, I'm not a fan of being called a bitch. Or rather, if I'm going to be called a bitch, I like to *really* deserve it.

I sidestep the last few people so I'm standing right at the edge of the tiny stage. The man looks down at me smugly from his stool, thinking he's won.

I make direct eye contact with him as I hold up my cup, smile and then slowly pour its contents into his lap.

"WHAT THE FUC—"

I walk swiftly away from him and out of the pub, leaving behind one incredibly irate, soggy man, and a whole crowd of others laughing their bloody heads off.

Well? Anything for my fans.

I emerge into the dark streets outside, shaking my hands out to try to help me regulate my nervous system. I cast an anxious glance behind me, very conscious that it's night and that I've just royally pissed off a very large man.

"IMOGEN!" a voice calls and I jump out of my skin before realising that no one in the pub knew my name and that the voice doesn't sound angry at all.

"Oh. Hi!" I cross the street hastily to join a beaming Amelia and a regular Josh walking along the opposite pavement.

"Are you OK?" Amelia asks, taking note of my shaking hands and my repeated glances behind us at the thankfully still-empty street. "You seem upset."

"How astute." I try to be flippant. Amelia still looks concerned for me, however, and I wonder what it must be like to be a nice person without having to try. "I'm fine. Just slightly concerned I'm going to be chased down by a very large, sexist-joke-making gentleman whom I may have accidentally angered when I poured my coffee in his lap in retaliation for said sexist jokes."

She looks at me with a blank expression for a second before realising I'm not joking. She lets out a burst of laughter. "Wow. That's badass, Imogen. I'm obsessed."

Josh is less impressed. "That probably wasn't the smartest idea," he says curtly.

Amelia's head snaps towards him, frowning. "Josh. It's not Imogen's fault that the men in there were being gross." She turns back to me, curved red lips returning to a crescent-moon shape. "I support your coffee-based retaliation. I think it was brave of you."

"Thanks," I say, taken by surprise at how earnestly admiring she sounds and the unreserved well of kindness in her eyes. Deep brown ones, I notice. With tiny glints of gold that look like glitter.

I jump as a door behind us swings open, letting a burst of sound – revelry and clinking glasses – escape into the street, breaking my gaze with Amelia.

"Oh, God, it's not a tall, angry-looking guy in wet jeans, is it?" I say, ducking between Amelia and Josh and doing a very odd, crouched walk, using them both as a human shield. Amelia laughs, her face momentarily shining in the amber glow of the streetlight as we pass under it.

Josh remains unamused as he casts a quick look over his shoulder. "Nope. It's two pretty short men going the other way."

"Phew. Well, I think it's been long enough that I'm not going to be chased, so I'll leave you to whatever you were doing."

Josh nods. "Thanks."

"Oh, don't worry about that!" Amelia says. "Actually, I've been meaning to message you. Josh and I are having a New Year's Eve party at my house, and I was wondering if you wanted to come? Everyone from the group should be there – no pressure if not, though!"

Hmm. This is unexpected. On the one hand, Amelia and Josh hosting a party together like they're an old married couple already is sickening and I don't want to encourage that. But, on the other hand, it would mean I could skip out on my parents' party and not have to contend with Dad's boring colleagues and Mum's yoga ladies asking me whether I have a boyfriend and telling me how 'cute' I am as they get progressively drunker until one of them throws up on Mum's peonies. Yeah. That settles it.

"Sure," I say. "I'll come."

Amelia looks surprised. (As does Josh, but at least Amelia's pleasantly surprised – I'm starting to think Josh isn't my number-one fan.) "Oh! That's great!" She blinks at me with those perfectly curled eyelashes. "I'll— We'll see you there, then."

This means I only have eleven days of obligatory family time to endure, and then I get to see in the New Year with people who possibly aren't entirely terrible. I think it's fair to assume that Ollie'll be there too, but whether that's a good or bad thing, I guess I'll find out.

CHAPTER THIRTEEN

OLLIE

Christmas seems to be rushing towards me this year, the fairy lights flickering twice as fast as usual, mocking me as they say, 'Oh, you're not looking forward to Christmas this year? TOO BAD: here it comes at warp speed.'

I wake on Christmas morning and groan, stretching out my limbs and accidentally whacking my arm on the wall next to my bed.

"Fuck!" I rub my wrist and grimace as I spot the bulging stocking in my doorway. I guess there's no stalling. Time to pretend to be feeling all *holly jolly* for Maya's sake.

Speaking of Maya, the floorboards across the landing creak and a voice high-pitched with excitement cries, "Can we go wake Ollie? *Pleeeeease?*"

"Ten more minutes, Maya."

I climb out of bed, grabbing a jumper and tugging it over my head, plastering what I hope is a convincing excited smile on my face as I grab my stocking.

"I'm here," I say, going into Mum's room where she and Maya are now situated in her bed.

"Ollie, Ollie, Ollie!" Maya squeals. "Santa's been – look!" She heaves up her stocking to show me and I smile for real this time.

"Wow. Santa must have seen how good you've been this year."

I personally find the idea of a random old man watching you all year and deciding whether he thinks you're 'naughty' or 'nice' incredibly creepy, but it's kind of adorable that she's so excited.

Mum shuffles over so that I can sit down with them on the bed. "Merry Christmas, honey."

"Merry Christmas."

"Come on, present time!" Maya pleads, wriggling impatiently.

"All right, all right, let's see what Father Christmas brought you," I say. I reach into my stocking and then retract my hand, looking around the room. "Where's your stocking, Mum?"

Her expression is blank as she clears her throat. "I – erm…" She sees Maya looking over with a frown on her tilted face. "I told Santa that I didn't need one this year so he could buy the reindeer some extra treats."

"That's nice." Maya nods, satisfied with her answer. I'm far from satisfied, however.

Mum and Dad always did each other's stockings – it hadn't crossed my mind for a second that she wouldn't get one this year. I'm such a *dick*. That settles it – I'm going to have to get a job before next Christmas so that I can make sure she gets one too. God, why didn't I think about this before today?

I glance at Mum and find that she's watching me.

She smiles reassuringly, trying to tell me it's OK. I bite my lip and turn away. It's not OK.

Maya's already tearing into her first present. "Yay! Ollie, look! I got a new horse!" She thrusts a plastic horse in front of my face.

"It's pretty," I say flatly. "What's it called?"

She takes it back and considers it carefully, stroking its fake mane. "I think I'll call it … Blackbeard. Because it has black hair."

She's been really into pirates recently. Last time Imogen was here, they played in the garden for ages, using sticks as swords and shouting words like 'swashbuckling' and trying to get me to walk an imaginary plank.

I wonder how Imogen's Christmas is going – we haven't spoken for a while. I didn't reply to her text after we had our fight on *that* day. I meant to talk to her at school, but then she ignored me in the corridor. I guess she's still annoyed with me for making that comment about her not being normal, and I don't blame her so I've been giving her the space she obviously wants. Everything's felt oddly quiet without her, though. We might only have been hanging out since September, but now we've stopped I'm realising how much I genuinely enjoyed being around her.

★

We finish opening our stockings, then go downstairs to eat breakfast and open the rest of our presents. After I've helped Maya assemble her brand-new toy pirate ship and played a great many rounds of 'mermaids versus pirates' (I was the mermaid, naturally), I dig out my camera (I've been neglecting it recently – beautiful moments have felt a lot harder to spot as of late) to take the usual Christmas family portrait of us all sitting under the tree. It's not really usual, though: it's the first time a 'family' portrait hasn't included my dad. This reminds me of something; I check the time on my phone. Yep. Twelve o'clock. Time to go. *Great.*

Mum and Dad spoke for the first time since he moved out about what they were going to do for Christmas, and the amazing plan they decided on involves Maya and me leaving Mum alone for the afternoon while we go to his flat and watch him attempt to make us Christmas dinner. I protested when I heard, saying that we could just go round on Boxing Day, but apparently Dad insisted on seeing us at some point on actual Christmas. Or Maya, at least. I'm fairly sure he doesn't give a rat's ass about me. I've been brusque with him (at best) ever since I found out about his affair – although he still doesn't know that I know. In a twisted way, I'm kind of enjoying sitting in mutinous silence and watching him get progressively more pissed off with me.

The divorce hasn't exactly brought out my best side.

★

The buzzer is answered by a "Hello?"

"It's us," I say. (Who the hell else would it be on Christmas Day?)

The buzzer makes a grating noise, signalling that we've been permitted entry.

"Welcome, welcome!" Dad opens the door upstairs, wearing a drab red jumper with a vaguely festive white pattern on it.

I walk in while Maya hugs Dad and take a seat on the edge of the sofa, scanning the room for decorations. The dining table has a plastic tablecloth with reindeer on, and there's a foot-high fake tree standing on a side table with a smattering of wrapped gifts on the floor beneath it. Nice to see he's pulled out all the stops.

Maya comes over to sit next to me and spots the tree. "More presents!"

Man, kids are materialistic.

Dad takes a seat on a chair opposite us and

smiles. "Of course there's presents – you didn't think I wouldn't get you anything, did you?"

Maya blinks up at him innocently. "But I already had my presents."

"Not from me, you didn't," Dad says. "You've only had your presents from your mum."

"What do you mean?" she asks, and I glare intently at Dad, trying to tell him to choose his next words very carefully.

Dad continues to be oblivious, however. "Well, Mummy bought the presents you had back at the house, and I bought these ones. You're lucky: you get two Christmases in a way."

"OH MY GOD!" I blurt out, and he closes his eyes for a second before nodding his head to placate me.

"Well, not 'lucky' as such," he says, not getting that the lucky comment was irritating, but only part of the issue.

"But – but—" Maya struggles, fiddling with the tinsel at the end of one of her plaits, "why did Mum buy my presents? I thought they were from Father Christmas."

Dad jerks up his chin, finally looking as panicked as he should be. "*Oh.* Erm, yes, of course they're from Santa. Sorry, Maya."

Maya's lip trembles. "Gracie said that Santa wasn't real at breaktime, but I told her she was being silly."

"She *was* being silly, Maya," I insist, stroking her hair. "Dad just made a mistake, *didn't you*?"

"Yes," he says, nodding wildly. "Yes! I was being silly too. Come on, Maya, let's see what Santa brought you here. He must have known you were coming."

"But you said – you said that you bought them?" she says, not letting it go.

Dad has the gall to look over at me for help. The audacity of this bitch.

"Let's just see what you got, shall we?" he says when I don't answer his plea for support.

Maya sits, looking half grumpy, half confused, saying nothing.

I lunge over and grab a present that's got her name written on it. "Here you go, Maya-moo. I wonder what it is? Maybe it's a dinosaur."

She giggles weakly. "It's not big enough, silly."

I smack my head comically. "Of course." I drop my voice to a hushed whisper. "Unless it's just a dinosaur egg, and it'll grow up to be a big one."

She wiggles her shoulders excitedly and starts unwrapping it.

Dad smiles at me as if to say, *Phew! That was a close one!*

I give him my best side-eye and pick up a present labelled 'Ollie', unwrapping it to reveal some sportswear. Dad's clearly still wilfully ignoring the fact that I don't share my friends' affinity for wearing sports clothing when you're not actually playing sports.

"Thanks," I say, pulling the thick cream cardigan Mum (sorry, Maya, *Santa*) got me more tightly around me.

★

Maya grows quiet again during our dinner of an annoyingly well-cooked turkey paired with stone-cold vegetables and lumpy gravy. Neither Dad nor I are feeling particularly chatty, so it's an awkward, silent meal. Once we've washed up (also in silence) and I see that Maya's still staring at the pile of wrapping paper and presents with her concentrating face on, I decide that we've fulfilled our family obligation and we walk home.

Mum's curled up on the sofa with a book that she's clearly just picked up to pretend she's been doing something and not just sitting being sad and lonely while we've been gone.

"Did you have a nice time?" she asks tentatively, and I don't know which kind of answer would make her happier. Actually, no, I do – she's the parent that genuinely wants us to be happy regardless of her own feelings.

Maya goes and snuggles next to her, gazing up at her and saying earnestly, "I don't know if I think Santa's real any more."

Mum's eyes widen. "Why would you think that?"

"Dad," I mouth to her with narrowed eyes, watching as a dark look pass over her face.

★

The week between Christmas and New Year passes as it always does, with everyone feeling stuck between some great ending and a new beginning, not sure whether we're more nostalgic for the past or impatient for all of the unknowns to come.

On New Year's Eve, I spend the day at home watching TV, helping Mum check for any last bits of dust so that the house is ready to welcome the New Year, and making our traditional osechi ryori with Maya's 'help'. Once we've eaten our delicious feast together, I get ready to leave for Amelia and Josh's New Year's party.

"Are you sure you're going to be OK?" I ask Mum as I put on my shoes.

"As I told you the last four times you asked, we're going to be fine," she replies. "Go and have fun – just be back home for sunrise."

I've always really loved the tradition of hatsuhinode (waking up to see the first sunrise of the year) so I'll definitely manage that. I leave them both to celebrate the fact that it's already New Year in Japan, bundle up in my coat and scarf, and walk across town to Amelia's house.

"EY, Ollie's here!" Josh shouts as he opens the door to me, already looking slightly dishevelled with one side of his shirt collar folded upwards.

"Hey."

There are already quite a few people here scattered around on chairs or chatting in the kitchen. The whole footie team is here, as are all of Amelia's friends from the orchestra and student council. I even spot Louisa and Clem looking cosy in an armchair and Maryam adjusting the speakers in the corner.

"Ollie." Amelia smiles, stepping back to let me into the kitchen. "I'm so glad you came. Would you like a drink?"

"Thanks." I pour myself a cider, marvelling at how chill Amelia's parents are to let her throw an unmonitored party and also buy her alcohol.

Josh comes through to pour himself a drink too, and Amelia tuts at him before straightening his collar.

Josh grins and lunges forward to kiss her.

"Josh!" Amelia laughs nervously, taken by surprise, and bats him away. "Stop it!"

I grimace at the floor, manoeuvring myself round their PDA to go back into the lounge.

I make conversation for a bit, graze from the professionally catered spread, even dance when coerced by a progressively more inebriated Josh. But part of me still wishes that I'd stayed at home, having a quiet night of family time and self-pity.

I collapse on to the sofa after a particularly

energetic dance to 'Mr Brightside' that I was forced into with the rest of the football team and let out a long, slow sigh.

"You not having the best time either?"

I turn to my side and see Maryam sitting with her legs curled next to her.

"Oh. Yeah, I'm just kind of tired and not in the mood for a party. I'm fine, though," I insist.

She nods knowingly. "Same. My mum wanted me to go out and celebrate. I normally do, even though it's not the Hijri New Year until July. She says that your teen years are the best years of your life—"

"God, I really hope *that's* not true," I say and then immediately feel awkward, but Maryam just laughs.

"Me too. I don't think they will be. Everyone's trying so hard to be *something* and I feel like it only makes them happy maybe half of the time."

I notice her looking over at Amelia and Josh who are now dancing to some jazz music that must have been an Amelia addition to their playlist.

Maryam must feel me following her gaze and stops to turn back to me. "Sorry, that was a bit deep for so early in the night, wasn't it? I'm usually more of a *stay at home watching Netflix and baking my troubles away* kind of gal."

"That's fair," I say. "I saw your cake, by the way," referring to the ginormous two-tier chocolate cake with 'Happy New Year' written on it in perfect iced calligraphy, with buttercream swirls around the edges, that's taken pride of place on the dining table. "It's awesome."

Maryam looks pleased. "Thanks! I saw your photography page too. We should team up more in the group. With your photography skills and my knowledge of how to game social-media platforms, we'd be unstoppable. We should talk to Imogen about it when she gets here."

I'd been nodding along in agreement the whole way through until she got to the last sentence. I didn't realise Imogen was coming. She's not going to want to talk to me, even if it is about the group.

Maryam's clearly waiting for a response, and I feel bad, but I suddenly can't seem to force myself to do anything but smile half-heartedly and then turn my attention back to the room.

We sit in silence as the song finishes and another one starts. I immediately recognise it as 'Gimme! Gimme! Gimme!' by ABBA. Charlie and Josh make eye contact with each other and run over to me.

"DUDE!" Josh shouts. "This is your shit – come on."

"I'm good, thanks." I'm fine just nodding along and enjoying it from the safety of the sofa.

"You have to dance," Charlie says. "You made us come to the cinema with you to watch the second *Mamma Mia* film – you love ABBA."

"I do love ABBA – it'd be a crime not to – but I'm really fine here," I insist.

Josh moves to grab my arm and I jump up to escape him.

"I'll be back in a second," I say, leaving the room as quickly as I can.

"Fine, you come dance with me, then, babe." I manoeuvre round Josh, who's now grabbing Amelia's hand and trying to pull her in towards him.

"I can't," Amelia says hastily, yanking her hand out of his. Josh's jaw hardens. "I think someone's at the door."

I go out into the hall with Amelia, leaving her to open the door, and stride up the staircase, my heart thumping a hurried beat inside my chest as I sneak into the bathroom to hide.

What's wrong with me? Why can't I just have a good time?

I should have been better at at least pretending to enjoy myself – I don't want to bring anyone else down with me. I sink slowly on to the cool tiles, leaning my head back against the side of the bath.

Yeah. I think I'll just stay up here a while.

CHAPTER FOURTEEN

IMOGEN

I actually love New Year's Eve.

Not the usual parties with my parents' friends, but the moment after everyone's gone home and you're left on your own to stare at the night sky and think about how, at that precise second, people all over the world are hoping for better things. It's nice to feel slightly less like I'm screaming into a void.

I practically skip the few streets over to Amelia's house, flared green velvet trousers swooshing round my ankles, leaving a trail of glitter behind me.

I push open the gate with a horrible grating noise that makes my shoulders tense up under my blazer. I can see through the tinsel-strewn windows that the lounge is already full of people seemingly having the time of their lives, dancing and talking, drinks in hands and smiles on faces.

Someone must have been listening out for new arrivals because a bleary shadow behind the glass approaches the door before I can even knock.

"Imogen! You came!" Amelia opens the door in a red silk dress, hair perfectly wavy, looking like some kind of goddess of New Year's Eve.

The hall is far more bohemian than I was expecting. The walls are painted a deep green and there are paintings of famous composers or musicians with the heads of various animals going all the way up the stairs. We walk past Sheep Beethoven and I nod to him. "No one thought to go with Baaach for that one, huh?"

Amelia snorts and then immediately covers her mouth like she can't believe she just made such an un-demure noise. "Um, no. Apparently not." She recovers from her character-shaking outburst. "Not everyone is blessed with your top-tier punmaking abilities."

"Probably for the best."

She offers me a drink, listing an almost comically expansive selection that I cut off halfway through to just ask for a lemonade. She pours me out a generous measure of some fancy lemonade in a glass bottle and even fetches a lemon slice and star-shaped ice cubes. "I'm not drinking either," she says conversationally. "Josh drinks enough at parties for the both of us. I prefer to stay in hostess mode."

"That seems on brand," I say, and she glances at me like she's not sure whether I'm complimenting or insulting her. I'm not sure either.

I follow her through to the lounge and then head straight for the corner of the room that has huge knitted cushions. To my surprise, Amelia follows me and takes a seat on the other cushion.

"Gosh, I'm tired already. Josh has been in a very dancey mood tonight – if he insists on any more, I don't think I'll make it until midnight. Poor Ollie already had to take a break."

I sit upright. "Ollie's here?"

"Uh-huh, he's about somewhere."

I knew he would be. I think I'll try to talk to him at some point, even if it's just to wish him a happy New Year.

"I'm really excited about the talent show – it's going to be so good," Amelia says, her voice raised so I can hear her over the too-loud music. "And hey." She taps me lightly on the arm. I turn back from watching our classmates dancing terribly to face her properly (after briefly blinking down at the place on my arm her hand just vacated). "I can't wait to see you do your stand-up for it."

"Don't get too excited," I say. "I'm not super sure how I feel about performing at the minute."

Amelia looks instantly concerned. "Why not?"

"Well … the last time I was going to do it didn't exactly go to plan," I say, flicking at the pompom fringing on the cushion, "as you know."

"Yes, but that wasn't your fault," she starts, but Josh spots us both in the corner and immediately makes a beeline for Amelia.

"C'mon, babe, come dance – I love this song."

An Ed Sheeran song is currently playing, and I have to battle so hard against the urge to laugh as Amelia lets herself be led away by Josh, tossing an apologetic glance at me over her shoulder as he drags her into the crowd of sweaty teen dancers.

It's fine. I'll go and see where Ollie's disappeared to. There are too many different noises going on in here anyway, and then, when you throw Josh shout-singing along to Ed into the mix, I'm no longer just in sensory overload, I'm in my own personal hell.

I climb the stairs, almost knocking a picture of Mozart with a goose head off the wall with my shoulder. There are five doors on the landing, all of them firmly closed – Amelia doesn't seem like the kind of person who would let people get up to salacious shenanigans in any of the bedrooms. I start with the first door on the right. The room beyond looks like half office space, half home for more instruments than I've ever seen in one place outside the school music room.

The next door I try can't be anything but Amelia's room. There's a nook that houses her double bed with a collection of perfectly colour-coordinated cushions, three sets of bookshelves, a dressing table with make-up and skincare products (Ollie would approve) neatly lined up in rows, and a desk with everything at right angles. The wall above her desk serves as a gallery with framed prints of classic literature book covers, all hung on a wall covered in delicately patterned wallpaper. It's Amelia in a room.

I close the door slowly behind me, feeling like I'm trespassing. Besides, there's still no sign of Ollie anywhere. I try the next door but find it's locked.

I knock on the door and a voice rings out from inside that I recognise instantly. "Hello?"

"Ollie?"

There's a pause. "Yeah?"

"It's Imogen," I say. "Are you doing a shit, or can I come in?"

There are noises like he's scrambling to get up from the floor and then a click as the door unlocks.

Ollie stands there, hands in the pockets of his wide-legged trousers. "H-hey."

"Hey," I echo as I walk past him and climb into the claw-foot bath, sitting there cross-legged.

Ollie just stares.

"Come sit," I say, patting the tub in front of me.

He quirks an eyebrow. "In the bath?"

"Chill. I promise not to turn the tap on."

He shrugs and comes to sit opposite me. "It's cold," he says.

"Yup."

We survey each other, neither of us saying anything.

"We should—" I start, at the same time as Ollie

says, "I'm sorry—"

I smile. "You can go first."

He nods, pulling his sleeves further down over his hands. "OK. I'm really sorry things got so messed up. I was just so *mad*. At my dad," he adds.

"Nice rhyme."

"Thank you." He carries on staring at his hands in his lap. "But I took it out on you, and I shouldn't have done. And I especially shouldn't have said that thing – you know, about you being normal or whatever. I've thought about it a lot recently, and I think I knew it was a shitty thing to say at the time, but I didn't realise quite *how* shitty until afterwards. I like that you don't give a fuck what other people think, and you get excited about things, and you come up with these crazy plans and then actually do them. I don't want you to be anything else. I need you to know that." His voice wavers. "I really didn't mean it – I was just pissed off. I – I never should have said it." He finishes talking and lifts his head up hesitantly to see my expression.

My eyes crinkle as I smile at him, and he blushes. That was a pretty good apology. "Hey," I say firmly, "it's OK. I always forgive."

He nods, mouth beginning to curve upwards.

"*Once*."

My lip twitches as we look at one another and burst into simultaneous laughter.

We laugh for a solid thirty seconds before collecting ourselves.

"Man, it's good to laugh," Ollie says. "It's been a very laughter-free few weeks."

"Well…" I reply, "we'll just have to have lots of uproariously good times now to make up for that, then, won't we?"

"Sounds good." His smile is audible.

I feel lighter, like maybe things really will be OK between us from now on. There's still something left for me to say, though, before we draw a line under this whole unfortunate situation.

"Erm…" I pause – I really need to get this right. "I, erm – I need to apologise too."

Ollie shakes his head firmly and looks as if he's about to interrupt me, so I forge on, needing to say my piece.

"No, I do. I should have taken how you would feel into consideration and been more understanding. I shouldn't have pushed you to basically stalk your dad. I thought it would help you, but really I think I was just thinking about what would help *me*, and I know you said you'd be OK, but I shouldn't have—"

"Imogen," Ollie says loudly. "Imogen, stop. It's OK."

"Really? Because I have two more apology verses to go, and I could probably even improvise an apologetic interpretive dance if I needed to."

"As much as I would love to see that, it's really

fine," Ollie says. "I *am* glad that I know. I wasn't at the time, but I am now. And," he adds, "it *was* kind of fun getting to Sherlock it up."

"Excuse me, I'm clearly the Sherlock in this friendship. You're such a Watson."

"We can take turns being Sherlock."

I fold my arms across my chest. "We'll see. I'm not very good at taking turns."

"Why does that not surprise me?"

"Because you know me pretty well."

"I suppose I do."

I grin to myself, watching Ollie do the same out of the corner of my eye. "So…" I say, trying (and failing) to act casual, "are we … friends again?"

"I didn't realise we were friends before," Ollie says, a teasing glint in his eye.

I fall for it, nonetheless. "Um, EXCUSE ME – of course we were. What did you want, a friendship bracelet?"

"That would have been nice."

I glare at him sulkily and he shakes his head, starting to laugh again.

"Yes, we're friends again, Imogen. No friendship bracelet necessary."

Thank fuck for that – the friends part anyway: I'm absolutely making him a friendship bracelet now.

"So how have your holidays been?" I ask once he's stopped laughing.

He sobers up quickly, the frown lines between his

eyebrows crumpling. "How were *your* holidays?" he says.

Like I would ever let him off the hook that easily. *"So how were your holidays?"*

"No, how were—"

I give him my most withering stare.

He sighs. "Fine. Not great. Dad basically told Maya that Santa wasn't real, the bastard, and I mostly ignored him. He still doesn't know that I know," he adds. "And, apart from that, I've just been hanging out in my room, feeling sorry for myself. I'd just quite like a break from so many terrible things happening, you know?"

I attempt to look sympathetic, but am wildly unsuccessful. "Dude, no," I say frankly. "We need to get you out of that headspace immediately; it's not going to help anything. You've got to learn to see life not as a series of unending tragedies, but as a series of not-terrible moments occasionally interrupted by tragedy. That's the only way to survive in this dumpster fire of a world."

Ollie leans back. "You know, that was almost wise."

"I am frequently *almost* wisdomous, yes."

"You're ridiculous," he snorts.

"I'm ridiculous? Says the guy sitting in an empty bathtub. Hey." I realise something. "Why are you hiding out in the bathroom anyway?"

Ollie shrugs. "Just wasn't having a great time downstairs. Too many people being happy."

"Ah, yes, people being happy are the worst," I say sagely. "To be fair, the music was very loud and there was a lot of Amelia and Josh-ness going on down there. I was glad to escape to come and find you."

"Maybe we're just not party people," Ollie says.

"Nah," I respond. "We're definitely party people; we're just not *people* people."

He laughs again. "That might be true."

"Here," I say, pulling out my phone and opening Spotify. "I'll prove to you that it's definitely true." I press play on my *Soundtrack for the Revolution* playlist.

Ollie listens for a second, rudely not joining me in bopping my head to the beat. "Why does all your music sound like angry women having breakdowns?" he asks.

"Because that's what the inside of my head feels like, except now it has killer beats."

"Killer beats," he repeats.

"Is what my alter ego would be if I was a DJ slash serial killer? Yes."

He raises an eyebrow. "Would you kill your victims by making them listen to this music?"

I open my mouth in mock outrage. "DUDE, how dare you? This slaps and you know it. But go on, then," I challenge. "You put on something better."

He takes the phone off me and scrolls for a while as I look impatient.

"Aha!" he says at long last, pressing play. The

unmistakable intro of 'All Too Well' by Taylor Swift begins playing.

"Of course." I think about rolling my eyes, but the song is a certified bop.

I stand up, awkwardly clambering out of the bath, and offer Ollie my hand to do the same.

He tilts his head at me in question, but follows my lead.

"Now," I say emphatically, facing him on the tiles, "we were about to prove that we're definitely party people by having a dance party."

"We were?"

"We were."

I turn the music up full blast and then start headbanging.

Ollie just stands there, looking amused, so I headbang even more furiously.

He laughs and then joins in. By the time it gets to the infamous bridge, we're both headbanging while we fling our limbs energetically in every direction and scream along to the lyrics.

The music continues and I can't hear anything but the song and our shouted words – whatever's going on downstairs and in the rest of the world fading away into irrelevance as we dance and sing, our voices and bodies colliding in a golden frenzy as we get lost in our movie-perfect moment, with Miss Swift's angst as our soundtrack. Ollie twirls me under his arm, and I keep going until I'm dizzy and we collapse on to the floor at the final 'all too well', our laughs interspersed with pants as we try to catch our breath.

"Well, that was the best thing ever," Ollie says, his chest heaving under his loose shirt as we lean back against the bath.

"Agreed." I press my hand to my side and grimace. "I think I pulled something."

Once our breathing's returned to normal and the world's no longer spinning, Ollie grabs my hand and pulls me up. We dance and shout along to 'New Romantics' and then catch our breath again to 'New Year's Day' back in the bath, the only sound our breathing and the lyrics that cause goosebumps to graze my forearms.

As the song finishes, despite my protests, Ollie gets out his phone and takes a photo of me – portrait mode and everything, the little photography bitch – cross-legged in the bath, cheeks flushed and sparkling as I smile back at the camera, despite myself. Then he suggests that we should probably go back downstairs and join the others before it gets to midnight and I agree, feeling much calmer now I've danced all the anxious energy out of my body. He grins and I take his hand, squeezing it three times.

We rejoin the party and dance several times with everyone from the activist society, I eat my own bodyweight in crisps, and then it's almost midnight.

Amelia puts the countdown on the TV and

everyone gathers in a glittery clump in the middle of the room, party poppers in hand.

"TEN, NINE, EIGHT, SEVEN," we all count in unison, "SIX, FIVE, FOUR, THREE, TWO, ONE!"

I cover my ears as everyone pops their party poppers and cheers, then I remove my hands as I gaze round the room – Amelia and Josh are kissing, and a couple that was making out in the hall earlier are *really* going at it. Louisa hooks her feather boa round Clem's shoulders and pulls them down on to her lap for a smooch.

I turn to Ollie who's looking slightly ill at so many displays of affection.

Once he spots me watching him, though, all traces of a frown vanish from his face. "Hey, come here." He winks at me in a very disconcerting manner and I shove him away.

"Gross," I say. "Besides, I'm sure you don't want a cliché romantic moment given your current aversion to all things love-related."

"I think I can deal." He lifts my hand up and I let him kiss it. "M'lady."

I shake my head at him, trying to pretend like I'm not the happiest I've maybe ever been. "M'lord."

"Happy New Year," he says.

I smile with aching cheeks. "Happy New Year, Ollie."

CHAPTER FIFTEEN

OLLIE

I start the new school term in a much better place than when the last one ended. Things are fixed with Imogen. Things are most definitely not fixed with my dad (I've been blanking him since Christmas Day), but what with lessons and the preparations for the talent show, hopefully I'll keep myself busy enough to drown out the little self-pitying gremlin that keeps piping up in my head.

My first lesson of the term is Photography, in which we learn how to blend images together in Photoshop. At the end of the lesson, the teacher tells us all to listen closely. I sit up straighter and tear myself away from editing my photo of Maya on a pirate ship.

"All right, lovelies," says Miss Casey as she strides to the front of the class. "This term and the next are really important. You're going to have to plan, photograph and edit your own portfolios for assessment. This year's theme is a broad one and I'm excited to see how you interpret it." She writes the words 'This is what [blank] looks like' on the board.

"You can interpret the theme however you like," she says. "But all your photos need to tell a cohesive story of whatever you pick as your 'blank'. The world is your oyster, so get brainstorming!"

This could be cool, I think to myself as I pack up my things. I've felt my love of photography gently simmering inside of me again ever since New Year's Eve, and I'm always open to more distractions these days. I get thinking about what I could pick as my topic as I walk to the Drama corridor for our group meeting.

Rounding a corner, it appears as if the meeting's been relocated to the slightly inconvenient location of the middle of the hallway. Imogen, Clem and Louisa are all clustered round a door.

"This is a 'dynamic solution', is it?" Imogen's saying, anger ripe in her voice.

"What's going on?" I ask, walking up to them.

Clem just points at the door. Louisa is looking too pissed off for words.

"Oh." Attached to the door for the disabled loo, in addition to the disabled toilet logo, is a sign with the traditional 'male' and female' logos divided by a vertical line. "I guess this is the 'gender-neutral' toilet we were promised."

"I suppose so," Clem says carefully.

"Well, I think it's fucking ridiculous," Imogen says less carefully. "I know we shouldn't have expected the heads to put more than three seconds of thought into something, especially something as unimportant as, I dunno, ensuring all students have a safe place to piss, but—" Her words morph into a very articulate screech.

"So…" I attempt to take over, but I'm not really sure what to say. "What do we do now?"

"Now," Louisa says, "we hope that this means they've magically fixed the lift to the second floor so that I can access the only other disabled toilet in the building. Or that my Ehlers Danlos syndrome miraculously ceases to impact me on school days so that I can leave Judy at home and skip into the regular toilets when this one is inevitably in use."

I raise an eyebrow. "Judy?"

"My chair," she says, patting Judy's arm.

"Of course."

"As *dynamic* as this solution is," Imogen says, "it's not OK. They don't get to just shove all disabled and non-cis people into one category and restrict access for both just because it's *convenient* for them."

"C'mon," Louisa says, gesturing with her head towards the Drama classroom and starting to manoeuvre away. "Let's go to group and tell the others. Maybe we can come up with a different idea that solves this and they'll change it again."

"Or maybe Ms Greenacre 'accidentally' falls off a cliff," Imogen mutters, looking much too pensive about the idea for my liking.

The first meeting of the year begins, and we launch straight into getting the others up to speed.

"So, when they told the student council that they'd taken our idea on board last term, this is what they meant?" Amelia looks affronted to her very core that they would perjure the student council in such a way. "They meant that they were planning to do something that requires the least possible amount of effort and doesn't really solve the problem. I suppose they thought the disabled loos are already gender-neutral so what could be a simpler answer?"

"That's the crux of the matter, yes," Louisa says dryly. "I guess now we just wait and see what happens. But if lots of people do start using it and it becomes inaccessible for disabled students then we'll have to fight them on it again."

Everyone in the group (Mr Holland included) is suitably irritated by this turn of events. Clem chews their lip anxiously the whole time and Imogen continues to vibrate next to me, even as the conversation drifts away from possible alternative solutions to the bathrooms and moves on to the talent show.

Louisa, the only art student in the group, shows

us a mock-up of the posters she's made – first to find people to perform in it, then to advertise for the actual event – which look fab, and then we move on to talking about who within the group is planning on performing so far.

"We've been talking about what songs we should do in the school band group chat," Amelia says, "so we're definitely in." She clears her throat awkwardly. "Imogen, are you thinking you—"

"I don't know," Imogen interrupts in a flat tone.

She filled me in about what happened at the open-mic night. It made me so furious that I told her that if she ever sees any of the guys from the pub again then she needs to point them out to me, and I'll bash their heads together in her honour. She laughed and thanked me, but then also said I needed to 'chill the heck out with the toxic masculinity' otherwise I was sinking to their level, which, fair, I guess.

Amelia twists her hair in silence, clearly picking up on the *I'm not talking about this now* vibe that Imogen's crossed arms and blank expression are exuding.

The bell rings and almost instantaneously Josh, who hasn't said a single word for the entire forty minutes, is by the door.

"Ollie?" He jerks his head towards the corridor. "You coming?"

"Oh. Sure." I tell Imogen that I'll talk to her after

school and follow him down to the changing rooms for PE.

Josh stays silent the whole walk down the path to the sports centre and as we get changed into our matching school joggers and jacket. Usually, we'd be bitching about things together or planning strategies for our upcoming matches. Something's definitely wrong.

"Josh?" I venture tentatively. "Are you all right, man?"

A muscle in his cheek twitches, but he brushes me off. "Yeah. I'm fine."

I don't dare say anything else; we start our warm-up laps without another word.

Charlie jogs to catch up with me as Josh forges ahead. "What's his deal, then?" he says. "He nearly bit my head off earlier when I asked if he wanted to come with me to get a sausage roll. Has he gone vegan or something?"

"Not that I'm aware of. He's upset about something, though; he's barely said a word all day."

Charlie grins as he wheezes his way round the perimeter. "He probably just needs to get la—"

"NOPE," I cut in. I'm not in the mood for his misogyny today. Or any day, really. "Don't be gross."

"You're such a prude, Armstrong."

"Why is Ollie a prude?" A voice comes from behind us; Josh has caught us up again.

"Nothing. It's not important," I say firmly, giving

180

Charlie side-eye.

"Well," Charlie starts, ignoring me to be a brazen dick as per usual. "We were talking about how you're clearly in a mood about something and—"

"I'm not in a mood. Why are you saying I'm in a mood?"

"I dunno…" Charlie flounders. "You seem tense – that's all I'm saying."

"Well, don't," Josh bites back, jogging so closely behind Charlie that he keeps looking over his shoulder nervously. "Don't talk about me when there's no need for it."

"Ah, yes," Charlie mutters. "You're clearly super-fucking chill."

"What?" Josh gets even closer, basically talking directly into Charlie's ear now. "What did you just say?"

"Whoa." I think it's time to intervene – people are starting to stare. "Guys, come on: there's no need for that, just take a breather."

Josh glares at me, a ferocious glint in his eyes. "I don't need to take a breather. Charlie's the one with the issue; *he* should take a breather."

"Look," Charlie starts, "I'm fine. You're the one that's got an issue. Just be a man like me and Ollie and tell us what your deal is. Well, not a man exactly like Ollie," he adds with a snort, "but you get the gist."

Excuse me?

"What the fuck are you trying to say?" Josh says, shoving Charlie from behind.

It's pretty clear what he was trying to say. Be a man – not a gay man, but a straight man, a *manly* man. And there might even be some racist shit mixed in there too.

"That's messed up," Josh says, fire in each word. "Sort yourself the fuck out."

"HEY—" Charlie says, stopping in his tracks so quickly that Josh nearly topples over. "What's your *problem*?"

"My problem is that you're an asshole," he spits out. "That's my problem."

They stand facing each other, both their upper bodies puffed out in aggression.

"Guys…" I say. "Let's just—"

Charlie eyes Josh and then moves forward like he's going to shove him.

Josh reacts quickly, grabbing his arm with a vice-like grip.

"GUYS!" I shout. "Calm down!"

I should have known better, really. Telling someone to calm down has never, not in all of history, made someone actually *calm down*.

Charlie scrambles to yank his arm out of Josh's grasp. Josh does let Charlie go, but then makes a motion with his own arm like he's going in for a punch.

I react quickly enough to grab his fist and get in between them.

"FUCKING TRY ME, MATE!" Charlie yells, trying to dodge round me.

"CUT IT OUT!" I shout.

Josh squirms, trying to get past me as well, but I don't let go of him even as he contorts and twists like a furious boa constrictor to reach Charlie.

"Come on," I say again as firmly as I can. "Let's go get a drink. Mr Yarbury's going to come over any second now and give us shit."

No one says anything, so I take the opportunity to pull Josh away, keeping a tight grip on both his arms so he knows not to even *think* about going back for round two. I'm pissed off at Charlie too, but Imogen made a good point. Starting a fight with him isn't exactly going to help reduce the amount of toxic masculinity in the world.

We burst through the double doors back out into the changing area and I finally let Josh go.

He storms across to the other side of the room, punches a wall, lets out a yell of frustration (and also probably *pain* because he just punched a concrete bloody wall) and then he throws himself down on to the floor, banging his head down on to his knees.

What the hell is up with him?

I sit down as close next to him as I dare without being in the danger zone for getting punched.

"All right," I say, in what I hope is a soothing tone. "Now do you want to tell me what just happened? Because I'm honestly confused."

"I don't want to talk," he says quietly.

"I think you need to," I say, trying to be gentle but firm. "Charlie can be a prick, yes, he often deserves a punch, but that's the first time – probably – that someone's tried to actually do it. I get the urge, I do," I continue and Josh exhales through his nose. "But what was it that pushed you over the edge?"

He lifts his head up a little more. "You heard what he said. He's always making stupid comments. He's fucking toxic, man. I'm sick of it."

I nod. "But you were upset before PE? And unless it was the sausage roll thing from earlier, which I still don't really understand—"

"It wasn't the sausage roll thing."

I think that's the most murderously anyone's ever uttered the words 'sausage roll'.

"Right…" I say. "Then what was it?"

"I just…" He lets out a long groan. "ARGH. Everything's going to shit."

Ah, yes. Been there, I think to myself. Out loud, however, I say, "What's everything?"

"Just everything. I want to do well these next two years so that I can get into a good sports academy, but things with Amelia are—" He looks like he's about ready to cry. "Things have been weird, well, since September, but especially since New Year, and I just want everything to go back to normal. I'm spending loads of time with her, but that means I can't train as much as I need to, and it's not even fucking working."

I'm not sure how to respond to that. "Why are things with Amelia weird?" I ask.

"I don't know, man. I don't know." He finally snaps his head up properly and looks at me. "Have you noticed it too?"

"Erm…" Do I tell him the truth? Probably not. "I don't think so?"

"Well, I have," he says firmly. "She's always been busy, but this year's even worse. All she wants is to do things for the *group* or talk about the *group*. Like, I'm glad we're making a difference and all, but I feel like Amelia cares more about that than she does me."

"Ah…" I start, trying desperately to be careful with what I say and keep my expression neutral. "That sucks?"

Josh takes one look at me and lets out another groan. "I sound pathetic, I know."

I shift over closer to him and pat him awkwardly on the shoulder. "You don't sound pathetic. You're just going through a bad patch right now."

"I don't want to be jealous," he says quietly. "I just want things to go back to the way they were."

We lapse into silence, listening to trainers squeaking against the linoleum and shouts drifting through from the main hall.

"We should go back and join the others," Josh says finally.

"You sure? Do you promise not to try to batter Charlie?"

"He'd deserve it if I did," he grumbles.

"Maybe just give him space this lesson actually," I say, deciding that's safer. "That's probably for the best."

"Probably," Josh admits. "And I'll—"

But I don't find out what he was going to say because Mr Yarbury bursts through the door, whistle bouncing up and down on his chest.

"BOYS!" he barks. "Stop having your little tea party and get out there. Ten laps, NOW."

Great. I have to break up a fight, do some couples counselling, and now I'm stuck with extra laps?

We don't dare argue, however. We return guiltily to the hall and start our punishment.

Charlie eyes us from across the room where he's doing reps over the tiny hurdles.

Josh ignores him. "Hey," he says in between focused breaths. "Thanks for listening to me moan, man. Means a lot."

"No problem. I know you'd do the same for me."

He nods. "Yeah."

And then I realise that I haven't given him the opportunity to do the same for me. Maybe I should try and let more people in. God knows I don't want to be like my dad, bottling stuff up and acting like everyone around me is irrational for not repressing their emotions.

"Um," I start, and Josh turns his head slightly. "There actually is something I've been meaning to talk about for a while."

He gives me a glance. "If you're going to tell me that you're gay then I already know, dude."

I snort. "No, not that. Um … my parents are kind of getting divorced."

"Oh." He pulls a face. "Sorry, man. I remember when my parents split; it was rough."

"Yeah, it's not been the best time."

"LADS, STOP CHIN-WAGGING AND GET ON WITH IT!" Mr Yarbury yells again, hands squarely on his hips.

We exchange glances, trying not to crack up, and finish our laps off without speaking. I'm glad I told him. And Charlie can piss off with his flawed ideas of what masculinity is.

Oh.

That gives me an idea. Once we get back to the changing rooms, I hurriedly scrawl a note in my planner. This could be so great … if I'm brave enough to do it. Either way, thanks for the inspiration, Charlie, you misogynistic prick.

★

Once we're changed, Josh and I head out of the sports centre, chatting about Ardenpool United's performance in their latest match, and spot Amelia waiting by the doors.

"Hey, babe," Josh says, kissing her cheek.

"Hi," she says, giving him a quick smile and then turning towards me. "Hey, Ollie, I wanted to talk to you about something. It's about Imogen and the talent show."

A dark flicker passes over Josh's face. "I'll just go wait over there."

Amelia doesn't sense his frustration. "OK, I'll just be a sec," she says. Josh shakes his head as he walks away.

"What is it?" I ask.

She tucks her hair behind her ear. "I'm worried that Imogen's not going to do the show. I think it's important that she does. She needs to get back in the saddle again after that terrible open-mic night or she'll lose momentum."

"Yeah," I agree. "But if she doesn't want to then I don't see how we can convince her. Imogen's not a big fan of doing things she doesn't want to, believe me. I tried to get her to eat some salad with her pizza last week and she literally threw the cucumber I gave her out of the window and told me if I gave her any more then she'd just 'defenestrate the slimy bastard again'."

Amelia laughs. "That does sound like Imogen. But I had an idea."

"Yeah?"

She explains and I smile. It's a really nice plan.

"I think that sounds great," I say.

She claps her hands together. "You do?"

Josh, tired of waiting for us, comes back over, scraping his trainers across the concrete. "Are you done? Can we go home now?"

Amelia nods. "Sure." She turns back to me again and says more brightly, "I'll message you once I've talked to Imogen. See you tomorrow."

"Bye."

Josh attempts to meet my eyes, but doesn't manage it, instead looking somewhere around my ear as he mutters, "Bye, Ollie."

I know it was about time Josh and Amelia revealed that they weren't, in fact, *completely* perfect for one another, but still ... poor Josh. It looks like it's going to take a lot more than a changing-room pep talk to sort out whatever's going on between them.

CHAPTER SIXTEEN

IMOGEN

The talent show sign-up sheet in Mr Holland's room taunts me from the noticeboard every time I go there for Drama class. As do all Louisa's posters – Amelia was very thorough with putting up three of them in every corridor and at least one in every classroom. They're absolutely shitting everywhere. To give begrudging credit where it's due, we do now have at least fifteen people wanting to perform, but the posters provoke a moderately panicked thought spiral every time I see them.

I'm already stressed enough about the fact that we're behind on fundraising – we've raised around three thousand pounds now and we're hoping that the talent show will bring us up to five, but that's still only halfway, and June is getting closer every day. And when I think about having to perform too...

I just don't know whether I should do it. I want to be a comedian and I know I need to practise in order to be great at it. But what if it goes badly? I don't want anything else to put me off doing comedy: it's one of the few things I actually feel like I'm good at.

Amelia keeps trying to put in little words of encouragement here and there and, a few days later, while Ollie's trying to teach me how to play *FIFA* on his PlayStation, she starts again.

"Imogen, stop scoring own goals. Your goal's the other end of the pitch," Ollie says, his eyes darting about the screen as he presses all the doodahs and whatsits on his controller.

"I know where my goal is," I insist. "I just know I'm not going to win so I thought I may as well help your team out. OOH, NICE GOAL, tiny football man."

Ollie laughs. "That's very noble of you, but it does kind of defeat the point of the game."

"There's a point to the game? We're pretend kicking pretend footballs into pretend goals."

My phone buzzes on the floor. I move to pick it up and Ollie sighs, pausing the game.

"Ugh, it's Amelia again," I say. She's sent me a screenshot of the calendar for one of the other pubs in town, *The Golden Goose.* It includes an open-mic comedy night on the tenth of February, and Amelia has added a message that says, Look!! You should do it, my parents go to The Goose every week and it's a much nicer crowd than The Lock and Key, it's all artsy people and students. Just something to think about! x

I snort and show Ollie. "She's really not letting this go, is she? I'd say she needs more hobbies, but she already has like a billion of them."

"Yeah," Ollie says, shaking his head at the phone screen. "But erm," he continues uncertainly, "it's not such a bad idea, is it?"

"Not you too." I roll my eyes. "Why is everyone so obsessed with me trying stand-up again?"

"Because we think you're good," Ollie says with the air of someone explaining something very obvious. "And we don't want one bad experience to put you off doing the talent show and showcasing your comedic talents to the world."

"I don't think one auditorium full of people exactly equals the whole world."

"Well, that makes it even easier, then, doesn't it? Far fewer people to impress. But –" he shrugs with a dangerous-looking smile – "if you *really* don't think you can do it, if you *really* want to give up that easily, then I won't stop you."

I put my controller down. "You can stop that right now. You're not going to goad me into doing this."

He raises an eyebrow. "Aren't I?"

We stare at each other, waiting for someone to break the stalemate. I wish we had cowboy hats and guns in holsters to make it more like a stand-off in a saloon in a Western movie (and also because I'd totally rock a Stetson).

I let the tumbleweed blow past for a few more

moments and then heave a sigh, breaking eye contact. "I suppose … if *The Golden Goose* is as chill as Amelia says and I decided I could perform, and that performance went OK, then *maybe* I could do the talent show. Maybe."

"AHA!" Ollie cries in triumph, doing that *get in there!* thing with his fists that boys always do when they watch sport.

"Did you not hear all those 'maybe's and 'if's I used? It's all very tentative so you can stop looking quite so pleased."

"Tentative is a start," Ollie says, still grinning.

I shake my head at him and pick up my controller to restart the game and see how many more goals I can get for Ollie's team. "If it goes well, then I guess it would make for a nice birthday," I say, offhand. "Although, alternatively, if it went terribly, then it wouldn't exactly be an auspicious start to my eighteenth year."

"Wait." Ollie pauses the game again. "The tenth is your birthday?"

"Yup."

"Why didn't you tell me?" he says incredulously.

"I don't know." I shrug. "It's not a big deal, really. I didn't have a lot to do with me being born; it's my mum that put all the hard work in squeezing me out of her vagina."

Ollie pulls a face.

"Grow up, it's just science. VAGINA."

He lets out a burst of laughter and tries to wrestle a cushion over my face. "I'm fine with the *science* of vaginas existing. I'd just rather not have to picture your head crowning in your mum's one. Shut up!"

"VAGINA!" I yell again, my voice only slightly muffled by the cushion. "HEADS," I burst out between breaths, "CROWNING!"

"Imogen, I swear to—"

I pretend to go all limp, flopping like a wet fish on to the floor.

"I know you're not dead. I can see you smiling."

I stay still.

"If you stop pretending to be dead," Ollie says, "we can go and get iced coffee downstairs."

I leap up immediately. "OK!"

He shakes his head. "God, you're easy."

"That is what it says on the bathroom wall at school, yes."

"Eww. Does it actually?"

"*No.* Now give me coffee."

Maya runs over to hug me when we get downstairs. "Imogen!" she squeals, pronouncing it 'Immy-gen' like she always does.

"There's my favourite pirate." I pat her on the head. "How are we doing, me hearty? Taken any captives or found any treasure today?"

She giggles. "Not yet."

"Well, there's still time," I say, extracting myself gently from her hug to retrieve the coffee from the fridge. "Do you have any ice?" I call over to Ollie, but he's distracted, typing something on his phone. "OI!"

He looks up. "Yeah, just a sec."

"Who are you texting so furiously?" I ask him, eyes narrowed.

"…No one?"

"Sure. That's not suspicious at all."

He puts his phone down. "It was Josh – he just wanted to double-check the homework we got in PE. And we do have ice, yes, bottom drawer of the freezer."

Unconvinced, I get out the ice. Maya then drags me over into the lounge to play fairy pirates with her, while Ollie sits on the sofa behind us and continues covertly texting.

The tenth of February rolls around quickly, bringing with it both my day of birth and dense grey clouds heaving with the threat of snow.

It's a quiet Saturday, and not too many people reach out to wish me a happy birthday, but that's nothing I'm not used to. I get dressed in the evening, ready to go out in my chunky rainbow-striped jumper that's about two sizes too big for me, flared corduroy trousers, and new boots with stars all over them that my parents got me for my birthday. I even manage a fairly successful sixties make-up look with pastel green eyeshadow and eyeliner arching over my eyes.

I'm running through my routine one last time when the doorbell rings. I hear footsteps padding down the hall to the door, and a few moments later Mum's voice calls up the stairs. "Imogen? It's for you, darling."

What's for me? I need to leave – well, five minutes ago, really.

I grab my coat and run down the stairs two at a time. Mum swings the door open further to reveal Ollie, dressed smartly in a green turtleneck jumper and grey tartan trousers, a gift bag in one hand and a bunch of multicoloured tulips wrapped in brown paper in the other.

My mouth edges into a grin. "What are you doing here?"

"I'm here to escort you to your gig," he says, grinning back. "All the best comedians have an entourage."

"Do they?"

Ollie waves a flippant hand. "I don't know – just go with it."

"OK." And I do go with it, shoving on my coat and following him out of the house, where we walk down the icy pavements, occasionally grabbing on to each other to stop us from falling on our arses.

"Are you all rehearsed and ready to go?" Ollie says.

"As ready as I'll ever be, I guess."

"That's sort of the spirit," he says. "Oh, happy birthday by the way." He hands me the tulips and the gift bag. I peer into it, but I can't see past the tissue paper covering the top.

Ollie pokes me in the arm. "You can open that later. We're almost here."

We reach the entrance of *The Golden Goose* at the end of the street.

"Are you ready?" Ollie says, his expression so close to smug that it raises my guard instantly.

I narrow my eyes. "Ready ... to perform? Right?"

"Sure. To perform."

As we enter the pub, Ollie casts darting looks round the room filled with people chatting and drinking, all bathed in a flattering glow by the warm lights. "C'mon," he says, "let's go round the corner. There are better seats there."

I do as he says, and the second we turn the corner I realise why he's been acting so weirdly.

"HAPPY BIRTHDAY!"

The activist group – Amelia, Josh, Maryam, Louisa and Clem – is sitting at a table that takes up the entire corner, with a huge bunch of balloons that keep floating around and bopping a grumpy-looking man at the next table on the back of the head.

"What the...?"

Ollie links his arm through mine, looking very pleased with himself. "We wanted to celebrate your

197

birthday as a thank you for starting the group. Plus, now you have an audience of people who already believe in you and know how hilarious you are."

I could cry. I won't because everyone's beaming up at me and that would be embarrassing, but I could.

"I can't believe you're all here."

"We've already signed you up, you're going on second, but come sit down!" Amelia says, making space for me and Ollie next to her and Josh on the sofa.

The second I've sat down, Maryam slides the fanciest cake I've ever seen across the table at me: smooth buttercream covering the outside, expertly controlled chocolate drips going down the side, chocolate-covered coffee beans artistically piled up on the top.

"Here." She smiles shyly. "I made you this – it's a coffee cake. Ollie said that was your favourite."

"It is – thank you," I say, hoping I sound as grateful as I am, but feeling a little overwhelmed. This is the nicest thing anyone's ever done for me, these beautiful rascals.

There are twenty minutes until the open-mic portion of the evening begins, so there's time to chat and open my presents. Ollie's bought me a new plant in a funky pot for my room and enough flapjacks to last me – well, a lot less time than it should. Realistically they may not even make it home. Louisa, who I bonded with a few weeks ago over our mutual love of Harry Styles, has done me a painting of him that I screech over. Clem gives me a badge with my pronouns 'she/they' on a rainbow background that matches their own they/them one, and I immediately pin it to my jumper. Amelia thrusts a box into my arms that she says is from her and Josh, although Josh's expression suggests this is the first he's heard of it. It's so perfectly wrapped that I actually hesitate for a second before ripping into it, but I'm too intrigued as to what it could be to then not dig into it like the feral raccoon that I am.

I lift up the lid – inside is an eyeshadow palette with dozens of glittery shades, and some patches like the ones I have on my denim jacket, including a pastel rainbow and one that says *zero fucks given* with flowers around it. Hot damn. How did she get it so spot on?

I turn to Amelia. "Thank you so much – they're amazing! I'm going to sew the patches on first thing in the morning."

She smiles serenely. "You're very welcome."

I lean round Amelia to look at Josh. "Thanks, Josh."

He nods his head and then breaks eye contact with me as quickly as he can. Most people would think that was rude, but eye contact's hard. I get it.

"Hey." Ollie nudges me. "I think it's starting."

Ah, fuck. I was having such a nice time I'd almost forgotten that I have to perform. I take a few deep breaths and pretend like I don't need a nervous shit, while a woman sets up the microphone and announces the first performer.

A man, with heavy-framed glasses and lanky limbs, probably in his early twenties, walks up to the microphone and begins to talk.

He's clearly nervous, as he keeps fiddling with his glasses, but he's not half bad. He tells some funny stories about his colleagues at the research lab he works in, which get a lot of laughs. Amelia was right – it's definitely a much more chill, younger crowd here, and everyone seems relaxed and happy.

The man finishes up with a joke that I don't hear because I can tell he's wrapping up and I'm too busy trying not to have an anxiety attack.

"All right," the announcer lady says. "Thank you for that, Eric – that was wonderful! OK, and up next we have…" She looks down at her list. "Imogen Quinn!"

Everyone at my table whoops and claps as I stand up. I only just manage to place one shaky foot in front of the other and make it to the microphone.

I gulp, looking out at all the expectant faces, lower the mic and then, inexplicably, I start talking.

CHAPTER SEVENTEEN

OLLIE

Imogen's about ready to begin. Everyone finishes clapping as she moves the microphone down to her height – the guy before her was a bit of a beanpole (quite a cute beanpole, in a nerdy kind of way).

I'm nervous – mine and Amelia's plan to boost her confidence only works if this goes well… "C'mon, Imogen," I whisper under my breath. "You've got this."

Microphone suitably adjusted, she tosses her hair back and then starts talking.

"Hello, everyone!" Gone is the resting bitch-face, replaced with a confident, engaging smile. "If you don't know me…" They pause. "Then what the hell are you doing? Stop being so self-absorbed and be aware of my existence – I'm delightful."

A laugh ripples round the room and my nerves start to ease.

"Just kidding," they carry on. "If you don't know

me, then I'm Imogen Quinn, and if you do know me then I'm still Imogen Quinn, but I'm also … *sorry*."

This gets another laugh, and her shoulders loosen as she relaxes even more into the flow of it.

"So," she says, removing the mic from its stand and tossing it from hand to hand. She must be relaxed – that's the most coordination I've ever seen her display. I threw a ball to her once and when she tried to catch it she accidentally batted it into Amelia's face. Although now that I think about it, that may not have been an accident.

"Some fun facts about me," she says. "Well, the first fact should be that I love fun facts. In fact, I've been told that I tell people so many fun facts that they cease to be fun. But you know, that's just their opinion. What could be a more fun time than listening to me recite endless facts about the seasonal changes to the neuropsychobiology of squirrels, am I right?"

People laugh again. It's all right for them – they don't have to actually hear about how squirrels' hippocampi grow in autumn and winter because they're using their memory more to remember where they hid their nuts.

"OK, a couple more fun facts about me – for starters, I'm bisexual, so lock up your daughters. And your sons. And your non-binary offspring."

I give a solitary whoop at that and she purses her lips to try and stop herself from smiling.

"And *lastly*," she continues. "I'm also autistic as hell."

There's a ripple of awkward laughter at that like people don't know quite how to respond.

Imogen nods their head with a knowing smile. "Yeah, that was pretty much my reaction when the doctor told me too. I was like, I'm autistic? But I don't like trains, my maths skills are terrible, I don't resemble Sheldon Cooper in any way – this can't be right."

People laugh a little more easily this time.

"That's what people always think of when they hear the word autism – little Timmy who's obsessed with trains and doesn't understand social conventions, and while that can be what an autistic person looks like, so is this." She gestures down at her body. "This ravishing creature standing before you today."

"I feel like, being autistic," she carries on, "I have to announce that I'm funny. People don't expect me to be funny, you see, and when I am they assume I'm not doing it on purpose and so if they laughed it would be mean."

A few people in the audience are nodding thoughtfully. She's making people laugh AND she's promoting acceptance of neurodivergence – *that's my friend*.

"So," she says, "this is me standing here and saying, 'Hi, yes, I'm Imogen. I'm autistic. I'm also fucking hilarious. Those things aren't mutually exclusive, and I hereby enthusiastically invite you to laugh, and to find me as hilarious as you would a person that did understand social conventions.'"

This gets another big laugh and Imogen chuckles to herself. "Actually, it's a really common misconception that autistic people don't understand social conventions. Most of the time we do understand them." She smiles with a nonchalant shrug. "We just think that they're stupid. Like, for example, who decided that wearing hats indoors was rude? Because unless my hat is calling you a bell-end then I don't see how it can be rude. I swear allistic people just made all these rules up hundreds of years ago and now, when they're challenged, they're like—" she makes an exaggeratedly horrified face. "*But – but*—" she stutters. "*It's tradition.*" She shakes her head and sighs before smiling slyly. "And y'all think it's autistic people that don't like change."

This gets another big laugh, and it's not just people in our corner that are entertained; everywhere I look, around all the tables in the room, people are smiling and laughing – she's done it: she's won the crowd over.

I pull my camera out of my bag to take a few pictures – landscape and framed with Imogen on the right-hand side, and the audience's faces smiling up at her filling the rest of the picture.

As she moves on to do a bit about how pointless

perfume adverts are, Amelia notices me scanning the room and snapping pictures and nudges me again.

"I'm so glad we did this," she murmurs to me. "She looks in her element, doesn't she?"

Imogen keeps on going, delivering punchline after punchline, and people keep on laughing. I can't help but grin at her, completely at home up there, a natural with her comic timing, everyone engaged. This is her *thing*.

"Yes," I answer proudly. "Yes, she does." I take another photo, this time zooming in so it's just her and the microphone, her eyes glistening with the reflection of the lights around the room, her smile wry.

She continues her set for another five minutes, including a couple of minutes on her hatred of both soup and useless binaries, including a bit about what the actual definition of soup is as opposed to a smoothie ("Don't even try to tell me it's a temperature thing because then how do you explain gazpacho, you *bitch*") that they then somehow link to gender in a bizarrely insightful way.

I didn't actually know they used they/them as well as she/her pronouns until today. It absolutely tracks with how much they hate people saying things have to be staunchly one thing or another, though, and I make a mental note to make the effort to swap between them from now on.

Imogen winds up, taking a step back to survey the room with a grin, before putting the microphone back on its stand. "All right, thank you for listening to my tirade, everybody," she says. "*I've* been Imogen Quinn – *you've* hopefully been amused. Peace out."

And then they give a solemn bow and leave the stage to applause, claps and, from our corner, wolf whistles and whoops.

Imogen throws herself down on to the sofa next to me. "Whoa." She blinks a few times, I think just processing, before sitting up a little. "So … what'd you think?"

I take their hand and squeeze it with a grin. "Oh, shocking. Truly, truly, terrible."

She smirks back at me with affectionate eyes. "Thank you."

"You were amazing!" Amelia blurts out. "You were so funny – everyone loved you."

Maryam nods. "You should let me film you next time for our social-media pages."

Imogen looks unsure at this, but is quickly distracted by everyone else telling her how great she was (besides Josh, who stays slumped on the sofa).

We listen to the other four performers – none are as good as Imogen in my entirely unbiased opinion – then Maryam suggests that Imogen cuts the cake.

She's looking a little overwhelmed, so I announce that we're going together to find a knife and pull her away for a second.

"You OK?" I ask. "You're looking a little dead behind the eyes."

They smile dopily. "I'm good. Really good. Just a tad overstimulated."

"Ah, right, got it. Cake and then home?" I offer.

"*Cake and then home*, my favourite phrase. Hey." They touch me on the arm while the man behind the bar fetches us a knife, and I know they're about to be sincere. "Thank you so much for organising this – I'm going to need to spend all of tomorrow sleeping to recover, but it's genuinely been the best birthday I've ever had. No question."

I accept the knife from the barman. "You're very welcome. But I can't take all the credit. It was Amelia's idea really," I add. "Now, come on, let's go back to the others."

I start walking but Imogen stays where they are, immobile among all the bustling patrons, so I retreat the few paces back to them.

Their brow is furrowed as they just stand there. "It was Amelia's idea?"

"Yes?"

"But…" She struggles to find words. "But that's so nice – why would she do that?"

"Well," I start carefully, "maybe because this whole weird rivalry thing you think you have going on is all in your head and you're actually somehow … friends?"

"Friends," they repeat dubiously. "Amelia and I are friends."

"I think you are," I say, trying not to laugh at

her mildly horrified face. "She's always nice to you; maybe you should try being nice to her back sometimes."

"Hey, I'm nice to people," she objects.

"Sure. Occasionally."

They put up a middle finger. "Bitch."

"See? You're so good at being nice."

Imogen opens their mouth to retort, but then decides against it, instead crossing their arms and glaring at me as I laugh.

"Come on," I say, putting my arm round her and leading her away. "Let's go stab that beautiful cake."

And we do, or Imogen does – I wouldn't usually be too thrilled about handing her a weapon, but it's her birthday so she has to cut it herself. Hmm, we allistics do have weird rules; she's right. She starts cutting slices, handing the first one to Amelia.

"Here," she says to her. "And er – thank you. For everything."

Amelia looks taken aback, her throat tensing as she swallows before replying. "Oh! You're— You're welcome."

Imogen hands the next slice to Maryam, also thanking her for making such a kick-ass cake – they're definitely taking my comments about being nice to heart – and then give out slices to the rest of us. We sit and talk and stuff our faces with Maryam's beautiful cake; but I can tell that Imogen's fading, her responses getting shorter and her eyes glassier over time, and so after a little while longer I suggest that it's time I walk her home.

She smiles sleepily. "Yes, please."

We all head outside where I say bye to Amelia and tilt my head up at Josh, adding quietly, "Hey, you all right?"

His expression stays blank. "Yeah. Fine." I follow his eyeline and notice that he's watching the rest of the group as they say their goodbyes.

Amelia and Imogen stand talking. Imogen looks hesitant, but then moves in for a hug. Amelia seems even more taken aback now, but goes with it, and when they break apart they're both smiling. Blimey.

Imogen waves a final goodbye to the others and returns to my side. "I'm sleepy."

"Let's get you home, then. Bye, Josh."

He grunts in response and goes to link arms with Amelia.

"Oh, MAN," Imogen exclaims as we walk down the road. "That was so great, but I'm EXHAUSTED. What with all the lights and noise and trying not to throw up before my routine, I'm fully going to sleep for seventeen hours. In fact, I may just fall asleep in the street right now."

"Please don't," I say, swinging our joined hands as we stride out, long silhouettes cast on the pavement beneath us from the light of the streetlamps. "I mean, I could probably just about carry you home, but it would be a lot harder if you were unconscious."

Imogen grins a very concerning grin. "Now, there's an idea."

"What is?" I ask dubiously.

"You giving me a piggyback home. That's so nice of you, thanks, Ollie."

"Hold on. I don't think that's quite what I said—"

"TOO LATE." They spring up on to my back, taking me by surprise and whacking me in the face with the balloons and in an entirely different area with their present bag.

"OOF," I groan, wishing my hands weren't now taken up holding on to her legs so that I could a) punch her and b) attend to my poor bruised balls.

"Sorry," Imogen says brightly. "Now, onwards, my trusty steed!"

"It's a good job it's generally frowned upon to murder people on their birthdays," I say darkly as I resign myself to my fate and begin plodding on back through town towards their house.

"Yes," Imogen says. "Because on any other day people would be like, *sure, go for it, murder as many people as you like, just make sure it's not their birthday beforehand because otherwise that'd be a bit of a dick move, mate*."

"Shut up."

★

It's Thursday, the eve of both Valentine's Day and the talent show, and it's going to be quite a busy day if the ever-growing to-do list in our *Ardenpool Activists/Absolute Bloody Legends* group chat is anything to go by.

Once I get to school, Imogen, Amelia and Clem are already in the auditorium, hanging up the abundance of heart-shaped bunting and red-and-pink paperchains that Louisa made. It looks like Cupid threw up in here.

"OLLIE!" Imogen yelps as she spies me lurking in the doorway, wondering whether I can sneak off and hang out with Josh before they see me. Damn it. "Come help – I'm not tall enough."

I clamber up on the stage and help Imogen pin up their end of the paperchains that Clem's sticking up stage left, while Amelia examines them to see whether they're level.

"It's all looking good – but where are the others?" I ask, curious (particularly as to why Amelia let Josh off decorating duty when *we* all have to help).

"Josh has disappeared somewhere," Amelia says, uncharacteristically unbothered by this.

"And Louisa's just nipped to the loo," Clem adds. "She'll be back in a sec."

In actuality, it's several hundred secs before Louisa appears, pushing her way through the double doors in her chair, face streaked with tears.

"Lou?" Clem leaps down from the stage. "What's wrong?"

"What's wrong is exactly what I thought would

happen has happened," she says, sniffing, shining eyes hard. "People have clocked the gender-neutral sign on the door of the toilet and now everyone's using it because it's big and they can do their make-up with their friends in there or something. And, like, everyone should be able to use it, I don't know what people feel safe with, but I've tried to go three times today and couldn't get in, and then I tried to use the lift to go upstairs but, *surprise, surprise*, that's still broken, so I ended up screaming at it in front of several classmates before going back to the loo on this floor and knocking on the door until eventually three people came out and glared at me, and just *UGH*." She finishes all of this with another big sniff as Clem leans over to hug her tightly.

"This isn't OK." Imogen verbalises my thoughts, then her mouth sets in a straight, furious line. "I'll ask Mr Holland to get Ms Greenacre to come to our meeting at lunchtime. She needs to listen to us explain things and actually *hear us* for once. We can't have this keep happening."

"Agreed," I say firmly, my heart clenching as I look at such an obviously upset Louisa.

After PE, Josh and I walk up to the main building – a brief calm interlude before our inevitable confrontation with Ms Greenacre. As we reach

Mr Holland's classroom and see Imogen and Amelia in conversation outside the doors, however, Josh pulls me aside.

"What's up?" I ask, concerned.

He just stands there with a panicked expression for a few beats before he gulps. "I … I don't know how much—"

"Hey, guys!" Imogen's spotted us and is waving us over. "Come on – we should sort out our game plan before she gets here."

I glance at Josh who's back to wearing the blank expression that's become standard for him over the last few weeks. "Are you…" I trail off as he starts walking into the classroom. "OK?" I finish to myself, now standing in an empty corridor.

A few minutes later, we're all seated round the table, staring up at Ms Greenacre with matching expressions of hatred.

"Hello, everyone!" Ms Greenacre stands over us in her tweed skirt and matching jacket, a saccharine-sweet smile on her face. "Now, I understand that there's a situation a couple of you delightful young people aren't particularly happy with?"

I place a hand on Imogen's arm, hearing her yell in her head, '*Not particularly happy with*, my arse.'

"That's correct." Amelia is the first to speak up. "You see, when the school council unanimously voted to instate a new bathroom for students who aren't comfortable using gendered facilities, we were under the impression that the facility created would, in fact, be a new one, and not just combined with the disabled bathroom."

"I see." Ms Greenacre nods mock-thoughtfully. "And you're not happy with the solution we landed upon?"

"No," Imogen spits out. "We're not."

Louisa's gaze flicks to Imogen, subtly telling them she'll take over. "You see, while it's great to have a gender-neutral bathroom, combining it with the only disabled toilet that I can actually access in the building has meant that I *can't* access it because it's never vacant: everyone's using it."

"Wasn't that your intention?" Ms Greenacre asks. "To create a facility that all could use?"

"Yes," Clem says, clearly anxious, but pushing through for Louisa. "But we can't *all* use it because now disabled people can't get in it when they need to."

"Which is essentially a human-rights violation," Imogen adds.

"I see," Ms Greenacre says, in a tone that suggests she very much does not see.

"Let me put it this way, Ms Greencare," Louisa continues, faux-pleasantly. "It's not just a simple matter of access, of us being able to go to the toilet or not; it's also about what that lack of access says. And it's saying that I'm not valued, that my needs are supplementary, an afterthought – if they're indeed a thought at all."

Imogen nods vigorously. "Exactly. It's saying this world is not yours, it's mine, and you're lucky I'm allowing you into it. But we don't believe that we are lucky to be invited in. We want to kick the fucking door down so that no one ever needs an invitation to enter again."

Ms Greenacre closes her eyes for the briefest of moments. "Language, Miss Quinn," she says while I squeeze Imogen's hand three times under the table. I don't understand what it's like to be a disabled, neurodivergent person. But I do know what it's like to be a gay, biracial person, and I know how the world likes to shove everyone that doesn't fit the 'norm' into a corner, to listen to us only when it's convenient to them, and to ignore us in our wholeness. And, suddenly, I feel the need to speak up too.

"Look," I start, feeling everyone's gaze turn to me, "we're just saying that there has to be a better solution than this. There must be some other location where a gender-neutral bathroom could be created. I get that this seemed a convenient choice for you, but accessibility is important, even when it's not *convenient*. That's kind of the point."

"Thank you for your contributions, everybody," Ms Greenacre says, pursing her lips tightly as Imogen beams at me with unadulterated pride. "Unfortunately, this is the situation we decided is appropriate. And, while I'm sure this is important to some of you, I hope you can also see that you simply can't always have your cake and eat it too."

She did not just say that. I mean, she did in fact, just say that, but she did *not* just say that.

She pauses like she's waiting for us to say something. When no one fills the silence, she carries on. "We pride ourselves on our inclusive ethos here at the academy, and I'm sure you would all agree that we are a very inclusive place. Especially since we were so generous as to allow you to form this little group in the first place." She lets out a false laugh. "It's just that we're rather limited with the changes we can make, especially as any other solution would reduce the number of bathrooms available for the other students who are in the majority when it comes to their views on gender."

What the fuck does that even mean, 'views on gender'? And did she really just openly admit that she cares less about disabled students than she does about non-disabled ones? Jesus.

"Now," she says, clasping her hands together; the noise rings out in the deathly silence that's fallen over the room. "I think I'll say goodbye and let you boys and girls get back to whatever it was you were doing."

And with that she exits the room, leaving many furious people in her wake.

Louisa grabs Clem's hand over the table, but we wait until the door is fully closed behind

Ms Greenacre before making any noise – in Imogen's case, an infuriated pterodactyl screech.

"I think what Imogen's trying to say –" I jump in, knowing she still has several more seconds of incoherence in her – "is that that was horrendous."

Imogen nods violently, their hair bobbing up and down with them. "And this is exactly what we've been talking about the whole time with the pride festival – we need spaces that are accessible for disabled *and* LGBTQ+ people. That's why we started this all: it's precisely what we're fighting for."

"Yep," Louisa says, tiredness weighing heavy on her face and audible in her words. "But God forbid we get anything that even acknowledges intersectionality without having to fight tooth-and-nail for it beforehand."

Amelia's expression is furious, but also focused. "Let's get the talent show out of the way tomorrow so that we can raise some of the money we really need," she says, "and then we can dedicate all of our energy towards fixing this mess. They can't get away with this; we won't let them."

"Actually," Clem says, and they look more determined than I think I've ever seen them, their usually slightly nervous, freckled face set hard, "I have an idea. Maryam, I'm going to need your help. And yours, Imogen."

Maryam looks surprised but nods. "Of course!"

There are a lot of grim expressions around the

room but, as Clem explains their idea, they're gradually replaced with mischievous grins.

Look out, Ms Greenacre. You've just said a whole lot of things you're going to regret.

CHAPTER EIGHTEEN

IMOGEN

It's the day of the talent show, and Ollie and I have just finished some last-minute first aid on the decorations in the auditorium. Our lessons out of the way, we spend all of lunchtime frantically rushing through the corridors to get everything ready before the show starts, and then there's nothing to do but get ourselves ready. And, in my case, try not to have an anxiety attack.

Ticket sales have been pretty decent, but hopefully takings on the door will bring us up to an even better figure. We've already had to start paying deposits for a few things for the festival now we're only four months away (a couple of performers, a BSL interpreter and some sound equipment) and that's put quite the dent in our funds. I want this so badly. And not just for me any more. I've turned my rage into hope and I've given it to other people. I can't let them down now.

Hence why I've been struck with a big ol' case of executive dysfunction and can't seem to make a single decision. I'm already dressed in my outfit (bright red dungarees over a pink-and-white striped T-shirt and a messy attempt at space buns in my hair); all I have to do is finish my make-up. And yet.

"Just pick one and get on with it," Ollie says, perching impatiently on a chair in the empty dressing room while I look blankly in the mirror.

"The red would go with my dungarees, but the pink would match my T-shirt. It's a hard decision, Ollie – you can't rush these things."

"I can try," he mutters, before sighing at me weighing up the two pallets in my hand. "Do the pink to match your shirt and put red hearts on your cheeks like you did the other week to match the dungarees."

"Ooh, that's an idea," I say, tossing the red palette aside for now, at least one crisis averted.

"You're welcome. God, you have so much make-up," he says, sidling over to come and investigate. "How is all this necessary? You only have one face."

"Oh, you naïve little man," I say. "This isn't even that much – some people have whole-ass dressers full of it. Besides, it's not all for my face; there's nail polish in there and just general glitter – biodegradable, of course. Feel free to help yourself if you fancy a touch of sparkle."

I expect him to roll his eyes at me, but instead

he extracts a glittery highlighter. "What do you do with this?"

I look back at him in my filthy mirror. "Use the dropper and dab it on to your cheekbones."

"Cool." And he does, very clumsily, but it looks cute, his cheeks glimmering with silver glitter in the dim light of the dressing room. "How long will you be now?"

I'm still working on my second eye. "Five more minutes?"

"Fine. I may as well paint my nails, then."

"Like you could do that in five minutes," I scoff, but he's already picked a glittery black polish and is applying it with far more skill than he did the highlighter. "What the heck? How are you so good at that? I get it bloody everywhere."

He shrugs a shoulder casually. "I do it for Maya sometimes."

Figures. Kid has the best brother in the world; of course he knows how to do nail polish.

By the time I've finished, Ollie's nails are done and he's wafting them around to dry them, stealing sneaky glances in the mirror to examine his glittering cheekbones from different angles when he thinks I'm not looking. Hmm…

When his nails are dry, Ollie goes off with his camera to take some photos while I head to the official changing room next to the stage to make sure everyone else is on schedule.

"Just tell me what we're doing." Josh's raised voice from around the corner makes me freeze. "I don't care what it is; I just want to know that we're going to be doing something together later. It's Valentine's Day, Amelia. It would be nice to actually spend some time with my girlfriend today of all days."

"But *I don't know*, Josh," Amelia's voice replies. "Can we just get through the show and make plans afterwards? We might be celebrating with the group or something. Now, please, I need to go and warm up. The show's starting soon."

"But—"

The sound of footsteps fades away, so I decide it's safe to move again, but as soon as I walk round the corner I crash into a very irate-looking Josh.

"JESUS CHRIST. Why are you *everywhere*?"

"Excuse me?" Why is he taking this out on me? It's not my fault you're not happy in your relationship, pal.

"Never mind," he says mutinously, storming away as quickly as he can with a gait that's not unreminiscent of an angry Sesame Street character.

Lovely talking to you as always, Josh.

I enter the changing rooms a few moments after Amelia and see a gaggle of girls surrounding her.

"What did Josh get you?" asks one of the dancers, peering into the gift bag hanging off Amelia's arm.

"Oh my God, that's so cute!" says another.

A girl brandishing a French horn puts a hand

over her heart and sticks out her lip. "You guys are so perfect together. You're legit relationship goals."

"Amelia, there you are." I stride over and touch her arm.

She stares at my hand before looking up at my face, wearing a panicked expression.

"We need you over in the corner," I say, doing a cheeky bit of improv. "Someone's, erm … having a wardrobe malfunction."

"Oh? *Oh*," she says, catching on. "Yes, sorry, girls. Duty calls!"

We extract ourselves and head to the opposite corner where there's a free expanse of bench for us to sit on.

"You looked trapped."

"I was," she replies, staring at the speckled vinyl floor.

"It doesn't seem like you're having the best day."

"Not exactly." She swings her legs, scuffing the floor with her pink heels. "Well," she adds, "I mean, it's fine. I'm looking forward to the show."

"Sure…" I say awkwardly. I don't want to pry but also it is clearly *not* fine. "Look, if there's ever anything—"

"I need to get ready." Amelia stands up abruptly, cutting me off. "Good luck with your performance; you'll be great. Bye, Imogen." She walks away to the rest of her orchestra friends and starts tuning her violin.

There's something weird in the air today. Everyone seems on edge. It's sort of contagious. I feel like I need to go do some yoga or commit arson or something to stop my body (and my stressed brain) feeling like it's going into hyper-speed mode. A feeling I'd rather avoid right before I hop on a stage in front of a huge audience and do something some people are definitely not going to like.

After about twenty minutes of trying not to combust and going over my routine in my head, I hear chairs squeaking and the cacophonous din of everyone filling up the auditorium next door. Ten minutes after that, Mr Holland starts talking about fire exits, pretending to be a flight attendant, before announcing the start of the show.

A group of girls doing A Level Dance open the show with a bizarre but not entirely unimpressive half-ballet, half-hip-hop routine, followed by a Year Eight boy singing one of the more depressing songs from *Les Mis* (which is saying something given 'miserable' is literally in the title).

I make my hands go in and out of stars as I watch, trying to quell the rising tide of tension in my chest. I'm not nervous about my routine exactly – Ollie and Amelia's dastardly plan worked and I feel much more prepared this time – but still. There's this pressure for everything to go well for the sake of the festival and the people I care about, and there's been a lot going on today, a lot of noise and stress and— *Oh*.

Amelia and the orchestra are onstage. Amelia begins their set with a solo, her violin pressed to her shoulder, playing each note perfectly. I watch as she gets completely lost in the music, eyes closed and notes cascading out one after the other. She's focused, that much is clear, but it's also the most relaxed I've ever seen her. It's just her and the music, the music and her. And, as I stand in the wings and watch her, I feel my own anxiety slowly fade out of my body and be replaced by another infinitely preferable feeling that I can't quite pinpoint.

And the anxiety doesn't return, not even when the orchestra exits stage left and it's my turn to step out and watch all the expectant faces following me to the centre of the stage.

As the spotlight focuses on me, I put on my best weatherperson smile and grab the microphone off the stand. I launch into some of my material that got a good response at the open-mic night. It gets a similarly positive response here, and then I try out some new things I've written recently.

"So," I say casually, "you know how you lie awake at night, and you can't get to sleep and so your brain goes, 'Oho, I know what will help – playing a montage of every stupid thing you've ever said or done'? Yeah, the older I get, the more I lose hope I'll ever stop saying things that will haunt me in the early hours of the morning. I think we all just have to be reconciled to the fact that we have done a great number of stupid things and that we'll keep on doing stupid things until we die."

Some people are laughing; some are looking mildly traumatised. So, you know, my sweet spot. "Maybe even our last words will be something stupid like poor Louise-Marie-Thérèse de Saint Maurice." I wander up and down the stage, eyes grazing over the sea of heads in front of me. "Who, as she was lying in her sickbed, farted, then said, 'Good, a woman who is farting is a woman that is not dead,' and then IMMEDIATELY DIED."

This gets a loud burst of laughter from the crowd and dispels the tension I'd created in the room with wonderful juxtaposition.

I look down at the first row of seats. We had to reserve it for all the 'important' school staff, including Ms Greenacre, who has a posed, polite smile on her face.

This makes my body positively *quiver* with all the anger that resides in it on standby at any given moment. I'm well aware that she doesn't like me, and she's well aware that I'm well aware that she doesn't like me. I hate people who fake things at the best of times, but especially when everyone knows they're faking. I'd respect them much more if they just said what they meant' it would save everybody time.

"Speaking of saying stupid things," I say, initiating phase one of the group's potentially dangerous plan, but too enraged to back out now, "we've had a bit of a situation going on in school recently. And no, I don't mean Mr Holland's new novelty ties, although there is *a lot* going on with them, sir."

Mr Holland chortles, holding up today's tie covered in garden gnomes for everyone to see and nodding like the good sport he is.

I wait for the laughter to die down before smiling more soberly and laser-focusing on the hypocrite in the front row. "No, what I actually mean is a certain situation we have regarding bathrooms."

Ms Greenacre freezes in her seat.

"You see, me and the activist society, and I'm sure many other pupils too," I add, "think that Ardenpool Academy should be inclusive of all pupils. However, this view is not shared by some of the staff, who decided that instead of creating an actual gender-neutral toilet for any pupil that doesn't feel comfortable using one that's designated ladies or gents, they'd just *whack* a logo on the only accessible disabled toilet in the main building.

"Which has created an unacceptable situation," I carry on loudly, "where disabled students can no longer access that bathroom when they need to because it's being used much more frequently – and often they have specific needs that have to be addressed more urgently than those of non-disabled students."

A couple of people look uncomfortable. Well, most people look uncomfortable, but a few look

227

especially uncomfortable, knowing that they've been using that toilet with their friends for non-essential reasons. That group includes Jen and Hannah (a turn of events that doesn't surprise me in the least). It's always nice to have a reminder that you made a good decision. I shake my head and continue.

"And I know, I know –" I throw the microphone from one hand to the other – "I'm here to make jokes. I'm here to make you laugh. And it's definitely not funny that members of staff, even after becoming aware of this situation that they've created, have decided not to make any further changes. It's not funny at all."

Ms Greenacre now looks like she's trying to set me on fire with her gaze, and several of the other heads are shifting around uncomfortably.

I make the signal and Clem and Ollie quietly move from their posts at the side of the room (while Maryam is filming everything). They head up the stairs, holding giant tins, and begin to hand out perfectly baked and decorated cupcakes. Louisa also wheels over to the front row, a devious grin on her face, another tin on her lap, and hands more cakes out to the heads, who frown quizzically as they accept them.

"In fact, one particular member of staff informed us we couldn't have facilities for both disabled and gender non-conforming students because that would be *having our cake and eating it too*. Well," I say, "we'd like to invite you all now to say a hearty FUCK THAT and eat your damn cake."

As the full realisation of what we've done sinks into Ms Greenacre's mind, her hand freezes, the first piece of cupcake halfway to her lips. I've never seen someone look quite so incandescent with rage before.

I like seeing her this mad.

Shocked laughs ripple round the room, and a lot of people do, in fact, dig in to Maryam's cupcakes. Another good portion of the audience doesn't seem to know what to do or where to look, which tells me that I've royally fucked the comedy aspect of this routine, but also that we're doing something important. The only way for everyone to feel comfortable in this world is to disrupt the comfort of those who've been far too comfortable for far too long.

"Well…" I say, chuckling to myself, "I'm so glad that you're all enjoying this performance. And the cake."

People laugh a little more now, probably hoping that the serious portion of my routine is over.

"If you know me, then you know how much I love a captive audience, and since you're a captive audience – seriously, check the doors: they're all locked. Just kidding, wouldn't want to break fire-safety rules, am I right, Ms Greenacre?" I wink at her. She doesn't laugh, which, like, *fair*.

"Since you're my captive audience today," I repeat, "I had to talk about something that's important to me and my peers. I thought about telling a knock-knock joke, but 'knock, knock,' 'who's there?' 'a staff member at the academy,' 'a staff member at the academy who?' 'a staff member at the academy who doesn't think trans, non-binary and disabled students deserve a basic human right' was a bit of a bummer – I think you'd all agree."

Most of the students in the audience are laughing again and I feel that fire rise up in me. Not everyone is agreeing or understanding with what I'm saying, but plenty of people are, and that's something. *More than something.*

"Now, some of you may already know that I'm autistic and might think that this explains the whole portion of the routine where you were all thoroughly uncomfortable and I couldn't tell, but NOPE," I say brightly. "I was aware that you were all wishing you were anywhere else. Shout out to Ms Greenacre who definitely won the prize for most horrified expression. That wasn't because I was autistic; it was because I have an entirely different diagnosis, one that I believe is called 'being a little shit'. Thank you and goodbye!"

And with that I skip off the stage, leaving half the audience whooping and clapping and the other half glancing around, wondering what in sweet Lucifer's name just happened.

CHAPTER NINETEEN

"Imogen!" Amelia rushes over to me in the corridor from where she was listening at the door. "That was… Well, I knew it was coming, we planned it all, but I can't believe you actually did it."

I laugh maniacally, still processing what I've just done. "Yup, neither can I."

"You really have no fear, do you?" she says, shaking her head at me, but still wearing an incredulous smile.

"Oh, I have fear. A lot of fear," I add, grimacing. "I just only pay attention to it to decide whether a thing is worth doing or not. This made me super scared and so I knew that meant it was worth doing."

"Wow." Amelia looks impressed for a moment, but then her smile flickers and fades. "I wish I could be more like you," she says quietly.

"Erm, what?" I snap my focus directly on to her, not believing what I've just heard. "But you have everything so annoyingly together. You're literally perfect."

"No. I'm not," she says fiercely, fire somehow still blazing in her eyes even as they fill with water. "I'm messing everything up."

Josh sneaks through the double doors from the auditorium, hearing Amelia's raised voice in the silence just before the next performer starts singing. "Babe? What's wrong?"

Amelia's head jerks round to him.

He frowns and then nods at me. "Hey, Imogen, could you give us a minute?"

"NO," Amelia blurts out. "Stay, Imogen."

"Erm…" It's my turn to be an uncomfortable audience now. I don't know what to do.

"Of course," Josh says sarcastically. "Why would you want your *boyfriend* to comfort you when you're upset? Silly me."

Amelia's lip trembles wearily. "Josh, just stop."

"No. Not until you tell me what's going on." Josh walks round in a circle, fists clenched at his sides like in the Arthur meme. "Not until you tell me why you've been so weird with me recently, why you never want to be alone with me or let me kiss you, why we always end up talking about Imogen and the fucking activist group over any other topic."

I'm just wishing that Amelia had let me leave when Josh asked me to when she turns to me and says, "Imogen? Would you actually mind giving us a sec now? Please?" She swallows hard. "I'll explain everything in a minute."

I nod. "Sure. I think I'd better run anyway: the show's almost over and Ms Greenacre looked *pissed*. I'll be hiding in Mr Holland's room if you need me." And, with that, I scurry away as quickly as I can like the little rat boy I am at heart. Valentine's Day really isn't all it's cracked up to be, is it? I'm supremely glad I don't have to deal with the relationship politics those two crazy kids do.

I pick a spot on the floor of the Drama classroom and sit down cross-legged on the makeshift stage in the corner, watching raindrops wriggle down the windowpanes, just as an enraged shout sounds from somewhere down the corridor, followed by heavy footsteps thundering past, a pause, and then much slower, steadier ones approaching.

My body tenses as I wonder if Ms Greenacre has decided to come and murder me before the curtain call, but when the door opens it reveals Amelia just standing there, tears streaking down her face.

I put my hand up in an awkward wave and she enters the room, coming to sit down across from me on the stage, the room's silence only interrupted by her sniffing.

She smooths out her skirt, lets out one final shuddering sob, gulps and raises her gaze to meet mine, before saying something I don't think anyone ever expected she would say.

"Josh and I broke up."

I focus on her, ignoring the rain drumming against the windows, ignoring the voice in my head asking whether I'm making too much or not enough eye contact for the situation. "You did?"

"Yes."

"But … why?" Sure, they haven't exactly been the picture of a healthy relationship recently, but they've been together for *so long*. I figured they were both into the 'better the devil you know' thing.

Amelia stays quiet, gazing down into her pink-and-white polka-dot-clad lap.

Oh, fun. I get to guess.

"Did you have another argument?" I suggest.

She starts to shake her head and then switches to nodding. "Kind of. We've been arguing a lot recently."

"And it just got too much, huh?"

"No." Amelia is still staring intently at her skirt. "I mean, yes, but that wasn't why I broke up with him."

"OK…" Why else do people break up? Hmm. I give her a side glance. "Did he cheat?"

She shakes her head.

"Good, I don't have to rip anyone's balls off."

She laughs weakly but doesn't say anything else.

"So … is there someone else for you?" I'm running out of reasons. She's going to have to start talking soon.

Thankfully, she lifts her head at this. She looks right at me, a sad smile on her face. "There are millions of people."

I'm confused. "Huh?"

"There are millions of people I'd probably be happier with than I am with Josh."

I try my hardest not to, I swear I do, but I can't help but laugh. "Ouch. Is he really that bad? I mean, I know there's that whole smell thing going on, and he's never been the sharpest dresser, but—"

Her eyes flick towards the ceiling. "There was nothing wrong with Josh."

"Then why—"

"I'm trying to tell you that I'm *gay*, Imogen," she says, her words growing in volume. "And as amazing as Josh is … for someone – he was never going to be the one for me."

Holy. Fucking. Shit.

"Wow," I say, and then I repeat it because I have no other words. "*Wow*."

"Yeah." She laughs. "Wow."

I watch as the smile remaining from her laugh falters and then completely subsides, her eyes flooding with tears again. "I'm a terrible person."

I'm still desperately trying to process the fact that Amelia Valadez has just told me that she's gay, but I'm not having that. "You are NOT a terrible person," I say, so loudly that the words echo round the room. "Being gay is nothing to be ashamed of."

Amelia laughs emptily again. "I'm not upset because I'm gay, Imogen."

"Oh," I say. "Good?"

"I'm happy that I'm gay. I mean, girls are just..." Her voice trails off.

My curls bounce around in my peripheral vision as I nod, grinning at her.

Her. Amelia. Beautiful, perfect Amelia. Perfect Amelia who's a lesbian. It's going to take a while for this new information to sink in. "I know, right?"

She shakes her head, removing herself from her little gay reverie. "But I am upset that I hurt Josh. He didn't deserve this. I treated him like *dirt*."

"No, you didn't," I offer. She gives me a look that plainly says, *Come on, be real.* "Well, you didn't treat him, like, amazingly or anything, but you were figuring things out. And he'll feel better with time."

Amelia sighs and twists her hair round her finger absent-mindedly. "You know," she starts, "at New Year's Eve, I felt more in the three minutes I spent with you than I did when Josh kissed me at midnight."

Her eyes meet mine, and it's like there's meaning in them I'm meant to decode. I keep looking back at her, but clearly I'm not giving the answer she wants because she turns away again. I wish I spoke Amelia but I'm not quite there yet. I'm at least trying now, though. That's something, right? I hope she thinks it's something.

"It should have been one of those perfect moments, you know?" Amelia continues. "But it wasn't. I don't love him, not in the way I thought I did when we started dating. I was so happy back then. This cute, popular boy wanted to date me," she says, brushing a stray tear off her cheek. "It felt like proof that I could do it, that I could be this perfect person that I knew I was supposed to be."

I never thought I'd relate to Amelia Valadez. But I'm not unfamiliar with all-encompassing, rib-crushing pressure from the world to be something you know you're incapable of being. I try to think of what I should say that'll be helpful, but she carries on before I can come up with anything.

"I let this carry on for so long because I didn't want to hurt him," she says. "I thought it was easier to just try to make him happy and forget that I was hurting too, but I haven't been very good at that this year, and now I've ended up hurting him even more than if I'd just been honest in the first place. I SUCK," she finishes in a very un-Amelia-like way, throwing her hands up in her lap.

"You don't suck," I say. "I'm awful with pressure – I'd hate to have been you in that situation, everyone thinking you're in the perfect relationship, trying so hard to be a perfect person."

I've never thought about how hard it must be to be Amelia before. I've been too busy being jealous of her if I'm totally honest. But now I am thinking about it… Yeah. It must be hard. Panic attack every morning before school, hard. Pretending to be straight for seventeen years, hard.

Amelia's tears begin to stream again. She doesn't move to wipe them away, so they drip on to her dress. "I'm sorry I'm such a mess."

"Um, you're not a mess," I protest. "And, even if you were, I wouldn't mind. It'd make you seem more human and less like you're the goddess of having perfect hair every single fucking day, or of having impeccable handwriting."

Amelia sniffs. "You like my handwriting?"

"And your hair. Come on – if I'm going to be nice to you, at least pay attention."

She smiles a soggy smile, adjusting her position so that she's facing me and not the wall. "You know … I think that's the first time you've ever paid me a real compliment," she says.

"Huh." I consider this. "You know? I think you might be right."

She smiles an even more real smile this time and opens her mouth to say something, but then she freezes as the classroom door opens.

I twist round too. Oh, phew, it's just Ollie.

"Um, hey, guys." He looks very uncomfortable. "Sorry to disturb you, but I just ran into Josh. He, erm… He looked really upset and now I don't know where he's gone."

"Probably home?" I suggest.

"OK…" Ollie says. "Did something happen?"

"Erm, kind of," I start, ready to cover for Amelia, but she just jumps right on in there.

"Yep. We broke up," she says. "Because I'm a lesbian."

Ollie's expression goes through so many different emotions in such a short space of time that I can't help but burst out laughing.

"Oh … right," he says eventually.

I keep on laughing and Amelia giggles, laughing at me laughing, getting us trapped in a hyena-esque vicious circle.

"Am I laughing or crying?" she asks, pressing her hands to her cheeks.

"Both, I think," I answer between cackles.

Ollie stares at us both absolutely losing our minds before saying he's going to leave us to it and go find Josh.

We giggle for a little longer until a loud cheer comes from the direction of the auditorium and Amelia jerks up, back completely straight. Unlike her. Too soon? Maybe too soon.

"Oh, God," she says, groaning. "I have to do my speech as head girl at the end of the show. If they'll still let me," she adds. "I need to go and get ready."

"Yeah, where are your priorities?" I jest. "You couldn't wait to break up with your boyfriend and come out as gay until *after* the talent show? You waited seventeen years."

She stands up, smoothing out her slightly soggy skirt. "I did. But I think seventeen years was long enough, don't you?"

I offer a lopsided smile. "Probably."

"All right then." She walks towards the door, a determined expression on her face. She pauses when she reaches it. "You coming, Quinn?"

My mouth drops open a little. I think I'm going to like this new, uninhibited Amelia. "Absolutely."

CHAPTER TWENTY

OLLIE

"Run me through it again."

It's Saturday, the day after the talent show. I'm with Imogen (and Maya, who's absorbed in a serious game of horses in the corner) in my lounge, trying to wrap my head round all the many things that happened yesterday – and not just our cake protest.

It was a stroke of genius from Clem (and wizardry from Maryam, making all those amazing cakes overnight), but I'm very glad we did it on a Friday so the teachers have the weekend to cool off before our 'mandatory meeting' with Ms Greenacre on Monday morning. She did *not* look happy yesterday. Although, somehow, still not as unhappy as Josh. He was so upset when I ran into him, in floods of angry tears, his fists clenched so tightly it was like he was clutching the broken pieces of his heart inside them.

And then there's this other thing. The way I felt when I looked at myself in the mirror of the dingy changing room when my cheeks and nails were sparkling. I love taking photos of other people and watching them have that '*oh*, that's me,' moment when they look at them. But I've never had that feeling when looking at any version of myself, photographed or otherwise.

Or, rather, I hadn't until yesterday.

Imogen rolls their eyes at me as they take a sip of their lemonade. "I've already been through it like ten bazillion times. I think things started going wrong because Amelia wouldn't make solid plans with him for Valentine's Day, and then they had all the pressure of everyone at school saying they were goals and had built shrines to them in their rooms—"

"An exaggeration, but carry on."

"Then they had an argument that I was sort of on the periphery of, they broke up, Amelia and I went to hide in Mr H's room, she told me what had happened, and that's when you found us."

"And she just told you she was gay? Just like that?" Something doesn't make sense: why would Amelia suddenly decide to be so open after so long? Don't get me wrong – I've been there, I'm really happy she feels like she can be more authentically herself now – but there has to be more to this story.

"Pretty much." Imogen picks at the skin around their nails distractedly. "She said that she's known for a long time. And then at New Year she said she felt more talking to me than she did when Josh kissed her and that—"

"Whoa, whoa, whoa," I interrupt. Now we're getting somewhere. "You didn't include that little detail last time."

"What?"

"She told you she felt more talking to you than she did when Josh kissed her?" I say, needing to make sure Imogen's telling me what I think she's telling me. "She actually said that?"

"Yes?" She looks up from her hands and frowns at me. "Why are you freaking out?"

I stare back at her in absolute incredulity. "*Imogen*. Amelia likes you. She was telling you that she liked you. That was why Josh was getting so jealous, because she kept talking about you, not because she kept talking about the group. It all makes so much sense now." I mime my head exploding.

They wag their finger at me, still somehow in denial mode. I try to grab it to make them stop, but they dodge it and poke me in the stomach instead. "Excuse me, I'm not a homewrecker," they say as I lift up my T-shirt to see if my belly button's bruised. Can a belly button be bruised? "She doesn't like me; she was just trying to explain that she doesn't love Josh like that."

"I can't believe you're in denial about this." I grin. "Amelia has a crush on you."

Imogen whacks me in the face with a cushion.

"OW."

"You take that back right now."

"I will not."

They hit me again, so I drop the subject and pick up another cushion, initiating a vicious cushion fight that would probably have ended in at least one of our deaths because neither of us is exactly great at admitting defeat, but we're interrupted before it gets to the last-rites stage. First by Maya, who runs to join the fight with gleeful screams, prompting us to be much gentler in our attacks so as not to punt her tiny body across the room, and, secondly, by a series of beeps from my phone.

In the activist group chat, below the notification that Josh Hudson-Scott has left the chat, is a message from Maryam.

> Hey guys. Something's happened that I could do with telling you about in person. I'm with Amelia, but is anyone else free to meet up and talk about it? Like asap?

I sit up, trying to ignore the panic still lingering from remembering my parents asking me to 'come and talk' back in September. "This sounds ominous."

"What sounds ominous?" Imogen says, glancing up at me as Maya tries to say the word 'ominous', but keeps getting stuck halfway through.

"Check your phone."

Imogen shuffles over to her jacket and fishes her phone out of the pocket before pausing a few seconds to read. "Hmm," she says. "Ominous indeed."

I type out a message explaining that I can't leave Maya, but that the others are welcome to come here. Maryam replies and says that she and Amelia will be over in about ten minutes, and a few moments later Clem and Louisa say that they're on their way too.

"OK," I say, clicking away from the chat. "They're coming over now."

Imogen stops brushing the mane of one of Maya's horses, slowly twisting round to me in horror. "Wait, what? Like, they're all coming here? Everyone? Now?"

"That's what I just said, yes," I reply, and she bats my phone out of my hands like a cat with an attitude problem. "HEY! Smashing my phone won't unsend the message, but it will P-I-double-S me off."

"They can't come here." She looks at me with her wide, swamp-green eyes.

"Why not?"

"Because—" They don't finish the sentence.

"Oh." I smile knowingly. This is interesting. Very interesting indeed. "Because you're freaking out about Amelia."

"No," they say immediately. "*You're* freaking out about Amelia."

"No. That job is very much taken up by you right now. But if Amelia doesn't like you as you're so insistent that she doesn't, then why is it a big deal if she comes over?"

I've got them at checkmate, and they know it.

She gives me her best stink-eye as she cautiously says, "I suppose it isn't."

"Good. Then everything's fine."

"Everything's fine," she echoes.

While we wait, I send yet another message to Josh to ask how he's doing. I can guess the answer, however – my previous five messages are still unread.

I sigh, before looking up and immediately breaking into a grin. Imogen's fiddling with their hair in the reflection of their blank phone screen, fighting a losing battle against their curls.

I lean my head up on to my fists. "Whatcha doing?"

"What?" She throws her phone to the floor. "Nothing." The doorbell rings (a lucky distraction, but we're absolutely going to be discussing her sudden need to appear presentable later on) and she leaps up. "Oh, good, the door. I'll get it."

She returns thirty seconds later with the rest of the group.

"Sorry to bother you, but I knew you'd all want to see this now," Maryam explains, lifting her laptop out of a bag.

They all take seats around the room; Louisa sits down in the armchair, her cane by her feet, Clem perching on the arm of the chair, Maryam and Amelia on the sofa, while Imogen stays hovering in the doorway, surveying the room.

"Do we need drinks? I think we need drinks. I'll go get them."

"I think we're good," I say.

"What about snacks?" they say, still clinging to the doorframe. "Or … better lighting? It's quite dim in here – I could go ask the sun to move. Or I could buy a higher wattage bulb; that's probably more realistic. I'll go do that."

"We're really good, Imogen," I say more loudly this time, trying to tell her with my eyes to chill the bloody hell out.

They take a deep breath and come into the room, sitting carefully down next to me.

Amelia suddenly clears her throat. "OK, so you know Ollie and Maryam took lots of pictures and videos of the talent show, including of your performance, Imogen, and the erm, cake protest?" She focuses her gaze on Imogen, who just nods.

"Well –" Maryam takes over – "I edited some clips of your performance together and posted it to our page online. And, when I was baking the other day, I may have also baked a big sheet cake and piped the words *Accessibility is essential even when not convenient* on it. I posted a picture of that to my main page with a caption explaining what's been happening and linking people to our page and …

the photo and the video kind of blew up."

"*What?*" we all say in unison.

Maryam swivels her laptop round to show us. "Yep. It now has over forty thousand views – and counting."

Oh my God.

"What?" Imogen repeats. "But … *why?*"

"Well, there are a few trolls," Maryam says, "but on the whole it seems like people really enjoyed your routine and connected with what you were talking about. They're commenting about how their own schools don't have gender-neutral bathrooms either and sharing their own experiences of inaccessibility."

"And there's more." Amelia shows us her phone screen. "Someone started a petition called *Get Ardenpool Academy REAL gender-neutral toilets* with a whole impassioned caption about how terrible it is that the staff aren't being held accountable for their behaviour and how it's hurting people. It's just a stranger, they don't even go to our school, but it has six hundred and seventy-nine signatures."

"Wait." Imogen unfreezes. "*Six hundred?* What the actual fu…nky potato waffles?"

Maya giggles at 'funky potato waffles' from the corner.

"People really engaged with what you were saying." Amelia smiles at Imogen. "You've helped start a real conversation."

Imogen tries to smile back, but only manages something more akin to a grimace, so instead opts to finger gun – something that definitely doesn't help the awkwardness factor.

"And the cake idea was a great one, Clem," Maryam says, pulling my attention away from glancing between them both, thoroughly enjoying this whole show. "We needed to make a statement—"

"And, *oh boy*, did we," Louisa laughs, while Clem looks bashful but pleased.

"They need to listen," Clem says, and I know that they're not that comfortable with attention as a rule, but they look calm and proud, as they should. "And now they have no choice but to."

The room grows quiet as we let the knowledge that this has grown bigger than all of us sink in. With the cakes, the mildly viral video and the petition... I don't know what they're going to do on Monday, but we all know that something big is coming. It has to be.

CHAPTER TWENTY-ONE

OLLIE

When I get to Mr Holland's classroom on Monday morning, Imogen, Amelia, Clem and Louisa are all lingering there, anxiously awaiting my arrival.

"Finally," Imogen says, immediately making a beeline for me, the others close behind. "Let's get this over with."

Everyone moves from their positions and we make our way down the corridor to Ms Greenacre's office. I glance nervously around at my friends before taking a breath and knocking on the door.

It's opened immediately by Ms Greenacre's secretary.

"Ah," a voice from within the room calls out in a heinously sugary tone. "Our famous activist society. Come in."

The secretary steps aside to allow us entry, looking grimly at each of us as we file in to stand in two rows in front of Ms Greenacre's desk, where she seems as if she's having to work even harder than usual to maintain her calm, callous demeanour.

This doesn't look good.

"Well. I don't quite know where to begin."

Definitely not good.

"Before we address your clever little protest the other day," she says, "and, believe me, we'll be getting to that later." She emits a false little laugh. "I believe we have another situation on our hands. I was contacted this morning by a journalist from a county-wide newspaper about a petition that, until that moment, I was entirely unaware existed."

Very, *very* bad.

"Let's start there, actually. Would one of you care to explain how this petition came to be?"

"It came to be because you—" Imogen starts, voice raised and wavering.

Amelia puts her hand on Imogen's arm. She stops talking and nods, allowing Amelia to take over. (A very good call. Amelia's far more likely not to accidentally – or just intentionally – insult her.)

"Well, Ms Greenacre," Amelia says, her hands folded neatly in front of her, "we decided early on in the meetings of the activist society that we needed to have a social-media presence as a group, so that we could share important info and publicise our events – things like that. Until very recently, this page only had around three hundred followers. But after we posted clips from the talent show, the page grew to just over four thousand followers." She omits the fact that minor internet baking celebrity Maryam had more than a passive role in that. "And many more people besides that had viewed our content," she continues, "including one particular video of Imogen's performance at the talent show."

"This is all very interesting, Miss Valadez," Ms Greenacre says, "but could you please skip to the part where a petition was started that directly opposes the actions taken by the faculty of this school? Actions that I took care to explain to you were the best solution for your issue."

There's too much emphasis on the word *your* in that sentence for my liking.

"We don't know who started the petition," Maryam says, voice wavering as she speaks. "It wasn't a member of the group."

"It wasn't," Ms Greenacre repeats, her gaze sliding over to Imogen.

"No," I say quickly. I'm not letting her accuse Imogen of anything they haven't done. They've already legitimately done enough things to piss her off. "It was a stranger. Their username's something random like poppyfields05 or whatever – it was just someone who felt passionate about the cause. We have no connection to them whatsoever."

I know that no one in this room did it – I saw how shocked we all were yesterday.

Her eye twitches. "I find that very difficult

to believe. However, regardless of whoever the individual was that posted it, it exists, and it currently has almost one thousand signatures."

Bloody hell. More people must have signed it overnight. I'd feel proud of how we can all come together so easily to fight for things we feel passionately about if I wasn't busy facing down my incensed headteacher.

"And frankly –" Ms Greenacre's voice is high with a hint of a tremor that tells us just how pissed off she is – "I do not take kindly to you bringing such negative attention to the school, and actions must be taken."

We all exchange nervous looks.

"Before I discuss those actions, however, I want to inform you of a decision that was made this morning between me and the governors of the school. After your little *performance* at the talent show, we discussed the matter at length and have decided that it is no longer appropriate for an *activist group* to function within the school. Schools, as institutions, have to remain politically neutral, and we simply cannot allow a group that is actively politically minded to exist any longer within the walls of Ardenpool Academy."

No. My stomach twists with rage as everyone's jaws drop. "But you were perfectly happy for us to exist before the talent show," I blurt out. "This isn't anything to do with politics."

"YEAH." Imogen nods at me. "This is because of the cake and the petition and you not wanting to look bad."

"I would like to remind you that you are speaking to the headmistress of this school." She smiles grotesquely. "Now, I understand your frustrations—"

Do you? I add in my head, hearing it echo silently from the rest of the group too.

"But that is what is happening. The money you raised through your bake sales and the talent show will be reallocated to our funds for school improvements."

No.

"WHAT?" Imogen blurts in horror. "We raised that money so that we could put on Ardenpool's first-ever pride festival. *We* raised that money. And we've already spent some of it on deposits, people are counting on us."

"Well, whatever remains of the money, including the two thousand five hundred pounds raised from the talent show on Friday, was raised by you all as a school society," Ms Greenacre says calmly. "And, as that school society no longer exists, you are no longer entitled to have access to such funds."

It's a giant punch in the gut to learn that we exceeded our fundraising target for the talent show and would now have been back on track to reach our total in time. We've worked so hard, done so many bloody bake sales, so much planning… And the fact that we were getting so close to it and yet now I'm not going to get to march through town with Imogen, Louisa and Clem aren't going to get to go to the first Pride together that they can actually access, and Amelia won't get to march with us all for the first time as an out-and-proud lesbian makes me want to flip Ms Greenacre's desk. Like, yes, we weren't naïve enough to think that there wouldn't be consequences to what happened, but none of us could have thought they'd do *this*. "That's bullshit," I mutter mutinously.

Ms Greenacre raises a single plucked eyebrow but doesn't say anything.

"I can't believe you're doing this," Imogen says. "It isn't fair."

"Well, Miss Quinn, unfortunately, life—"

"If you're about to say that life isn't fair, then you can shut the fuck up right now," she says furiously. "We're all very aware that life isn't fair; that's exactly why we started the society in the first place."

The room falls into a very tense silence.

"Well," Ms Greenacre says, putting her hands together, "if everyone has said their piece, then I suggest you all go back to class."

I stare at her incredulously. This is not how this was supposed to end.

Amelia drums her fingers on the edge of Ms Greenacre's desk, lingering like there are lots of things she would dearly love to say but knows she shouldn't. She glances at Ms Greenacre who simply stares back at her in challenge. There's a pause and then: "Come on," Amelia says in defeat. "Let's go."

Ms Greenacre's secretary stops lurking silently at her desk in the corner and walks over to hold the door open; we start to file out in silence.

"Imogen?" Ms Greenacre calls out. "If you wouldn't mind staying for a moment."

Imogen stops dead in their tracks, so I almost walk into them. "Not at all," they say, in a way which, coupled with their expression that's clearly the product of many tumultuous thoughts raging inside their brain, could not more obviously mean, *Yes, I fucking mind*.

I squeeze her arm firmly and whisper, "Good luck," before very reluctantly leaving her behind in the lion's den.

The second the door is closed, everyone's reactions erupt out of them.

"GODDAMN IT!" I yell, raising my middle finger at the closed door.

Maryam looks close to tears. "I can't believe they're doing this."

"I can," Louisa says, each syllable imbued with fury. "But I wish I didn't."

Clem collapses over to lean on Louisa, looking entirely miserable.

Amelia, however, stays quiet as she stands staring intently at the door.

She feels my eyes on her and seems to jerk out of her trance. She only glances at me for a second, but the desperation in her eyes is undeniable. "I hope Imogen's OK."

"Yeah," I say quietly. "Me too."

We wait for another anxious minute before the door opens again.

Imogen emerges, already small but looking frankly diminutive now. "They think I started the petition. I've been suspended. I— I tried to " Their voice cracks and my heavy heart aches for them, for *us*. "But they won't listen. It's over – it's all over."

It's all over.

I step forward and move to hug her, but she steps back slightly, and I get the message. She needs space right now.

I hover, helpless. I don't know what to do.

Ms Greenacre's secretary pops her head out of the door. "Miss Quinn? Ms Greenacre's ringing your parents now to inform them of your suspension. If you just head to reception, then I'll be along shortly to escort you to the gates."

Imogen just nods as the secretary retreats into the office/lair of evil once more. They look so un-Imogen-like, so sad, so *resigned*.

They look around at us all, but I don't think any of us know what to do, what to say to make this better for them. After a moment, they turn and walk slowly away down the corridor.

As I watch her shrinking in front of us, I feel something calcify in my ribcage. I can't just let this happen. I have to do something.

"Imogen," I blurt out. "Don't leave just yet. Give me five minutes, OK? I'll come find you. Just … wait."

They pause in the doorway, so I know they've heard me, even though they don't say anything. I turn back to the others. "Right," I say, courage rising. It's time for me to put everything being friends with Imogen has taught me into practice and bloody well *do something*. "I'm going back in. It's not fair that we've been disbanded, and I don't think I can change her mind about that, but—"

"There's a but?" Amelia queries.

"There's a but," I confirm. "We raised that money, so if we can't have it for the pride festival then it should at least go to towards making the accessible bathrooms. That's a school improvement if ever there was one. You guys wait here," I carry on. "But I'm going in."

"So am I," Amelia says forcefully, her voice contrasting with the way she's biting her lip that lets me know she's scared as well as determined. "C'mon, Ollie. Let's do this."

I nod in reply, knowing better than to try and talk her out of it.

"MS GREENACRE?" I burst through the door

without bothering to knock.

Her head jerks up, eyes narrowed. "I thought I told you to go back to class."

"You did," Amelia says. "But we need to talk to you."

"Miss Valadez, I suggest you do as I say before you make things any worse for yourself," Ms Greenacre says. "I would have thought you of all people would know better than this. You are our *head girl.*"

"Thank you for your concern, Ms Greenacre," Amelia says innocently. I suddenly feel like I've got front-row seats to the best showdown in history. "But, as head girl, I represent the best interests of all Ardenpool Academy's pupils, and it's because of that that I'm here today."

"We understand that the group has been disbanded and we won't bother trying to change your mind about that," I jump in. "But we want the money *we* raised to go towards creating the separate gender-neutral bathrooms that this school needs."

Amelia's brown eyes narrow. "The ones that the school council unanimously decided were an important and necessary addition to this school, so that the disabled toilet can go back to being actually accessible for disabled students."

Ms Greenacre and her secretary exchange unreadable looks.

"We raised that money," I say, voice shaking

with anger. "It deserves to go towards something important like this. And if you're still determined to be bigots then—"

"Mr Armstrong!" she interrupts. "That is no way to speak to school officials. I suggest you monitor your language unless you wish—"

"THEN I'LL RESIGN AS HEAD GIRL."

I turn my head, eyes so wide that they begin to prick in their sockets. Bloody hell.

"I don't want to represent a school that doesn't practise inclusivity," Amelia says. "And so I'll be happy to resign and to remove all mention of inclusivity and accessibility from the school promotional materials. You know," she adds, "the ones that I wrote for you."

"Yes," I say. "And who knows how many more people have signed the petition since we've been in this room? I'm sure as a school with such a famously *inclusive ethos*, you'd hate for it to gain even more traction and misrepresent the school any further."

Ms Greenacre looks as if she's about to go into cardiac arrest. "I don't think there is ANY NEED for such ultimatums."

I lean forward, my hands on her desk, black glittery polish still sparkling on my nails, apparently possessed by an incredibly ballsy ghost. "Isn't there?"

No one says a word for what feels like a very, *very* long time.

Ms Greenacre takes in a stiff but deep breath

through her nose and then slowly lets it out. "And what would you suggest as an alternative to the present facilities?"

My heart leaps.

Amelia speaks up eagerly. "We've talked about it before – the main girls' toilets downstairs can be entered from both ends of the corridor, with two separate doors. We thought if you put up a simple divide you could easily separate a couple of stalls on one end and put a sign on that door indicating that those stalls are now gender neutral."

There's another lengthy silence.

"I suppose," Ms Greenacre says slowly, "in the interests of not prolonging this discussion any longer, that that may be an appropriate solution, and we could allocate those funds to purchasing and installing that divide. We pride ourselves on being an inclusive environment here at Ardenpool Academy and we wouldn't—"

I'm sure she finishes her sentence but neither of us hear it – instead, we turn to beam at each other in disbelieving celebration.

"YOU'RE BOTH ON PROBATION, however," Ms Greenacre says loudly. "Your behaviour today and at the talent show has been highly disturbing and irregular, and if I hear word of any similar instances then you will ALL be suspended. I'm going to be keeping quite the eye on you, so consider this your warning."

"Oh, I feel thoroughly warned," I say.

"As do I. Thank you so much for your time, Ms Greenacre," Amelia says, using sarcasm for possibly the first time ever. "Your empathy is an inspiration to us all."

We leave her spluttering behind us as we shut the door and emerge back out into the corridor.

The other three have been standing outside the door, waiting for me and Amelia. "Well?" Louisa prompts us immediately, Clem and Maryam looking incredibly tense beside her. "What happened?"

I glance at Amelia. The corners of our mouths quirk up ever so slightly.

Louisa emits a celebratory screech, punching me in the arm in glee. "No fucking way."

"I don't believe it," Clem breathes, and we all become a hooting, hollering mess, jumping up and down together in a clump in the corridor. Only for a moment, though, before I pull away. Because we're not 'all' doing anything.

"Wait," I say. "Where's Imogen?"

They're nowhere to be seen. Frowning, I walk down the corridor to reception and ask the man behind the desk if he's seen them.

"I did," he says, a harassed expression on his face. "I told her to sit on the bench and wait for Miss Erikson to come and fetch her, but she just walked out anyway."

"Ollie?"

Amelia's followed me, her face crumpled with … worry? Fear? I'm not sure. She doesn't say anything, instead just holding up her phone so I can see the screen. Imogen's messaged the group chat.

Thank you all for everything. I'm sorry I let you down.

And then underneath:

Imogen Quinn has left the chat.

Shit.

CHAPTER TWENTY-TWO

IMOGEN

A cheer echoes from somewhere behind me. I don't know what they're celebrating – certainly nothing I've done for them – but I've personally never felt less like celebrating. The sounds of jubilation fade as my feet pick up the pace and carry me out of the main doors of school. The school I've just been suspended from. Because it wasn't enough just to dismantle everything we've painstakingly built together, to take my dream of fighting back against a world that tells me I'm too much – along with all the money we raised to make it happen – and make it an impossibility, splitting up the group and the community we found in each other too.

Although this *we* that I keep thinking of – there's no more *we*. It's just me, walking through town to my house, feeling so disconnected from the world that I worry I've slipped into another dimension while also feeling so full of everything that I think my organs might go into failure just from the intensity of it all.

I reach my house and climb the stairs to my room, my brain still flicking from one horrifying thought to the next, and lie down on my floor, staring up at the ceiling. There's a cobweb swinging from my lampshade, I notice.

My phone buzzes next to me, the noise of it against the floor setting my teeth on edge. It's another notification from our group's page — someone's commented on the video of my performance.

You're so inspiring <3 if this doesn't get them to listen then nothing will !!

They weren't wrong, I suppose. A tear sneaks out, coming to rest on my horizontal cheek. And then it's joined by many others, the river bursting its banks as I take my phone, turn it off, and slam it away in my drawer so I don't have to look at any more uninformed comments and the absence of anything else.

I've always felt this tugging inside, telling me when things are right and things are wrong. This intense sense of justice has carried me through the last few years of my life and guided pretty much all of my actions.

I really, truly believed we were *doing* something: we were actually helping to make the world a kinder place. The group, coming up with plans for our fundraising events, going to protests, making signs and writing captions on our page online, baking stupid, ugly fucking cupcakes – it's all I've thought about for six months; it completely took over my brain – not to mention the actual serial-killer-style vision board I've got going on on the wall above my desk.

And now it's gone. If it wasn't a cliché (and I had the energy to move even one of my limbs off the floor), then I'd reach up and tear it all down, strings and pins and plans and photographs of pride protests through history flying all round my room like they used to fly round my brain.

I don't know what to do. I'm so tired of the fact that no matter how hard I try, I always come back to feeling like things are never going to change and that people are always going to step in to tell me that I've gone about things the wrong way, despite the fact that no one's passing out handy instruction manuals to tell me what the 'right' way is.

I thought I'd made peace with muddling through and blazing my own trail. But now, instead of just being a little confused and a whole lot of angry, I also feel achingly sad. I messed up. I let the group pull this stunt. It wasn't my idea but I was the one that actually carried it out. I filled all their heads with my dream and they made it their own, then I messed things up and let other people snatch it away from them.

And the worst part, I think, as my chest rises and falls with alarming rapidity, is that even though the pride festival has been my focus for so long, and the loss of even the possibility of it happening is entirely devastating, it's only half of a whole. Right this second, there's something I'm grieving even more.

I thought I was starting to make friends – real friends – and now that's all gone. The *group* is gone, and along with it all our shared goals and time together. Clem will go back to making music in the band room that Louisa will haunt too when she's not busy covering herself in paint with her art friends, Maryam and Amelia will still have each other and Amelia will still have all the God-knows-whatever else she overschedules herself with. And Ollie…

My throat grows so thick that I worry for a moment I won't ever be able to breathe again.

I suppose he'll go back to hanging around with his friends, with Josh and Charlie and the football team, and it'll be like I never walked up to him in the corridor in September at all. I'll go back to being the weird, obnoxious person with too many opinions, who eats her lunch with a teacher because the canteen's too loud and overwhelming to brave alone.

It'll be better like that. The group didn't have anything to say to me earlier after I ruined everything. I saw them flounder in front of my eyes. Besides, they can clearly manage much better without me, if the cheering's anything to go by.

This is how it always goes. I ruin things, other people fix them, and then they realise that maybe they'd be better off without the person who fucked things up in the first place. You'd think I'd be used to it by now.

This time, though, I think it is a little different. It's me that's realising they'll be better off without me, not them. I can't control a lot of things – most things, even. Not all the injustice in the world, not Ms Greenacre disbanding our group and ruining our plans to make school an even slightly more inclusive place. But I can make sure that the others don't ever get their hopes inflated by me again, only for me to watch as anchor chains are looped round their ankles, tying them back down to earth, feeling heavier than ever before.

"IMOGEN."

My eyes open some indeterminable amount of time later, as I hear the front door slamming in its frame, then they close again while I take one final breath. And I do mean final. He does NOT sound happy.

Heavy footsteps thunder up the stairs.

"IMOGEN." My dad's at my door now, pushing it open. I don't raise my head, but I can feel his presence looming, feel the waves of anger lapping at the doorframe. "What the hell are you doing on the floor being all dramatic for? And, more to the point, why in God's name did I get a call from your headteacher today informing me that you've been SUSPENDED from school for FIVE DAYS?"

"Probably because they decided that five days was the appropriate number of days to sufficiently punish me for my rebellious actions," I say without irony, staring at the cobweb on my ceiling again.

"My issue," my dad spits out, coming further into the room, "as I'm sure you are well aware, *madam*, lies not with the number of days of the suspension, but with the fact that you were suspended at all. *Explain*."

I don't know what does it, whether something in me malfunctions or whether I just don't care any more, but I do as he asks – I explain. I start right from the beginning, not looking directly at my dad, or at anything, in fact. I tell him how I felt when the confetti cannons went off. I tell him how alone I was, about why I started the group and about the pride festival I dreamed up. No, not just dreamed up. I tell him about the plans that I made, the countless hours of research and finding vendors and performers and researching which stage lights have the most adjustable settings for different needs, and reaching out to people like the BSL interpreter who was just as excited by the idea as we were and was going to bring her wife and kids along on the day too. I tell him about the protests we attended, and our protest at the talent show. I tell him exactly how much money we raised and then exactly how it was taken away by people who care more about protecting a false reputation than protecting their students. I tell him about our online pages and the comments we got from people that wanted all the same things as us. I tell him that there *are* people out there like me, and lots of people that aren't like me but who've still felt similar things that they don't deserve to feel either.

Throughout all of it, he just stands there, saying nothing.

"And I'm not lying on the floor to be dramatic," I continue because frankly why the hell not at this point? "I'm lying on the floor because something about it helps regulate my body when everything feels overwhelming like it does right now. I learnt this when I was ten.

"It was Mother's Day and you gave me ten pounds to go to the shop and get Mum a present and I saw the roses on the trellis on my way out and I figured I already knew Mum liked them, and if I just cut them then I could use the money to get you a present too, because I didn't fully understand the concept of *Mother's* Day. So I did, I cut them, and I went to the shop and bought you some chocolate-covered peanuts because you always got them at the garage when we stopped for petrol and I didn't want you to have to wait until the tank ran low for you to get to have something you liked.

"But then, when I got back home, you'd seen the roses and were so mad that I got scared and

I couldn't talk; the words just wouldn't come. And you got madder and madder about me not answering you so I ran upstairs, and I lay down on the floor until I remembered how to speak. Then I threw the peanuts out and we never talked about it again.

"I know I've never been what you wanted. And I'm OK with that. I have people now that do like me for who I am. Or," I remember, lead filling my stomach, "I did anyway."

The silence stretches on until— "I don't remember the roses," he says.

"I wouldn't expect you to," I say simply. "Things have always been bigger for me than for anyone else."

There's another wait. "You've been busy." It's a statement, but it's also a question.

"Yes," I answer. "I have."

"Imogen?"

"Yes?"

He doesn't say anything in reply. My curiosity gets the better of me. I sit up. He's still just standing there, but he's also looking right at me.

"You've done so much," he says, still looking.

"Yes," I say again. "*I have.*"

"We'll talk about your suspension later. OK?"

I nod.

"What … what do you need right now?"

Everything stops. I imagine all the clocks in the world halting their ticking. My dad is looking at me, the question hanging in the air and in his eyes.

He really asked that. He's never asked me what I need before. And, more than that, he wants me to answer.

"Could I—" My words cut off, not because he's staring at me with anger and disappointment and frustration and my brain's shut down, but because he *isn't*. But then I force out the words because there is something I need, and I've never been one to waste an opportunity when it's been given. (Or to force opportunities to happen for myself because they rarely *have* been given.)

"Dad? Could I have a hug?"

His eyes flare in surprise and he doesn't move for a moment, but then he does and he's kneeling down and holding me in his arms.

"Is … this all right?" he asks, sounding unsure but doing it all the same.

"A bit tighter," I say. "I need the pressure."

He squeezes tighter.

We stay like that for a really long time – his arms around me, me crying until my body feels like it's mine again. I still feel broken: there's no getting round the fact that there is a time stamp on the day, marking the destruction of everything I thought I'd built and everything I had yet to.

But.

My dad is here, in my room, and he's holding the pieces of me in his arms. So that's something, right?

CHAPTER TWENTY-THREE

OLLIE

Amelia grabs me on my way down to the sports hall after school. We've got a match against Dunston High that I could really have done without today, but I'm the captain. I can't abandon the team.

"Maryam and I were chatting at lunch," she says, ignoring Josh's hostile stare lasering into her back (and my front) as he walks past us down the stairs, "and we've had an idea. We need to set up a group outside school. We've built up all this momentum, and I think the reaction online shows that other people would be interested in joining too. What do you think?"

"I think it's a great idea," I say. "What do we need to do?"

"Well, first we need Imogen." She bites her lip. "Have you heard from them yet?"

I shake my head. I've sent her multiple texts and I tried to call her at lunch, but nothing. I'm getting worried. If I didn't have this stupid match, I'd just go straight round to her house and see how she is.

"Me neither. I hope they're OK…" Amelia's voice trails off. "But, when we do get Imogen back," she says determinedly, like she's trying to convince herself Imogen's going to appear midsentence, "then we'll also need a venue for our meetings and ideas for some more fundraising events to kick us off."

The words 'kick us off' prompt a thought. "We never did a football fundraiser. We could do a family fun day with a couple of friendlies, maybe sell some food and tickets for spectators. Not at school any more, for obvious reasons," I add – there's not a chance in hell Ms Greenacre would let us do an event on school property now. "But maybe in the park?"

"Ooh, yes," Amelia says. "That'd be great. I'll start putting in the forms to register us for a new group. Are you all right to sort the, um, football side of things?" I know from her sudden awkwardness that she's thinking about Josh.

"Yeah, course. I'll message Imogen too and see what their thoughts are."

Amelia heads off home and I make my way down to the sports hall, my brain feeling full. I'm really glad we're not letting this stop us – I think a new group's a great idea. I just wish Imogen was here to plan it all with us – and that they'd reply to one of my messages so I know they're OK.

★

We manage to just about scrape a one–nil victory against Dunston – I was distracted the whole time and kept fumbling the ball, and Josh played a very aggressive game, quite possibly motivated by seeing me and Amelia chat earlier. I do feel bad for him, but I can't avoid her just for his sake. Everyone else played well, though, and they seem to be in a relatively good mood as we collect our stuff from the changing rooms. When I ask whether they'd be willing to play in a couple of matches as part of our potential football fundraiser, they all agree readily (except for Josh, who scrolls on his phone in the corner, pretending not to listen to what I'm saying).

He slopes out just as I'm finishing getting changed, so I quickly shove my boots into their bag and rush out after him.

"Hey! Josh!"

He doesn't acknowledge my call so I jog up to him as he's leaving and clap him on the shoulder.

"Hey, man, I was shouting for you," I say. "Didn't you hear?"

He doesn't look at me. "Nope."

"Oh. Right. Well … I didn't see you at lunch today. Are you doing OK, or are you…"

I don't finish the sentence but we both know I mean 'or are you in a deep Amelia-based depression?'

He doesn't answer for a while, instead staring

straight ahead like he's surveying the horizon for ships. "Does everyone know?" he says eventually, his tone as bitter as burnt lemon.

"Does everyone know...?"

"Does everyone know I've been *dumped*?" he spits out before lowering his voice as one of the Dunston team comes past us, and I can hear the anxiety hidden under the anger this time. "Has everyone been talking about it?"

"No, I don't think people know yet," I say, trying to tread carefully. "It's only been a couple of days. I don't think anyone's noticed anything different."

That's only half true. I've definitely heard rumblings from the school's rumour mill today that there's been a rift between him and Amelia – they weren't exactly subtle with their conflict on Valentine's Day. She's told everyone in the group what happened, but no one else seems to know the specifics yet.

"They'll find out soon enough, I guess," Josh says.

I wish I could reassure him that no one cares about his love life, but he and Amelia have been a more enduring feature of the school than most of our teachers. I really do feel for him. I feel for Amelia too: what she went through isn't easy, but she at least seems freer since it happened. Josh, on the other hand, looks defeated. And also like he maybe hasn't showered in a much longer time than I would recommend.

"C'mon," I say, tossing an arm round his shoulder. (And then hastily removing it when I catch the look on his face.) "It'll be all right. Come hang with me down here tomorrow lunchtime – we can focus on prepping for our next match against the posh pricks at St Michaels and you don't have to face everyone at the upper school."

"Nah. You've got your group and I don't need your sympathy. I'm fine."

Ah, yes, everyone who's fine ignores their friends and nearly maims people by going in too hard with tackles. "It's all right. I don't mind," I say. "And I don't have the group any more anyway, we got disbanded after the talent show. I'm actually kind of worried. Imogen was suspended and I've not—" I stop. He's looking at me with an Arctic-cold expression.

"I really could not give two shits, Oliver."

I bite my tongue, then say, "Not two shits, huh? OK, well—"

"I don't want to hear about whatever happened," he says, voice rising. "I don't want to hear about whatever the group's doing or not doing, and I especially don't want to hear anything about Imogen. So go be worried about her somewhere else and leave me alone from now on, all right?" He claps me on the shoulder with a very passive-aggressive smile and storms away across the courtyard.

I stay standing where he left me for a few seconds

and take a couple of deep breaths. I want to be there for him, and I get that he's upset, but it's not Imogen's fault. Regardless of anything that's happened this school year, Amelia would still be gay and still be unhappy being in a relationship with him.

I'm not going to waste my energy trying to comfort someone so determined to be angry with the world, and yes, I do see the hypocrisy of that statement.

I tug my phone out of my pocket and fire off yet another message to Imogen.

> Josh update: still hella pissed.
> Ollie update: missing you. Video call at six? xoxo

★

"I'm home," I call out into the house, kicking my bag under the stairs a little harder than is strictly necessary, but, you know, it's not been the best day of my life.

"Hi, honey!" Mum calls from kitchen. "Could you come in here a sec?"

My sigh deflates my entire body. So much for my plan to slip quietly upstairs. I had big plans to light a scented candle, listen to Taylor Swift, and attempt to decompress while I try (again) to make contact with Imogen. I need to know that they're OK.

Mum looks up from the book she's reading

over in the corner of the room, her legs curled under her in her chair. Maya's at the table doing her 'homework', which, as far as I can tell, is just sticking animal stickers into her project book.

"Hey." I pour myself my leftover cold brew from the fridge and hover over Maya to try and postpone whatever's coming from Mum a little longer. "You all right, Maya?"

"Yep, I'm doing my rainforest project," she says impressively, smoothing out an elephant sticker.

I point at something, nudging the book. "Do they have elephants in the rainforest?"

"They discover new species all the time in there," Mum calls over from her chair. "Who's to say whether they have elephants or not?"

"I think the new species tend to be smaller things like frogs, not stinking huge elephants," I say, subtly pushing the more geographically correct monkey stickers towards Maya.

"Wow." Maya grabs my hand. "Pretty," she says, looking down at my glittery black nails. I get a pang in the pit of my stomach as I remember how much simpler things felt when I painted them last Friday.

Mum looks over again to see what she's talking about and smiles. "That looks nice, Ol."

"Thanks. I got bored waiting for Imogen to get ready, so…" I shrug.

"Will you do mine after tea?" Maya asks, looking up at me hopefully.

"Sure, we can match."

She reaches forward to take my hand and then drags the backs of my fingers across the page of her book.

"Excuse me, I'm not an ink-pad, Maya," I say with a laugh, dodging her coming back for more. "You've got enough glitter upstairs to fill a bath with; you don't need my hands."

She turns quickly to Mum, wide-eyed. "Can I—"

"*No*," Mum says firmly. "You cannot have a bath in your glitter."

Maya turns back to her stickers, disappointed.

"Sorry," I mouth as Mum glares at me from over the top of her book.

I catch my reflection in the darkened window and something inside me jolts as I once again remember looking at my reflection the other day and seeing someone who looked a lot like me, but was also brave and glittery, his cheekbones sharp and gleaming, contrasting with their dark floppy hair and the threat of stubble on their face.

I think I liked that person.

"So, Ol." Mum's voice brings me back into the room and I look over to find her unfurling herself from her chair and moving to stand at the counter. "How are you feeling today?" she asks, starting to slice some ginger on the chopping board.

Ah. The old parent trick of trying to get your teenage child to engage in conversation by avoiding eye contact so that they feel safe and non-threatened. She read that in a magazine; I saw it open on the sofa once. I slope reluctantly over to her.

"*Maamaa.*"

"You sure you're OK?" She keeps chopping.

"Uh-huh…"

"Your dad called earlier. He wants to know if you and Maya can go over on Friday night. He says the football's on and he'll cook so you can stay for dinner too."

Great. Dad's company *and* his cooking: two of my favourite things.

"I can't," I say. "I'm busy. I'll walk Maya over, though, if you need me to."

"Ollie." She puts down the knife. "You've missed three weekends in a row now. You have to spend time with him at some point."

"Um, no, I don't." Trust me, I'm getting pretty good at avoiding it. I did see him a few weeks ago, but only because I didn't think I could claim to have flu for the fourth week in a row without him being concerned for my immune system. Not that I think he would actually care.

"He's still your dad, Ollie. You can't stay mad at him forever."

"Oh, I think I can. Don't underestimate me."

Mum leans back against the countertop. "I wish you wouldn't be angry with him."

I mirror her by leaning against the doorframe.

"And I wish you *would*."

"I'm not an angry person, Ol – you know that."

I raise an eyebrow. "Excuse me, I've seen you watching *The Bachelor*."

She looks back at me, working hard to maintain her serious expression. "I just don't understand why they're all chasing after one terrible man. Or why they're all called Becca. But stop distracting me. Will you please just go and see your dad?"

I look up at the ceiling, letting out a guttural groan. "Next week, maybe."

"*This* week," Mum says firmly. "Definitely."

UGH. "Why *aren't* you angrier with him?" I say exasperatedly. "I saw you when he first left: you were a mess. He did that to you."

She flinches at that last part, and I feel a twinge of guilt at bringing it up, but the fact that she doesn't want to bitch about Dad or, I dunno, run him over with her car is *infuriating*.

Her voice goes more hushed, probably not wanting Maya to overhear. "It was a tough time, Ollie. I was in shock for a while," she starts. "I didn't see it coming, and I always saw divorce as a kind of failure. *But*," she says more loudly as I open my mouth to interject, "now that I have more distance, I can see that it was the right thing. For all of us."

"What?" I can't see that. "How?"

"Because everyone, even cowardly idiots that, yes, have made a fair few mistakes, deserve to be happy. And I wasn't happy being lied to, he wasn't happy doing the lying, and you guys wouldn't have been happy growing up in a house with parents who didn't love or respect each other. Not enough anyway."

I would argue that he seemed perfectly happy lying to her for a very long time, but that doesn't feel like a necessary thing to say out loud.

"I know I was a bit of a mess at the beginning," she continues, "but, overall, I'm a pretty strong woman, kid. I'm fine without him. And at the end of the day, whether he's happy with this *Lisa* or not, I still won. I got to keep you guys – the two best things that ever happened to me – and I get to go to sleep at night knowing that I haven't treated anyone badly. He doesn't get to do that."

"No, he doesn't," I mutter.

"So, if I'm not angry – most of the time anyway – can you work on not being angry too? It's not going to change anything, sweetheart. Your dad is your dad, and I know he loves you."

"Yes, and he has an excellent way of showing it."

Mum purses her lips and shakes her head again. "I get that you're hurt. You're entitled to be. But you're going to work things out with your dad eventually, and maybe then you'll wish you hadn't wasted all this time being angry beforehand. Just think about it."

"Fine."

"So." She pulls a really irritating face. "Where did we land on you seeing your dad on Friday?"

"I swear to— Hey, Maya."

She's flung herself at me and is tugging at my shirt. "Are you coming with me to Dad's house?" So much for her not hearing us. Her tiny face is so full of excitement that I want to scream. I would literally rather eat my own foot, toenails and all, than go and see my dad.

But she's my sister. She doesn't need me to be angry; she needs me to be her brother and go with her to see our stupid dad. I heave a soul-suffering sigh. "Yes, Maya. Yes, I am."

Maya dances away with a series of *yay*s while Mum twists round to beam at me. I wish doing the right thing for her didn't feel so wrong for me.

A feeling that only intensifies when six o'clock comes and goes and all my calls to Imogen ring out to silence and my phone screen fades back to black.

CHAPTER TWENTY-FOUR

"Hey, kids!" Dad opens the door to us on Friday night wearing a football shirt and a broad grin. "Nice to see you, Ollie. Are you ready to watch the game? I've spread tea out in the lounge buffet-style so it's like the Superbowl. I thought that'd be fun."

Fun. Sure. He's in a good mood. He must have taken me coming over as a sign that everything between us has been miraculously fixed. Idiot. I'm just repressing everything for Maya's sake and exploiting you for your food and TV.

We get settled in on the sofa, an array of snacks laid out on the coffee table that are exclusively beige except for a plate laden with plain spinach (delicious...) and a bowl of Skittles. I make a note to keep an eye on Maya so that she doesn't pour them all straight into her mouth and have a three-day sugar high like she did at her last birthday party.

"Who's ready for some football?" Dad moves to

sit down between us, making me hutch up to the edge of the sofa.

I grab a spinach leaf just for the heck of it. "Sure."

The game begins. By half-time, Liverpool are winning two–nil, I've removed the Skittles bowl from Maya four times, I've checked my phone seven trillion times for a still non-existent message from Imogen, and Dad's said three things that pissed me off – not an all-time high, but there's still room for improvement.

Maya reaches for the Skittles yet again as they cut to the adverts.

"Look at your fancy nails," Dad says patronisingly. "They look nice. Did you do them all by yourself?"

"No, Ollie did them," she says, proudly thrusting her hands in his face. "We're matching. Show him, Ollie."

I hold up my hands, my own polish a little chipped now from all the nail-biting I've been doing the last couple of days.

His smile goes taut. "Ah. Right," he says tersely. "I'm going to go get a drink. Do either of you want anything?"

Maya shakes her head.

"Nah, I'm good," I say. I'd recommend he pour himself a glass of 'chill the fuck out, they're just nails', but he's probably all out of that.

On second thoughts, this spite is kind of making me thirsty. I get up and stroll across to the kitchen side of the room, opening the fridge to see what he has. I pour myself a sizeable glass of a gross-looking green organic fruit pressé purely because it probably cost him an exorbitant amount of money. He was never exactly a proponent of green stuff before – it must be another example of him either losing his goddamn mind or catering to this *Lisa*.

Dad frowns at my glass of juice as we sit back down but chooses not to say anything about it, instead selecting a more infuriating topic. "Did Maya make you paint your nails to match, then?"

"No. It was the other way around. I did mine first."

"But…" He flounders, struggling in his limited capacity as a cishet White man to recognise experiences that don't exactly match his own. "Why? Why would you do that?"

"Because I was waiting for Imogen to get ready and I was bored," I say carefully, focusing very hard on not rising to him. I can do this – I can choose not to let it bother me. "And why not? It looks cool."

He leans back in his seat, letting out a burst of air through his lips as he does so. "Blimey. I didn't think—" He stops. "Nah. Forget it."

I exhale slowly through my nose, knowing exactly where this is going. "You didn't think what?"

He rubs his stubbly chin. "Well, I knew you were gay. I just didn't think you were, you know, that—"

"That *kind of gay*?" I narrow my eyes. "Is that

what you were going to say?"

He shrugs, one hand up as if to say, *well ... yeah*.

"And what kind of gay would that be, Dad?" I put my drink down on the table deliberately next to (and not on) a coaster, and turn to face him.

"Come on, you know what I mean," he says, daring to look at me like I'm the one being unreasonable.

"No, I don't know what you mean," I say, still fighting to keep my voice level. "Please elaborate."

"Look, Oliver, I dealt with you being gay – you know I'm fine with that—"

"Maya?" My voice is quivering with anger now. "Go and ... see what kind of soap Dad has in his bathroom."

It wasn't my best suggestion, but she trots off out of the room all the same. She doesn't need to listen to this, and I have a feeling I may have to use some words not appropriate for her ears.

I twist back round the second she's out of earshot. "I don't know that you're fine with it actually, given that you've literally *never* mentioned it to me since I came out."

"Well, what did you want me to say?"

"Oh, I don't know," I say sarcastically, "that you love me, that you support me no matter what, that you're proud of me."

His eyebrow twitches at that last one, like he can't possibly conceive of a world where he would ever be proud to have a gay son.

"You know," I carry on, "all things that Mum has told me countless times. But I don't know what I expected: you were never the caring parent."

His jaw hardens. "That's not fair."

"Isn't it? You never talked about anything hard or complicated or messy. That was always Mum's job. And then you'd have the balls to complain that Mum was *too emotional*. What the fuck did you expect when you never showed emotion about anything?"

Dad's face goes Medusa-stony. "There are just certain things that men are supposed to be and do, Oliver, that's all."

"What, like cheat on their wives and abandon their families?" I spit back.

Oh, shit.

Dad's hand flies to his mouth. "I didn't— How did you…"

"I saw you with her. Lisa," I say, turning away to look out of the window. "I saw you kiss her. And then I talked to Mum."

He lets out a derisive snort. "Of course."

I turn back from the window immediately, my eyes boring into him like the barrel of a loaded gun. "Don't you fucking *dare* blame Mum for this. She didn't tell me anything until I outright told her I knew. And the fact that you thought you had the right to even ask her to protect you in the first place fucking *blows my mind*."

"All right," he says loudly. "You can stop with

that language right now."

"Oh, yeah. Because God forbid a man shows emotion, right? Got to keep it all buried in there to punish others with, right? That's how I'm supposed to do it?"

"I don't deserve this," he mutters, getting up to walk away.

"Yes, Dad. You do. You deserve to know exactly how shit you've been."

"This isn't your fight, Ollie," he says flatly. "You're just angry because your mum is."

"Mum isn't angry! She should be, she has every right to be, but she's a far better person than you are." My voice cracks. "I'm the angry one. You hurt my mum, my beautiful mum, who's never done anything bad to anyone her whole entire life, and you broke up *my* family and my *sister's* family. She's never going to grow up knowing what it's like to have a family with two parents who love each other, and I'm always going to wonder whether I ever had that too or whether it was all a sham."

Dad goes very still, standing with his back to me at the sink. "How did we get here?" he says quietly. "I was just trying to say that I'd accepted that you were gay, but I didn't like you wearing make-up, that's all."

"Sure, that's all," I say with a hollow laugh. "But I'm secure enough in my masculinity to wear make-up if I want to. I don't associate femininity with weakness. Something that clearly is not the case for you. And accepting only straight-passing queer people isn't acceptance anyway. You either accept all of us, every queer person, even the loud, outlandishly, *in your face* queer people, or you don't accept any of us. And until you decide which it is, I'm done. I don't want a dad who only tolerates my existence. I deserve to be loved *because* of who I am, not *in spite* of it."

His shoulders droop but I don't wait around to see if he's going to reply. I've heard enough, and finally, *finally*, I think I've said enough too.

"Come on, Maya," I say, opening the bathroom door to find her diligently checking the cupboard under the sink for soap. "It's time to go home."

Poor Maya trails along behind me on the way back, almost jogging to keep up with my rage strides. "Go see Mum," I tell her when we get through the front door. I rush into the garden, wanting to escape the memories of sixteen years' living in the house with my dad that echo round the walls inside.

I close the back door behind me with so much force it shakes in its frame. Then I sink down on to the grass, staring up and into the night sky and wishing my body didn't feel quite so affected by the pull of gravity.

I don't really know what I'm feeling. On the one

hand, I got to say some stuff that I've been bottling up for years, but on the other hand... Yeah. *On the other hand*.

"Ollie?" Mum's head pokes slowly into view above me. "Daijōbu?"

Yep, I'm fine. That's why we're back two hours early and I ran straight out into the garden.

"Did your dad say something?" she ventures cautiously.

I snort in derision. "What *didn't* he say? Oh, and he knows that I know about him cheating now. I told him," I say, still staring up above me.

"Oh, Ollie..." There's a pause (and a thud) as she lowers herself down on to the grass next to me.

"He's just such an asshole, Mum," I blurt out in an almost-whine, turning to face her fully.

"I know, honey," she says, reaching out to rub my shoulder. "He definitely can be – I'll give you that. I don't know what he's said to you, but ... but fuck him, OK?"

My mother just swore. She just said the f-word about my dad.

Finally.

Mum smiles wryly at my half-shocked, half-pleased face. "Yeah, I said what I said. But we don't need him. We're a complete family with or without him – you know that, right?"

I nod.

"Good," she says, clambering up with a groan.

"I'll give you your space, but you come inside if you need anything." She hovers above me again. "Why don't you message Imogen and see if they're around. They always cheer you up."

"I will," I say, but once she's gone again my eyes flood with tears. All I want right now is to rant to Imogen and have them be full of rage on my behalf and then say something so ridiculous that I burst out laughing, puncturing the giant red ball that's inflated inside me. But they're MIA, still ignoring my messages. Still ignoring everyone's messages, if the group chat's anything to go by.

I check it again. It's still just all the same messages from earlier. From Louisa:

> Absolutely fuck Ms G, but shit, guys!!
> We did the thing, we got the bathrooms!!

And Clem:

> So proud of us. What comes next tho?
> This isn't it, right?

Louisa again:

> Hell no. We've celebrated and now it's time to plan.

And two from Amelia, the first one explaining what her and Maryam spoke about and mentioning my football plan, and then a second, which just says:

Anyone heard from Imogen yet? I'm getting worried.

I scroll back up to Imogen's last message.

Thank you all for everything. I'm sorry I let you down.

She doesn't really believe that she's let us down, right? I messaged her privately after I saw it (You've not let us down, you dickhead, we love you) but I've not had time to really think about her message and what it means until now. I know what she's like when she gets an idea into her head, how her brain is built for things to latch on to. What if she really *is* blaming herself for all of this?

I want to cry even more now, imagining her spending the week alone and thinking she's to blame for us losing everything. She doesn't even know that we *haven't* lost – she's not opened any of my messages, including the one where I told her the whole story about the bathrooms.

I have to fix this right now.

My dad might not love me for all that I am. But Imogen always did. They put their hand in mine and glitter on my cheeks and they made me *brave*, and I'm only realising now that I've never told them any of this out loud. I've been too busy with my parents' divorce to realise that even though their love story has ended, one of my own has begun.

A plan forms in my head and I smile properly for the first time in five days. I fire off a message to the group chat, fingers frantically flying over the keypad, firstly, to explain the plan and then to reply to everyone's enthusiastic responses.

Back inside in the warm, one chaotic, three-hour-long video chat later, the plan is fully afoot. It's late now, and all I can do is sleep off this shitty day. But first thing tomorrow, I'm going to go tell a tiny, glittery, ridiculous gremlin, who made me laugh and dream when I had no interest in doing either, that I love them.

CHAPTER TWENTY-FIVE

IMOGEN

At first, I think it's raining. It didn't look like it was going to rain earlier when my mum made me sit and mope in the garden while we ate breakfast (instead of sitting and moping indoors for a change), but I figure it's just the weather doing me a solid with some pathetic fallacy.

My dad and I seem to have reached a grudging impasse where he tries to remember that I'm a human being – a confusing human being, but a human being nonetheless – and I tell him how I feel in an honest, non-flippant, no joke-cracking style that feels equally foreign to me. But apart from that, everything still feels irreversibly changed for the worse. My group's still disbanded, all the money we raised is gone, the pride festival is back to being a pipe dream, and I've ruined everything for people I care about.

I took my phone out of its drawer of shame

yesterday in a moment of weakness and turned it on. I ignored the overwhelming flood of notifications, instead deciding to torture myself by reading some more of the unintentionally upsetting comments on social media telling us how amazing everything we're doing is (was). When I did, though, I noticed a post lurking in the drafts folder. A post about a new group they're all starting, asking whether anyone wants to join. Anyone but me, obviously – I'm still not wavering in my self-imposed restraining order from them all. Their plans sound great too – I'm really happy for them. Or I would be if all the sadness would leave some room for it.

But then the rain stops. And something heavier knocks against my window, startling me upright in bed where I've been hiding all afternoon. Hmm. My window is indeed wet, peppered with shining droplets like it's been raining, but there still isn't a cloud in the sky.

Curiosity may have killed the cat, but I'm not a cat, I'm an Imogen, and I'm willing to risk it. I'm just clambering out of bed to investigate the sky when I hear another *bang* – and this time I see the pebble bouncing off my window frame to accompany the sound. The sound that, as I fling my duvet off from around me, is followed by blaring music. It's a familiar song, one from the playlist I renamed as *angry girls having breakdowns* after Ollie's comment at New Year's Eve. It usually fires me up, igniting my rage and making me productive, but today it just confuses me. Why is it playing outside my house? Who is throwing rocks at my window? And where did the rain come from/go to?

All of these questions are answered and replaced by approximately a million new ones as I stand at my window, unlatching it so I can lean out and peer at the scene before me.

There, in the middle of my front lawn, stands Ollie, an actual, literal boombox held above his head, looking damp and shiny because someone (Amelia, I suspect, if the toned legs attached to pink Mary Janes poking out of the garden hedge are anything to go by) is crouching in the aforementioned hedge, pointing my garden hose high in the air so that water rains down on him.

Like I said, I have many questions. Primarily:

"What the fuck?" I mutter to myself.

"Imogen!" Ollie calls up to me. "Thank God you're here. I was getting worried."

"Of course I'm here. Where else would I be?" I ask, still not one hundred per cent sure I'm not in the middle of a very strange depression-induced dream. "But … why are *you* here? You shouldn't be," I add soberly. "You've all got your own lives – you don't need me. I don't blame you all for hating me for messing this up for us."

"I hate a lot of things, Imogen!" he shouts, still holding the boombox aloft. "I hate that our group was disbanded. I hate that my dad was even worse than usual to me yesterday. I hate that we lost all the money. But I don't hate *you*, you idiot."

I can't let myself believe it. "You don't?"

"No, I don't. Why on earth would I?"

"Because," I say, almost shouting over the music, "in the end, it was my performance and the fact that Ms Greenacre already hated me and so went straight to blaming me for the petition that tipped her over the edge. If it wasn't for that, we'd still be on track to put the pride festival on. We were going to create a safe space for so many people, and I got you all excited for it and then I wrecked it."

Ollie is quiet for a second. Only the music and the white noise of the hose still raining all over this whole weird tableau remain. But then he says, "Imogen?"

"Yes."

"Would it ruin the moment awfully if I put the boombox down? It's heavier than I was expecting, and my arms are starting to feel like mayonnaise."

"For God's sake, no, put it down. I don't even know why you have it in the first place, or where on earth a person would acquire a boombox in this day and age."

"Oh, well, that last part is easy. Amelia borrowed it from the music graveyard in her parents' attic."

She pops her head out from the side of the bush and gives me a wave. "Um. Hi, Imogen."

"Hello," I say, not getting any less bewildered

(although this does explain who had the presence of mind to wrap the boombox in clingfilm to stop it getting wet).

"The other part will become clear momentarily," Oliver replies. "Now, there are two wolves inside me right now—"

"And both are gay?" I offer.

"No. Well, yes. They are. But also, one wants to tell you you're being absolutely ridiculous—"

"Says the guy who's dripping wet in the middle of my lawn. For reasons I still don't understand."

"Patience, Imogen, patience. And *the second wolf* wants to tell you that I'm sorry."

"*You're* sorry?" I can't be hearing any of this right.

"Yes," he says simply. "I am. You're my best friend."

My whole body goes light, like I'm going to need to weigh myself down so as not to float out of the open window.

"And I didn't listen to what you were telling me." Ollie runs his fingers through his (very damp) hair. "I didn't realise how far you'd spiralled; I didn't realise you were being serious when you sent that message to us. And then I was so busy this week *missing you*, getting annoyed with Josh, planning things to keep us going, and having the fight of all fights with my dad, that I didn't think to just show up here and make you listen."

"You confronted your dad? Are you OK?" I ask,

but I can't overlook what else he said. "Also, wait. I'm your best friend?" I say weakly.

His eyes crinkle as he offers up a wry smile with his response. "Yeah. I think you are. And I'll tell you about my dad later, but for now –" his tone is reverent – "listen to me. We love you and you have ruined *nothing*. To start with, even if you had, it would be rude of you to take all the credit when we were all involved."

"Technically, the cake protest was my idea." Clem steps out from behind a car because of course they're here too.

They're closely followed by Louisa, wheeling round to the edge of the grass. "Yes, if you're going to blame anyone for the situation at school, then blame Clem. I mean, don't blame Clem, *no one* is to blame, but still."

Maryam pops out of another hedge, adjusting her hijab. She looks a little like she's been dragged through a hedge backwards, probably because she sort of has. "And I baked the cakes, so I helped too."

"Exactly how many people have you stashed in my front garden?" I yell down at them all. "Is this everyone or am I about to be subjected to some kind of flash mob?"

"Damn it, we should absolutely have done a flash mob." Louisa looks despondent at having missed such an opportunity. "Next time."

"This is all of us now," Maryam says reassuringly.

"And, by the way, if you haven't checked your messages, then you won't know this, but after you left we got Ms Greenacre to agree to make *actual* gender-neutral bathrooms, so not everything is terrible."

"You did?" I can't keep from sounding downright incredulous, mostly because I am. I thought I heard them celebrating something when I ran away from school, but I didn't think it could be something that good. "*How?*"

"Blackmail, mostly," Amelia says sagely, and I've never been prouder of her.

"Incredible."

"Now," Ollie says, "are you going to come down or do I have to keep doing this?"

"Just to be clear," I reply, "you don't *have* to do any of this. I didn't ask you to come and drench yourself on my front lawn for reasons that I'm still not entirely clear on."

"Oh, aren't you? Sorry, I'd hoped it would be clear by now. This is my big romantic gesture, baby."

I just look at him. "Your *what?*"

He has the gall to roll *his* eyes at *me*. "You know, guy realises he's been a dick – or in this case just a bit dense – and comes to fight for the girl – or in this case not really a girl – and stands on the lawn with a boombox playing her favourite songs until she comes down, he tells her he loves her, and they kiss in the rain."

I pull a face. "Eww."

"Yeah, I'd rather we didn't do that part if it's all the same to you. But, for the record, I have been an idiot. I'm sorry that we all got busy and didn't make it clear enough how important you and this group are to us and how we're in this for the long haul. *Together.* And I'm sorry I forgot that you always assume people hate you until proven otherwise and I didn't come over here sooner."

For some reason, Amelia looks pensive at this, frowning thoughtfully, hands still clasped round the hosepipe.

"So, this is me proving otherwise," Ollie continues.

I let out one last disbelieving breath. "You really don't hate me?"

"No, Imogen, haven't you been listening? Quite the contrary, in fact. *I love you.* We all do."

"Yes, and we need you to come down – firstly, so that Ollie can complete the gesture by not kissing you," Louisa calls up, "and secondly so that we can tell you the plans we've made for what comes next."

I don't know what to do with myself and all this information that's just been shouted up at me. *Ollie loves me. Something comes next.*

I grin. I'm about to run down and into the arms of one or all of these absolute buffoons when...

"What in GOD'S NAME is going on out here?"

Uh-oh. My dad bursts out of the front door to stand on the lawn, looking around at the scene with not entirely invalid confusion.

"Oh. Hi, Mr Quinn," Ollie says. "Don't mind us – we're nearly done."

"Done with what, exactly?" he demands. "And will you turn that awful music down – you're disturbing the neighbours."

Ollie nods up at my window. "With mission *recover Imogen from their lair of despair and get them back on board with our plans.* And, with respect, I don't give two figs about the neighbours. Or a singular fig, even."

My dad wheels round and spots me hanging out of my window.

I wave down. "Hi, Dad."

"You know what?" Ollie continues to my dad. "While I'm here, I may as well use this chance to try to shamelessly exploit your privilege for our benefit. We have big plans to keep making the world a less shit place – plans Imogen started for us and that you should be incredibly proud of them for – and we need a base to do that from. I think I know what the answer will be, but how would you feel about letting us use the town hall for meetings? And one of the football pitches in the park for a fundraising event?"

"Sure," my dad says and, if I hadn't already reached my emotional bandwidth for the day, I might be more shocked at this response. But, thankfully, Ollie looks shooketh enough for the both of us.

"All right, so maybe I didn't know what the answer would be."

"Imogen's told me what you've been up to recently," Dad continues, "and while I can't say I agree with all your methods—"

I feel my cheeks go a tad magenta. He may have been unprecedently chill this last week on account of the minor menty-b I've been having, but I still didn't manage to escape a lecture on how getting up onstage and swearing at my headteacher was not appropriate behaviour and I was letting down the good Quinn name by resorting to such language.

My dad glares at each member of the scattered group in turn before speaking again. "But nor can I say I don't admire your ambitions. And, if you'd like to stop ruining my lawn and come inside for a discussion, then I'd like to hear these new plans and we can figure out a time for you to have your meetings."

There's a slightly stunned silence.

"Th – thank you, sir," Ollie says. "We'll be right in, if we could just have one more minute."

My dad bristles like a moderately irate hedgehog, but, after a quick glare at Ollie and another one up at me, he says, "Make sure you all wipe your feet," and turns round and goes back inside.

Ollie's eyes flare back to me. "What the fuck?"

"Yeah. Things have been weird around here," I say. "I'll catch you up later."

"Please do. Now, are you coming down, or what?"

I grin. "Oh, I'm coming."

For some reason, in my brain the most direct route to Ollie's arms is not via the stairs, but rather climbing out through the window and on to the sloped roof above the front door. And the reason is that I've always wanted to do it and now seems as good a time as any.

"Please be careful." Amelia steps fully out of the bush and rushes forward, tossing the hose to Clem, panic in her eyes.

"Careful, shmareful," I say, but when I've shuffled myself to the edge of the roof, my legs hanging over the drainpipe, I kind of see her point. "Um … now what?" I say, looking down at the drop that seems a lot higher than I'd imagined it being in my head.

"Jesus Christ." Ollie shakes his head up at me. "Come here."

He moves to stand underneath me, Amelia following behind him, and I have to restrain myself from kicking them both in the head. "Right, lower yourself as far down as you can, and I'll catch you."

It says a lot about our friendship (our *best* friendship, I remember, grinning even wider as I do so) that I both listen to what he says and also trust that he will catch me.

In the end, I do a very ungraceful shimmy down through Ollie's arms, as he strains to stop us both from falling, but then…

"SHIT!" Ollie topples backwards and thuds on to the soggy grass.

You would think a muddy butt would be the most embarrassing result of such an incident, but personally I think my fate is worse. A thought that occurs to me as I blink down at Amelia, who I've just flopped on top of like a dead salmon.

"Um…" she says. "Hello."

"Hi. Come here often?" I quip, to try to cover up the fact that I'm very aware of the way her body feels underneath me, and the proximity of her face to mine.

"Here." Ollie's hand appears in my peripheral vision. I quickly look up at him so I'm *not* looking down at Amelia, whose chest I can feel rising and falling very shallowly and quickly underneath mine. Probably because of all my dead weight pressing down on it.

I take his hand, letting Amelia scramble up after me, and end this embarrassing display by sticking my arms out like I just performed an epic double-pike vault and didn't nearly kill myself, Ollie *and* Amelia in an act of ridiculous triple manslaughter. "Easy-peasy."

"You're an idiot." Ollie shakes his head, but his smile is warm and my happiness reaches down to my toes. "Come here."

He drags me into his arms again, this time not to save me from an embarrassing, squishy death in my mother's petunias, but to envelop me in the tightest hug known to humankind.

I let it happen, sinking into his lanky frame. "Ollie?" I whisper.

"Yeah?"

"I love you too."

I didn't think it possible, but he holds me even tighter, the 'rain' still pouring down on us.

After a few long moments, I pull myself away. I've got something to say. "Romantic gesture complete." I turn to the others. "Please will you turn off the hose, for the love of all things unholy. Think of the polar bears."

"Told you they'd mention the polar bears," Clem says, smiling wryly as they do what they're told.

"Right, come on. Let's go inside and get to work," Ollie says.

I'm not sure what exactly we're going to be working on, but I'm excited for whatever it is.

We head inside (first wiping our feet and then removing our shoes) and arrange ourselves in a circle on my living-room floor. I wrap one of my mum's many blankets round me and Ollie to warm us up (and to protect the cream carpet from his butt), the pair of us having borne the brunt of the 'rain'.

"Well?" I say, looking around at them all. "What are we doing?"

"We're getting our heads back in gear and making plans," Louisa answers. "We've got the bathrooms sorted, now we have to keep going."

Amelia swoops in. "We had an intense planning

session last night, and we don't think we should let a small thing like getting disbanded stop us." She grimaces. "Yes, losing the money is a bit of a blow—"

That's one way to put it.

"—and it's unlikely we can put the pride festival on now, but…"

Maryam smiles a surprisingly mischievous smile. "*But* unlikely doesn't mean *impossible*. We don't need school. We can start our own group and let people from other schools join if they want. We can make a difference even without a classroom as a base."

"We've built up some great momentum." Clem looks right at me, their face kind and open. "People are listening to us for once. It'd be a shame to let that go to waste, don't you think?"

"And sure, we've got some stuff we need to figure out," Louisa says. "We've already paid some deposits, and there has to be *something* we can do about the pride festival, even if we can't have the huge event we wanted."

"We still have our online fundraising page," Maryam says, "and, like Clem said, we've got momentum; we've got people listening. Ms Greenacre can't take any of that away. And she can't stop us continuing to raise money on our own."

"We're not back at the beginning." Amelia's honey-brown eyes are soft as she looks at me. "We might have to start from scratch with fundraising, but we've still come much further than any of us could have hoped, in other ways. We've planned out logistics for the group and it's all sorted – especially if your dad does let us use the town hall for it. We just need you to say *yes* and we're on our way again."

I feel Ollie's careful gaze on me. "So?" he says. "Do you? Say yes?"

The room feels golden – warm and light like the sun rose right here inside it while they were speaking. I can scarcely remember how low I was feeling earlier; right now, I'm here, in this golden room, with people who care. About me, about our group, about making a real difference. I know I will always have to live with the uncertainty that comes along with existing in this world as the person that I am. But this, right here – *us* – this is something I know for certain I got right.

I swallow back the swell of tightness in my throat that formed while they were all speaking. I think about teasing them all a little longer with feigned hesitation, but I just can't do it. "Yes." I grin. "I say yes."

Everyone beams.

"Hell, yeah," Ollie echoes behind me. I do a little grooving happy dance, and everyone laughs and joins in and then suddenly we're all dancing and laughing and *yes. Nothing has changed.*

An hour later and they've updated me on

everything they've been planning. They've got forms filled out and ready to go to register us as an official community organisation and they show me the draft post to share to our page to invite others to join. I don't tell them I saw it while I was in my depression cave. Instead, I tell them how proud I am of all the work they've done to keep us moving forward. We also decide that if we can even just raise a couple of thousand pounds, we'll be able to pay the performers and equipment suppliers we've already booked instead of just losing those deposits, and we can put on some kind of event, at least, even if it's not the huge pride extravaganza we'd imagined.

There's a slight break in the joy when an uneasy silence falls while I'm midway through an improv comedy roast on Ms Greenacre – my mojo apparently thoroughly restored – and I look up to see my dad hovering in the doorway. But even that doesn't last long. Instead of berating us for our performance outside, he offers us a room in the town hall for Sunday afternoons and says he'll take our forms into work with him on Monday. As he's looking over them with Amelia, advising her on the application process, Ollie nudges me to get my attention, eyes twinkling.

But then I notice that when he looks towards my dad, his excited expression slips away and I remember what he said earlier about fighting with *his* dad.

That evening, after we've exhausted our brains and my stomach's started making noises akin to a fighter jet full of grizzly bears, we decide to call it a day. I ask Ollie whether he wants to stay a while longer, though.

"I have frozen pizza and an excellent listening ear, or so I've not been told," I say. "Truthfully, my mouth is better at the talking thing than my ears are at the listening one, but I'll make an exception for you?"

CHAPTER TWENTY-SIX

OLLIE

Imogen's standing in their hallway, concern hazy around the edges of their usually focused green eyes, and it's making me want to cry. I've not had time to process my argument with my dad yet and the offer of pizza and a person to rant at is too tempting to resist.

I nod and follow Imogen up the stairs to their room, where I flop dramatically backwards on to their bed, the mattress sagging beneath me.

"That good, hey?" Imogen looms over me, a mildly amused expression on their face before they flop on down next to me.

"Pretty much," I say, turning to face her again.

"D'you need to rant?" she asks, and I take a deep breath before letting not just a rant but a rant of truly epic proportions spill out of me.

Once I've finished relaying the details of this batshit couple of days (and they've finished calling my dad a bastard many, *many* times), they fold their arms across their chest. "He really is a ten-out-of-ten dickhead, isn't he?"

"YUP."

"I'm very proud of you, though. We love a man who fights toxic masculinity."

I chuckle (and then sigh). "Thanks. I just… I don't want this any more. I'm so sick of it."

"Sick of what?" Imogen asks. "Your dad?"

"No," I say. "Well, yes, but it's more than that. It's just, you hear stories all the time about men who get angry and shout and throw things around the room, but never about the men who stay quiet and let their silences grow so loud and heavy that they fill up every room they're in. People always blame the women who snapped, not the men who drove them to say too much by saying nothing at all. And I'm sick of there being so many things to be angry about and not knowing what to do with it all without making things worse for the people around me and being part of the problem. I don't want to walk this fucking tightrope any more; I want to take a pair of secateurs to it and plummet down to somewhere different, somewhere kinder."

"There's some in the shed," Imogen offers. "My dad put a padlock on it when I went through my topiary phase and turned the front hedge into what was meant to be a porpoise but ended up looking more like … a mangled hedge. But we can hack the code, I'm sure. There's nothing we can't do."

"Thank you." I gently bump my head against theirs. "I've actually been fine recently just ignoring my dad's existence," I say, absent-mindedly twisting the braided bracelet round my wrist. "But he was just such a *dick* yesterday, and seeing your dad being so helpful just reminded me of everything I've lost out on. I don't know how I'm supposed to be chill about that."

"I don't think you *are* supposed to be chill about that," Imogen says. "Or any of it, in fact. I've found that the more I push my anger away, the harder it comes back. It's like the world's worst boomerang. And boomerangs were already a silly concept."

"So what, then? I'm just meant to be full of rage twenty four seven?"

Imogen shrugs. "Rage can be pretty productive sometimes. Anger's what we're going to use to change the world, BEBE."

"But I just … I feel like I'm a little bit angry. Like, *all the time*," I add quietly.

"Me too," she says. "But that's why we're friends."

I scoff. "We're friends because I have anger issues?"

"No, doofus, we're friends because you care about things enough to be angry. Not the kind of pointless, malicious anger that makes people punch walls or hurt other people, but you're angry because there are reasons to be. I couldn't be friends with someone that wasn't at least a little bit angry all the time when there's so much to be angry about."

I nod. She put it so well. And yet… "It's just so exhausting, you know? Aren't you tired?"

"Oh, God, yeah. Constantly. You?"

"Yeah. Yeah, I am."

We lie on the bed in the quiet for a little while, wrapped up in our togetherness, letting our feelings expand out into the room and leak out of the cracks into the world beyond. And by the time we've finished talking and eating our pizzas, it's so late that when Imogen suggests I just stay over I go straight to fetch my phone to text my mum and let her know what's happening.

Imogen's parents look vaguely panicked when they tell them I'm staying, even when Imogen reminds them that I'm gay and that she 'has taste' (harsh). Her dad firmly insists on the door staying open and Imogen's mum pops her head round to peek at us every half an hour. It's a little funny, really, and I know they won't be alone in their assumptions about our relationship.

But I love Imogen. There's no one else I'd rather eat pizza with and fall asleep next to after whisper-ranting about things until 3 a.m. There are as many versions of love as there are people, and this one is ours. Maybe some people won't get it, but that's OK.

This isn't for them. This is for us.

★

"Imogen? Oliver?"

"Urghhhhh," Imogen groans right in my ear, an impressive amount of their body overlapping mine. Apparently, they like to sleep in a starfish position, regardless of whether or not there's anyone else in their bed that might quite like to sleep without a limb flung on top of them. "That's my dad. What does he want so early in the morning?"

I glance at the clock on her bedside table. "It's quarter to eleven."

"Exactly. Heinous behaviour."

We shuffle downstairs, blankets round our shoulders like fuzzy capes, still groggy from staying up quite so late last night, and find Imogen's dad in the hallway, packing his golf clubs away in the hall cupboard.

"Ah, there you are!" He casts a discerning eye over us. "You're not just waking up now, are you? It's nearly midday."

"What can we help you with?" Imogen says, her words businesslike, her tone sleepily apathetic.

"It's more what I can help you with. I just spoke to Hugh at the club – he works in our town-hall office – and he's confirmed that we can give you a slot there on Sunday afternoons for your meetings."

"Oh!" Imogen perks up a little at that, the blanket slipping off one of their no-longer slumped shoulders. "That'd be perfect. Thanks, Hugh. And thank you. Heh. Rhyme."

"Yes, thank you, Mr Quinn," I add – that was quick. But you know what they say: nothing like two White men on a golf course to help society progress— OK, so maybe no one's ever said that ever. Mr Quinn keeps standing there, however, still looking very smug. Too smug for this to be it, surely? He already basically said we could have the hall yesterday.

Imogen notices this too. "What is it?" they ask. "Why are you doing that with your face?"

"I have no idea what you mean," he says, clearly lying as he follows it up with, "although there might be something else too."

"We're listening…" Imogen says.

"Well, after I updated Hugh on your plans, he realised that he'd seen your application for the Community Enrichment Events Grant recently – the one you sent through in October. And – you didn't hear this from me – but he says everyone in the team agreed it was a great idea. As soon as your paperwork to register your new group goes through, Ardenpool Youth Activist Society will officially be in the running for the Community Enrichment Events Grant."

Imogen and I turn to each other, eyes wide with excitement.

"You'll need to send in plans for everything you'd spend it on, and raise five grand yourselves," Mr Quinn continues, "but once you've proven you've done that, the events team will match that amount to help you put on your festival."

Imogen grabs my arm with a vice-like grip. "Wait – we raise the first five grand, and they'll give us that much again? Another *five thousand pounds*?"

"Yes," he says.

"HOLY FUCK."

He winces. "IMOGEN—"

"Yes, sorry for swearing, but—" She lets out an absolute *screech*. "This is HUGE. We have to tell the others. Like, now."

"It's not official yet," he calls after us as we make for the stairs. "It all still needs formal sign-off, so don't get your hopes *completely* up."

"Too late!" Imogen calls merrily back.

I toss what I hope is a grateful smile back at Mr Quinn before nearly crashing into Imogen as they pause stampeding halfway up the stairs and rush back down. I watch (feeling only slightly bittersweet) as they nearly flatten their dad with a hug.

"Get away with you," he says, but you can detect the note of affection in the midst of the disgruntledness. "And make sure you make the most of this, OK? Don't let me down."

Imogen nods, beaming all the while, and then comes back to join me on my way upstairs, where I then join her in singing along, "*We got the grant, we got the grant!*"

"I can't believe it," I say, flopping on to the bedroom floor next to Imogen. "This is so great."

Imogen kicks her feet against the floor. "Right? Like, I know five grand is a LOT to raise and we'll need to work our butts off and come up with some really big fundraising ideas. But if we did manage it," they continue, "we'd basically have half of what we needed to put on the entire original festival, not even the smaller event, and if we did do that then we'd get the other half anyway. I know it's unlikely we can do it in time but there's still a *chance*."

"Yeah," I say. "There is."

We grin at each other for a beat before Imogen leaps upright.

"Right. First, I propose toast. And then coffee. Lots of coffee. Second, we need to tell the guys, make a fundraising plan and share that post. It's time to get Ardenpool Youth Activist Society 2.0 on the road."

"Both excellent proposals," I say. "I'm in."

★

"Holy SHIT," is Louisa's response to the news about the grant. A sentiment swiftly echoed by everyone else on the video call, all beaming and glimmering with excitement in their own houses.

"I'll share the post now," Amelia says. "I'll make a couple of edits to say when the first meeting is, add in the link to the new fundraising page Maryam set up yesterday and say we'd appreciate any donations, and then we'll see what happens!"

"Let's not tell anyone about the grant just yet, though. Not till we get it in writing that it's all gone through," Maryam adds, ever the pragmatist.

We all agree, but even that does practically nothing to grey the sparkling sheen of hope permeating across town and lighting up all of our rooms. And by the time we've finished collectively basking in the excitement, the post has been live for about twenty minutes and we've already had six people RSVP to the first group session, several people congratulate us on the bathrooms, and our first few donations to the new fundraising page.

"Guys…" Imogen breathes. "This is going to work. We've started a new group, we're raising money again – we can definitely put on some kind of pride thing this year! We need to keep this going, keep spreading the word."

"We've done lots of online stuff now," Clem says. "What if we go and hand out flyers and put them up in queer establishments to advertise that way too, try to engage directly with people in the community? Plus," they add with a twinkle, "I reckon we deserve a chance to celebrate."

We all agree that this is a great idea, and decide to go into the city next Saturday to visit the Gay Quarter ahead of our first meeting on Sunday. Our primary objective is to target the queer population with the flyers Louisa's now working on, but we'll also (again, at Clem's suggestion) watch a drag performance in one of the venues we're going to visit. I've never seen drag live before so I'm not exactly sure what to expect. Clem's right, though – we do deserve to celebrate. And if this is how the others want to do it then I'm willing to come along for the ride, just so long as they're all along for it with me.

CHAPTER TWENTY-SEVEN

OLLIE

After a thankfully uneventful week at school (besides Josh continuing to ignore me, which, you know what, *fine* – he can come to me when he's ready), Saturday arrives, and Imogen and I are getting ready to head to Amelia's to get a lift into the city with her and Maryam. We are, of course, running late, thanks to Imogen fussing with their make-up choices again. This time, however, her dilly-dallying does seem to be motivated by two new factors.

Firstly, her not wanting to get there early and be left alone with Amelia should I mysteriously vanish to the loo or anything, not that Imogen would admit that.

'We don't want to get there super early," they say. "No one wants to feel rushed by people arriving exactly on time."

"Imogen, Amelia notoriously loves punctuality."

Cue their panicked expression and petulant retort. "Why would I care what Amelia loves?"

And then secondly, while they're digging through their make-up drawer, supposedly in search of the perfect shade of 'periwinkle' glitter, they also dig out a midnight-blue nail polish and a silver glittery highlighter.

"I'm nowhere near done, Ol – you've got time to have a play around. These would work well with your whole vibe right now."

"Is that vibe impatience?" I ask, taking them off her anyway.

Imogen responds by giving me the finger. I shuffle next to her to use the mirror, scattering the glitter over my cheekbones. Something else sparkles at me, nestled in Imogen's box of chaos – a vial of silver stars. I extract them carefully and then scatter a few down my temples to my cheekbones, making my face into a constellation.

Imogen, *finally* fucking done, grabs their rainbow tote and looks at me with a grin. "You look cool as shit, bud. The stars were a great choice."

I shrug, feigning nonchalance. "Whatever."

In reality, I couldn't be further from nonchalant, though. Every time I catch my reflection glimmering back at me in the windows we pass on the way to Amelia's, constellations twinkling on my cheekbones, a twinge of newness unfurls a little more in my chest.

★

After an hour's drive in Ladybird, Amelia's eyeball-affrontingly red car, we arrive in the city, where we meet Clem and Louisa outside a hipster-looking coffee shop where they've been dropped off by Louisa's mum; Louisa now reassembling Judy in a seamless routine.

Things are significantly less seamless, however, as we roam the surrounding streets to hand out flyers before the drag performance. To start with, too many cars are parked on the kerb, so there's no room for Louisa to get through to all the different shops and bars. And often the doorways are too narrow or up a couple of steps, so she and Clem have to wait outside and hand out flyers to passers-by while Imogen, Amelia and I go in and talk to the owners.

We do have a productive morning and start to the afternoon, though, with about fifteen places agreeing to put our posters up in the windows, and several of those even offering to donate to our page themselves and tell their patrons about it.

Clem and Louisa also prove to be a dream team when it comes to the general public. What with Clem's beguilingly innocent appearance and subtly mischievous ways (I spotted them poking a rolled-up flyer into a man's open bag – the good chaotic version of pickpocketing) and Louisa's whole *I'm so cute in my cottagecore gingham dress but I'm also deeply uninterested in the idea of letting you past without hearing what we have to say first* thing, they manage to hand out a good chunk of our flyers.

However, the lack of accessibility only gets worse when we arrive at the drag bar. Despite Louisa ringing up before to check and being told, 'Yep! The venue's totally accessible,' totally accessible in this case apparently means 'besides the two steps up to the seating area'. Louisa seems unimpressed but unsurprised by this discovery, but Imogen darkly proclaims her intention to leave them a scathing review online, and I can't say I blame her.

After *de*-assembling Judy, three of us carrying the chair up, and Louisa having to climb the steps aided by Clem, we finally manage to commandeer a couple of tables. There we alternate between an intense discussion on what our drag names would be and stuffing our faces with chips, until the lights dim and a voice on the loudspeaker calls out, "Are y'all bitches ready for some drag *royalty* all up in this joint?"

We cheer along with everyone else who's filed in while we've been sitting there. (It's mostly other students who aren't allowed in at night either, because of the 'the law' or whatever.) They lower the lights even more before brightly coloured ones begin to beam round the room.

"ALL RIIIIGHT, PLEASE WELCOME TO THE STAGE..."

I join the others in doing a drum roll on the table.

"MERYL … AND … THE … STREEEEPS!" The voiceover booms out as three drag queens strut on to the stage in perfect time to the unmistakable sound of ABBA's 'Dancing Queen'.

My jaw drops. ABBA. It's like they knew I was coming. And, in some ways, this whole thing does feel as if it has been waiting out here for me.

"You are the dancing queen, young and sweet, only seventeen…"

As the queens shimmy across the stage, lip-syncing and flirting with the audiences on either side of them, I can't help but stare at those perfectly styled wigs, that winged eyeliner sharp enough to kill a man.

I'm briefly distracted from my staring by Imogen nudging me in the ribs. "Hey. I know her!" They point excitedly at the queen in the middle with a foot-tall lilac wig.

I give them a look – I wasn't aware they had a secret double life where they're friends with drag queens. But then again, it's always best to expect the unexpected with Imogen.

The first part of the show lasts for about half an hour, all three queens dancing to ABBA bops and occasionally stopping to tell jokes and insult people in the audience, like one idiot who thought it was a good idea to wear socks and sandals. He really shouldn't have needed a drag queen to tell him it wasn't; I would have told him for free. (Imogen'll never dare wear Crocs and socks in front of me again. Not if she knows what's good for her.)

"That was so much fun!" Louisa says as we clap them off the stage.

"YASS, QUEENS!" a girl in the audience screeches, eliciting eye rolls from a number of us around the table.

After a couple of minutes, the queens come out of a side door to discuss something with the man in the sound and lighting booth and – to my great amazement – the lilac-wig-wearing queen looks around the room, her face lighting up in recognition as her gaze reaches our group.

"Oh my God, she's coming over here," Amelia whispers, echoing my thoughts.

The drag queen stands at the head of the table and points at Imogen. "You. I know you."

"Told you," they say smugly to me.

"Babycakes!" She grins. "How are you doing? It's been a while. Come on then, shove up. Tell me everything." She makes Clem shuffle further along the bench so she can sit down with us.

"I'm good! I've been pretty busy," Imogen says. "After the pride festival, I dumped my friends, set up an activist group, made some better friends, exposed a man who'd been cheating on his wife, started doing stand-up, poured my coffee into some guy's lap, had my birthday, did more stand-up at the school talent show and accidentally got the group banned from the school – although we did get the headteacher to agree to our gender-neutral bathroom proposal, so that was good. And now we're starting our own group anyway because a) fuck 'em and b) we have to keep fundraising to make the first five grand we need to put on our own accessible pride event – the main reason why I started the group in the first place." The end of Imogen's spiel overlaps with my snort. That's my best friend, folks.

"Is that all?" Auntie Septic blinks with her long lashes. "You've been slacking. Pour coffee in all the men's laps, not just one."

"I'll take that on board, thank you," Imogen says solemnly.

"Erm … how do you two know each other?" I muster up the courage to speak at last.

"Auntie Septic gave me her handkerchief and made sure I was OK after I had a meltdown at Pride last year," Imogen says. "The one that made me decide we needed to start our own pride festival."

"That sounds exciting!" Auntie Septic claps her hands together, acrylic nails clacking. "Can I come?"

Is she serious?

"Absolutely," Amelia butts in enthusiastically. "We're still fundraising for it after the, er, situation Imogen mentioned."

"When the accursed school staff stole all the money we raised," Imogen adds darkly.

"*But*," Amelia continues, "if we get enough, we might have the budget for more performers."

Auntie Septic, as she's apparently called, plucks a rectangle out of her cleavage and places it down on the table. "Here's my card. Email me the deets and I'll see what I can do. You say you're fundraising for an 'accessible' thing? What does that mean?"

I pick up the (uncomfortably warm) card and join in with the explanations from the rest of the group about how we're including fewer overwhelming spaces and performances for people with different sensory tolerances, sign-language interpreters, and accessible parade routes and venues to make sure everyone can celebrate.

Auntie Septic takes it in, blinking at us through inch-long lashes and nodding along with our words. "Well, this sounds fucking marvellous – I've been to hundreds of Prides and I've never seen anyone consider any of that before."

She takes Imogen's hand as they say, "Exactly! That's why we're working our butts off trying to raise money so that we can do it all. We want to be the first and set the bar."

"Right. Then, what can I do to help your little tushes out? What do you need?"

"Really?" I say, a little breathless. "Well, we have posters and flyers…"

Louisa extracts a stack from her bag and slaps them on the tabletop. "If you could put them round the bar or up in the window then that would be amazing," she says. "The links to our page and the place to donate are on there. We're trying to come up with more fundraising ideas because we've exhausted our original list, but we need all the donations we can get in the meantime."

"Oh, come on, my lil peach, I can do better than that," she says, taking the entire stack and shuffling them together neatly. "What do you say I hand these out at the end of the performance and announce that anyone who doesn't donate is getting kicked in the rear by these." In a display of impressive agility, she kicks her leg up and then rests it on the table. Her silver heels are staggeringly high and would definitely cause you great physical pain should she follow through on that threat.

"That would be *incredible*." Imogen beams up at her. "Thank you!"

"Not a problem, angel. Now, you all have a *fabulous* day. Oh, and I'm loving the look." She does a flourishing gesture round my face and I feel my shining cheeks flush from the unexpected compliment. Then she waggles her fingers at the table, grabs the pile of flyers and posters, tosses her yellow feather boa dramatically over one shoulder, winks at us and heads back to her friends.

Cheeks still red, I try to sift through everything I'm feeling. Something clicked in me recently and, though my dad tried his best to tug it back out of place, I don't think he has the power to do that any more. I'm not *giving* him the power to do that any more.

If he could only see me now, I think to myself as the show resumes, having the time of my life with my friends, the lights reflecting off my cheeks, greedily soaking in every ounce of drag and ABBA that's raging in technicolour in front of me.

OH. I've just had an idea. A giant, unignorable, wonderful idea. And I'd like to thank my dad for invoking it, and Imogen's constant tardiness (and general existence) for giving me the nudge to let this feeling of infinity start to unfold in my body.

I turn to Imogen, wanting to tell them immediately, then hesitate.

They've sunk down low in their seat, shoulders stiff and hands fidgeting under the table. They look trapped.

"Hey." I nudge her lightly. "You OK?"

CHAPTER TWENTY-EIGHT

IMOGEN

The performance starts back up after our exciting interlude with Auntie Septic, but it's darker outside now and the lights feel even harsher, like they're shining straight into my eyes and hardening the surface of my skin with their brightness. I sink deeper down into my seat as the speakers blare and everyone starts clapping in time to the music.

"You OK?" Ollie whisper-shouts at me.

I nod, trying to focus exclusively on the grain of the wooden table. It's not an easy task; all my senses feel like they're being bombarded at once. The music feels like it's blasting actually inside my brain, and there's a strong smell of alcohol and a general musty bar scent that I've managed not to notice so far, but now can't *stop* noticing, the temperature is slightly warmer than is comfortable, and the lights are switching rapidly between scarlet, neon pink and vivid blue, green, yellow and orange and bouncing off the wall behind us, reminding me of standing in the path of an ambulance as its beacon flashes its urgent warning.

I jiggle my leg under the table, trying to shake away the feeling that's fizzing up inside of me like my body's a bottle of Diet Coke and someone's just lobbed a fistful of Mentos into it.

I can do this, I tell myself. I can stay here – I managed the first performance: this one shouldn't be any different.

Except I'm becoming acutely aware that if I sit here much longer then I will have to physically wrench my head off my body.

"I CAN'T HEAR YOU!" the voiceover shouts, and everyone starts cheering even louder, all of the different voices forming one obnoxiously loud sound that's overwhelming my entire brain, along with the thousand other sounds layered on top of each other like a delicious sensory-overload lasagne – the clinking of glasses, the speakers playing ABBA's 'SOS', people clapping and cheering, their chairs squeaking and NOPE NOPE NOPE.

I stand up abruptly, accidentally shunting the table forward a few inches, muttering an apology as I squeeze past Maryam. I sprint towards the door, shaking my hands as I go, to give me something, *anything*, to think about, until I reach the sanctuary of the not-too-loud, not-too-smelly, not-too-hot outside.

I burst through the doors outside and sink on to the ground, leaning my back against the side of the building and looking out at the canal, feeling my entire body exhale. I hold my hands up in front of me and stare at them as I let the cool wind brush against them until they've stopped trembling.

"Hey."

I twist round to see Ollie standing over me. He must have been right behind me as I left.

"What happened? Are you all right?"

I push out a long, shuddering breath and wait a few moments until I'm able to speak again before replying, "I will be."

"Can I do anything to help?" He sits down next to me. "Do you want to talk?"

"I don't know," I say. My brain's still cooling down from being so assailed by quite so many things.

"Can I?" He lifts his arm up.

I nod and let him put his arm round my shoulder, adjusting his hand so it's holding my arm properly instead of resting loosely. When I'm overwhelmed, I need a firm touch or none at all; people just lightly touching me makes me shudder.

I lean my head on his arm and breathe out fully. We sit down on the cobbled street and stare at the family of swans bobbing around on the canal. The reflection of the setting sun flickers in the water, calmer pinks and oranges painted in watercolour ink above us.

"What—" Ollie starts after a while, before changing his mind. "No, never mind."

"No, go on," I say.

"What's it like for you … when things like that happen?" His voice is curious but in an entirely non-judgemental way that I'm still getting used to. "I could see you getting overwhelmed. I've seen it happen before at school, like when we're in the cafeteria and people are being particularly rowdy, but what actually happens for you at those times? You don't have to talk about it if you don't want. I guess I've just been wondering."

I chew my lip, mulling it over for a minute. I know that most people will never understand me, and many don't even want to try. But, I suppose, here is a person who does want to try. The least I can do is let him.

Ollie jumps slightly as I begin talking, I think having decided that I wasn't going to answer.

"Sometimes," I start, "I think that I was born to experience the universe more intensely than most people. And, in some ways, that's great. I can feel really connected to things. I can feel light and joyful and appreciate everything around me, but then there are other times – times when it's really hard. Everything feels turned up a little more than is comfortable – sometimes a lot more. Colours are too bright and hurt my eyes; noises are too loud and fill up my head so that I feel like there are people shouting or fridges humming directly inside my brain and I don't know when they'll stop – if ever. Everything just hurts a little more than it should. I can enjoy my capacity for more and also hate it sometimes, you know?"

I feel Ollie nod next to me.

"And sometimes," I add absent-mindedly, "like today, it feels as if I'm trapped in a burning building, and everyone around me is completely calm and I just don't understand why they're not running around and screaming and trying to get out too. It doesn't make any sense to me how they can be so relaxed when there are literal flames burning all around them."

"That must be frustrating."

"Yeah," I say. "It can be." I turn to face him. "Thank you for coming to check on me – I'm sorry I'm making you miss the show. I know you're a slut for ABBA."

"You're not making me miss anything. I'm a slut for ABBA, yes, but I'm a slut for you too," he says, and it's such a ridiculous sentence, said in such a fierce tone of voice that I have to let out an involuntary cackle, before he says more quietly, "and there's nowhere else I'd rather be."

And as I smile up at him and he smiles right back, I realise that I believe him – I really do.

We sit there for a while, chatting about how great Auntie Septic was and all the flapjack I'm going to eat when I get back before passing out on my bed, until the others appear outside.

"Is it over?" I ask. "Did we miss the announcement about us?"

"No, we just wanted to make sure you guys were OK," Amelia says as they gather on the ground in front of us. "Are you?" she continues, looking concerned. "OK, I mean?"

I smile, fighting back a yawn. "I'm fine. It was just a bit much in there. You can watch the end if you want. I'm fine out here and I don't want to make you miss the grand finale."

"No," Amelia says, almost as fiercely as Ollie did when I suggested it to him. "We've seen enough – it's OK."

Louisa laughs. "And there's no chance I'm going through that whole palaver to get back in again."

I nod. "See – that's exactly why we need this. We can have performances that will suit people's needs, we can have quiet rooms, we can make sure places are *actually* physically accessible, and we can let everyone revel in queerness."

The others agree heartily and my spirits rise a little more. They don't think I'm stupid or too sensitive or that I should just 'deal with it'. They actually get it; I don't think I'll ever take that for granted.

"Agreed." Louisa nods. "This is what we're fighting for, for us and for everyone else who just wants to celebrate all the parts of themselves at once. Anyone who doesn't want to be seen as a fucking pie chart to be separated out into convenient sections, but as a chaotic abstract painting, a whole colourful mess with all its overlapping lines."

I grin up at her as Clem looks at her with so much ardent love in their eyes it makes even cynical *me* melt, never mind Louisa.

Ollie, I notice, however, has his eyes narrowed in thought and I wonder briefly what he's thinking about before I turn my attention fully back to Louisa.

"I love that," I say. "I've always thought that queer people and disabled people have a lot in common – we're all existing in the world in our own ways; we're all breaking convention. And there's something really cool in that. We get to carve out our own spaces where we get to make our own rules."

I gaze around at the group but my eyes land on Amelia. Her brown eyes are swimming as she looks back at me.

"I've never thought of it like that before," she says quietly. "I always thought of my queerness as breaking the rules. I've never considered that maybe it's just a blank slate to write my own rules on."

"That's what being non-binary is like for me," Clem confesses, running a hand through their hair. "I've never identified as either a man or a woman, and being non-binary to me means that I get to decide exactly what I want my gender to be or not be, with no expectations to be anything but myself."

"That's a really cool thought, Clem. It sounds freeing," Ollie says. He looks down at his hands, the hazy setting sun making the glitter on his nails shimmer.

"It is," Clem responds simply.

Amelia sniffs and blinks several times, trying to compose herself.

Maryam looks around at us all, shaking her head. "Guys. We need to talk about this online. I know we've discussed how important accessibility and visibility are there before, but it's all been in the abstract. And this isn't an abstract thing: it's personal. People should hear our stories, hear exactly why it is we're raising money for this."

Right on cue, the music cuts out inside the building, and we hear Auntie Septic's voice boom out, muffled through the windows, telling the audience about our cause and delivering the promised threat to people who don't donate.

I smile as I turn to Maryam. "Maybe you're right. What if –" I start – "what if we filmed something now, while we're all thinking about it?"

They all agree and so we do – Maryam and Ollie set up the shot and we gather and talk about *why* each of us feels we need our event and what exactly it all means to us. And, when Maryam presses stop five minutes later, for once I don't feel uncomfortable about having been vulnerable in front of an audience. I feel proud. Somewhere out

340

there, there might be someone who feels the same way as us, who just wants to celebrate their whole selves, and, when the video's posted, they'll know they're not alone in that feeling. Not any more.

"It's been a good day today," Amelia says, and we all grin at each other. "It's really nice here," she adds, gazing out at the canal: a skyline of old brick industrial buildings on the other side of the water, their windows reflecting the blazing orange sky.

Amelia shudders. It is getting chillier out here.

"D'you want my jacket?" I offer, enjoying the cold after the overheated bar.

"Oh!" Amelia starts. "No, no, that's OK."

"Take it," I insist, already shrugging it off and passing it to her.

She smiles nervously. "Thank you," she says, putting it on.

"It suits you," I say, and Ollie clears his throat next to me. "I mean … it goes well with your outfit."

"Thank you," she says again. "I feel special getting to wear this – the denim jacket is like the iconic Imogen look."

I snort. "There's no iconic Imogen look. I just wear whatever I think is funky. And you are special – I don't let just anyone wear my things – they might ruin them."

Maryam looks down at her phone to hide her smile, and I realise what I just said.

"I mean that … you were cold, and you're so

responsible and…" I look to Ollie for help, but he just smirks at me in reply.

Louisa starts asking Maryam questions about the video and when she's going to post it, and under the cover of their conversation I lean towards Ollie.

"I hate you," I whisper to my favourite person on this whole stupid planet. "This is all your fault."

"I accept no responsibility for your awkwardness," Ollie says, "but I am enjoying the show."

"Fuck you. Can you not— Ugh, hold on." I pull out my beeping phone from my pocket. "Oh, it's my dad."

> Hello Imogen, Hugh just sent confirmation that your paperwork's gone through and you've been approved for the grant. If you check your emails you should have one from the team going into more detail about it all. Hope you've had a good day, see you later. Dad.

"HOLY MOTHER OF ALL SHITS!"

"Eww." Ollie pulls a face, and the others all stare as well. "Why?"

I don't have any more words right now. I just hold the phone in front of him and he promptly takes it off me so he can actually read it and I can keep jumping up and down and squealing.

"OK, upon reflection that was a warranted turn of phrase." Ollie hands me back the phone, trying not to grin.

"Care to share?" Louisa demands, and I pass the phone around. "Hell, yeah," she adds.

"This is incredible." Amelia looks awed. "We can tell people about it now, right?" she says, addressing Maryam specifically.

"Oh, absolutely. We'll let the rest of the group know tomorrow."

"What a nice way to start our new group," Clem says dreamily.

"And then we should also make another video celebrating getting the grant as a push to get people to donate, now that we definitely have this concrete goal."

"Great!" Amelia claps her hands together. "We could all—"

"You and Imogen should do it," Maryam carries on swiftly. "You two did most of the hard work getting the grant."

"Yeah," Ollie adds, his eyes flicking towards Maryam – something unspoken passing between them. "You could do it tomorrow morning before the meeting. We're all nearer the town hall anyway so it'll be easier to go straight there. You guys can film the message and then walk over together."

"OK," I say brightly, nodding to Amelia. "I'll stop by yours first thing tomorrow morning. Shall we say eleven?"

"O-OK," she stutters, looking to Maryam for some reason.

Maryam just smiles serenely back at her.

"Now," Ollie says, also sounding decisive as he changes the subject. "Speaking of celebrating the grant – and in the interest of never letting a golden-hour photography op be wasted – any objections to taking a group photo?"

There are no dissenters and so Ollie gathers us with the canal as our backdrop, camera set on a timer to capture this moment, warm light cascading over our smiling faces.

As we're staggering back to the car park (staggering because I conned Ollie into giving me a piggyback again, on the condition that I wouldn't hit him in the nads this time), Ollie says something, his tone careful so I know it must be important.

"Hey, Imogen? Now we've got the grant, we're going to need some big fundraisers to help us, you know, actually *get* the grant, and … I kind of had an idea to make the football fundraiser even bigger. What if…"

His next words result in me accidentally screeching directly into his ear.

"OW!"

"Sorry, sorry. Just—" I let out another (quieter) excited scream. I really wish I didn't need to use my hands to hold on so that I could jump around and shake them. "This is a *delicious* idea, my dude. Yes. Absolutely yes. We have to do it."

I can't see his face, but I can tell that he's smiling.

He shunts me up a little further on his back like he's suddenly finding me a lighter load.

"We do, don't we?" he says. "Or I do, at least. And I'm going to need your help with my Photography project too. And probably all the others' as well, if they're in."

"Oh, we're in," Louisa calls back to us, twisting round in her chair. "Sorry, didn't mean to eavesdrop, but, to be fair, Imogen was literally screaming."

"We're all in," Amelia says.

"One hundred per cent." Clem's eyes find Ollie's and he nods back at them without words – I think he's been as brave as he can for now.

Back at the car park, we say goodbye to Clem and Louisa and start the drive home. Comments and donations begin to stream in as Maryam posts the video from the front seat while I'm lulled to sleep by the monotony of the motorway, my cheek pressed to the cool glass of the window, utterly exhausted and completely, utterly content.

CHAPTER TWENTY-NINE

IMOGEN

Ding-dong!

Amelia opens her front door the next morning wearing a very Amelia-y outfit consisting of bright red lipstick and matching cardigan, a white shirt with bumblebees all over it and a blue skirt. "Hi," she says, stepping aside for me to come in.

I walk through to the lounge, expecting that to be where we're filming, but quickly stop in my tracks.

"Oh. Hello," I say. Amelia's parents are snuggled together on the sofa, looking up at me.

Amelia comes up behind me. "Mum, Dad, this is Imogen – we're just filming that thing for the group and then heading out. Imogen, these are my parents, Manuela and Seb."

"Oh, *you're* Imogen," her mum says, smiling. Her hair is the exact same colour as Amelia's but styled in a short crop rather than in Amelia's long, tumbling tresses. "It's lovely to meet you at last."

"Yes," her dad says, his eyes twinkling up at us. "The famous Imogen."

I raise an eyebrow. "I'm famous?"

"Oh, very," Seb says. "We've heard all about you and what you've been up to. We can't thank you enough for getting Amelia out of the house and away from her books."

"DAD!"

"No, mija, you were driving yourself potty with all the studying. And the boy."

Amelia's shoulder twitches. "Yes, well, you don't have to worry about that any more, do you?"

"Nope." Manuela lets out a tinkling laugh. "If you raise the money then, we'll be at all your pride events, Imogen. We're very excited to see if you can pull it off – and to support Amelia. We're so proud of you, sweetheart."

"Yes, we love you no matter *who* you love," Seb adds dramatically.

"Thank you," she says stiffly. "We're going to go film in the kitchen now."

I wave at them both and follow Amelia out of the room.

"Sorry, they're in super-proud mode," Amelia says, lips pursed as she pours us both a lemonade. "I think they googled 'things to say to your gay daughter' and are now working their way through all of them."

I snort. "Adorable."

We set to work filming and uploading the video online. We immediately get lots of excited responses, and even receive a few more donations to our fundraising page, which brings our total up to a very tidy two grand. It's nearly time for the meeting to begin, so I'm about to suggest that we go and meet the others when Manuela pops her head round the door.

"Knock, knock," she says, which is entirely redundant seeing as she's already looking at us. "Can I come in? I need my glasses."

Amelia stares at her. "Why are you knocking? Of course you can."

"I didn't want to interrupt you filming, or —" there's a significant pause "— anything."

Or anything.

My cheeks burn hot in what I'm sure is a violent shade of pink. It's been a while since I've been accused of getting up to any kind of shenanigans.

"You're not," Amelia says quickly and pointedly. "We're just leaving now."

Her mum nods slowly. "Good, then we'll see you in a bit. And it really was lovely to meet you, Imogen — you're welcome here any time."

She grabs her glasses case and leaves the room again.

Amelia closes her eyes for a beat, messing with the ends of her hair. "Sorry about that."

"It's fine," I say, trying so hard to sound breezy

and natural that it comes out the exact opposite. "So should we—"

"She didn't mean to imply anything." Amelia picks up speed twisting her hair. "I haven't said anything to her about … anything. She's just trying to be supportive."

"Sure," I say, wishing she wasn't making this more awkward than it needs to be. And that's coming from me.

"Not that there's anything *to* tell her about, obviously." Amelia blunders onwards, her cheeks a blazing reflection of my own. "I mean … that's not to say… I do like you a lot—" She finally stops talking.

I wait for her to continue but she doesn't, instead choosing to stare intently at her high-heeled boots and prolong the discomfort.

"You like me … as a friend … right?" I say slowly, giving her the chance to make things more normal again.

"Sure. As a friend." Her throat bobs as she swallows thickly, still looking at her shoes. "And, I don't know, maybe—"

"We really are running late now," I say, inadvertently cutting her off as I notice the time on the clock on the wall. "Oh, sorry, you weren't done. What were you saying?"

"Nothing. I— I was done."

"All right then." I slap my knee. "Let's go."

"NO." The word bursts out into the quiet and rings round the room.

"No?" What's her deal today? She's normally so eloquent – this is all highly disconcerting. "We're five minutes late already and I know how much you value punctuality."

"No, I meant no, I wasn't done." She fixes her eyes on me, looking at me like I'm the only thing that exists *to* look at, and I stare back, trying to remember how regular human beings breathe.

"I spent a really long time hiding how I felt, and I promised myself at New Year that this was going to finally be the year I stopped doing that." She places her hands formally in front of her and lets out a shaking breath like she can't believe what she's about to say. "I like you, Imogen Quinn, as more than a friend."

I can't feel my face. Wait, can I ever feel my face? Never mind, not important. *Fuck*.

"I've known that I liked you since Year Nine." Amelia forges on, no turning back now. "We were in a Maths lesson and Sara Young had been having a really bad day. Her dog had just been put down and she had a headache from crying so much, and she wanted to go and fill up her water bottle, but Miss Simmons wouldn't let her go because she said it would waste time and she should have gone before class. She harped on at her for so long about better planning and organisational skills that Sara started crying again, and you… You stood up, looked at your watch and then at Miss Simmons, and you said: 'You've been yelling at her for four minutes and seventeen seconds now. She could have been and gone four times, and now you're wasting our lesson time that I very much need because I still don't have a clue what you're going on about with these quadratic equations. So could you leave Sara the fuck alone, please?'"

She smiles a lopsided, rueful smile. "You got a whole week's worth of after-school detentions for that, but I realised something about you that day that I know is true even more now. You can see when things are wrong and when things are right, and you would never sit there and let anyone treat the people you cared about badly." Her voice tremors with vulnerability. "All I've *ever* wanted from that day onwards was to be included as one of those people. I just, *I like you*, Imogen. And that's, that's all."

Holy shit.

I'm so annoyed Ollie was right.

Amelia shifts in front of me as I try to focus and let the words she spilled out fully enter my brain, but my entire body seems to have gone into shock.

"So … is there anything you … want to say?" she asks.

"Oh. I don't— I don't know." My brain continues to refuse to cooperate with me and produce anything even vaguely resembling a full sentence.

Do I like Amelia? I mean she's gorgeous, obviously, that goes without saying, she's like unfairly pretty, and she's smart, and yes, watching her play the violin at the talent show was basically a religious experience she was so talented, and yes, arguably objectively hot, and she makes people feel *good* about themselves – she's kind in a way that I know I'll never be… But these are just things people know about Amelia, factual observations; it doesn't mean I'm in love with her or anything.

"Imogen?" she says, and the softness of her tone makes me relax, just a little.

"Yes, sorry." I take a resolute breath – I have no idea what to say but I know I have to say something. "I guess I just need some time to think. To process. Is that OK?"

She looks down at the parquet floor, nodding slowly. "OK. Yes. You have a think. Um… So we should get going, then."

"Yes, we should. We've got a group to start and a world to change."

Amelia fakes a laugh as I turn away, trying to pretend like my world's not just been cracked right open.

When we walk up to the town hall, Ollie can immediately tell something's happened. He pulls me over behind one of the stone pillars of the building while Amelia goes on in without us.

"What's going on? You and Amelia look tense."

"We're always tense," I answer with a flippant hand gesture.

"I mean tenser than usual. What's up?"

I let out a garbled noise. "ARGH. Fine. So Amelia may have said that she liked me? No-no-homo style."

Ollie seems puzzled but then suddenly looks around to check no one's within earshot before saying, "Wait, sorry ... the double negative confused me – as I'm sure you intended it to— Are you saying that she likes you? Like, romantically?"

"SHH!" I whisper furiously. "And yes."

"AHA!" he bellows in triumph.

"Ollie! Shut the flip-flop up, please."

"So does this mean that I was right?" he says, grinning, just like I knew he would.

"Ugh," I groan. "Yes."

He cups his ear with his hand. "Sorry, I can't hear you. What did you say?"

"You were *right*." He's enjoying this far too much.

"One more time."

"YOU WERE RIGHT. Now, can you focus, please?"

"Right, right, sorry." He stops grinning, eyes wide in question. "What're you going to do?"

"I have no idea."

"Do you like her back?"

"I don't know."

"But do you—"

"Take the hint, Ollie," I say. "My head is an on-fire garbage can right now. I have no clue what to think."

He pats me sympathetically on the back. "Right, right, I'm sorry. But she's probably going to want an answer at some point."

Louisa and Clem wave at us from across the square and I try to arrange my face into something resembling an expression a regular human would wear.

"We'll workshop later," he says, moving over to lower the lift for the steps down for Louisa. "This is so exciting!"

I'm glad he thinks so. I hardly ever know what I'm feeling (except unadulterated rage and indignation, of course) and I have no idea what I'm going to say to Amelia.

It takes a lot of effort to put the morning's events out of my mind as I stand up from my chair half an hour later and start the meeting.

"Right, everybody, listen up!" I'm standing in a circle of about twenty people, aka the new and improved Ardenpool Youth Activist Society. I'm jazzed that so many people have turned up.

"Thank you all for coming," I say. "I'm Imogen Quinn; I founded the original Ardenpool Youth

Activist Society along with the rest of these dashing folks." I gesture to the gang around me. "We're so excited that you're all here and we can't wait to see what we can achieve together to make this world a slightly kinder place, starting right here in Ardenpool."

I go over everything we've done so far and everything we hope to do very soon, including Ollie's *incredible* idea for a fundraiser. Several people let out laughs or joyful exclamations when I explain the added twist.

"If anyone wants to be one of our football players then I'll leave the sign-up sheet by the door. All genders are welcome, and no sporting ability is necessary. I'll be joining in, and I've been known to trip over my own feet before we get any balls involved, so take comfort in the knowledge that you won't be the least capable player out on the field."

This gets a few laughs from some of the adorably eager faces currently staring up at me.

In the end, everyone's so keen to talk about their own experiences at their schools and suggest ideas that we end up overrunning by ten minutes. You can feel the hopeful, excited energy pinging round the room, everyone here with their own story to tell and their own plans for writing better chapters for themselves and others in the future.

As I gaze around proudly, I notice a Black girl with bright pink hair hovering awkwardly by the door, waiting for her turn at the football sign-up sheet.

I make my way over there and tap her on the arm. "Hey, you're Poppy, right?" I say, remembering her name from when she spoke about wanting to fight for gender-neutral bathrooms in her school too.

She starts in surprise. "Oh, hi!"

"I just wanted to say thank you for speaking up earlier," I say. "And for giving us the idea to reach out and try to take our campaigning into lots of local schools too."

"That's OK." She smiles. "I'm glad I felt brave enough to do it. Everyone here seems really nice." She looks down at the floor. "Um..." she starts. "Can I... Can I tell you something?"

Ooh, intrigue. "Of course."

She gulps and then lets it out in a rush. "It was me that started the petition."

Whoa, OK. Whatever I was expecting her to say, it was not that.

"You did?" OH – *poppyfields05*.

"I did," she says, pulling anxiously on her sleeves. "My stepsister had been telling me what happened at your school, she's in your group, and I didn't think. I just did it. I told her not to tell you. I didn't mean for it to get so big, or for you to get into trouble for it. I'm really, really sorry."

She looks agonised, still not able to bring herself to look up at me.

"Hey," I say. "*Hey*."

Her gaze lifts a little.

"You absolutely, one hundred per cent have nothing to be sorry for," I say firmly. "We got the bathroom and that was the important thing. And the group getting disbanded just meant that we had the opportunity to create this new, bigger group. I should be thanking you, really."

She finally meets my eye. "You're sure?"

"Completely."

She breathes out in relief. "Good."

I smile, trying to reassure her even more that I'm really not mad at all, but then a question enters my head. "Wait … who did you say your sister was?"

"Oh," she says, "Maryam. My dad married her mum last year. She's been so great; she's really been there when things have been rough for me at my school, and I don't know – I just really wanted to help, and all I could think to do was start the petition."

"Wait. Maryam's your sister?" I repeat. "She knew about this?"

"Uh-huh. She did."

Well, cover me in sauce and call me a prawn cocktail. That's quite the juicy little nugget she's just dropped on me. No wonder Maryam was so on it with the petition – she had inside information, the cheeky little minx. She's good at keeping secrets, I'll give her that.

I scan the room for Maryam and spot her standing next to Amelia across the room. Maryam was already looking in our direction, and she glances down when I make eye contact with her, cheeks a little flushed and an impish glint in her eyes. Then I flick my gaze towards Amelia and feel *my* face flood with warmth. I don't know what I'm going to do there. I really don't know.

CHAPTER THIRTY

OLLIE

It's Wednesday afternoon and our football team have just won a match against Dunston High. The sun is still shining, the air and everyone's mood is imbued with a touch of gold, and so, once we get back to the changing rooms, I decide that it's a good time to tell them about the slight change of plans for the football fundraiser next week.

I climb up on to one of the benches and clap to get their attention. "That was a great game, everyone!"

Charlie whoops. "Three–nil – we wiped the floor with those sons of bitches."

A few of the others cheer in response.

"Damn right we did." I clear my throat. "Erm … there's something I'd like to talk to you all about. So I know most of you are playing in the match next weekend at our football fundraiser, and I just wanted to say thanks again for agreeing to be involved and also give you a quick heads-up about something."

I swiftly explain what the other team – my team – will now be doing and am immediately met with a mixture of panicked stares, laughs and a few *what the hell*s thrown in for good measure.

"You're having a laugh, mate." Charlie scoffs loudly. "We can't do that."

"*You* won't have to," I clarify. "You'll be on the other team, playing against us."

"Wait," one of the midfielders, Rob, says. "*You're* going to be wear— Doing – that?"

"Yes," I say calmly. "I will be."

Far more people laugh this time. I'd expected this but it's still annoying. I'd hoped that maybe we'd got past this kind of thing – me needing to keep two separate worlds, one where I'm Ollie the team captain, just one of the lads, and one where I'm Ollie the gay British-Japanese guy who cares about things, isn't ashamed of expressions of femininity or emotion, and is in an activist group. I just want the world to see that I'm everything at once, that I'm not half anything or some impossible walking oxymoron.

Flipping out isn't going to convince them, though. I need to stay calm.

"This is really important, guys, and it'll be a laugh. Are you all still good? I have to confirm numbers so we know how many players we need on our side."

The room goes quiet.

"I'm still in," says a quiet boy named Ewan, the only other out-queer person on the team. "I think it sounds fun."

"Great, thank you!" I smile warmly at him. "Anyone else?"

I wait about ten seconds. No one speaks up. I don't know what we're going to do. If we don't have another team, then I don't see how it can go ahead; we can't play against ourselves. I hop down off the bench. "Great," I say sarcastically. "Thanks, guys."

Josh puts his phone down on the bench and leans back in disbelief. "Wait, seriously? None of the rest of you have the balls to play any more?"

No one answers. He lets out a derisive snort. "Cowards, the lot of you." He gets up and stands next to me. "I'll do it. I could do with a win."

There are a few scattered smirks from people in the room. News about why he and Amelia split up has well and truly broken in the school – Amelia posted on Instagram with a caption 'guess whose straight As are the only straight thing about them?' with a whole bunch of rainbow emojis, and the gossip mill promptly went *wild*.

Josh juts his chin up. "Now, are you dickheads going to join me, or are you all fine being homophobes?"

Hmm, that's an unusual tactic. It clearly makes an impression, however.

"WHOA!" Charlie puts his hands up. "We're not homophobes."

The jury is definitely still out on that actually. There's a long pause.

"*Fine*," Charlie says eventually. "If Armstrong and Hudson are in, then I'm still in."

"I'll do it too," Rob says, frowning at me. "I'm not a homophobe, mate; it's chill that you're gay, you know that."

I nod, amused. "All right. Cheers."

"I'm still in too." Matteo puts his hand up, closely followed by Harry, Oscar and Muhammed.

Soon we have ten players confirmed, which is one short, but frankly they could have three players and still batter us, so it'll do. Who knew all it would take to get a bunch of vaguely homophobic football players to agree to the plan was to imply that they were actually homophobic?

I get changed back into my clothes ready to walk home. As I step out of the sports centre into the sunny courtyard, however, I'm accosted by a loitering Josh.

"Oi, Ollie."

"Yeah?" I shield my eyes from the setting sun as we start walking back up the steps. "Thanks for stepping in back there. I really appreciate it, man. I think I'd have lost them all without you and then the whole plan would have been screwed."

"That's chill, no worries. They were being pricks."

"I've got to say, I was kind of surprised you agreed. I'm really grateful – don't get me wrong," I add quickly as a muscle in his cheek twitches, "but I kind of thought anything to do with the group was a no-go with you."

"I mean, I'm not going to be rejoining or anything," he says flatly, "but that doesn't mean I don't still respect what you guys are doing. And you were a good friend to me, even when I was a bit of a dick to you, so I kinda feel like I owe you one."

"Well, thanks, I appreciate that." He *has* been a bit of a dick, but I know he's a good guy underneath all his recent angst. "And thanks for doing the match," I say. "I hope you know you don't have to, though. If you decide it's going to be too hard then—"

"No," he says firmly. "No, I want to. It'll probably be hard seeing … you know."

I nod. I do know.

"But I need to stop letting that upset me. Amel—" His voice cracks and I pat him sympathetically on the shoulder. "Amelia was my life, man. We were together for so long and she always knew exactly what to do and who she wanted to be. Being next to her was the best thing. After a while, I started believing that I knew what to do and who I wanted to be too. But then we broke up and I felt like I was thirteen again – it was fucking scary. I didn't have the protection of being 'Amelia's boyfriend' or part of

'Josh and Amelia'. Now I'm just me, just *Josh*."

He's still not looking at me but I'm glad he's finally talking about this. Keeping stuff inside is a recipe for disaster (as I know all too well).

"You know, I knew you before you even met Amelia," I offer. "You were a great guy before her and you're still a great guy now."

He smiles, a slightly sad smile, but a smile nonetheless. "Thanks, man." He heaves a sigh and then laughs, kind of hysterically. "God, I've been a mess. I've been so fucking lonely, man. You've no idea how good it feels to finally talk to someone about all this."

"I'm glad," I say sincerely. "I've missed you – it's not been the same without you around."

"Maybe," he says, voice tentative, "we could play *FIFA* together at the weekend or something. You know, if you're not busy or anything?"

"Sure," I say with a smile. "I'd like that."

He purses his lips, looking pleased. "All right. Nice one."

Josh walks with me the rest of the way back to my house. We talk about tonight's match and then he even asks about what we've been doing with the new group, so I fill him in on all the goings-on. When we part ways, he seems in a better mood than I've seen him for months.

★

A week later, we're all squeezed into the church hall opposite the park football field, and I have to admit that I'm getting a little nervous.

I thought it would be fun – it *will* be fun – but there's a whole lot at stake here: we need to raise a decent amount to get to the five thousand. I can hear the crowd gathering out on the field and it's prompted my stomach to decide now is the ideal time to get into literature by recreating the storm from *The Tempest* in there.

We've divided the hall into sections with screens and sheets hung up all over the place, and the activist team section is an absolute bloody mess.

"We've got half an hour to go," Imogen calls out. She's tightly clasping a clipboard, looking frantic as she strides over to me. "T-minus thirty minutes, people. Make sure you're ready – over ninety people have RSVP-ed to watch."

"Are my armpits sweaty?" they say more quietly to me, raising their arm.

"Gross." I wrinkle my nose. "And yes."

"It's this fabric." They scratch at it. "I hate it."

I pat them on the head, and they swat my arm away. "Not long now," I say. "What was it, T-minus forty minutes?"

"THIRTY MINUTES, Oliver. THIRTY."

"I *know*. Jeez, you're worse than Amelia."

Imogen twitches. "Shut up. And don't say her name: she'll think I'm talking about her and she's already not happy with me."

"Well, no," I say. "When you tell someone you like them, you kind of hope you'll get a response in less than a fortnight."

"It's not been a fortnight. Yet. And my feelings are very complex, OK? I don't want to get hurt. Not that she could hurt me," she adds. "I'm a strong, independent person – I don't need no lady."

"Sure, but consider this," I say. "You could still be an independent person in a relationship, *and* you would get to kiss Amelia."

Her mouth goes completely straight. Ironically.

I snort. "Thought so."

"I have no idea what you're talking about, so you can stop thinking whatever you're thinking," she protests, jabbing me in the chest with her clipboard. "And do you not have somewhere to be instead of attacking me? Aren't you supposed to be taking photos of everyone getting ready?"

I sigh. As fun as it is to tease Imogen, she makes a good point. "Yeah, yeah, fine."

"Hey, Ollie?" Imogen calls, and I turn back towards her. She smiles. "You look really great."

"Oh. Thanks," I reply, not bothering to hide how pleased I am. She knows, somehow, that this isn't just a game for me; it's something more. And I do look great – I *feel* great. I catch a glimpse of myself reflected from across the room, and that new but increasingly familiar thrill courses through my body.

I shake my head and snap myself back into the room to take pictures of everyone at various stages of being ready, quickly getting engrossed in finding the perfect angles to frame the lighted mirrors we borrowed from a local shop for the day, before a tap on the arm alerts me to Mum's presence in the tent, Maya by her side.

"Wow," she says. "There's a lot going on in here."

"Yep. It's a little bit wild right now – it's nearly time." I look down at Maya who's completely transfixed gazing up at me. "You all right, Maya?"

"You look pretty," she says solemnly, eyes wide.

"Thank you." Bless her.

Mum pats her on the head. "Maya, why don't you go talk to Imogen over there? I'll be over in a second."

"OK," she says, immediately sprinting across the room to pounce on Imogen, who picks her up and spins her around, almost taking out a smiling Amelia who's standing nearby.

"Is everything OK?" I ask, focusing back on Mum.

She takes a deep breath, composing herself like she's about to deliver some seriously terrible news. "Ollie, your dad's out there in the crowd. He came."

"He did?" I say in shock, before letting out a laugh. "Well, I hope he enjoys the show."

Mum surveys me carefully. "Are you still sure? You definitely want to do this?"

"Positive," I say with grim determination.

"Well, OK then." She takes in the whole picture of me. "I'm really proud of you, Ol. This is quite something you're doing."

"Thanks, Mum," I say, before voicing my own concern. "Are you sure you can face being around Dad?" We hadn't known whether he'd come, whether he'd believe that I was randomly inviting him to a football match after we'd not spoken for weeks. But now he is here, he'd better bloody not upset Mum or I'll be ordering everyone to pelt the ball in his direction at every opportunity.

"Oh, I'll be fine – don't you worry," she says, smiling to herself. "I'm a tough cookie. And, besides, it'll be good practice for seeing him in court next week."

"Wait—" This is news to me. "You finally got your last court date?"

"Sure did. I got the letter this morning. As of next week, your father and I will be officially divorced."

"Whoa." I chew my lip, trying to gauge how Mum's feeling. "And you feel … good about this?"

"I feel great," she says, and I believe her. She looks lighter, less encumbered by invisible weights than I've seen her in a long time.

"No more dealing with solicitors or email arguments about child support," she says. "We can finally move on as a family, start to properly adjust to our new lives."

She leans forward to kiss me on the cheek before I have time to push her away. "Now, I'd better retrieve Maya – I want to make sure we get a good spot. I love you, kid. See you out there."

I let her hug me and then she's gone. That was kind of a lot – my parents are very nearly officially divorced. I don't know how I feel. Last year, I definitely would have known and it definitely wouldn't have been good. I think maybe my parents' marriage ending fucked up my ideas about love for a while there. But Mum's doing OK now, and maybe sometimes things do work out. Or at least all the good times and memories from the in-between make it all still feel worth it in the end.

"OLIVER ARMSTRONG."

I snap back into the room and stop contemplating whether love is real or not. Just casual things. "What?"

Imogen appears in front of me. "You were fully zoned out then. You need to get your head in the game, and no, for the first time ever, we simply do not have the time to sing a *High School Musical* song."

I snort. "Wow, this must be serious."

"We have like three minutes to go," she says, slight panic in her eyes. "Everyone's about ready: time for a quick pep talk."

Both teams gather in the centre, the boys from school who agreed to play, our gang (me, Imogen, Amelia, Maryam and Clem – Louisa did the art for our posters and is filming the livestream of the event from the sides), and then six others from the new group on our team. So many of them wanted to join in that we're going to have to sub people in at half-time so that they all get a turn.

"OK, everyone," I say, "thank you very much for agreeing to be part of this absolutely ridiculous scheme. I'm so glad that I had the idea to do this and that you were all so eager to take part." Some people (teams) were more eager than others, but we don't need to go there. "It doesn't matter who wins – we're going to have a great time, we're going to raise lots of money to help us put on Ardenpool's first-ever pride festival, and we're going to look cool as fuck while doing it."

Everyone claps and whoops and I grin around at the array of excited faces.

"All right then – let's do this!"

We all gather just inside the double doors. Imogen pokes her head out and waves to Mr Holland, who insisted on doing the commentary for the match after he heard our plan and is sitting up on a lifeguard-type chair with a speaker and microphone ready to announce our arrival. We hear his voice boom out, asking the crowd if they're ready, getting them hyped up for us.

I let out the longest breath of my entire life. We're really doing this.

Imogen whispers next to me, "We've got this.

This is so cool."

I swallow and nod.

"And here they are," Mr Holland calls out, "the boys' football team…"

The team heads out to cheers and shouts.

"And now…" He pretends to do a drum roll. "THE YOUTH ACTIVIST QUEENS."

We burst out through the double doors, high heels on our feet, adorned in bright dresses in all colours and fabrics, hair teased up into elaborate styles or wigs pinned tightly, and dramatic make-up covering our faces – bold, winged eyeliner, electric shades of eyeshadow, arching eyebrows drawn up high, and finished off with beautiful, pouting lipstick.

We walk out on to the pitch and hear the crowd go *wild*, all of them stamping their feet and cheering their voices hoarse already, the atmosphere palpably electric.

I look at Imogen next to me, the bright purple curls of their wig draping across the dramatic shoulder pads of their dress. "Let's fucking *go*," I say.

Her shoulders wriggle as she grins back at me. "Yes, bitch."

The whistle blows.

CHAPTER THIRTY-ONE

I have no idea how this happened but I, Imogen Quinn, am playing a sport. And yes, we did somehow get this past the council's health-and-safety department.

Ollie manages to get the ball first and kicks it down the pitch towards our goal. I run after it in the hottest pursuit I can manage in three-inch heels.

Josh (unsurprisingly) gets there before me and deftly passes it to Rob.

The ball disappears up the other side of the pitch and there are plenty of our team already trying to fight for the it, so I take a second to look around me.

There are well over a hundred people here; there must have been lots of last-minute arrivals. At a minimum donation of five pounds in lieu of tickets – and hopefully a few donations from whoever watches the livestream – we'll have raised a very respectable amount to help us on our way towards our goal.

We have our first fall only five minutes into the game. Maryam takes a dramatic tumble after one of her heels gets stuck in the mud, and then Clem and Briony (a girl from the group) trip over their dresses not long after, letting the opposition score their first goal.

"GOAL!" Mr Holland shouts. "That's one–nil to the Academy. Come on, Queens – show us what you're made of!"

"C'MON, TEAM!" Ollie yells, surprisingly light on his feet in his bright-red chunky heels. He darts forward to tackle Ewan and dribbles the ball all the way back down the pitch.

"GO ON, OLLIE!" I scream at him as he takes a shot at the goal. "You can— *Ughhh*," I groan along with the crowd as Charlie manages to deflect it.

Twenty minutes later, Mr Holland's blowing the whistle for half-time, the school team having scored three goals, while our team is yet to score one.

Ollie gathers us all in a huddle. "OK, we're not doing too badly – honestly, I thought the other team would have already scored way more goals than they have by this point."

"Excuse me, ye of little faith," I protest. "We're not completely hopeless."

"Oh, no, *you* absolutely are," Ollie says without

missing a beat. "You're staggering around like an inebriated giraffe and haven't touched the ball once, but the rest of the team's pretty decent."

"You're a giraffe," I mutter petulantly, offended but also aware that that's likely an accurate description.

"Amelia, that was a nice move you played at the start. See if you can do that again – aim for Rob and Harry; they're huge misogynists and will definitely underestimate you."

"Got it," she says with a determined nod.

"Maryam, we'll sub you out if your ankle's sore," Ollie carries on, and she grimaces in thanks. "Clem, you keep covering the goal; try to distract Charlie. And, Imogen … just try not to die out there. I love you, but you're shit at this."

I put my finger up at him and he blows me a kiss.

"Right, let's get back to it." Ollie claps, jogging backwards – how the hell is he doing that?

"Um, guys?" Louisa calls out from the sidelines, glancing between us and the phone attached to a tripod beside her.

"What?" I shout, but Mr Holland's already calling us back.

"Never mind," she says as the whistle blows.

★

With eighteen minutes to go, the other team's scored yet another goal. And while part of me is

374

having a blast watching our team of impeccably dressed drag queens running-slash-staggering round a football pitch while the whole crowd fiercely cheers us on, the other part of me really wants us to score a goal, just *one*. The school team's getting far too cocky – they need to be taken down several pegs or else I'm going to have to do me some more elbowin'.

The people we subbed in from the group do seem to be slightly better than the first lot. A boy called Michael has definitely played a lot of football before – maybe not in heels, but he's still got skills. Ollie passes the ball to him, and he narrowly dodges Harry. He's getting ready to pass it back to Ollie when his heel gets caught on the hem of his dress and he jerks forward, faceplanting on the ground with an impressive *splat*.

Mr Holland blows the whistle for a timeout.

"I'm OK!" Michael shouts, stumbling back up, but I've had enough.

"ALL RIGHT, QUEENS, SHOES OFF!" I yell, looking to Ollie who nods in agreement.

"But none of us are wearing socks!" Amelia says.

"Doesn't matter – the mud'll wash off. We need our feet for this."

I remove my originally aggressively purple but now very brown shoes and toss them into the crowd like a bouquet.

Amelia laughs and does the same. "There you go!"

Ollie chucks his shoes to Maya and surveys the

We fare much better back on solid ground. However, with only ten minutes left, we've just managed to defend against the other team's advances and still haven't scored a goal of our own.

Josh comes towards me with the ball, getting dangerously close to the goal.

"Come on, Quinn," I mutter to myself, "we can do this." I go in for a tackle, a clumsy one, but it catches him off guard nonetheless and Ollie's able to steal the ball as it drifts away.

"*NOW* WHO'S AN INEBRIATED GIRAFFE?" I screech happily, dancing around as the crowd laughs. "Oh, shit, yeah, the game."

I run back up the pitch in pursuit of Ollie.

He passes the ball to Michael to avoid Rob.

Michael passes it back.

"*Yes*," I breathe. "*Come ON.*"

Ollie's within scoring distance. Charlie crouches down and dodges from side to side, ready for him to aim.

Ollie's jaw is set, concentrating intently on the ball. He skips round Josh, he shoots and…

"YES!" I scream as the ball flies past Charlie into the back of the net. "THAT'S MY BEST FRIEND!"

I run up and pounce on him, shrieking, and we both fall to the ground, laughing. The rest of the team piles on, forming one giant, tangled mess of limbs and grinning faces.

"Guys," Ollie wheezes as we all laugh. "We're still playing. It's not over yet – there's still a minute to go."

"It doesn't matter, we've won!" I say, high-fiving Amelia.

"We very much have not – it's four–one."

"Yeah, but we got the best one," I insist. "And we should get at least fifteen bonus points for style."

Ollie's trying to tell me that there are no bonus points in football, but we're all distracted by the other team yelling for us to keep playing.

"We're having a moment! GOD!" I shout, but then we all get up and prepare to finish the match (slightly) victorious.

Fuelled by the joy generated from our single goal, we manage to stop the other team from scoring again before the final blow of the whistle.

"AND THAT IS IT!" Mr Holland shouts. "The Academy beat the Queens four–one, but what a game it was!"

Both teams are mobbed by the crowd, and there's an electric buzz in the air as everyone talks about how great the match was. Clem joins their family and Ollie's accosted by his mum and Maya, his dad watching them all from a few metres away.

Louisa, closely followed by Maryam, moves on to the pitch towards me and Amelia. "That was amazing, you guys – everyone loved it!"

"Yeah, the crowd seems to have had a good time," I say, trying to absorb all the good vibes. "Everyone looks happy."

"It's not just the crowd here." Maryam beams. "We have news."

My ribcage contracts in anticipation.

"What?" Amelia says quickly. "What is it?"

"The livestream went viral," Louisa says. "Like *fully* viral. We had just over one hundred thousand people watching it when I left," she says, motioning towards her phone propped up on its stand in the makeshift commentary tent.

"*One hundred thousand?*" Amelia clutches my arm.

"Yep. People were sharing it and saying how great it was and how amazing you looked."

"But that's not all." Maryam bites her lip, still beaming. "When I was setting it up with Lou, I linked to the fundraiser in the stream description and explained why we were doing it in the first place, and we got some more donations. A *lot* more donations," she adds.

"How – how many more?" Is this really happening? Somebody pinch me.

Louisa's eyes flit towards Maryam in glee before she speaks. "Our total is now at six thousand five hundred and thirty-eight pounds. Maybe more since we've been over here."

I pinch my arm. It hurts. "What the—"

"But that means…" Amelia says, eyes wide.

"That means that, with the grant we now qualify for, we're well over ten thousand," I say, breathing heavily. "If we get a move on, if we book everything we originally planned, if we can organise it all in time, we can do it – we can put on our dream pride festival *this year.*"

"We should go and check the stream again and tell the others. We did it, you guys!" Maryam says, clapping her hands together with a look of complete joy, before running off into the crowd to share the incredible news, Louisa following close behind and yelling something about finding Clem.

I turn to Amelia. Her mouth is curved in an open, disbelieving smile.

"We…" she starts, "we did it."

"We did it," I repeat. "Holy shit, WE DID IT!" I shout, grinning.

"YES!" Amelia says – we make eye contact and just absolutely *scream* at each other in celebration.

Once we've stopped screaming and jumping around, Amelia moves in for a hug then hesitates, knowing me well enough now to ask.

"Oh, wait— Can I hug you?"

I give a definitive nod. "Sure."

She wraps her arms round me. My head rests on her shoulder. I can feel her hair brushing my left cheek. She smells so nice, like the deliriously sweet warmth of a Parisian bakery. Oh, fucking hell, what's happening to me? I'm not the kind of person who compares other people to *Parisian bakeries*.

The world blurs around us, hordes of people laughing and talking and celebrating; the hug lasts a moment too long and we both realise it. We pull apart just enough to survey each other's faces. When our eyes meet, both our laughs are a little too high-pitched.

Her eyes flick slightly lower down on my face. We're still standing close – too close. I can see every perfectly curled eyelash, every gold fleck in her brown supernova irises, the deep black of her pupils. My breath falters as I realise my hands are still resting on her lower back, her arms still wrapped round my shoulders.

Amelia swallows tightly. "Well … we should…"

"We should."

Neither of us moves.

The clamour of a hundred people on the football field around us has faded to white noise. Everyone is happy, celebrating, but I'm still standing here, far too close to Amelia Valadez, and oh, FUCK IT.

My eyes dart up to meet Amelia's. She looks terrified in the absolute best way.

"Do you— Can I—?"

She nods vigorously.

I lean in swiftly, pressing my lips to hers like I've just realised that this is something I should have been doing my entire life and why the hell did I wait this long?

Amelia meets me with equal, if not even greater, enthusiasm.

I pull her towards me with my hands laced behind her back as she cups my face with her hand, the kiss increasing in force and hunger as she does.

God, she's good at this.

A minute passes in a blissful stupor before I stumble backwards from her, trying desperately to catch my breath. "Whoa."

"Yes," she says, breathing shakily. "*Whoa.*"

I just kissed Amelia Valadez. And it may well have been one of the greatest moments of my horny little bisexual life.

We stand opposite each other, both trying not to grin, both doing an absolutely abysmal job of it.

As I stare at her, what just happened begins to fully sink into my brain. The quiet between us stretches on a little too long, as Amelia's teased up pastel-pink wig drifts like candyfloss in the wind.

"Imogen?"

I realise she's now scanning my face carefully.

"We should … talk?"

"Sure, yes, talking sounds good," I agree. "It's really loud out here, shall we go back to the hall?"

"OK."

I grab her hand and snake us through groups of people back to the empty hall. Everyone else is far too busy celebrating to want to get changed yet.

I take a seat in a far corner on an uncomfortable

bench and Amelia sits next to me, staring down at our still-entwined fingers atop our matching pink and purple silky dresses.

"You wanted to talk?"

She looks up from our hands. "Oh. Yes. I just wanted to check in."

I tilt my head to the side. "About what?"

She looks at me incredulously, dropping my hand. "Imogen! We just kissed?"

"I'm aware."

"And you're feeling … what, about that?"

"Erm, I dunno."

Her shoulders sink.

"I mean, it's hard to narrow it down," I continue. "I'd say happy, excited and weirdly proud are the top three, though."

Her neck snaps back up so quickly I'm surprised she doesn't get whiplash. "Wait – really?"

"Well … yeah?" I say. "Why? What are you feeling?"

"I was trying not to get my hopes up or expect anything from one kiss – incredible as it was," she adds, and I can't help but smirk at that, my cheeks flushing red. "But yes, I'm feeling the same. Definitely the same."

"All right then." We stare back at one another. "Want to do it again?" I offer cheekily.

She doesn't hesitate for a second. "God, yes."

We meet each other in a hurried blur again

and for several minutes everything but *her* disappears, everything else in the universe suddenly seeming deeply inferior and irrelevant. I never really understood the concept of kissing before or why people liked it so much – you're just kind of smushing your faces together, after all – but I get it now. I really, *really* get it.

"OK, no," Amelia says, finally pulling away with a laugh that sounds like summer. "We really do need to talk. This is all –" she gestures vaguely between us – "very lovely and I look forward to many repetitions of such behaviour, but I think I'm still processing. Up until five minutes ago, I had zero clue how you felt about me. And until a few months ago I thought you actively disliked me."

"Oh, I did."

She laughs again. "Great."

"But then I realised that I didn't even really know you," I say, "and I think I *may* have been using you as a way to feel insecure about myself and I forgot that those feelings were entirely my own responsibility and nothing to do with you. Which wasn't very groovy of me, and I apologise."

She shakes her head, but she's smiling. "I accept your apology."

"And then on my birthday, Ollie kind of pointed out how nice you were to me and suggested that I try to be nice back, and it was easier than I thought it would be," I say. "Sometimes, at least. I'm aware

I was mostly just weird around you."

She doesn't deny that.

"And then I found out you liked me," I carry on, trying to adequately explain everything I've been repressing for so long, "and I panicked again because I'd never thought of myself as a person people like in that way. Before this year, I've always been treated as a kind of pet, the cute, awkward person you keep around because they say weird things you find amusing, not because you actually like or respect them as a person and definitely not because you find them attractive."

Amelia's eyes are right on me, this time not in a way that makes me sweat and want to poke her eyeballs out, but in a way that makes me feel seen. "For the record, I respect you *and* I also find you very attractive."

"I respect you too, and you're hot as hell."

She lets out a burst of laughter. "Thank you. This is so bizarre. I never thought this would happen. Like, *ever.*"

"Right back at you," I say, and it's true. Yesterday's Imogen would never have been able to comprehend this current situation, never mind the Imogen of last year.

"So?" Amelia shakes her hair back so it bounces behind her shoulders. "What now?"

"Well," I say, "I think the proper protocol involves me asking you out on a date."

"And we wouldn't want to break the protocol, would we?"

"I mean, that is generally our thing, but just this once I think we should respect it." I clear my throat, shoulders square. "Amelia Valadez, would you like to get coffee with me tomorrow?"

She smiles a golden, radiant smile. "Imogen Quinn, I would love to."

Mr Holland's jarringly loud amplified voice carries from the field outside into the hall, thanking everyone for coming and announcing that we've hit our fundraising goal. There's a further uptick in noise from everyone's applause and cheers.

"We should probably get back out there," I say. "We should celebrate with the others."

"Probably," Amelia says, but then she smiles wryly, her warm brown eyes narrowing between their ridiculously long lashes. "Or we could stay here for another minute."

"We could also do that, yes," I reply, and we laugh. Amelia settles in closer, our legs overlapping on the bench, heads close together.

"GUYS, WE DID— Oh, hello."

We look up guiltily to see the whole gang – Ollie, Maryam, Louisa and Clem – staring at us with matching grins.

Amelia bites her lip, then says, "We were just…"

"Celebrating the good news?" I suggest.

Amelia nods. "Yes, that."

"Oh, I bet you were," Ollie says, in a tone of voice that absolutely necessitates me flipping him off again.

"FINE," I say forcefully, putting my hands down. "We were talking about how we liked each other. And also doing a teensy bit of the kissing."

Amelia lets out a hysterical peal of laughter but doesn't deny it or remove her legs from over mine.

We let the others gather round to tease us and talk about 'how great this is' as more people file back in to start getting changed. We gradually transition to doing the same, the room filled with the pervasive smell of a dozen cans of hairspray. Bobby-pins are scattered on the floor; dresses in bright jewel colours are draped over the backs of chairs.

At some point, Josh comes in, clocks the lack of distance between me and Amelia (and our matching smudged lipstick…) and freezes.

I meet his eyes, also frozen, feeling more guilty than I'd expected to. But then he just blinks, nods almost imperceptibly to me, offers an equally faint smile to Amelia and walks behind the curtain.

I turn to Ollie, who paused in removing his eyeliner to witness this interaction. "D'you think he'll be OK?"

"Yeah," he says, looking over at where Josh was just standing, and nodding his head. "I actually do."

I can't help but sneak glances at everyone as I unpin the lilac wig and shake out my curls.

I've never felt quite so happy to be among people before. We all did something incredible together. My best friend's on one side of me, smirking at me in an incredibly irritating way, Clem and Louisa are talking enthusiastically behind him, and the most beautiful girl on the whole planet is laughing with Maryam in the chair on my other side, occasionally turning round to smile happily at me or reaching across to squeeze my hand firmly in hers, both of us just wanting to remember that we're near each other. It's all so new, and I'm usually not a fan of uncertainty (i.e. I loathe everything about it) but for once I'm just excited to see what happens.

My entire body feels light and giddy, my veins filled with subtly fizzing champagne instead of blood, as I sit here and let it truly sink in that the pride festival, my passion project, my dream event, is really going to happen *this* summer. I now get to go into hectic planning mode with my dream team around me. A team that makes me feel like whatever is coming, whatever shape it takes, it's going to be something great.

CHAPTER THIRTY-TWO

OLLIE

The game was a total success. Not only did we have an amazing time, but we raised more money than any of us could have dared hope for. I could hardly believe it when Maryam told me – I'm actually going to get to march through Ardenpool with all of my friends and have a blast and celebrate the joy of being queer and how far we've all come together (and how far there still is to go).

Speaking of how far there still is to go, once I've changed back into my clothes and removed all the make-up from my face, it's time to head back out there and talk to my dad.

I spoke with Mum and Maya straight after the match and they both rhapsodised about how great the match was and how amazing we all looked (just before I heard the truly shocking news that Imogen had *finally* got their shit together and kissed Amelia) but Dad just hovered a few metres away. I truly have no clue what he's going to say; I spend the walk back into the gradually dispersing crowd preparing myself to greet any ignorance.

I wave to Mum and Maya who are waiting for me over in the playground (Maya now pinging around on a spring-loaded donkey) and approach Dad with as much confidence as I can muster.

"Hi."

He turns round from staring at a group of people, which includes several members of our team still dressed in drag. "Ollie. Hey."

Silence laps between us, made even more obvious by its contrast with the happy buzz of people chatting and laughing all around the field.

"That was quite a game," he ventures eventually. "You played really well, especially considering your choice of footwear. The crowd went nuts when you scored that goal."

"Yeah, it was a good moment," I say, still waiting for the blow to fall.

"It's a shame not all the members of your team have your level of skill, otherwise you might have actually stood a chance."

"Well, we weren't really playing to win," I say carefully.

"No, no, of course not. I just meant—" He rubs his face, looking annoyed – but not with me. I think his anguish is more internal. "Look, Ollie, I'm really sorry about what happened at the flat the other week.

I hate that things between us are the way they are."

"Well, yeah, me too," I say, and bite my tongue to keep from adding, *but you made them that way, so now what are you willing to do to fix things?*

"I do—" He shifts his weight awkwardly from one foot to the other on the trodden-down grass. "I do love you, Ollie. I know I don't always show it—"

I have to stifle a chuckle at that. "I mean ... not always, no."

"But I'm going to work at being better, I swear," Dad says seriously. "A lot of what you said was right – I've never been particularly good at emotions."

Bit of an understatement.

"But I need you to know that I –" he meets my eyes, not blinking – "I'm proud of you, Ollie. I am."

I feel some of the sharp edges inside me begin to be sanded into something slightly smoother. It's a start. "Thank you."

"And I can't pretend to be entirely comfortable with everything you do," he continues, "but I'll ... I'll try to work on that too."

I arrange my face into a calm smile. "I don't need you to be comfortable. Sure, it would be nice if you were, but I'm comfortable with myself – I don't need anyone else to be."

He gives a very slight nod. "OK then. I respect that, but I will try all the same."

"And I appreciate that."

"Good. OK then," he repeats. "Now I know that not everything is fixed—"

I try not to laugh again because I know that he's trying and I do appreciate it, but yes, that is one way of putting it.

"But if you feel like coming round to the flat some time soon, or we could go out somewhere, I don't care … then I would like that."

I consider for a second. "How about tea tonight?" I say. We postponed our group celebrations until tomorrow's meeting so that everyone can be there, and I figure there's no time like the present to start trying to repair our fraught father-son relationship, particularly if he's in an apologetic mood. "We could go get pizza with Maya?"

Dad blinks at me. "Tonight? Oh— Sure, yes, let's go get pizza."

"OK. Maya's over there." I nod towards the play area. "I should probably check with Mum first."

"Yes, you do that," he says, before pausing. "Or … you know, she could come too."

I think I need to clean my ears out. "I'm sorry," I say slowly. "You want to invite Mum?"

"Why not?"

Jesus, he's actually serious.

"All right, you can ask Mum." I'm not sure what the chances of her coming to dinner with the man who cheated on her are, but I'm going to enjoy watching him ask her all the same.

We go over to the play area and lean over the fence. "Hey, Maya?" I call, and she bounces over, Mum trailing behind her. "You fancy having pizza for tea with Dad?"

"Pizza, pizza, pizza!" she squeals.

"I'll take that as a yes. Is that OK, Mum?"

She nods. "Of course."

"Hey, erm, Keiko," Dad says nervously, "you're welcome to join us if you're not busy."

Mum does not move an inch. There's a very long pause before she says, "Sure, I'll come. For the kids," she adds, and I cover up my smile by rubbing my nose. Good on her for making it very clear that she's happy to be the bigger person, but that she's not even slightly doing it for his benefit.

"Great!" Dad says, a touch too enthusiastically, so that he sounds slightly unhinged. "Let's go for dinner. All of us. Great."

"Yep. Great," Mum says.

They come round to our side of the fence, and we all start walking back through the park towards the centre of town.

Maya skips ahead a little with Mum by her side, and I'm left to make conversation with Dad.

"So," I say. "What did you think of my dress?"

Dad's face turns beetroot red and he looks gloriously panicked. "I didn't think anything," he says quickly. "Or no, I thought it was … it was lovely?"

I laugh to myself all the way to the restaurant,

Dad looking perplexed beside me. This is going to be fun.

★

The next couple of months pass by in a flick-book blur of group meetings, frantic preparations for the festival and, of course, many days spent with Imogen, drinking quantities of iced coffee that no doctor would condone and talking about anything and everything. Including getting Imogen to tell me every detail of her and Amelia's dates and annoying her with comments like, "So are we ready to admit that maybe we didn't hate Amelia for how 'perfect' she was – we were just secretly in love with her the whole time?" that get me promptly biffed in the face with cushions/told to piss off.

I also work on my Photography project harder than I've ever worked for any school project before, as well as documenting pretty much everything the group does. Inspiration never feels far away these days, and life is full of moments that I want to remember.

The last weekend before the festival, the whole group is at my house to help me out with a couple of shots before they go back out into town to deliver a final batch of flyers to local businesses and I head off to take some last photos with Josh and Charlie. Once we're done, we gather round my camera to have a look at the results.

"Not half bad," I say, grinning.

"They're better than that," Imogen says. "If you don't get an A for this then I'm going to personally go to Miss Casey's classroom and remove all the memory cards from the cameras."

I fake-gasp. "You wouldn't." Losing memory cards is a photographer's worst nightmare and, annoyingly, also a far too frequent occurrence.

"You know she would," Amelia says dryly, and unfortunately, yes, I do. "Right, well, we'd better head off before..."

She means before Josh gets here and plunges us all into an awkward situation, but before she can finish there's a knock at the door, followed by Josh and Charlie's faces peering round it.

"Oh... Are we early?" Josh says.

"No, we overran," Maryam tells them smoothly. "We're just going."

"No rush to split or anything." Josh comes into the room, nodding calmly at us all in greeting. "I'm sure Ollie'll need help making us two look good on camera."

"I dunno about that," Charlie says, striking an awkward-looking pose and not proving the point he thinks he is.

Josh rolls his eyes at me, but there's no malice in his look any more. I spoke to them both the day after the game, reviving our old group chat, and thanked them for playing. When Charlie replied to say it was no problem and that he 'has to respect anyone who can put up a fight against me in a game while wearing shoes like that', I privately messaged Josh to say I thought it was time we all tried to mend fences. Fences that will make it clear they won't tolerate homophobia or misogyny or racism of any kind, but fences all the same.

Charlie's not a perfect person, but I also don't believe he's a bad one – he's just grown up in a world that's taught him certain things. But that doesn't mean there's no room for him to evolve and learn something new. Tides come in and out, starry skies fade to cerulean and people change. God knows I have.

★

A week later, the Photography classroom has been transformed into a gallery with screens dividing the room, featuring our final projects, along with the feedback sheets showing our grades. None of us have been allowed in to see the final displays yet and so we're mingling outside in the hallway, impatiently waiting for Miss Casey to open the doors. Imogen's with me, of course, looking even more impatient than I am.

"I swear to God, if she doesn't come out in the next thirty seconds, I'm going to—"

The doors open.

I raise my eyebrows. "You're going to do what?"

"It's irrelevant now – come on." They take my hand and drag me past my classmates into the room. "Where's yours?"

"Erm… Aha!" I spot it and we walk over past the other *This is what [blank] looks like* projects to stand in front of my board, which features all of my photos printed out on gleaming paper.

"Whoa," Imogen says, stepping back in awe.

Staring back at me are over a dozen of my favourite photographs I've ever taken.

Under the words *This is what masculinity looks like*, are photos of me, Charlie and Josh with our Xbox controllers, shoving each other and laughing. There are some of us outside with me holding a football in the air, Charlie and Josh playfully trying to fight me for it; one of me in goal, grass a green blur at the bottom.

And then there are others too, ones of me wearing make-up, my cheekbones glittering, nails displayed as they frame the side of my face, branches of cherry blossom held around me, just out of focus so it's a haze of rosy pink. One of me and Maya at a 'fairy tea party' that I took at home, both of us wearing fairy wings, a fuchsia feather boa flung round my neck. There's one of me with blue ink running down my face, a blue backdrop with white teardrop shapes stuck to it behind me. There's one of me taken through a thin Pride flag so there are distorted rainbow lines across my face, and there's one of me and Imogen, my arms round her waist as I try to kiss her cheek, while she laughs and pretends to wriggle away.

I grew up believing that the only acceptable kind of masculinity was the kind represented in the first set of photos. And then, when I came out, I internalised the idea from people around me (my teammates, my dad, the wider world in general) that being gay was only acceptable because I could fit in with my straight White friends and their ideas of masculinity.

But I'm done with that. What Clem said that day at the drag bar really hit home for me. Only *I* get to decide what my gender means to me – masculinity is whatever I decide it is. It's football, it's passion, it's wearing make-up, it's being affectionate, it's fairy tea parties, it's being gay. It's both separate from femininity and intrinsically linked; it's whatever I *damn well* please. The knowledge of that and how comfortably it fits inside me makes me feel giddily weightless.

Imogen shakes her head in disbelief. "Hot diggity dog, you're a talented little frog. And look at that." She points towards my feedback sheet, where a bright red 'A' is circled in the top right corner.

My stomach lurches up towards my ribs.

"Not half bad," Imogen says, linking her arm tightly through mine.

I laugh. "Yeah. Not half bad."

I stare at the scarlet 'A' and run my gaze over

the photos one more time, letting the abundance of joy that's so apparent in every image wash back over me. I couldn't have taken them last year; there's something kind of magical in knowing that your past self wouldn't recognise the person you are today because you've expanded the definition of who you are.

Imogen starts rummaging in their backpack. "Ah, here it is." They extract their phone and take a video, skimming over all the different photos and then finally zooming in on the 'A'.

"What are you doing?"

"Being proud of you. Deal with it."

I shake my head at her, but I can't stop smiling. "I love you, you idiot."

I couldn't be prouder to be a person that feels things and loves loudly now. And so yes, I love a lot of things, including the curly-haired gremlin currently shimmying around in a truly ridiculous fashion as they chant the words, "You got an A. You got an A!" over and over again. I love them a lot.

CHAPTER THIRTY-THREE

IMOGEN

It's here. The morning of the pride festival has *finally* arrived and the whole gang has assembled to get ready together in the town hall. I gaze out of the window into the square, where rainbow-coloured bunting criss-crosses between every building, banners are hanging everywhere, and a temporary stage is set up on the side of the square that runs parallel to the park, where I'll be announcing the start of the parade in just a couple of hours. People are already milling around outside, and some of the council events team are helping set up the sound systems or lining up chairs in the areas designated for anyone who might need them.

"Hey, Imogen." Ollie calls over from his spot in front of the mirror. He's dressed in a pale pink T-shirt with the word *PRIDE* emblazoned on a stripe of rainbow, and bright green high-waisted trousers. He looks very snazzy.

"Can I steal your highlighter, please?"

I stop looking out of the window and call back over to him. "Check your bag."

"Why would I check my bag? I don't have—"

He pulls out the highlighter that I bought him and snuck into his bag when he wasn't looking this morning.

"You're welcome."

"You're the actual best."

"I know."

I run through my speech one last time, muttering the words quietly to myself before calling over to Ollie to say I'm going to do a last check of everything.

"Hold up, I'm coming," he says, finishing glittering himself up.

"I hope you know that Maya's going to fully lose her shit when she sees your outfit later." Ollie links our arms together as we walk, taking in my glittery matching trousers and blazer and my eyeshadow in the bi flag colours. "She's going to want a matching suit."

"Yay, Maya's coming?"

"Yup, the whole family is. Just for the parade but still – progress," Ollie says, and I know he's referring to progress with a particular family member who's still on my list for now, but *has* been significantly less of a twat recently.

We walk out into the corridor, people bustling around us, Ollie's smile growing as he surveys the photographs that line the walls – a gallery of his work. They feature some of my favourite moments from the last few months, including the one he took of us celebrating hitting the fundraising goal, wigs askew and grins on made-up faces, or the one of the whole group out by the canal the day we went into the city for the drag show. It's messy, with some people laughing and others looking at each other and not the camera, but I think it might be my favourite. There are also portraits of us core six mixed in too – each one somehow capturing us exactly how we see ourselves. Ollie took the photos and Louisa painted around us all with swooping lines in bright colours and geometric shapes. They look cool as fuck.

We pop our head into the main room where the performers are getting ready – the musicians, the singers, the dancers and, of course, Auntie Septic, who's performing with her drag sisters later on.

"Looking good, darlings," she calls, waggling the fingers of one hand at us, while the other spritzes perfume on to her glittery décolletage – and on to one of our interpreters who's sitting next to her. trying to read. I notice that she's reading our event programme, something I'm particularly proud of. It's a guide to the whole festival that we're giving out to everyone, with detailed descriptions of everything that's going on, including the sensory aspects, whether that's flashing lights, loud music, or whatever. We're also doing two performances of everything – one that might be more demanding sensory-wise, and one that will be quieter, with no bright lights, and the seats more spread out.

The last thing on my list to check is the quiet room at the far end of the hall and, once we've discovered that the beanbags are in fact plump and the lights are dimmed, even I can't find anything to panic about. We're done.

The crowd is filling the square – glittering people all enjoying themselves, just waiting for me to go out and deliver my speech and start the festival with the parade.

Amelia appears at my side as I shake my arms around, standing in the entrace of the town hall. "You ready?"

"No."

She pauses for a second. "How about now?"

"Not quite." I lean forward and plant a kiss on her cheek. "OK, now I am."

"Imogen!" She laughs but she doesn't bat me away. I much prefer the way she says my name to the way people used to say it, which usually indicated I was about to get yelled at for something. She makes it sound prettier.

She turns to face me properly and I can feel her smile as she kisses me.

Someone sighs melodramatically behind us.

"Can you guys stop being cute, please?" Ollie

says. "We've got a whole crowd waiting. You can make out later."

"Oh, we will," I say, glaring at Ollie as Amelia's shoulders shake with laughter next to me. "But fine, let's do this thing."

I look back at the room. Louisa and Clem are hand in hand, Maryam's smiling in her rainbow-striped hijab, typing on her laptop, Ollie's pacing impatiently next to me, and Amelia's on my other side in her pale pink spotted dress, the lesbian flag draped comfortably round her shoulders. The rest of the new group is outside, waiting to march together at the front of the parade. The only thing left to do is go out there.

"OK." I swallow. "I'm ready."

"Hi, everybody!" I say, stepping out on to the stage to the applause of the audience. There are a few hundred people in the crowd, all excited to start celebrating. "I'm Imogen Quinn; thank you all for coming! I'm so happy to be standing up here and welcoming you to Ardenpool's very first pride event – it's about time this town got with it, isn't it?"

There's a huge assortment of whoops from the crowd.

I let out a deep breath and keep looking out at all the familiar faces right in front of me. I can feel them willing me on.

"It's been a very long, weird and wonderful adventure getting to today and I wasn't always sure that were going to make it here. About ten months ago, I was at a pride festival in the city – the first pride festival I'd ever been to," I say. "Now, I've known I was bisexual—"

A few people cheer at that word and I laugh. "Thank you, thank you very much. I've known I'm bi since basically forever. Everyone who knows me knows I'm very comfortable with who I am. I don't really listen to what anyone else says – occasionally to my detriment."

This gets a few laughs from the people who know me, including a chuckle from my mum and dad and a nod from Ben, who's back from uni for summer.

I take in another deep, steadying breath and say with a determined smile, "I'm also autistic. And very proud to be, just like I'm proud to be bisexual. But other pride events wouldn't let me be proud of both of those things. In fact, I realised that most of them were completely inaccessible for disabled people, and I decided that needs to change. Because everyone deserves to feel pride in who they are – all of who they are, not just some of it," I say, and I'm pleased to find a good number of people nodding along.

"And so," I continue, "I decided to start an activist group in my school to try to find people to join me in making changes, and hopefully raise some money so that we could start a pride event of our own – one where *everyone* could feel welcome and be safe.

"And spoiler alert," I add, looking out into the sea of faces, "I think we managed it." I exchange smiles with the group in front of me before returning to rest my gaze more vaguely outwards. "I know today won't be perfect, but hopefully it's a start."

I dive into explanations of all the accommodations we've made, the BSL interpreter signing along as I speak, mentioning things like the ramps at all the venues, our entirely flat parade route, the audio descriptions and transcripts available to anyone who asks. A lot of people look bored, but I don't care. It's worth it for the ones who are listening carefully or just absolutely beaming, maybe on their own behalf, or perhaps for someone that they love. Those smiles are the whole reason why we did this.

Finally, I list all the acts – my stand-up (!), the drag performers, the singers, Clem, Amelia and the rest of their band and the exhibitions like Ollie's photos and the other gloriously queer art that Louisa and other people in the group have done.

"OK, I think that's everything. Again, please feel free to ask any of the Pride officials if you have any more questions." I grin and let out a long sigh.

"I'm just so happy that you're all here and I hope you have the best time ever – I know I will. I also want to quickly thank everyone in the council who's helped us with the logistics of the event, everyone who's volunteered their time today to help out, the original activist group who joined with me when no one else did – and who are maybe some of the greatest people that ever existed – the rest of you that joined further down the road and who've been absolute legends at getting things done. And I want to thank my girlfriend, Amelia—" *Oh, shit.* I pause to grimace. "Who I'm now realising I've never called my girlfriend before – we haven't exactly had that conversation yet."

I search for her face in the crowd. "HEY, AMELIA, I'm sorry I called you that, I hope it's OK with you— You know what? Never mind: we'll talk about it later—"

"It's very OK with me!" Amelia yells up at me, igniting a tremendous cheer and laughter from everyone else.

"All right, nice." I grin. Score. "Thank you to my *girlfriend*, who wants to make the world a better place as much as I do, i.e., so badly we will probably have a mental breakdown about it in the future," I add, and there's a ripple of laughter led by a viciously nodding Amelia. "And who somehow manages to do it all in a kinder way," I continue, not caring that hundreds of people are seeing me be vulnerable. "She doesn't just let her words stand for her; she leads by example.

"And finally, thank you to Oliver Armstrong," I say, spotting his already glistening eyes and wondering how in sweet hell I'm going to make it through this without weeping too. "My best friend on this whole damn planet." My voice breaks a little as my vision starts to swim despite my best efforts. "And the person who made me realise that being yourself and being loved aren't two incongruent things, just so long as you surround yourself with the right people."

I stare down at him and gulp furiously as we both brush away tears. "PHEW, OK." I let out a blurt of laughter, tearing my gaze away. "That's everything, I swear. If you would like to see me ramble away about hopefully slightly more amusing and coherent things, then feel free to come to my stand-up performance later on. Now, let's start this festival off with a bang, huh?"

There's a collaborative cheer from everyone, people brandishing dozens of different Pride flags and banners and shaking them in the air, causing a blur of colour, including Mr Holland with his husband, who winks at me from the middle of the crowd, and, right at the front, Maryam and Poppy, trans Pride flags wrapped round their shoulders as they supervise the team that will be documenting every detail of the day on social media.

"Have the absolute best time, everyone," I say. "Now, let's start this dang parade."

I climb down off the stage to uproarious noise, people clapping, shouting and stamping their feet.

I greet Ollie at the bottom of the steps where he kisses my forehead and gives me my bi flag to tie round my glittery shoulders like a cape. "We ready?"

All the people who are part of the parade gather behind me in the high street, ready to march through town and tell Ardenpool (and the world) that – despite everything – we're here and we're super fucking queer. We've fought for this moment, this moment of joy and protest, and we'll keep on fighting until everyone (and I mean *everyone*) gets to experience the joy that I'm feeling right now.

The banner for the activist society that we all decorated at our last meeting is propped up against the wall, ready to go with all our other signs. Amelia grabs one end of it, causing Ollie to frown. "D'you not want to march with Imogen?"

"Oh." She looks at me. "Well?"

I swoop a kiss on to her cheek. "We'll do the evening parade together, if that's OK? There's no way I'm not marching through town at least once with my beautiful *girlfriend* by my side."

She smiles radiantly back at me, lifting up one side of the banner. Maryam takes the other, Louisa and Clem in front of her, both glowing with happiness as they prepare to set the pace for the parade. "You're on," Amelia says.

I kiss Amelia's cheek again before looking at Ollie and sticking out my arm. "What d'you reckon? You want to lead the parade with me?"

A broad smile grows over his face as he grabs my hand. "Of course I do. Jeez."

"All right then, let's go."

I lead Ollie to the front of the march, peering around me at my beautiful friends (and girlfriend!) and the glittering crowd behind them.

This isn't the kind of place I thought my life would end up, but now that I am here it seems entirely implausible that, even in a million alternative universes, this isn't *exactly* where I'm supposed to be, surrounded by a kaleidoscope of colour and joy, hand in hand with the people that I love. Nothing else would make sense.

Ollie spots me gazing all around and nudges me gently so that I look at him.

"You did it," he says. "You actually did it."

"*We* did it," I reply firmly.

He shakes his head at me, smiling lopsidedly, that one dimple making a reappearance. "I guess we did."

Exuberant, lilting music begins to play, a cascade of notes tumbling out of instruments into the air behind us – our cue to begin the parade.

"Hey." Ollie scans my face carefully. "You OK? You ready?"

I look down at our joined hands and then jut my chin up determinedly, meeting his eyes again with a grin. "You bet your sweet ass I am."

AUTHOR'S NOTE

Dear Reader,

Something to be Proud of started life as my lockdown passion project, a way for me to escape all of the Trying Times™ and create something joyful and funny, with a healthy measure of hope for a better future – my act of rebellion against all the fear and anger that was rife in 2021. (And, also, an excellent way to procrastinate from writing my dissertation.)

The story quickly grew to mean even more than that to me, however. Imogen Quinn is a queer, autistic person with a lot of feelings, even more passion and an incredibly strong sense of justice. She learnt pretty early on that her power comes from using the unique parts of who she is to make other people feel things too – whether that's laughing at her ridiculous jokes, or rousing people to make a difference in the world. This both was and wasn't my story when I was their age. Imogen was diagnosed as autistic when they were quite young – well before our story starts. Imogen has the answers that I didn't get until I was an adult, but they're not lucky enough (at the beginning of our story at least) to have people around them that celebrate them for who they are.

That's when our other main character, Oliver Armstrong, enters. He's a bit of an angsty lad on the outside, but inside he's a soft-boy with a heart of pure gold. He loves his mum and younger sister Maya (and Taylor Swift), and he's just trying to figure out who he wants to be as opposed to who he thinks he should be/who he's been raised to be. The COVID lockdowns sparked some intense self-questioning around sexuality and gender for lots of people, and Ollie's story was partly inspired by this. Who would you be if no one else was watching? And then how do you learn not to care when they are? A huge thank you to Will Dobson – who read an early version of this story to make sure that Ollie's experience as a British Japanese teenager rang true.

Most of all, this story is a love letter to all the loves of my life – everyone in my life who loves me because of who I am, not in spite of it. But it's also a question: how can we use the work of everyone that came before us – the activists, the rioters, the artists – to help create more of the change we need so that everyone gets to celebrate all the different parts of themselves at once?

And finally, I wanted it to be a message of defiance for LGBTQ+ and disabled people everywhere. Oh, you don't like who we are? Well, too bad, because we do.

Something to be Proud of has brought me so much joy from the moment Imogen and Ollie burst into my head and demanded to be written about, right up until today. I couldn't be prouder (*ba dum tss*) that now I get to pass some of that joy along to you.

Thank you so much for reading,

Anna x

ACKNOWLEDGEMENTS

Being an author has always been my dream, pretty much right from when I knew what it was *to* dream. As I got older, I started to worry that it wasn't realistic, so I taught myself to dream of other things, all while my love of writing simmered stubbornly inside me. I couldn't be happier now, however, to have proved myself wrong. And I have lots of people to thank for helping me do that, so here we go!

To Lucy. I could not be more grateful to you. You've loved and fought for Imogen and Ollie (and for me) ever since you met them/us – I couldn't have asked for a better champion for this story. Thank you.

To Mattie. Thank you so much for taking a chance on this story and for your invaluable help making it what it is now. Also huge thanks to Sophie for your wonderful design skills, Jane for proofreading, and to George, Jade and Finn for marketing and publicity.

And, of course, thanks Lucía for perfectly bringing Imogen and Ollie to life on the cover, and to Will again for his infinitely useful help with making Ollie's British Japanese identity authentic.

To Alicia/Pasta Mum. You've been Imogen and Ollie's biggest fan from the very first notes app concept to now. *Thank you thank you thank you* for all the screaming, unhinged comments left on manuscripts, and endless support. This book wouldn't be the same if I didn't know you.

To Alannah for sticking by my side from *Roses Are Red... Or Are They Dead?* when we were eight (?) right to *Something to be Proud of.* And to Kate for changing me from 'that weird girl that hides in the cloakroom to read' to '*one* of the weird girls that hides in the cloakroom to read'. No beloved music groups die in this one. Maybe next time, though.

To Dan and Liv. Thank you for being there while the most bonkers part of all this occurred and for the Bluey/Glee and ice cream nights, and the late-night family IKEA trips that helped keep me (mostly) sane during it.

To Bill, for being my go-to resource on anything sports/teenage boy related and for your own brand of weird support – mocking everything I say (but, you know, *affectionately*). And to Mum, for everything. You're one of the strongest, bravest people there is. Thanks for passing some of that along to me.

To all the Hellions. I could not have done this without you, but even if I could, it wouldn't have been half as fun. Special thanks to El, Dervla, Audrey and Zoé for the use of your spectacular eyes on the very first draft, and to Lex for creating our weird corner of the Internet in the first place. Success rats to all.

To Nanny and Grandad. You've been asking me ever since I wrote my first story when I'm going to be published. Finally, I can tell you that – now! Right now! Thanks for believing in me from the start.

To Grandad. You were the recipient of my first ever 'book' (approximately five pieces of green card stuck together, with horse facts and very wonkily drawn vaguely quadruped-shaped creatures inside). This one is hopefully a bit better than that. And to Nan. We all miss you. I hope you are proud.

To everyone at New Writing North for giving me a huge boost (mentally and financially) in 2022. Special thanks to Will and Emily, and to Liz Flanagan for picking *Imogen & Ollie* for the YA Northern Debut Award. You all helped change my life.

To Rachael. I didn't know you when I first wrote this book, but I'm going to know you and love you for all the rest. I couldn't feel any happier or luckier to get to do all this with you by my side. I can't wait to marry you, my love.

And to every queer, neurodivergent and/or disabled person reading this right now. I wrote this for us. I hope you enjoyed it.

ABOUT THE AUTHOR

Anna Zoe Quirke is a queer and autistic
author and librarian from the North of England.
She currently lives in Manchester with her partner,
Rachael, and their very angry tortoise, Sheldon.
They're at their happiest writing stories about queer
and neurodivergent people finding and claiming
their place in the world, exploring the literary
wonders of the UK, or making a big ol' mess in
the kitchen baking things for their loved ones.
Something to be Proud of is their debut novel.

LOOK OUT FOR ANNA ZOE QUIRKE'S NEXT BOOK, COMING 2025...